Praise for
GEORGE TURNER

"BRILLIANT . . . A MIND-STRETCHER"

Arthur C. Clarke

"ONE OF THE CLEAREST, MOST CREATIVE
VOICES IN SCIENCE FICTION"

Austin American-Statesman

"TURNER HAS A DARK VISION OF THE FUTURE,
WHICH HE EXPRESSES ELEGANTLY"

Denver Post

"EXTRAORDINARY"

Locus

"GREAT SKILL AND ORIGINALITY"

Booklist

"BOTH EMOTIONALLY AND
INTELLECTUALLY SATISFYING"

The New York Times Book Review

Other AvoNova Books by
George Turner

BRAIN CHILD
THE DESTINY MAKERS
GENETIC SOLDIER

GEORGE TURNER

BELOVED SON

AVONOVA

AVON BOOKS • NEW YORK

The characters in this novel are totally imaginary and bear no relation to any person living or dead.

AVON BOOKS
A division of
The Hearst Corporation
1350 Avenue of the Americas
New York, New York 10019

Copyright © 1978 by George Turner
Cover art by Eric Peterson
Published by arrangement with the author
Library of Congress Catalog Card Number: 95-94931
ISBN: 0-380-77884-X

First AvoNova Printing: March 1996

AVONOVA TRADEMARK REG. U.S. PAT. OFF. AND IN OTHER COUNTRIES, MARCA REGISTRADA, HECHO EN U.S.A.

Printed in the U.S.A.

RA 10 9 8 7 6 5 4 3 2 1

For JOHN BANGSUND

without whose encouragement and
bullying I might have spent the
time writing something else.

The Truth about History

Nearer and nearer draws the time, the time that shall
   surely be,
When the earth shall be filled with the glory of God
   as the waters cover the sea.

                      From a hymn by A. C. Ainger

If I had been present at the creation, I would have
given some useful hints for the better arrangement of
the Universe.

            Attr. to Alfonso the Wise, King of Castile

Great men are almost always bad men.

          Lord Acton: *Historical Essays and Studies*

CHAPTER ONE

AD 2052—A REPRISE

"I wouldn't go into biology if I were starting again now. In twenty years' time it is the biologists who will be working behind barbed wire."

> Fred Hoyle from a conversation
> quoted by G. Rattray Taylor
> in *The Biological Time Bomb*

—1—

The Security Ombudsman for the Australasian Sector of International Security was tall but stooped, unmuscular and skeletally thin. His teeth were false; he wore glasses; he was quite bald and his skin, mostly bared in the manner of the time, was entirely hairless. He was unevenly brown—piebald, though no one used the word to his face—in the manner of an earlier time when bouts of exposure to hard radiation were a daily hazard. A greyness tinged the brown and with his splayed nose attested the quarter of aboriginal strain contributed by a tribal grandmother.

Wherever he went he would be recognized as a member of the pre-Collapse generation and an Ombudsman: only an Ombudsman could be so old—and be deferred to. Up to a point.

One such point was that they had not allowed him to breed. The youngsters (as he still privately thought of them) would concede much, even beyond reason, but not that. His genetic record was an outrage of damage and mutated combinations which even reverence could not tolerate. Because they had looked after him well he was healthy and potent,

1

but the issue of his fatherhood would certainly have been abominable.

He was sixty-eight, a rare age in the Reconstruction Years; that he had been permitted to live was a permission which entitled him to great respect.

He lived by reason of his intelligence, his devotion and his special knowledge; he was needed in this world belonging to the young and they knew it. (Though it was daily growing more accurate to say that he *had* been needed and they were becoming aware of it.) His kind were the anchors of the Reconstruction, the repositories not of knowledge in the factual sense, for that was plentiful and growing exponentially, but of the experience of the effects of the misapplication of knowledge, which was scarce in a generation still scrambling out of planetary disaster.

The role of the Ombudsmen—the original meaning had been distorted and lost—was to prevent mistakes happening twice and in spite of fallibility they had been more successful than otherwise. Else they would have been disposed of (gently but finally) long since, for the youngsters were not sentimental about incompetence.

This one's name was Jackson and he pushed at the plump folder on his desk. "I don't see why it should be my business."

The man who had placed it there was, at thirty-four, a Commissioner of International Security and his charge was the Australasian Sector. He answered familiarly, as an equal (which he was not, for he commanded far more than Jackson's fluid and undefined authority) and yet with the tinge of automatic deference which was an Ombudsman's tribute from high and low.

"Read it. These people—Raft and the rest—will need someone to lean on, someone who remembers their world to interpret this one to them. We can't assess the impact of cultural changes; you can."

"In some things." The youngsters, for all their steel-bright intellects, were a mixture of doubts and certainties, of truths and half-truths and outright myths; shrewd enough to reject his advice at times, they could be naïve in their assessment of his capacities. "I was twenty-six when *Columbus* took off for Barnard's Star, twenty-eight during the

Five Days, and at that age one didn't understand the world so damned well; great areas of my memory must be subjectively distorted. Besides, I haven't the time to devote to individuals.''

''In your age group——'' the Commissioner used the phrase hesitantly, for the implications of it were both honorable and shameful ''——I suppose there isn't much time for individuals. But this Albert Raft is one to be treated with kid gloves—whatever they were. Read the folder and you'll realize he's a problem, perhaps a whole horde of problems.''

''Such as?''

''Read it, Stephen; read it.''

Jackson smiled. ''I believe you're scared.''

''Uneasy.''

''Ready to be scared. Raft commanded *Columbus*, I recall, but the rest were scientists. I'd have thought them more of a problem.''

The Commissioner's gesture dismissed them. ''They're out of date; show them a modern laboratory and they'll unhinge their psyches trying to adjust. Raft is the worry.''

''But *Columbus* returned ten days ago. Why this only now?''

''We didn't know the facts about him. So much history has been lost, so many records destroyed. Do I have to tell *you* that?'' He tapped the folder. ''Most of this comes from the starship's own records and some of it is appalling—the picture of world conditions in 2010; the spying and backstabbing and double dealing; the treachery and distrust and duplicity.''

So much authority, Jackson thought, *so much competence but so much youth without a tradition*. He asked, ''Do you think your world is so different?''

The Commissioner was startled and showed it; in a life devoted to brave new beginnings the idea of such a primitive resemblance was outside his thinking. He returned to the safety of the Raft problem (but the question remained with him and rankled and burned): ''Have you heard rumors that someone called Heathcote is still alive from pre-Collapse days?''

''Is this germane? Of course I've heard the coffee-bar

yap; he'd have to be a very old man, probably centenarian, which is dismissably unlikely. Do you believe it?''

"True or not, a pointless rumor matters. A symptom of unrest. The folder bears on it.''

Jackson opened the folder, still thinking of Heathcote, whose existence he barely remembered; the rumor made him some sort of scientific messiah but his shaky recollection fixed the man as obscure save for some connection with the *Columbus* flight.

First on the heap was a transparent plastic envelope containing something he had not seen in forty years.

"Recognize it?''

"A pre-Collapse video-cassette.'' He felt unreasonably ashamed of its bulky clumsiness as though the world of his youth had betrayed him. "Where did you get it?''

"Canberra archives. There's a machine coming up that will project it. We had to have it made in a hurry and then view useless hours of the stuff because we had only the file labels for identification.''

As if the old artifact had rolled back time for him Jackson recalled Heathcote's connection with the starship. *So! And if he is alive, where is he? How could he have hidden so long? And why? All bloody nonsense!*

As if on cue a young man trundled in a bulky, untidy machine on a trolley, something conjured into existence from electronic theory and study of eroding museum relics.

"The projector.'' The Commissioner stood. "I'll see you in an hour or so.''

Jackson hurried after him into the corridor, out of earshot of the projectionist. "Where are the complement of *Columbus?*''

"On board their ship. In orbit. Quarantined. Out of the way until we have some idea what to do.''

"After forty-two years they return and ... For God's sake!'' The name of God was no longer a commonplace but the youngsters knew his habits. And most of the Security men had read the New Testament as a part of Hist. Phil.

"We simply don't know what to do with them, Stephen. We've fed them a tale of immunization against mutated bacteria and protection of ourselves against whatever oldtime beasties they may harbor. Satisfactory?''

"As they knew biology, probably. But possibly not; the twentieth century was not just a planetful of idiots.''

"The evidence says differently.'' Jackson would not argue over that but he had placed a previous dart into the Commissioner, who needed to ease its itch. "Is our world so bad? Even half-created as it is?''

Jackson said immediately, "No," because that was a brand of doubt the youngsters could do without. "In general it's an improvement, but the *Columbus* men won't see it so.''

"Surely they'll adjust?''

"They will conform; that's not the same thing. I grew up with the changes and have never finally adjusted to many of them.'' He considered a blow below the belt. And delivered it. "My prediction is that they will loathe your generation.''

The Commissioner absorbed that a word at a time; avoidance of overreaction was drilled into the service types; he did not speak until he thought he understood Jackson's point. "That will be very unfair. It was not our generation who carried out the Weeding.''

"No,'' Jackson said straightly, "it was mine.'' If he felt shame or regret or satisfaction no one was to know it. "They will realize that, in time, but their first reaction will be simply that this world killed theirs. Literally. And to them this world will be your generation.''

The Commissioner made the small gesture of respect, a token movement of the hand towards the heart, almost a ritual, given when an Ombudsman offered advice. "I will remember.''

He went off, very smart in black uniform, very efficient to the approving eye and very self-assured, which Jackson knew that at this moment he was not.

The young man had erected a screen and fed the cassette into his scrapyard machine. He seemed unusually young for his role even in this age of precocity.

"How old are you?''

"Seventeen, sir.''

"Technician?''

"First Class, sir."

At seventeen! "Are you cleared for classified material?"

"To a degree, sir."

The cassette had come in a folder color-coded black— Commissioner's Discretion Only. Sometimes he really feared the capabilities of these super-educated fledglings. From junk and theory they had built this machine, with an improvement to allow projection on a large screen, in a matter of days.

Aside from the brilliantly effective instructional techniques there were most secret and tightly restricted drugs for the enhancement of natural intelligence, the small beginnings of which had been known in his own young day, and plainly youth rather than maturity would furnish optimum test material. The damned biologists and biochemists; behind screens of secrecy and silence, what were they doing? Was there anything they were not doing, any area of human pursuit they might not bless or blight?

Campion, the Commissioner, might know and could safely be asked. Whether or not he would reply was another matter; he placed limits on confidence. Politics revolved around different possibilities in this era but they were still politics, ultimately concerned with protection and power and deviousness. And secrecy.

"Are you ready, sir?"

Caught dreaming, he said stiffly, "Yes, thank you."

The youngster told him conversationally, "This is from some collection of historical records, a bloody great batch of newscasts about *Columbus*." With the job begun, enthusiasm forgot to be deferential and Jackson wondered, like old men down the centuries, what these polite kids were really like. "The Commissioner picked this one to show you."

"To show me what?"

"Don't know; it seems pretty ordinary. Just interviews." *So I'm supposed to catch on to whatever Ian caught on to.* "But this one has been tampered with. We think this is the full record but that some sections were not shown on the newscast and the thing was later reassembled for preservation. They must have had a strong historical sense."

Ah, you trusting child! "Lord, boy, they recorded everything down to their retinal patterns; by the time of the Collapse they were literally bugging themselves for posterity." Actually for self-protection, but that would take too much explaining. "Can you recognize the doctored sections?"

"I've got them noted."

"Call them as we go."

"Right."

"What's the date of this thing?"

"March 11, 2088."

He had been twenty-four years old; he might well have seen this newscast. Within minutes he knew he had; his visual memory was tenacious but this returned with a clarity quite extraordinary after forty-four years.

A blare of theme music, four decades forgotten, set the period. A familiar pattern of dancing geometry capered, split, reformed into letters: MATTERS OF MOMENT.

Saturday night—Channel 2—Melbourne. He was seized by a violent, unhappy nostalgia. *Melbourne my lovely old monster! But we had to kill you; it was necessary.*

The voice-over (name eluding him) said, "We—the camera crew and I—recorded this in America only hours ago. It's another Matters of Moment scoop!"

COLUMBUS SIX screamed the title, brilliant scarlet against stars and darkness. *Six? Of course; there had been all those miniature unmanned test vehicles.*

The title skittered off into infinity past a cratered Luna and a ringed Saturn. *Standard, recognizable objects; after three decades of space most still hadn't appreciated the difference between a planet and a star.* The camera cut to a medium shot of *Columbus*, a tracery of metal struts sunlit against the stars. (Doctored, of course; actually the thing would have been hard to see.)

It was an ugly structure. "Blowing your way to heaven on a klaxon" had been the joke of the day, and it fitted. *Columbus* resembled nothing so much as the skeleton of an old-fashioned motor horn of the early years of the century, with the great flare of the monopole rim tapering to a wasp waist and expanding to a cylindrical bulge at the rear end. The bulge, housing quarters and nuclear plant, was solidly metal-walled but the rest was spiderweb, a frame surrounding emptiness. Wrap a sheath of polished brass around it and there would be your klaxon. And blow, Gabriel, blow!

The ship shrank swiftly into a lower corner of the screen and from its flare a shatteringly green line leapt across space, shimmering in an illusion of speed. The words BAR-NARD'S STAR appeared in at first tiny letters at its far end, then swelled to fill the screen.

The view cut to a studio technician's idea of Barnard's Star (or any goddamned star, what the hell?)—a slumbrous coal in the womb of night, crimson, menacing. A red dwarf. Round it, at accelerated speeds and in impossibly close orbits, swung two globes which, for an eyecatching composition, the technicians had lit in ice-blue and striated bronze.

"Barnard's Star!" cried the off-screen voice, building urgency as if the world was not fed to the teeth with similar spacecasts. "More than fifty million *million* kilometers from Earth! Already known to be circled by two huge planets and who knows how many more? The goal of *Columbus*!"

Cut to a shot of Earth from space (authentic, from the library, cyclone whirling like mad over the China Sea): cut to the announcer in the studio.

Barnes Falworth. The slightly soupy voice clicked recollection into place. *Poor glamor boy—gone with the wind, the pestilence, the famine, the March of Man. The staggering stumble of man.*

"You may think the last possible drop of interest has been drained from the starship while we have watched it building, strut by plate by bolt by weld, for three years. But tonight we have the final factor which brings the years of preparation home to us as human beings." Pause for a last squeeze at non-existent drama. "The names of the star travelers have been released!" Pause again, with small smile of promise. "And we bring you, first in the world to interview them, their faces and voices. Here they are—the fabulous men!"

Forgotten. All those years out there, and forgotten. Poor bastards.

The camera cut to an austerely military lounge-room and seven unfabulous-looking men. Two were playing chess, two reading, two chatting; one, a little separate from the others, merely sat. All save the last tried to look as though failing to be aware of a camera was their normal way of life; he simply looked uncomfortable.

The camera inspected the chess players. Falworth purred, "Doctor Ivan Doronin, physician-psychiatrist——" Doronin looked up on cue, smiled, nodded, looked down and moved a piece "——and Doctor Piotr Kulayev, biologist and radiologist——" Kulayev managed an abstracted smile while he scanned Doronin's inroad on his middle game "——both of the USSR."

The view moved to a thin blond gent with a pipe and a book which he laid on his knee before the camera could kick it out of his hand. "Doctor James Lindley, surgeon-psychiatrist. Of Britain." Lindley gave a clear "Good evening" in a voice as English as Oxford, money and a distaste for the camera could make it.

Two armed-forces types, clean cut and crew cut but not much at ease, were "Doctor Ewan Matthews, astronomer-physicist, and Doctor Gordon Fraser, astronomer-mathematician. Both of the USA."

Matthews offered a strained "Hi!" in a voice that owed something to education and something to the Bronx—the old, forgotten, pounded-into-rubble Bronx. Fraser said, "Howdy," trying to be gracious-relaxed. Despite his name the voice recalled a boyhood spent in the environs of Yoknapatawpha County. *And who, save for an unlikely specialist in literary archives, remembers Yoknapatawpha County?*

A slightly fleshy gentleman with spectacles and bushy eyebrows was Doctor Joachim Streich, bio-chemist and neurosurgeon, of Germany. He gave "Good evening" in nearly accentless English.

The lens examined the man sitting apart more thoroughly, from above and below and both sides. He was notable for an ugly face whose individually acceptable features seemed clumsily mated and for the fact that of the seven only he wore clothes he might have slept in. And for the additional fact that, forty-four years later, Jackson remembered him. And then thought, *It isn't memory; I have seen him somewhere. Recently. And that's not possible. Or is that one of the things I'm supposed to catch on to?*

Falworth positively smirked his climax. "Last and not at

all least—Senior Officer Albert Raft, Commander of *Columbus*.''

Raft opened his mouth, thought of nothing to say, glared at the camera with demented self-control and finally made a strangled sound of greeting.

Falworth moved with relief into a sequence better than a round of name calling and Jackson's curiosity noted that he made no reference to Raft's outstanding peculiarity— that alone in this galaxy of bi-disciplinary professionals he was credited with no scientific standing.

''Commander Raft is more than simply another member of an illustrious complement. He is the living symbol of a long-kept secret, for 'dinkum cobber' Raft'' (Raft flinched visibly) ''is an Australian, and with him Australia makes her début in the great adventure of star travel. She enters right at the top, in command of the most tremendous voyage in history. And Australia has earned her right to this accolade for—and this is the long-kept, well-kept secret— the discovery of the slow-metabolism technique which alone makes this voyage possible for human beings is the work of an Australian biologist, John Heathcote.''

Well, well. But why a secret, well-kept or any other kind? Memory scraped a few vague impressions regarding the man, who had made no splash in his time. A rumored connection with the starship . . . rumor again! But to the world he had been a nobody.

The picture froze to a still. The young projectionist said, ''Something funny here. That name—Heathcote—had a sound blur over it, as if it had been drowned in some background noise. It wasn't easy to remove. They must have wanted it suppressed because the announcer's voice had been tinkered with, too, re-handled to make a sort of downbeat as if the sentence ended at 'biologist.' Was it worth that trouble?''

''To them, apparently. Perhaps we'll find out why.'' But they did not.

Falworth jerked back into speech. ''I spoke to Commander Raft earlier in the day and of course we talked of the journey.''

The view cut to an unidentifiable country road where Raft and Falworth strolled in sunlight, Falworth impeccable in the featureless business suit of the eighties and Raft shambling and disreputable in timeless overalls. Grubby overalls.

Overdoing the common-touch Aussie bit. Or was—is— he really like that?

Falworth was hearty. "Your job puzzles me, Albert." Raft's resentment of familiarity did not escape the camera. "As I understand it the course is computer-controlled throughout, yet you are listed as, among other things, navigator and pilot. Will you be called upon to do any actual piloting?"

Raft's answering voice was identifiably Australian without being aggressively national, but his speech was slow and stilted.

The kind who can't repeat a scripted speech naturally.

"Quite a bit. The computer programming is only provisional for orbit. For one thing, we haven't an exact figure for the mass of Barnard's Star and satellites, so there will be corrections necessary to the basic orbit computed for rounding the star. That means the provisional course programmed for return to Earth will need corresponding correction. I'll probably bring the ship in manually over the last months of the home stretch."

It isn't camera fright; he knows too much, and classified facts keep getting between his thought and his tongue.

Falworth cried fatuously, "So man still rules his machines! Now, what can you tell us about the flight in general?"

Still in the tone of one crunching through a balky set piece, Raft had scarcely begun with, "We'll cover the first eight years at one-eighth g——" when Falworth broke in on him.

"Please, a question! Why only one-eighth g when the slowest rockets take off fifty times faster than that?"

This seemed unplanned and Raft showed some animation in replying. Animation and irritation. "Because that's the best optimum acceleration we can depend on getting. Our fuel is interstellar dust and gas and it's spread thin. And not evenly. We'd like a full g, but we must have as many constants as possible to keep formulae manageable, and one-eighth looks to be the likely consistent high. And that will give us a bloody sight higher final velocity than any rocket ever reached or could reach.''

''Thank you. Now, the trip itself . . .''

''Eight years at one-eighth g will bring us to eighty-seven L—that means eighty-seven per cent of the speed of light—and five-sixths of a light year on our way. Then we'll coast for about four and a third light years—not quite five years traveling—and spend eight years slowing for orbit of the star. Same routine to get home.''

It was a flat recital; Jackson imagined Falworth seeing his scoop fall apart in sheer inertia. ''Allowing a year for orbit, that makes forty-three years?''

''I'm only figuring approximately, so it'll actually be a month or so over forty-two years. We'll sleep most of the time.''

''In slow metabolism?''

''Yes. We'll have altogether thirty-seven years at ten per cent met. and a total of five years of waking periods each for the experimental work and observations.''

''Let's see—five years plus thirty-seven at ten per cent living rate''—classical rendition of rapid calculation—''will make you all just eight and three-quarter years older than at take-off.''

''A bit over eight. There's time dilation. Apparent time slows to exactly half at eighty-seven L, and that cuts the coasting in half for those inside the craft. The effect before that won't be much because it builds exponentially.''

Falworth was not getting himself into an on-camera tangle with time dilation. He mimed confusion and despair probably genuine. ''Please! I don't begin to understand accelerated time.''

What's all this scaled-down-to-the-public shop talk to me? For familiarization with the face? Where have I seen it—or one like it?

''Nobody understands it. It just is.''

''I'll take your word for it. And now the inevitable question: What sort of world do you expect to return to?''

Raft became ruminative. After ten paces he said, ''There'll be superficial changes, but they won't matter much. Basics don't alter in a short time; history only shows different facets of the human animal against different backgrounds.'' Then he delivered the line which earned him another nickname before he left Earth. ''If there's anything left at all, it'll be the same old shitheap.''

That was how we felt. Cold wars, hot wars, pollution, overcrowding, hunger, diminishing resources, fragmenting ecology, corruption, violence, greed. How right he was, and how wrong.

The rest was ten minutes of bland, uninformative interviews with the scientists. According to the youngster the thing had been chopped to pieces, apparently to eliminate even the most oblique technical references. Jackson could discover nothing worth hiding in the babble, but at that time he had been an Aboriginal Rights PR man, too close to protest and argument to pay much attention to science.

One amusing jolt of memory came at the end, as the youngster wheeled his gadget away. He recalled that his whole family had seen that newscast, and what returned to him was the remark of his teenage sister: ''I could do a drool over the Englishman, but isn't our Australian a drear?''

—2—

A note, signed by Campion, lay atop the papers in the folder: ''Transcript of material found aboard *Columbus*. The whole FYEO at present. Ian.'' For Your Eyes Only, i.e. keep your yapping mouth shut.

The first clip of typescript was headed: ''From the private journal of Albert Raft, Senior Officer (Commander) of *Columbus Six*, also Pilot, Navigator, Instrument Technician and Electrical and Mechanical Engineer.'' Raft was also multi-disciplinary in his highly practical fashion.

Jackson began to read.

Two days out after a flawless fare-thee-well. Much jubilation and radioed congratulation and a certain flatulence after meals, possibly due to the lightweight acceleration.

And so?

The great adventure may turn out to be the great boredom. I had a juvenile hope that some special feeling would emerge . . .

Nothing is changed—"Why, this is Hell; nor am I out of it."

Oh, dear, a literary gent. Who'd have guessed it of shaggy old "dinkum cobber"? Like hearing the garbage collector toss off an aria on his round.

Marlowe said it for himself as well as for Mephisto. I know how he felt—like a rat in a trap. In my case, the parent trap.

Perhaps my childhood was better than many, but it was bad enough. I lacked identity, which every child needs, early. I remember the sensation sometimes of splitting, of divorcement from self and environment, while some other "I" observed the unreality of me and my surroundings. It's common enough, I believe, but most seem to forget it, to give in, to accept the illusory "me" of dusty flesh as all there is.

I couldn't forget. The only child of two near-geniuses (neither of them with the faintest conception of a child's worth) has to find identity or be swamped by theirs.

An introvert's holiday. Who were the parents? Should check. Newspaper files, perhaps? We were able to preserve more than most areas.

But identity recedes; the last mirage. But there are moments of near approach, as when they told me: "You will pilot the ship; the stars are yours."

And excitement tore my silly heart loose from sense and Barnard's Star became heaven in a red dwarf.

The uncertainties, the dangers, all Earth itself lost in the paradoxes of time dilation and slow metabolism, could not shadow the dream of the ultimate journey with identity inevitably at its end. When I came home I would know who and what was Albert Raft.

Then I learned why—the real "why"—I had been selected and the walls of the trap snapped back around my hallucinated wishing.

My combination of talents and capacities could have been matched by dozens of men, hundreds. I felt the choice must have been a matter of millipoints of difference. Or mere chance.

It was neither.

I was chosen because physique and manual dexterity and a dozen characteristics not in themselves unusual are in me strongly defined. The list includes the shape of my nose (measured in three dimensions with nanometric exactness), the number of hair follicles in various parts of my body, the range of my color and sound perception, my encephalograph readings, my IQ tests over a period of years, my endocrine readings and God knows what else.

Out here, in this incarnation of everywhere and nowhere, I am still what John made me—an experimental rat in a biological trap.

John? Heathcote? No pie without a biologist's finger in it. I could almost hope there's a Hell, just for their judgement.

They're waiting on my return, after forty-two of their snailpace years, so that a new generation of cell carpenters and psychometrists can use me as a control for their examination of the others. Once and for all the great argument, environment versus heredity, will have its answer.

They must be damned sure we will actually get back. Ourselves think the odds are good but not all that certainly good.

As for those others, growing to manhood back there on the mudball, the less said the better. But how much will long remain private in this cul-de-sac of the cosmos? Before the years are through we will have investigated each other clear down to the synapses for lack of better amusement.

What others? Is this what we are after? Why can't people write their journals for posterity instead of the blowing-off of private steam?

*   *   *

Day 10. Some four hundred and fifty million kilometers
out, further than anyone has ever been. Probes have passed
Jupiter but no man. That's a nice big diary thought but quite
meaningless; you can't stay excited in a job already settled
into routine.

The first days were active while the schedules were set
up in ant-scurry efficiency; then the computers took over
and we lapsed into our first spasm of little to do. The real
work starts when we are free of the major impact of solar
radiation, and that won't be long now.

Meanwhile we talk, and talk circles endlessly around
homing year—2052. And here's a curious thing: when
these high-powered IQs attempt subjects outside their field
they produce ideas as woolly and flaccid as those of the
people next door at home. They throw their special jargons
at each other—and sometimes throw them clear over my
head—and I stay shut up until they stray on to ground of
my experience. And then they are little better than tattling
housewives.

Conventional! They confine their guessing to hardware
technology and their predictions are straight from the science fiction magazines. The older magazines, at that.

Cheap beamed power. (Nuclear of course; will they
never learn?) Synthetic foods. Deep ocean farming. Disposable clothing. Weather control. As though these things
are not already embryonically with us or at least on the
drawing boards.

But nobody mentions gerontology or gene manipulation
or a dozen related monster-weavings striving to break out
of the laboratories. Streich and Kulayev, who might be expected to point up such matters, stick to snappier computers
and labor-saving devices for the kitchen.

They may be afraid. Who knows what private orders they
may have had, in spite of the love-and-kisses international
nature of the trip?

Fraser and Matthews as Americans distrust the two Russians, who distrust them. That weed hasn't withered despite
the moving together of the two nations in the face of China's contemptuous isolationism; they see espionage and
subtlety feeding in with every computer tape. Britain and

Germany, those traditional enemies, get along as they always did in peacetime, keeping suspicion out of sight. The poor Australian bothers nobody; he isn't a scientist and so has nothing intelligible to say.

I suppose I'll have to put a stop to that eventually; not too roughly, I hope.

But even friendly Streich and Lindley can offer the rough edges of their tongues, as when Lindley said he hoped on return to find psychology established as an exact science, and Streich cut him down with an unpretty insolence.

"And so the end of psychologists, superseded by computerized chemo-therapy!"

Lindley remained placid (a tough training, English gentlehood) but I saw the sting enter. "That has been the direction since the early sixties, but therapy is not the only end of the discipline; the final uses have scarcely been glimpsed yet."

Said Streich, "Then guessing is useless," and talked of something else.

From Streich it was a fear reaction. They all fear the psychiatrists. They "know" that Lindley and Doronin are the ship's spies; nobody has said it but it hangs in the air. They "know" their actions and words will be analyzed, from take-off to planetfall, that "reports" will be made and that sharp and disastrous consequences may follow.

The idea clings in part because a harmless percentage of it is true. We know the working quarters are bugged for sight and sound, but this is overt. Our activities as a group will be the foundation of a whole new discipline dealing with the behavior—psychological, social and physical—of man-in-space. But the private cabins are not bugged; a measure of inalienable privacy was recognized as an absolute requirement.

But I'll bet that every one of them has searched his cabin for suspicious fittings and hollows and concealed leads. They know what manner of place their world is. (All right, little truth book; I've searched mine, too.)

Referring back to the 2052 discussion, only Fraser (speaking today's language incongruously in that cotton pickin' mammy accent) attempted to break the mediocrity barrier.

"Don't be surprised," he said, "if beamed transmission of matter is with us by then. It sounds long range, but technology's a-galloping."

They leapt on him, clawing. "We haven't the scanning techniques——" "We haven't a computer complex enough——" "We haven't the math——."

He answered them quietly. "We haven't the hardware and we haven't a suitably cheap power source, but the math was worked out in 'eighty-eight, just two years ago."

Was it indeed? Then there'll be some ratting of archives to see if those papers still exist.

It silenced them for a moment. From math to hardware is notoriously a short step and getting shorter, and Fraser's inside knowledge gave him an unfair advantage in augury.

While a little resentment spilled off on Fraser, Jim Lindley asked me, "What do you think, Old Silence?"

I don't mind that from Jim; his mockery is friendly and gentle, a long remove from Fraser's bouts of studied insolence. I said, perhaps feeling mildly fed up with their caution, "I don't waste time on it; technical change is too fast for prophecies. The face of the world—which isn't the part of it that matters—will probably be unrecognizable. Entering a room in 2052 we won't so much as know where to look for a light switch—if they still use anything so cumbersome as a switch—and if we can recognize a wall-less, electronically defined space as a room."

An effective gabble-stopper. It served pusillanimity right.

A touch of arrogance, Albert? Inferiority yelping? However, E for Effort, though we do use light switches and we prefer walls round our rooms, but the world will be strange to you. In unexpected ways, old "shitheap" Raft.

There was an aftermath; Lindley paid me a visit in my cabin.

I suppose I am a cold man; I have no feeling of closeness with *Columbus*'s complement and an active dislike for one of them. And only for Jim Lindley a positive liking. It is not as deep as friendship but at least it is positive.

He curled his narrow body (he's a most elegant scare-crow) in the spare chair and said, "I have a problem."

"Administrative?"

"Yes no maybe."

"Personal?" I had to grin—my last grin for a while. "Not a psychiatrist Dorothy Dixing the Commander!"

He smiled back, joylessly, and that was a warning. Within the limits of his professional competence he has therapeutic authority before which I must bow or show excellent cause why not.

He said, "You're the problem," and waited, giving me time to erect defenses against everything except the weaknesses I wasn't aware of, then referred to the discussion in the lounge. "You dropped that silly symposium in its tracks."

Naughty Albert! But I wasn't prepared to play erring child to his father figure. "They talk like schoolboys, the obvious passes them by."

"Such as?"

Though the trap was laid in the sight of the bird I wasn't about to flutter away from simple fact. "Biology is the shadow over the world, but nobody mentioned biological advances."

"Which are not necessarily advances?"

"You know it."

"They won't be mentioned for a while. Nobody will risk politics until the tribal instinct overcomes national distrusts."

"You agree that biology is politics?"

"It will be by the time we get home."

"Nice to know somebody sees it."

Then, having agreed with me, he hit me just as he had intended. "Albert, nobody could live with you through years of training schools without knowing your animus against biological research. It sticks out like a warning sign and the subject will continue tabu in your presence. A simple social safeguard."

What could I say? Offer reasons? Betray secrets? You don't betray secrets without great thought, certainly not in the early days of a voyage years long.

I tried with the slightest of shrugs to turn the matter off as unimportant, but I am an amateur and Jim is a *good* professional. He said, "And if you make a habit of killing conversations they won't speak in front of you at all. Tonight wasn't the first time."

"What I said wasn't much."

"You didn't hear your tone."

"I didn't intend contempt." It had been a weariness of profitless talk.

"Oh, but you did."

Only an idiot contradicts an expert. I waited.

"Think of it," he suggested, "as a defense mechanism."

"Against what?"

"You tell me." Before I could be resentful or impatient he said, "You aren't running a shipload of incompetents."

That was outrageous. "How could I think of it? They're frighteningly competent."

Just like that I tripped into his trap at the first prod, stumbling like a novice over the choice of an adverb.

He didn't bother to point it out, but went straight to the heart of it. "You're the Commander; you don't have to stand in awe of any of us. What are we? We're good at our jobs but we aren't research geniuses; our work is programmed, year for year of the trip, and we're trained like robots to do it exactly, but you are the all-purpose handyman who actually runs the household. We can afford spiky personalities and petulant grievances, but you're the one who has to put up with them and smooth them over and smack a recalcitrant bottom where necessary. You have to be final court of appeal, a little austere and removed as becomes the archetypal arbiter, but with warmth available. My bet is that they gave you the job because you are capable of those things."

I could have told him differently, but I said, "I can't talk to them. I have a good lay knowledge of all the disciplines but with these men I can only stand at the foot of the ivory tower, shouting up." I had enough restraint not to add a bitter "just as it was at home," but substituted something in retrospect nearly as bad: "My most profound comment on their work would be a naïvety."

"So you feel baffled."

It was wise in him not to say "inferior." Or perhaps he knows by now that I feel inferior to no man. I nodded.

"Because they don't make the first approach?"

"I'm the outsider, the non-specialist. And in fact I'm not much of a social animal."

"So that's one part of the Commander personality, the removed and austere bit. Don't let it dominate. For the rest, you are the supreme specialist aboard. You are the only one who can take us home when the course programming has to be corrected and the only one who can get us round Barnard's Star in an orbit that will fit the research curriculum. Without you we are useless. Make us understand it." And while I stared, aware of exaggerations and suspicious of deviousness, he added, "But please do it gently."

It was an unconscionable buttering-up. Fraser is quite capable of the calculations and so is Ewan, but neither could manage them with the simplicity of approach that has been trained into me, and either would have to abandon much of his other work in order to handle them at all.

Still, it adds up to an egalitarian aspect that hadn't impinged previously, and he left me thinking about it. Under doctor's orders to turn myself into a good Commander.

Why did they choose such a man? There must have been good reasons and he knows them. But what is it he knows?

Day 20 and the sun only a brilliant star. Life in a steel womb sighs with boredom and I am becoming a compulsive writer.

The others are busy with their second round of activities and small tensions are developing over the allocation of computer time. Lindley and Doronin are probably attending to this—imperceptibly, as should be. The potential of a competent manipulative psychiatrist (I'm pretty sure they have both been trained in manipulative schools) is daunting, but sooner or later I will have to assert authority and require reports from them. And then try to decide what they have considered unnecessary—unwise? inappropriate? indiscreet? or plain contrary to private briefing?—to tell me.

Oh, yes, there was private briefing. I had plenty that no one else did. And so, I'll lay, did each one.

What a bastard pack we were. In a condition of terrified peace we carried our wars underground—intrigue, espio-

nage, counterbriefing—even in a UN project. At least we have gained freedom from that. But, dear Christ, the price was high . . .

I took Doronin with me yesterday on web inspection, and we slid up and down and around the frame in our waldo shells—Inspection And Maintenance External Manipulation Capsules to you, sir—for two hours of irrelevant checking and testing.

The purpose of this exercise is, of course, to give complement practice in identification and use of the magnetic tracks connecting the salient points where trouble might conceivably occur. Doing this six times a year, once with each member, will soon become a vast nonsense, but with Jim's nasty little problem-and-answer session in mind I can use these dreary occasions to get closer to them, one by one. (Though there will be temptation, when his turn comes, to push Fraser under a passing meteor.)

I did well with Ivan once I had noticed his unwillingness to move without me close behind him; he is mildly agoraphobic and the sheer size of night sparks his discomfort. He asked too many artless questions about the magnetic tracks and the failsafe mechanisms of his shell; in all this emptiness his trust in the infallibility of engineering is diminished. It's a safe bet that he was repressing a vision of tiny Ivan floating helplessly away from the web, slowly starving while the inexorable air recycler refused a gentle death by anoxia.

We were almost chummy after an hour or so of permitting myself a shadowy role of daddy walking sonny boy. I didn't *make* him look to me; he wanted to, so I let him.

I won't tell Jim. He wouldn't appreciate me as professional competition, and I want his good will.

All the time out there I was haunted by the old "blowing your way on a klaxon" chestnut. It is too bloody accurate. The monopole flare may be a thousand feet in diameter and the horn a monstrous mile long, but the klaxon shape is there. It serves to remind that man's supreme technological achievement is a clumsy agglomeration of mostly inefficient junk.

We went up past the steering jets to the limits of safe

approach, a meter or so from the lip of the flare and its magnet rim. There, looking forever into the starfield, I realized *Columbus* as she really is . . .

Not a ship of metal but a shape of forces.

A blind, hungry maw, with the cone of the monopole extending the insatiable throat thousands of miles ahead, trapping and ingesting dust and gas and charged particles—sucking in and accelerating them and feeding them to the smaller monopoles in the body of the horn, to be whirled in the vortex which makes of the whole structure a helical accelerator until, concentrated in a white-hot stream of brutally enhanced mass and velocity, they are ejected through the tail vent at almost the speed of light.

And so *Columbus* moves.

Then the cartoon strip of seven self-satisfied little men puffing along intervened, and with it the incredulous amusement of the cosmos.

That was the end of the Raft clip.

Some introspection and a bundle of mystification; much arrogance muffling itself in "self knowledge." Even a paranoid touch, or is that the occupational disease of command? Not a very nice man, I suspect—but which of us is in his moments of unwitting revelation?

Writes well; even stylishly. No doubt the whole journal makes a useful record. Well, well, continued in our next.

He took up the next clip.

—3—

From the mentascript recording of Doctor James Lindley, surgeon and socio-manipulative psychiatrist:

(Collator's Note: We did not think that the twentieth century had done more than conceive of the possibility of direct thought-recording. The *Columbus* instrument is crude, possibly an experimental model; no mention of its existence has so far been located in archives. The recording is loaded with mental noise which has been sifted with some difficulty; it was necessary for the user to subvocalize to establish a recording line strong enough to override his own background noise. Transcription was by print-out; direct feed to another brain was not possible with this machine.

Lindley was not an experienced operator, as is witnessed by the rambling nature of the recording which he seems to have used as a personal journal as well as for notes of observations, with little separation of the two. Punctuation and paragraphing are by the transcribing technician.)

Oh, the indignant tone! World cataclysms don't change the urge to oneupmanship. Now, Mister Lindley . . .

Hello, little machine, disgusting snooper in a black box! You photographer of souls, you make man at last the pilferer of his own mind; in you the fleeting thought becomes evidence and menace; privacy is finally dead. I use you of my own will (albeit unwillingly) but how soon will your electrodes be clamped on some *protesting* head? One thing a man cannot do is stop thinking. There is no defense.

I had never heard of such a machine until this one was so slyly added to my equipment list, but I wonder if Doronin has one like it. Surely the spies spy on each other and silently jot their secrets. *Quis custodiet . . . ?* They do it themselves, of course.

To be safe in 2010 "don't move" is no longer enough. Don't think.

Better still, don't live.

But that won't be enough; soon they'll be able to extract knowledge from corpses. Wonderful biology, and its new handmaiden, psycho-electronics!

Perhaps by 2052 the whole place will be a radio-active puddle, and that may be for the best.

*   *   *

How nearly you were right. But there are worse things than radio-activity—equally lethal and infinitely more degrading. You'll be a sick man when you find out what we did.

If we come home to holocaust we can always go somewhere else; fuel is the one thing we won't run short of while entropy still dawdles down. That is, if there is anywhere else to go; how much chance of striking the one-in-a-million habitable world?

However, back to my spying.

The private quarters are, of course, utterly private. Each specimen has a retiring hole. For reading. Or keeping a diary. Or masturbating or whatever. *Utterly* private.

Except that some lies have been told. At least one cabin is bugged, undetectably unless walls and ceiling are torn out to bare the leads. Camera and microphone are not objects but sensitized areas of those same walls and ceiling. The recording apparatus is in my cabin and the bugged cabin is Albert's.

The system is so new that no word has so far leaked to the journals or the electronic world. Which raises a question: who does it belong to? To Britain, whom I represent? To Australia, wishing to keep an eye on its man? To the UN which in frail, frail theory bosses all of us? Or even to one of the others, playing a tortuous game? Due to the system of anonymity hilariously devised to give parity of authority to the participating nations I don't so much as know from whom half my orders have emanated.

But someone requires a report on Albert, psychological and physical, covering every aspect of his existence during the trip.

What's so special about Albert?

Quite a lot, but not matters that would interest a government authority. But this I am sure of—that introverts are not the stuff of which great commanders are made. Albert will be effective because prod by jolt by coercion I will see to it; but he will be acting the role, not much taken with it.

So why was he chosen? There must be compensating qualities.

Qualities? Why not simple factual matters, unknown to us? Political wheels turn through a queer topology, even out here among the stately stars. Who, for instance, is making notes on James Lindley? Doronin? Why not Albert himself? Ha-bloody-ha!

So let me consider Senior Officer (Commander) Albert Raft, non-scientist, pilot, navigator, mathematical and mechanical jack of all trades, mother superior *in posse*.

Is he diffident of command? Fraser, our hotshot cornpone astronomer, calls him "dinkum cobber" to his face, and his pretence that it's all in fun is only cover for his resentment of non-professional authority. Fraser is not stupid, merely self-ignorant. When I told him his imitation Australian slang is two generations out of date he replied, "So is Albert," meaning that laymen are just not up with the world.

Well, they never have been since the invention of politics, but neither have scientists. Fraser sees himself as a member of the coming intellectual élite when it arrives, as the portents say it will, but he may be in for a shock. IQ may not be the only requirement for membership.

But Albert is quiet, speaks when he has something to say, offers opinions only on subjects he knows—and always knows them exhaustively. The others, establishing pecking order, find him hard to peck while he, allowing himself perhaps one peck a week, infallibly draws blood.

He is capable of subtlety but some overt show of authority may soon be necessary, because nobody wants to be first to enter Slow Chamber.

Each wants to see whether the first sleeper turns black and dissolves into slime. They know he won't, but primitive fear asks proof.

(Here there was a break, possibly indicating the end of a recording session or perhaps the excision of non-germane material.)

At thirty-four, Albert is the youngest man aboard—another social strike against him; the older men feel they *should* be able to peck him.

His father was a distinguished (as distinct from great or

famous) mathematician, which may have some bearing on
his facility for mental calculation. (Or is that Lysenkoism?
Must ask Kulayev.)

His mother was something of a social scientist in a classy
amateur way, good enough and forceful enough to be a
thorn in the comfort of a succession of Australian governments. Her work in the aboriginal cause created a whole
series of electoral frenzies.

*My God, Annie Raft! That bitch his mother! She nearly
drove the abos mad, too, in spite of the good she did. I
think she wanted to be the Great White Queen of Black
Australia. Poor bloody Albert.*

He talks little about them or himself, but some reading
between the words indicates that they identified with their
work and had little time or feeling for the deeper instinct
of child rearing. I guess at a lonely child, smothering beneath the weight of public-figure parents, picking his way
through an environment alien to a child's needs.

The boy seems to have had a great affection for a family
friend, John Heathcote. Mysterious Heathcote of the Slow
Chambers, of course. What was the man really doing that produced the Slow Chambers as a by-product? And where does
little mate Albert come into it? Did it have anything to do with
his selection as Commander? That would need more than
plain or fancy nepotism. In any case, Heathcote has been kept
damned near incommunicado; few have ever heard of him. So
what was he doing?

I do love a good myst'ry, Mum! At least my spying will
have some personal curiosity to disguise the shabby taste of it.

(A cut.)

Heathcote's unknown work spins in my head. As a
group, biologists are the most dangerous men alive. The
bomb we've learned to live with and pollution we will handle. But biologists!

What they have achieved since the sixties is enough to
put the fear of hellfire into Jehovah himself. Artificial inovulation, the gerontological drugs, brain regrowth and the

mechanics of gene manipulation—these are already with us, imperfect and unready but with us.

They are only a beginning.

Consider the implications, and retch.

(A cut.)

Thirty-two days out and at last a little extra-curricular activity. Ivan and I are psychiatrists foremost; we didn't expect much call on our services as GPs, but today it came.

(Here an interpolated note in Campion's handwriting: "What the hell are or were GPs?")

You might imagine you would have to work hard to injure yourself in a one-eighth gravity field. Not so. What breaks bones is not weight or impact, but torsion. Fraser, climbing flywise up a set of store racks instead of using the platform jack, caught his toe under a bottom ledge with an armful of photographic plates, came down on his arse and elbow, breaking the elbow and jarring his spine. To do it he must have been flailing like a manic windmill.

There's not much serious about a clean break, though an elbow is a nasty place to have it, but his spine is painful and only rest and ray lamp will do much good. Therefore—

And here's the rub.

Albert suggested putting him at once into Slow Chamber. The idea was right but hasty. We must be sure first that the break is knitting correctly, and it is better to wait until the time, some twenty days from now, when the first three will undergo decelerated living.

It was only a moment's exchange of phrases but it made everybody suddenly aware of the imminence of sleep. And just as suddenly they came alive with reasons why their turns should be deferred, enlarging on the important work which will suffer from interruption at this critical time and . . . etc.

Such schemings among the intelligentsia will cut little ice with Albert, who can be a philistine bastard when he wants.

Fraser was not rostered for the vats so soon, but Albert

can alter the listing if he considers the circumstances warrant it. It means placing an extra workload on Matthews but he accepts it placidly and has made complicated arrangements with Fraser for splitting and re-programming their responsibilities. Fraser was resigned and presented no problem, but he sparked one.

(Another cut. The narrative picked up again in mid-scene but it was plain what had occurred.)

Only Kulayev persisted in demanding deferment. He wasn't noisy, only interminably reasonable in that fashion which makes refusal seem officious. Albert listened and said nothing at all, which is just as wearing a defense, until Pete talked himself into taking a step too far, pointing out in his still reasonable way that he could not be coerced.

"I have free will and the list can be adjusted."

Albert spoke at last and just as reasonably. "Only by making complicated accommodations with possible injustice to others. We must avoid that."

Pete pushed error petulantly further. "You have authority now, Albert, but it will be all one in forty years' time. In the long run you cannot force me against my wish."

"I can," said Albert, "unassisted."

It was not a threat. A statement, almost amiable. And naked. Those hands and wrists could deal with any of us.

"This is violent autocracy! You will have to answer for your actions eventually."

"It will be all one," said Albert, "in forty years' time."

Pete turned to Ivan, mutely asking backing, and Ivan, without readable expression, said a few sentences in Russian which froze Pete as though he had been assaulted in hard fact.

So much for the intelligentsia when they are afraid of the dark.

Later I asked Ivan what he had said. It was this, and I gather it sounds less stilted in Russian: "Does your psyche demand punishment? You asked for a spanking, saw the upraised hand and changed your mind. You should now be at peace."

Ivan is a tradesman and knows when to be rough.

*   *   *

(A cut of, apparently, two or three weeks.)

I gather that the great problem with anabiotic freezing
has been the cessation of the various metabolic functions
at differing temperatures rather than all petering out com-
fortably at a given point. Differential regulation would have
required several tons of machinery per vat to take over each
relinquishing function and so keep the subject—sleeper?
neo-corpse? cop-out?—minimally alive. And as much more
for the revival process, involving complex mechanical mas-
sage, heart stimulation, muscle toning and God wot.

Heathcote's chemical processes invade the functions at
their seat of operation and bring them to harmonized activity with only a mild temperature drop (about ten degrees)
to assist the slowing. All this is accomplished with a single
bank of machinery about the size of a double wardrobe,
into which the vat is sunk. And freezing is forever out of
date.

Fraser was first to go. He didn't like it any more than
the others but had nerved himself to a show of insouciance,
and of course overdid it.

With his still painful back and splinted arm, we had to
help him into the plastic overall after going through the
routine of plugging the orifices of the body (are you listening, Death?) which he resented stoically but which even a
man with the use of both hands can't do successfully for
himself.

Ribald jokes all round.

Then we ran the tubes into his nostrils, sealed the overall
and lowered him into the vat. He grinned comfortlessly as
the transparent carapace closed over him; air hissed out as
the lid lowered itself to the level of the immersion fluid.

Through the fluid a flexible arm snaked out, syringe-
tipped, pierced the loose plastic and moved slowly over the
left inner elbow, seeking a vein. And I wonder who devised
that piece of mechanical magicianry? The soporific went in
and the needle withdrew, hesitated a second as it heated
and sealed the perforation in the plastic, and snapped into
invisibility in the wall of the vat. Fraser seemed to sleep

immediately; there was a low hum as the refrigerators started.

The rest was repetition of syringes entering and withdrawing as one by one the telltales lit to signify that a stage had been completed. It took about an hour. Fraser was very white but hadn't the look of death; shallow breath, every couple of minutes, was perceptible if you watched for it.

We put the other two in simultaneously, Streich nervously talkative, Kulayev nervously silent. As Albert marked the resuscitation dates on the carapaces I couldn't resist asking him, "Mechanical and electrical faults you can handle, but how about chemical upsets?"

He told me, blank-faced, "We'd have to wake them and hope we were in time."

"And if? There's always an if."

"Then they die." He paused on that, then said, "And we break out the medical alcohol and get drunk and forget it for a couple of hours. For your interest, I helped design and build that machinery. It won't fail."

Did you indeed? Were you that close to Heathcote? Are the Slow Chambers relevant to what worries Ian? Is that what the "others" are? Preserves?

Can Albert be as phlegmatic as he seems? Ivan has asked and I have made believe to wonder with him.

Albert isn't.

At last I have done what breeding and instinct revolted against but which is part of my job; I have played back the film taken by his cabin camera. A dull business it has been, but productive after a fashion.

He reads, studies Russian and German from tapes and writes a lot. The ceiling camera catches most of what seems to be a private journal; I'll have to read it some day, but not yet; even a psychiatrist shies from final indecencies when he does not understand the necessity for them.

The others appear in his cabin now and then but their visits show more about them than about him. He is not an outgoing type; I keep remembering the little son of brilliant parents, enduring solitude.

One scene, private to the point of acute embarrassment,

enacted several times, holds my attention. I can make little of it and that little is only a dubious guess.

Albert stands before the mirror, birthday naked, observing himself in a series of gestures and postures. It is not a ritual; the movements are random, not repeated in a sequence, seemingly dictated by emotional whim. That is all, but what is he doing and why?

We know queerly little about each other. During our training we did not live together; we had private lives and weren't together as much as it seemed. Each had special functions requiring separate preparation; even physical exercise was tutored individually by instructors who treated each according to his body's need.

So we do not know what people in close contact usually know—what the others look like under their clothes. We know the obvious things—Kulayev is tall and thinnish, Streich inclines to pudginess, Albert is muscular—but I doubt whether any of us has seen the others stripped.

In Albert this seems important.

To the casual eye he is something of a shambles. He is fairly tall and you might guess his weight (wrongly) at seventy-five or so kilos. He is plain old-fashioned ugly; his is a coarse, over-nosed, over-mouthed, over-structured face, belonging to a wharf laborer who has had a hard life. Imagine if you can a wharfie who reads Russell, Plato, Pound and Joyce and will spend a happy hour splitting hairs in such realms as philology and the Minoan scripts—and likes to putter with machinery and to construct surreal models of indescribable visions from any material that comes to hand—and can play the piano with petrifying accuracy and no feeling for music whatsoever.

His hands, so dextrous and flexible, belong to a homicidal butcher and his shoes would be size 12.

His scruffiness is proverbial; at first I thought he simply had no clothes sense, but now I feel there is something deliberate about it, a meditated act of self-denigration. He can reduce a tailored suit to a flour sack simply by putting it on and in overalls he makes conventional shapelessness a joke.

Think of all that as Albert contorts before his mirror.

He is much bigger than he appears to be, having a physique to make the gods mutter surly envy. Yet he scowls at himself, examines himself with the distaste of someone picking over soiled underwear, and turns about and scowls again and flexes his hands and twists his torso and goes through a dozen meaningless acts.

But no behavior is meaningless and this private performance could be crucial.

From the past comes a memory of a book called, I think, *Goodnight, Sweet Prince.* It seems that John Barrymore, a famous Hamlet of the first half of the century, had a pathological aversion to tights. Accordingly he stood for hours before his dressing-room mirror, loathing the tights and getting himself accustomed to them, feeling that he looked like a posturing fool and forcing himself to overcome the feeling before it should permeate his playing of the role. Apparently he succeeded, as his Hamlet is part of theatrical history.

What to make of a man who hates a body anyone else would trade a sizeable stretch of his years to possess? This could be the key to his personality. If so it will turn in time.

That was the end of the clip.

Q: Why did they give him command?

A: Because he was no use for anything else. QED.

Q: Why, then, was he sent at all?

A: To hold him on ice for forty-two years while the "others" . . . did what?

In the back of Jackson's mind a watchful imp leapt a gap of facts to land on an idea. *Raft was thirty-four when he left and is forty-two (biological) age now. And it is forty-two years since they started out, so the "others" . . .*

The imp of intuition had done all it could. The coincidence was plain but not the connection.

—4—

The next clip consisted of two sheets only, from Raft's journal. They began: Fifty-three days from home . . .

Jackson was cheated, affronted, denied. Not even a prose-poem close-up of the red furnace of Barnard's Star!

Just a damned great jump to the end. *I'll have every word they preserved if it takes me a year to read them.*

Fifty-three days from home and *Columbus* has behaved as a thing of perfection. In an age of planned obsolescence she was built to function at top performance for centuries and is bringing us home without creak or murmur.

It hasn't been monotonous. The waking years were programmed to the limit and we needed every minute of them. Particularly Ewan who has had to do the work of two . . .

I must admit to having no difficulty in forgetting how we lost Gordon Fraser. He was an unbearable bastard. To the others he was an amusing personality, a joker and a teller of tales; to me he gave an unrelenting sarcastic bitching, as if my very presence insulted his professionalism.

Then one day he was no longer here. He woke from slow met on his third session, opened his eyes—and died. Looking back, it was an unsettling death. Just died—that was all.

We still don't know why; the machine seemed in perfect order and we used it again thereafter. Perhaps there are side effects of the process undetected as yet. Ivan wouldn't risk complete autopsy but insisted we bring him home in near-zero vat conditions for expert examination. There should be no decay at all.

His death put the terror of ending into them. Only determination kept them to the Slow Chamber routine once trust had been shaken. *My* determination, that is, plus the certainty of a food problem if we tried to spend the rest of the trip in wakefulness.

Otherwise the years have been undramatic. Until last night.

I don't know what possessed me. The pressure must have been piling up since long before we left Earth, but had become so much part of my life and thought that I had lost conscious notice of it. Like living on a busy intersection: after a week or two you no longer hear the traffic.

I am neither ashamed nor regretful, only surprised at the power of a private knowledge that has been battened down too long. I have broken the instruction to secrecy but, as

Pete said long ago, "It will be all one in forty years," and the forty years are up.

We were having a mild session with the ethyl alcohol, of which we have far more than we need, but I was not drunk. You don't get drunk on two fairly weak drinks, mostly orange juice.

Something in me wanted to create a sensation; perhaps dinkum cobber Albert wanted to show that he's really somebody, with or without a doctorate. He showed.

Jackson threw down the clip. What about it? Did the death of Fraser have significance, or the fact of a few bored scientists getting on the tank with home in sight?

Ah, the instruction to secrecy. *Raft actually knows something. It had better concern Heathcote or I stop trying.*

Then he thought that whatever Raft had revealed, six people now knew it, and those belonged to five different national groups, though their nations no longer existed as they had known them.

No, four groups. Forget unfortunate Britain.

All friendly at the moment, but who could see tomorrow?

Another damned big headache for the Ombudsmen, for if the revelation were of moment not even Security could simply suppress the voyagers. The general public might not care a hoot about space travelers but the physicists and radiologists would. And the bloody biologists also, he supposed.

With a premonition of disaster he took up the final clip.

It was headed: "Further Section From The Lindley Mentascripts."

Albert, Old Silence, tonight you scooped the pool! Winner took all and left the expert competition to contemplate its unconsidered futures.

I know now why that fine body bothers you so much, and with only seven weeks to planetfall I must break into that clutch of obsessions before it does you harm.

With home only a meteoric stone's throw away it was natural that community discussions should return to what we may come home to. Ivan and I have worked like moles to undermine personal and national barriers, and predictions have become much freer; politics and national propensities and the undertones of war have been added bluntly to the influences determining prophecy.

Yet it was to be expected that Joe and Pete would avoid their own subject; they are specialists enough to be uneasy but not "in-group" scientists enough to be sure.

They are sure now.

From the beginning Albert has only tolerated these harmless bull sessions, now and then silencing them with a brassy conversation stopper. Tonight he boiled over.

He thinks, like most people, that he can hold a little alcohol without interference to his mental processes; but no bodily function is strained without payment and in fact his tolerance is abnormally low. A couple of ounces of "starman's gin" was enough to snap a restraint leashed for years.

I must use the wardroom tapes to get this six-way conversation accurate. My recall is good, but not perfect.

So that's how you two produce dialogue like playwrights. I should have realized it's the real thing edited into English.

We were at the one-world concept again, Ivan and I arguing against the likelihood on political and psychological grounds and Ewan supporting us with practical points, such as "What would they do with the armed services? The unemployment problem would be staggering. And the financial aspect—big business couldn't survive the loss of military contracts. It would take a century of descalation to bring it off."

So we were left with our enemies and fears and national boundaries. He had some faith, though, in the emergence of an intellectual élite, a hierarchy of brains confined to about ten per cent of the population, a self-perpetuating genetic pool of wisdom, guiding government.

So had I until Joe and Pete pointed out simultaneously that specialized genetic pools tend to regress to the racial norm.

And Albert gave a short, sad laugh that seemed to be a comment without a point.

Politics reared its head with some talk of international socialism and Pete, of all people (he is a staunch communist), said, "That means only a central idea rent by national schisms and schisms within the schisms—like religion. The world has burned enough witches."

Albert showed some of his ungenerous impatience: "It will burn more yet. Probably biologists."

That was close to the bone and Pete, who once would have lost his temper, pretended not to hear. Joe commented neutrally that every discipline has potential for harm and, to divert argument, turned to Ewan. "Except yours. The starwatchers harm nothing but their eyesight."

"But our neighbors, the space physicists, have some capacity for damage. There was a project for making alterations to the Van Allen belts by shooting neutrons into them; it was pretty sticky and I hope nothing came of it. Or that it turned out harmless."

At about this point Albert's restlessness really registered with me. He glanced from face to face with compressed lips and took short, quick sips at his drink; some contempt colored his grimness as though he alone had an opinion worth giving but didn't intend to waste it on pigmies.

Joe thought that if the Van Allen thing had been feasible it would have been tried. "It was an age of interference; a project did not have to be useful, only possible. I am more concerned about pollution control. The influences against total success were powerful. Such greed and obstinacy!"

Pete suddenly made a speech in his pedantic English. "They succeeded or they are dead, or returned to tribalism. Powerful nations were frightened and when that point arrives something is done; big, drastic steps are taken. Pollution will have been beaten at the eleventh hour but the price will have been the changing of the shape of life. Cities, traffic, factories, the very wrappings of our goods— these things had to be controlled, modified, even eliminated before we should perish, and these things were the very shape of our lives. Forests, seas, fields, the air itself may all be new and strange."

Ewan, who never took these speculations very seriously, said, "If they've altered the women I'll have a sharp word with the man in charge."

Albert told him harshly, "They'll be changed too."

Ewan was undisturbed. "Depends how. Bigger tits and more extended frenzies? Let's never despair over that."

Albert stood up. Angry. Dominating. He blazed with purpose like a man who has taken all he can and means to bring the mob to order, half exalted, half paranoid.

"These *little* things!" Only the recording can carry the sound of his contempt; it threw every word so far spoken on the intellectual rubbish heap. I noted Ivan relaxing, settling back—his sign of alertness. Too late of course. "War, pollution, politics, boundaries! They aren't the point and never were. The point is not environment but the people in it. Look at the facts of human evolution—our personal, hell-bent, self-powered evolution—and start wondering what has been done to men and women. To their bodies and their minds. Think of things that began in the sixties and by the time we left had become snowballing horrors that governments were trying to sweep under carpets!"

He was raging. Lecturing a gaggle of incompetents. Revealing the Tablets of the Law.

"Artificial inovulation and insemination, to begin with little harmless things. Hope for sterile parents and gene-defectives! Great news for hemophiliacs! Great news for increase and multiply in a world already in progressive starvation! Biology's gift! There were consequences—emotional and legal traps that still hadn't been sorted out thirty years later. Who is Mum and who is Dad? Maybe neither is the one you've been taught to call so, and you don't find out until one of them dies that you can't inherit because legally you're a bastard and your particular administration hasn't got round to sorting out the responsibility. So much for biology's gift; it could be done so they did it, but no one thought of the consequences. Just as they didn't think until it was too late of the genetic consequences of the "clean" bomb, the one that didn't load the atmosphere with strontium 90 and all that harmful rubbish but released mainly mild old carbon 14. Not at all dangerous with that contemptible little emission, save that it will hang round for thousands of years instead of a decade or so and eventually do more damage than all the other bomb products put together, because radiation damage is cumulative. The bloody biologists knew, but did they say a word? They knew the old runaround: You can't stop progress so throw up your hands, look distressed and think up arguments for saying it won't be so bad after all. Don't get together and put out warnings so pungent they'll terrify governments; don't set up a united front. Then you'll have all those beautiful genetic variations to play with for generations to come—so long as you don't rock the fucking boat!''

He stopped, breathing hard and gathering a fresh avalanche, and Pete moved into the gap, piqued and taking it very personally. "Science is not criminal. These things are amenable to informed legislation. Governments are slow by nature, but by 2010 much had been done.''

Albert's anger hooked into him like a claw. "You men of good will! How about your interferences less easily legislated away?''

He wanted an answer; he wanted a biologist to convict his own calling. And Pete should have known that soft answers magnify wrath.

"There were admittedly dangerous experiments. That was known. They were not hidden.''

"Never?''

And Pete, knowing he had trapped himself, muttered defensively that exchange of knowledge had been very free after the Paris Conference of '82.

"It was? Then tell me what Heathcote was doing when he stumbled on slow met!''

That promised excitement. The man had dropped so suddenly from public view. There had been a misty hint of aversion to publicity, some reference to health, then nothing. Most of us had decided that it was connected with the nature of his research because secrecy of research was a fetish of the eighties, despite the Paris Conference. Then we had forgotten him.

Joe said, "We do not know that. Nobody knew but many thought, and I think now, that your government suppressed the information.''

Albert turned his ferocious grin on him, the tiger ready for its meal. "You can bet your Teuton balls it did. And how many other governments sat on information? Just how far did England and America get with gene manipulation? One major breakthrough after another—then silence, as if all the micro-surgeons had dropped dead. Why suppress knowledge unless secrecy promises power and domination and war potential?''

Even Ewan was interested enough now to protest. ''Like Joe said, all things are potentially lethal.''

Albert faced him like a fighter. ''What's merely potential about, say, mind control? I don't mean the simple-souled techniques of brainwashing; I mean the ability to alter minds permanently, or even create them from scratch.''

Pete muttered irritably that nothing much had been considered practicable in that line, but I for one didn't believe him and I don't think the others did. The world's journals had gone suddenly mute on that, allowing twenty years of work to fade out of mention.

Albert laughed at him. ''Then why did the planarian worm experiments go out of circulation when your country—*your* country this time—announced that acquired characteristics could be transferred on a more complex scale than mere learning ability in far more complex organisms than a lowly little notochord? Lysenko must have giggled in his grave when he heard that one. He'd been on the wrong track but not that bloody far wrong.''

''Those experiments were conducted with bees and mice. You cannot equate them with work on a human subject.''

''No? Listen while I do it. A step with a mouse, then a step with a pig—and the next must be taken with an ape. And the one after that?'' He was harsh with hate and disgust; only sudden violence could have stopped him. He had sought some enormous relief and would not be denied, and now he asked a question that pointed directly to it. ''Did you never wonder why I was sent on this trip when a thousand better men were available?''

Impossible question; there is a powerful inhibition against open criticism of a commander. But I answered it; I was caught up and couldn't help myself. ''We wondered.''

Anger and violence deserted him; he had reached the point of release and the struggling was over. He sat down.

''I was put aboard so that in the year 2032 I would be

the same physiological age, forty-two years, as some others born—if that's the word for it—in 1990.''

Joe leapt on it. ''A control! Do you mean that experiments in transfer of acquired characteristics were carried out with human fetuses and——'' he broke off, worrying at it. ''No, it could not be done with the fetus. The abilities would have to be in your sperm, which they are not. The chains cannot——''

Pete interrupted him. ''We have known since 1970 that DNA and RNA are not the only structures which influence genetic information. But that is not the same thing. Nor is a fetus, even one grown parthenogenetically, the same thing as a sectioned worm.''

Realizing that they contradicted certainty they shut up and waited for him to speak, probably wanting to discover that he was talking hysterical nonsense.

They had no chance. I saw the answer in perhaps the only real flash of intuition that has ever come to me—saw him twisting before the mirror and saw clearly the group of powerfully evinced characteristics which would make him the perfect directly observable control.

I said, dead sure of myself, ''Heathcote was engaged in cloning.''

Joe made a little, private, disgusted sound of contempt for a specialist venturing outside his discipline, but the others were silent. Except Ewan who asked, ''Growing people like buds or cuttings? Is that possible, like cutting a bulb?''

Albert answered him, still a bit off his alcoholic balance but with the strain gone out of him. ''Yes. You can save your snorting, Joe, because old John did it.''

Neat and, I suppose, useful, but for what? A hundred Jack-the-Rippers at once would be hard to take—or a hundred Albert Rafts or a hundred anybody. Identical dolls. Robots. Completely deindividualized. I don't see . . .

With a crawling of flesh he did see—imperfectly, as in a haze—why the Commander loathed his body and himself. He asked in silent agitation, *How many were there and did they survive? If so, where are they? Who has them?*

*   *   *

The biologists looked mulish but Albert went on for Ewan's benefit. "You start with a group of cells from the parent body—me. A single cell is theoretically all that's needed but in practice it doesn't work, so John told me."

Pete glossed grudgingly, "The making of a human body requires some hundreds of thousands of orders from the RNA chain and one cell could not handle them all. Cells of the adult body are too specialized, though it is possible to make them do work they are not adapted for. If Heathcote really grew a clone he must have used a large cell-group. A thousand cells or a hundred thousand."

Albert nodded. "The cells were grown in nutrient fluid and the genetic chains stimulated—don't ask me how because I don't know—until a fetus formed. I think it was first done with a chip off a carrot."

"Steward; 1963." Pete again. "Practically an accident."

"John raised his fetuses *in vitro*, in glass containers. That wasn't his own technique; if someone else hadn't perfected *in vitro* gestation his work would have been impossible. The fetuses would have had to be implanted in host mothers and born in the usual fashion."

Christ, but they were good; we still haven't caught up with some of their work. He was right to be afraid, though not sure of what.

"At any rate the set he chopped out of me were timed to reach crisis—the point of normal birth—a few weeks before *Columbus* left and on my last leave before take-off he called me to the lab to see myself as a baby. Understand that I wasn't keen. Apart from the eeriness of the idea of seeing myself only a few days old I'd begun to work up reservations about the whole line of research. But I was curious too.

"I drove over and a bloody peculiar feeling came over me as I got near the place. I can't properly account for it; I can only tell you. Like being alone and realizing with the back of your neck that you aren't alone at all, that somebody else is there; you turn your head and there they are and the uneasiness goes away. This didn't go away, because there was nobody there, and the closer I got to the lab the stronger it became. It was uncanny and profoundly unpleasant; it made me dizzy and I nearly ran the car off the road; finally I pulled up and vomited. And turned round and went home. I rang John and told him about it and he was as excited as all-get-out, yelling down the phone. He'd actually hoped for something like it. Hoped for it!''

I asked him was he talking about telepathy, but he wasn't.

"A sort of awareness. A high-powered empathy perhaps. It's documented in identical twins, though they don't all have it and I think none so powerfully. The difference is that with me it's a revulsion. I don't want ever to see any of them or be close to them; I don't think I could stand it.''

Pete pointed out that the clone-children were experimental and born in extraordinary circumstances, that the chances were fair that they did not survive to adulthood.

Albert seemed to have run down; he was sober now and somber. ''They did. Or some of them did.''

I didn't believe he could sense them at this distance and said so and he looked at me like a lost child. ''This distance? It's nothing. Out by Barnard's Star the dregs of awareness were there. The fact of them never leaves me.''

I could imagine a dozen counter-arguments to that conviction but he was in no state to accept reason; I kept my mouth shut. For the first time I really pitied him, living with a couple more hells than most of us.

That was the end of the clip and the folder.

—5—

Could that be all? Out of what must amount to millions of words written and mentascripted over the years Campion had thought these alone mattered. Jackson closed his eyes, summing up.

An experiment designed to come to conclusion forty-two years in the future . . . But the future they had counted on did not exist; history had stopped and begun again. Considering what had happened to hundreds of millions of people it was unlikely that a group of babies, unable to protect themselves, could have been brought alive through starvation and ruin.

But—"Even out by Barnard's Star the dregs of awareness were there."

Psychiatrist Lindley didn't believe it but Campion, with more to be cautious about, apparently did not discount the possibility.

So: What could be done with a dozen or a hundred Rafts?

There are soulless bastards who would appreciate regiments of identically dependable, dull-minded, uncomplaining factory hands who could be specialized from birth for specific dexterities and simple needs—a fully predictable complement as smoothly turned as the machines they tended.

But you wouldn't waste Rafts on factories.

You would clone for mental capacities as well as physical.

You could produce . . .

. . . powerful, high-stamina, high-dexterity, fully integrated, unbreakably group-indoctrinated—armies.

Not a hundred or a thousand. Millions.

All the uneasy tremblings of the experimental, half-formed, wholly vulnerable twenty-first century shimmered in his fears. He saw vividly the nature of the power latent in a process of endless, controlled duplication.

If Heathcote lives, who has him? Who makes rumors, and why?

He sat for two minutes frightening himself into paralysis, seeing his world crumble back into the wreckage from which it had risen. And for two more quietening himself after shock.

He reached for querulous hope. Only one miracle was required, that Heathcote's laboratory had been shattered, ruined, destroyed during the Five Days. Was that too much to ask of God? Probably it was; Old Testament God wouldn't give a damn while some remained for punishment.

Also, whatever had happened to Heathcote and his laboratory, something of his knowledge must be current still; otherwise the whole business of the rumors was fairy dust. Why should this historically obscure name be bandied in the streets when the very nature of his research was forgotten, unless someone or some group had not forgotten?

The rumors, then, were deliberately propagated, timed to gather impetus with the homing of *Columbus*, timed to climax with the return of the clone-father. If that was the word—parent? brother? broodmaster?

And Albert—hag-ridden, reserved, lonely Albert— would be the selected symbol of whatever movement was preparing its way. His willingness or unwillingness would not matter; any competent psycho-tech could handle that in minutes.

So the urgent questions were: Who? How many? Where?

Recalling his spontaneous recognition of Raft's face his scalp crawled. They could be anywhere, dispersed among the nations. He needed Campion, quickly.

Campion came at once.

"Ian, bring me up to date. What has been done?"

Campion leaned moodily at the window, looking out across Melbourne Town. Seeing what? In that direction lay only the great, squatting bulk of the Shrine of Remembrance on its garden hill. The rest of the city was gone long ago as all the great cities were gone, plundered for their metals and artifacts for the rebuilding of the world.

He said, "Not much. I saw that material myself only hours ago. We're looking for them, of course; there's a world search for doubles of Raft. This Sector is in charge— meaning that I am—because Raft is the focus and he belongs to Australia. Special groups are tracking the origins of the Heathcote rumor; with total recall examinations we should know that soon. Archives are being ransacked for papers of his that may have been preserved in the Pending Rooms. That will take longer; there are mountains of records we've never got round to cataloguing, let alone reading."

In the outside sky a cloud moved. A shaft of sunlight touched his profile, highlighting the long, hard nose and wide mouth. He looked enormously dangerous. So he was; that was his training.

He continued, "We need from you, first, historical advice. What do memory and experience tell you of the nature of insurrectionist movements? Which are the soft areas they attack first? What is the philosophy, the rationale of mass violence? The prognosis is that that could come, unlikely as it sounds."

"Unlikely? Try to remember that human instincts are under the leash of a saner outlook but they are not dead. Violence is always possible." Watching Campion's hard profile he said slowly, while he thought of something else, "Some thought will be necessary to reduce a mass of memory to essentials. A total recall session may be needed for me."

He wrote the note as he spoke: "Most Strictly Confidential. Obtain complete details of S/C Campion's background: birth, parents, associates, private interests and activities. Most Urgent."

He buzzed his secretary and Campion asked, "You've thought of something?"

"Unfinished business. I want my desk completely clear to concentrate on this affair."

When the girl came he handed her the note. "See to this for me please, Alice."

She read it, showed no reaction—that was *her* training— and left them alone. Campion turned from the window and Jackson felt a tremor of excitement at the investigation he had just begun. The hair color and distribution were wrong; the eye color was wrong; but these were matters easily arranged by a man who wanted to hide—or by those who wanted to hide him. Campion seemed a little thinner also, but that might be a matter of relative diets and activities.

And he, Jackson, who had had that profile with him for several years, had not at once recognized it. The invisibility of the familiar. He was visited by a peculiar idea: was it possible Campion did not know who and what he was?

Also it might be no more than remarkable coincidence, but he did not believe that; he was too thoroughly poisoned with fear for the young world he and his kind had built and preserved through its insecure years.

And Campion was speaking while Jackson brooded and worried and failed to hear, except at the end.

"... and then it may all be coincidental—there is no Heathcote and no plot and all the clones—or is clone a collective noun?" Jackson listened to the sharp edge of strain becoming clear. "Perhaps the clone died in its humidicribs and we have inherited too much fear. Do we start at shadows, Dad?"

"Often. But a shadow that shouldn't be there is worth investigating. There used to be a saying about the price of freedom being eternal vigilance."

Campion's gaze was questioning and his manner increasingly nervous. "You people liked your sayings, didn't you? 'Tomorrow never comes' and 'dreams go by contraries' and 'let sleeping dogs lie.' Are those what destroyed you? Did you believe them too much?"

"Don't mock." Or was he being obliquely threatened? "Our little defensive saws played their part, no doubt." *But he's only thirty-four and he has to be forty-two.* And at once came the counter-thought, *But is he?* Like Albert, the split tuber, the budded forefather, he looked older than his years. Alice would find out. Wary of too much silence he asked, "What will you do with them?"

"With all the little Rafts, if they exist? Nothing. They're no danger. What made them is dangerous; they may lead us to that."

"Depth questioning?"

"Later, perhaps. Now, nothing."

"Then why rope them in?"

"Did I say we would? We'll not touch them till there's a reason. We want to know who they are and where they are, to see who else looks for them, who their contacts are."

"Of course. I'm no tactician."

"But it's you and all you Dads who may have to advise us what to do with them. We don't want to harm them; it isn't their fault they were born, or bottled or whatever."

He turned back to the window and his profile dominated the light. He waited a long minute before asking, "Have I stood here long enough?"

"Meaning what?"

"No tactician and a poor evader. I have been told about my profile. Haven't you noticed?"

"I've noticed."

"And you are having me investigated? The note to Alice?"

"I told you about that."

"Dad, Stephen, Mister Ombudsman, you lied. If you didn't you're a fool. I'm having myself investigated; we can compare notes. I don't know much about my origins; how many of my generation do? But I'm too young for the role, aren't I?"

"Are you?"

He came to the desk. "I could swear it, but would that mean anything? Age is no guide; clone can be cloned in its turn, I suppose. There could be thousands of all ages, spread around the world."

Jackson decided for an impersonal approach, the only one emotionally possible. "If that's so, somebody spread them, and knows how to call them in. You may be contacted."

"No. I'm Security, which could be a development they didn't foresee. I have no nation, no loyalty except to the world. They wouldn't risk coming to me." But he was not sure and it showed. He said, so earnestly that suspicion rocked, "Stephen, if I'm a danger I want to be killed."

Jackson cut that away stolidly. "In your position that's the line I'd take." Saying the words hurt them both.

"Are we enemies, Dad?" He stepped back. "Enemies, Mister Ombudsman?"

"Not yet."

But they had become cautious of being friends.

—6—

The next morning he received a note from Campion, uncharacteristically skittish, the posturing of a wounded and worried man.

"Tomorrow has come, the dream has usurped its contrary and the sleeping dog has wakened. Two possibles in America, one dead ringer in France and one little Albert right here in Melbourne Town. We're going to bring the starman home and lay him out for bait."

From a back-of-the-mind ambush emerged a thought that should have come much sooner. Could Heathcote really have expected to survive as a practicing biologist for the forty-two years necessary to Raft's homecoming? And it seemed there was an essential silliness in waiting for the control to return, for if all members were identical did a control matter? Minor divagations could be checked for frequency and causation by further cloning of the clone members. The statistical approach would be sufficient; Raft was not necessary.

Then why had so doubtfully suitable a man been sent out . . . ? Raft's writings exuded the stink of complicity in high places. But why the complicity?

To get him out of the way?

If so, again why?

Because there was more to it than cloning, and the key lay in Albert rather than in the clone. So: what might lie in that solitary, bleak, unsocial mind?

Something he knew?

Probably. But quite possibly something he didn't know he knew.

Even something he didn't know at all.

He'll have to be scanned, cell by protesting cell, poor bastard.

While Jackson wondered, Campion agonized, in a fashion that would have surprised the Ombudsman greatly.

His stupefying resemblance to Raft was his lesser trouble, one that must find its explanation in a simple fact they would curse themselves for not having perceived. This he frenziedly needed to believe, and whatever the relationship turned out to be he had no urge to continue as anything but what he was, a guardian of the flowering world.

His work was the entire meaning of his life, and Jackson had stolen grace from it when he asked, "Do you think your world is so different?

For Campion it was a penetrating, unbalancing question which between them they had evaded answering until he, Campion, had returned to it to ask, "Is our world so bad?" and had not fully believed Jackson's immediate, too kindly "No."

The thing had dropped between them, but not out of sight. It stuck with the permanence of an idea fitted precisely into a moment prepared for it, and in fantasy he followed the conversation through the course it might have, should have taken, had he found the right words when they were needed.

"Do you think your world is so different?"

Himself, smiling, refusing to be baited: "Oh come, Dad, this is the world you Ombudsmen built to cut away the rubbish of history. You can't question it."

Jackson, somber: "You have trusted us too far."

No, that was not it. Too late his fantasy tried to recall, rehandle, but the dialogue had in the first exchange broken from his control. He fended desperately: "But where would we have been without you?"

And heard his mind betray him again: "Where are you *with* us?"

"Where it might have taken a century to arrive if you and all the world's Dads had not taught and guided."

The old face whispered inexorably: "Then what do you say of the American Soviet and the Kremlin Hegemony and the blood-feud systems of the Mediterranean groups? They also are the world we made."

Ah, he had the old man there! "You didn't expect perfection and it wasn't expected of you. These things have to work themselves out; they are the internal problems social groups have to evolve into workable systems. Security can't intrude. That's the ethic: freedom to seek and perfect their own systems."

"Yes, we gave you the ethic of non-interference. Is it right? Was it ever?"

"It must be right!" He could not see how his simple dialogue had reached this point of no return, of erupting answers to questions he had not known were in him. For peace of mind he must nail the problem for ever. "If it isn't right, our whole world is a sham. If the ethic doesn't hold, then the creation of Security was a vast error, and the national groups should have been left to their blood and savagery. And our system and all our lives have been wasted time."

That was unanswerable; the fundamental fabric of the universe cannot be challenged. He cut the mental tape while he had control, refusing to hear Jackson's fading whisper, "They have; they have."

CHAPTER TWO

PLANETFALL

There's no place like home.

J. H. Payne: *Clari, the Maid of Milan*

—1—

Between a gargantuan Earth and a resplendent moon *Columbus* pottered through a twenty-four-hour orbit.

The Security Techs (technicians? technologists? or whatever else within the language shift of four decades and a disaster) were polite and totally reserved. They imposed no restrictions (but the ship's controls were sealed in rock-hard plastic blocks), spoke only when spoken to and then only in variations of "Sorry, but we are not permitted to give information."

This, and indeed the very fact of their presence, did not sit well with the official quarantine story which Streich and Kulayev derided to their faces, pointing out that such viruses and bacteria as *Columbus* harbored would be relatively unmutated and amenable to remedies freely available in medical literature. But somebody with a caduceus on the breast-pocket of his black overall came aboard to give them hypodermic shots which he claimed would stimulate their abilities to manufacture antibodies; Earth's diseases would have mutated and they were'not immune to those. Streich and Kulayev were on him like wolves but he was only a medical assistant and had no technical information.

The biologists admitted, with reservations, the validity of this attention, but scouted quarantine as a reason for incommunicado confinement. They insisted that politics lay at the bottom of it, that shifts in the balance of power had upset the administration of the star flight. But they were by background and breeding children of state intrigue, seeing politics in everything.

Speculation died for lack of facts. There was only dullness with the Techs haunting the corridors like black ghosts. They realized the mass of boredom stored after years in each other's company and began to keep to their cabins. Only Matthews was professionally busy, hacking away at the immense backlog Fraser's death had wished on him; the computers, apparently considered harmless, had been left available, though the personnel record banks had been sealed.

Raft had his own ideas about their imprisonment and his inbuilt sensors told him what possibilities breathed on the planet below. The awareness amounted to little more than prickling apprehension and, save with Lindley, he kept these speculations to himself.

Lindley thought it likely that the "awareness" had imprinted itself so deeply that Raft would have it all his life, whether his "others" existed or not, for he had suffered a shock unique in history. He could not credit a vestigial awareness persisting so far away as Barnard's Star; it raised questions which clawed at the cornerstones of physics and he was not prepared to accept chaos while simpler explanations existed. He did not express these doubts to Raft, seeing no profit in arguing against a delusion which took light years in its stride. If, he conscientiously allowed, it was a delusion.

Raft busied himself with the log until on the third day this also was taken from him in an act of vandalism.

Small rocket ships—shuttles—flitted up from Earth and clustered like flies along *Columbus*'s flanks, and pressure-suited Techs came hand-over-hand on tielines because the shuttles' docking nodes could not lock into the starship's older design. Then they swarmed through her, general and private quarters alike, confiscating films, tapes, documents, journals, diaries, leaving nothing that recorded a moment of the voyage.

Raft protested officially and bitterly and met politeness: "Orders, sir." They knew what they wanted and they stripped *Columbus* clean, down to the most personal private papers. That most of their plunder could be reconstructed by the computers seemed not to concern them. They went, loaded, as swiftly as they had arrived.

Raft recognized helplessness but the others gave him the brunt of their fury as though he could pull administrative rabbits out of his authoritative hat; but he had no rabbits and they knew it, so they talked coals of fire, then cooled and sulked. He began a journal of this maddening interregnum, and that set him thinking over the few clues available. Eventually he formed an aggressive idea of how he might split the wall of silence.

On the twelfth day opportunity arrived in the form of the Senior Tech, whose rank was displayed in two vertical bars shining silver against the black breast-pocket. At the open door of Raft's cabin he stood briefly to attention.

"An official communication, Commander."

Raft, writing, did not look up. He completed a paragraph, read what he had written, made a correction, laid the sheet aside and casually met the man's patient gaze. And waited.

The Tech said, "Commissioner Campion will come aboard at 1400 hours. He requests that your party be prepared to leave for Earth immediately afterwards."

Expecting questions, he received not so much as a nod of comprehension. He continued sullenly, "Personal effects only can be transferred at this stage. You are requested to limit yourselves to six cubic feet of property per man."

That contained an ambiguity which forced Raft's tongue. He allowed one word: "Mass?"

It took the Tech by surprise. "I don't—ah, I see. Weight is not important, only the available space."

To one who knew intimately the mass-ratio problem of space flight it was a remarkable statement. Back in character as regurgitative mechanism the Tech said, "Other possessions will be ferried down within twenty-four hours," came briefly to attention again, turned smartly about—no mean maneuver in a null-g environment—and reached the door before a bored voice halted him insultingly.

"And who the hell is Campion?"

He repeated the about turn, less steadily, red-faced. "Commissioner Campion is head of the Australasian Sector of International Security and in charge of operations concerning this ship."

Raft turned the words over without pleasure. "Do you know," he asked, "that you have just answered two questions without a struggle?"

The Tech neither answered nor attempted to leave, recognizing a lesson in protocol. Raft held him to the edge of cruelty before he said, "As prisoner, internee or quarantined plague carrier I remain Commander of this ship and will exact every compliment due to me. Until superseded, *I* terminate interviews." He made deliberate and meaningless notes on the margin of his journal. When he was ready he said carelessly, "Dismiss."

Alone he pondered the words "Australasian Sector." *So this quarantine houha concerns me, uniquely me . . . and only one thing about me can interest Security, local or global . . . if they have lighted on that half-drunken tape . . .*

He had reacted violently against the cloning business as its implications became belatedly clear to him, had warned Heathcote to quarrelling point that what he proposed was more than a spectacular biological flourish, that the consequences could be catastrophic. And here came the consequences to greet him, with full Security honors. He could do nothing but set it to one side of his mind and remember his obligations as Commander.

He called the other five into the wardroom and told them of Campion's visit and how he planned that visit should run. They were curious, then amused, seeing well enough that simple nuisance making might achieve nothing, yet feeling the need for assertion. What Raft told them boiled down to: "Where you see a chance to needle, take it; if I give you a lead, follow it. They have to realize we aren't antiques to be stored until wanted."

In the sense of mere mischief, after days of restraint it appealed.

Columbus, having no fuel capacity problems, featured structural luxuries that were profligate by rocket flight standards. Among these was an extravagant wardroom which, lying against the outer shell, projected a blister window into space, allowing a full 180-degree view. From the blister Raft watched the Commissioner's arrival through a pair of filter-binoculars Matthews had produced from the Astronomy Store. They cut sunglare to a minimum and he had an excellent view of the two shuttles that matched speed with the starship with a precision arguing marvelously flexible control.

Previous shuttles had come without warning and the starmen had obtained only glimpses of them at odd angles, shadows against greater darkness or brilliant flecks lighted on a single face to obscure the shape of the whole. Closer view roused his space-trained excitement. First, they were far too small by the fuel-carrying standards of his day and their ventless noses made it certain they were not monopole ships. (A small internal voice nagged, *But why aren't they?* and was stilled for lack of clues.) Allowing for a crew of two and space for removal of *Columbus*'s personnel and baggage, no more than a third of their lengths could be propulsive system. This argued a sophisticated drive, and in his knowledge only the ion rocket could possibly fill the bill; he discounted the nuclear pulse system with its dangers and shielding problems.

The nearer shuttle swayed slightly as its tieline clamped magnetically to *Columbus's* hull, and he caught his breath as sunlight silhouetted what could only be an arrowhead airfoil. These were not space-to-space parasites but self-contained ground-to-space shuttles, postulating fully manual control and an accordingly high fuel capacity with an incredible waste allowance. He itched to come to grips with one of these tiny skybirds.

A porte opened and a suited figure moved clumsily out, fumbling along the tieline with an air of not knowing what to do with its useless legs. Sunlight caught the flash of insigne on the helmet.

The Commissioner was not accustomed to weightlessness; there were possibilities in that. An awkward man is vulnerable to indignity.

—2—

Campion's perfunctory hours of null-g experience in a Flight Branch school some years before had not been enough to immunize him against disorientation in a boundless environment or the shock of sudden reorientation—lurchingly downwards—when a movement of his head brought the huge Earth into view. He closed his eyes and felt his way along the line, anger rising at his ineptitude. (And always there was the subliminal sting of those Jackson-bred doubts, like a fortune teller's ambiguities.)

He snapped unforgivably at the Tech whose hand hauled him through the starship's porte and guided him right way up. Inside they stripped the suit from him and every movement was an error because his anger forgot to restrict exertion to a minimum.

His first impression was of waste. A space ship with a corridor and rooms opening off it like an Earthside hotel! He had been taught that conspicuous waste had been the identifying characteristic of the twentieth century; well, they had paid for it, poor devils. But the bitter result was that their descendants paid for it still and would for centuries to come.

He began to simmer down. He should not have made this trip; a deputy would have sufficed but the obsessive need to meet Raft face to face had overridden judgement.

While he clung without dignity to the shoulders of two Techs who tugged at his boots he saw the man himself. In shapeless, grubby overalls, with hair hanging over his eyes, hands in pockets, he lounged against the wall, observing the struggling group with professional contempt.

The likeness was fantastic and the Techs knew it; they also knew better than to refer to it or take obvious notice. In any case they must have been the first discoverers. So blue eyes under red hair stared into grey eyes under brown hair like feuding brothers, while Campion tried to comfort himself that a likeness between himself and this shambling ape must be fortuitous.

The ape raised himself erect in a movement Campion could not have duplicated and became suddenly the Commander shoddiness could not disguise.

"Commissioner Campion? Welcome aboard." It was a polite curse. "We'll wait for you in the wardroom."

He walked away with a shuffling gait Campion could not have achieved in weeks of practice, leaving the Commissioner to bite on the fact of having been effortlessly put in his place. He realized mismanagement of the *Columbus* affair from the start; her complement would be in no receptive mood.

He asked, "What the devil's a wardroom?"

"A sort of community lounge, sir. Derived from old seagoing speech." More damned waste! "Do we come with you?"

"No. Why should you? This isn't a job for——" He thought, *Steady!* and tried to undo brusqueness. "Sorry. I mean that this is still a classified matter."

There were handholds in the wall and he used them. Pausing in the doorway through which Raft had gone, he saw him again as one in a seated arc of dispassionately polite faces. Imitating Raft's shuffle he took a pace inside the room, steadied himself with a hand on the doorframe, shut the door behind him and positioned himself against it. He felt he had completed the maneuver without loss of presence and was aware of the impact of his tailored black and burnished gold against the pale paint of the bulkhead. Aware, too, that a careless movement could ruin it.

He recognized Lindley, excited and obscurely amused, as the one who relaxed first on a long breath and drew the eyes of the others with him to center on Raft. Raft was plainly puzzled by their staring, but a man does not readily recognize himself other than in a mirror.

Lindley said, "You read of it but never see it. Spitting image—almost. Albert, meet Albert."

Raft inspected Campion thoughtfully. Curiously his personality dimmed, withdrew, as though he listened to voices only he could hear. Then he smiled and shook his head but said nothing.

A slightly accented voice—ah, yes, Doronin—said, "Albert has brown hair and grey eyes. But it is astonishing, like different aspects of the same man."

"Hair and eyes are not conclusive." That was Streich. He and Kulayev chattered together about imperfect techniques, experimental sports and stimulation of recessives.

Raft said loudly, "Forget it; he isn't a clone-brother."

That was good, good, but also not conclusive. "You could have reasons for saying so, Commander."

Raft shrugged. "If you were a brother we would both know it and the point would not be raised."

"A statement impossible to corroborate."

So it was. Lindley said, "Take his word, Commissioner. It seems that clone-brothers have their own means of recognition."

"I have heard the Commander's recorded statement about that; it still remains only his word."

"You don't wish to be a clone-brother? I sympathize, and as a psychiatrist I have my own reasons for being sure that the Commander is telling the truth."

"And for convincing me of it." He continued sullenly, "I need to know, beyond doubt. Do you still say, Commander, that this method is not telepathic?"

Raft smiled at him, genuinely amused at an inane predicament. "I do. The awareness is strong and unpleasant; I don't know the pathology or psychology of it; I can only tell you that it exists. And who would want telepathy? Mental privacy is an essential need."

Campion said, without any lightness, "An outbreak of telepaths would be the last straw. I have to tell you all that you have returned at a moment of stress which nobody in authority understands or can explain to you. An underground movement exists and we don't know its meaning; it concerns that biologist of your time, Heathcote, and his experiments. You can accept, Commander, that a Security Commissioner takes no pleasure in being suspected as a possible member of your clone."

"You aren't."

"I wish I could be sure."

"You can. You don't make me vomit."

"I'm not laughing. Or do you mean that literally?"

"I do."

Campion thought about it. "You mentioned it on tape but I thought the revulsion might have been the passing aspect of a first impact." He continued, almost hopefully, "We still aren't sure but if this is so, then we're barking up a wrong tree. People with such reactions couldn't cooperate."

Raft nodded. "It could be a problem that knocks cloning on the head for ever; they simply couldn't stand each other's physical presences."

With a new line of thought opening Campion became careless; a slight movement displaced him and the attempt to recover lifted him six inches from the floor and turning slowly face down.

Raft came across the room in a sweep impossibly graceful in such an ungainly man, anchored himself with a hand on the door handle and with the other took Campion lightly by the shoulder to bring him upright, and steadied his floating with a touch of his knee.

"Stay still. Now—slide your feet across the floor to the chair. Don't push down."

It was humiliating but he needed the chair. He had lost his chance of dominating but had the sense to make the best of it, to assume a deprecating ruefulness and say, "Outside the Flight Branch we get very little orbital experience. I'm out of my element."

He saw a chance to recover the ball and added, "As you will be down there." That caught them; play what games of sang-froid they might, their curiosity must be consuming. "You will be babies in the new world, unable to stir without falling out of your unfamiliar cradles. Perhaps you'll like it, but my Ombudsman has his doubts."

He became conscious of an opposing stage management when Raft jumped his lead. "Nobody likes aggressive change but adaptability was a major requirement for our selection. When do we leave?"

"Now. With me."

None of them stirred and Raft asked only, "To whom will we be reporting?"

It was too cool; they were after something, but with six armed men in call he need not fear violence. "The administration that sent you out no longer exists and we don't know quite what to do with you. The scientists will want to have at you of course."

Doronin displayed the first eagerness he had seen in them. "Then perhaps we can go to our own countries?"

"Why, yes, I suppose so." With the words he realized that he had now a thoroughly nasty piece of business on his hands, one he had not given thought to. "With one exception."

The air tightened with defensiveness.

"I'm sorry, Doctor Lindley, but you cannot go back to England."

Lindley's face became wooden. "Why not?"

"There is no England—as you knew it." As the man's face became hideous he said desperately. "There was a period of—we call it the Five Days. I'll get the Ombudsman to explain it properly. Someone who lived through it. I wasn't born." He felt he was making excuses, pleading to be absolved of blame.

Lindley said in a stranger's voice, "There was a war? And England—disappeared?"

"Became uninhabitable. For another century, I think. There are a dozen such areas around the planet." No imaginable consolation was possible. He said drearily, "I'm sorry."

Lindley held a long silence nobody cared to break. At last he asked, "The island can be visited?"

"With precaution."

"Such as lead pants?" It was savagery, but the soul had gone out of him. "Albert! Can Australia hold us both, or have you seen enough of me?"

"No; stay with me." Raft left it at that and veered from the subject. "Was Australia damaged, battered?"

"Comparatively little. So little as to make us unpopular in a broken world."

"Then you are Australian?"

"In a way. I was born there. At least I think so; records were poorly kept then. But as International Security I have no country."

Lindley laughed. "One world! With an armed service to hold it together! We've had a few years in heaven, now let's see what hell on Earth is like. But Cap'n Albert said it all so long and long ago: 'It'll be the same old shitheap.'"

"Perhaps." There could be no reasoning with a man from whom tradition, kind and environment had been stripped in a sentence. "We should leave immediately."

No one moved. He rose cautiously from the chair to gain the mild superiority of standing over them. "It is time to go."

The German, Streich, said with an air of initiating a new phase, "After so long another hour can pass. We have had days to think on what we have seen and heard, which is little. What we have seen is only——" his fingers stabbed at Campion's black and gold "——that!" The detestation in his tone was dismaying. "We have had six black uniforms on six silent men. Now a seventh, who makes mysteries. This is menace."

"The uniform? The color?" Campion's mental footing was becoming as unsure as his physical equilibrium. "It is distinctive, immediately recognized. Nobody else wears black except for small dress contrasts; that is why we use it."

"So? A rainbow world? Pretty. But our century is not so forgettably far back in time. Do you really not think that black uniforms are ever the symbol of secret police, of arrests by night, of torture and blood and forced confessions?"

It was fascinating information, fitting his picture of their corrupt society. "That may have been. Not now."

"And the deaf ear to questions? What is hidden? Does the world even know we are here? Or are we something new and fearful to be kept in an administrative closet?"

Raft broke in on him, Commander of *Columbus* and all in it. "You sealed our controls and stole our records. For lack of understanding we let you do it, but we have had time to think and make our guesses." Campion tensed as Raft also stood and they faced each other, smart black authority against a shapeless overall loaded with command. Raft asked unexpectedly, "Are you armed?"

"Naturally."

Raft smiled. "You are probably as strong and fast as I am but not so agile in this environment."

As Campion's hand moved to the shoulder holster and he thought, *The idiot's going to attack me*, Raft was already upon him. He was swung about and the gun taken from him before he had properly freed it; he saw it tossed to Matthews before his arms were forced behind his back and up.

Raft spoke in his ear. "Aboard this ship *I* command and *you* request. That was law in my day and will remain so until I hand over command. When and if I find someone entitled to the handing over."

Campion remained still; he needed knowledge.

Matthews examined the gun and snickered, "It's a gas pistol!"

Raft asked, "What sort of gas, Commissioner?"

"A short time soporific."

Doronin said, "That tells us something. Let him go, Albert."

His arms were released. He tugged furiously at his rumpled uniform and at once drifted off the floor. Raft guided him back to his chair.

"As Commander I apologize, but it was necessary. What does the gun tell, Ivan?"

"He may also carry a lethal arm but he reached for this one—a peace weapon. Perhaps Security is basically a peaceful force. He came in here alone, arguing confidence and a lack of hostility. The black uniform is probably no more than he claims, simple melodrama. He is a man in an unimagined and possibly to him unimaginable position and therefore he is mishandling it. There would seem to have been some considerable changes in human attitudes. Jim?"

"Probably." But Lindley was in dead England and not much interested.

Raft said, "We'd better get the rest of them in here."

"I think not: they should not see him at a disadvantage. We must establish equality, not dominance."

Campion said. "Your methods are peculiar."

Raft laughed at him. "We don't much care for yours.

Let's begin again at the beginning. Commissioner, I am Commander Raft. Welcome aboard.''

Campion ignored the oneupmanship and the proffered hand. ''In your day was it customary to immobilize a protagonist and then offer a charade of formality to gloss violence?''

Lindley came viciously to life. ''In business, politics and diplomacy it was commonplace, and *Columbus* to your shuttle it still is.''

And that could be true in the sub-surface rough and tumble, though he had never considered it so succinctly. ''Very well, I'll play your game—when you return me the pistol.''

Matthews murmured, ''And balls to you, Fred.''

''Commander?''

''Give it to him, Ewan.'' Matthews did not move. ''Must I take it from you?''

No doubt that he could. Matthews handed it over with poor grace. Campion hefted it a moment and returned it to the holster. Gestures all round, he thought.

Doronin took up the attack. ''Our time is only four decades past; I feel that you are not so very much our technical superiors and certainly not our intellectual masters. You live in a different world, not necessarily a better one, and we are not country boys with straws in our hair. This had to be made clear.''

''Accepted—with reservations. It is your morality we distrust.''

Doronin's eyes widened. ''That? Perhaps rightly. Points of view——'' He did not pursue it. ''May I make an educated guess? You, a security officer, are capable of a kind of violence but not accustomed to it; your whole behavior pattern cries it out. So there must be a different relationship between law officers and the public than prevailed in the last century—more mutual respect, less distrust.''

Campion came in with exasperated force. ''Do you think I am some sort of muckraking policeman?'' The silence said that they most surely did. ''Security is non-national and it is not interested in civil crime; we guard the rights of people, not their possessions. We guard against encroachment and aggression and other less simple forms of anguish and disaster. We deal in population movements, conservation of resources, co-ordination of international projects, preservation of cultural identity in minorities and almost anything that concerns planetary welfare and what you could term fair play. You might call us international diplomats.'' Matthews squawked contempt and Campion surveyed him coolly. ''Very well—co-ordinating politicians. Politician was a dirty enough word in your time, wasn't it?''

''*Armed* politicians!'' Lindley jeered.

''Why not? Can authority preserve itself without a source of provable strength? Do you prefer anarchy? Ceaseless conflict? That was your life, wasn't it? We have certain police powers and military resources but they are rarely called on and have never seen massive use.''

Doronin was fascinated. ''An absolute authority? Unquestioned?''

''On higher levels it is continually in question. Among individuals rarely; we *are* their security.''

''That places a different aspect on your errors of handling us. What seemed arrogant authoritarianism was simple bad manners.''

Inwardly Campion winced. ''Have you been ill-treated?''

''Physically, no.''

Raft said, ''You seem to have lost some sense of individuality despite your talk of minorities. Your people insulted me personally by taking over my ship without explanation and without so much as a visit from an officer of any seniority. You impounded our records, which may have been your legal right but should have been explained. And the impounding of our private papers was theft.''

Campion chose words slowly. ''For these things I ask your pardon. I assume the blame.'' This was unfair to himself but the concession was wise. ''Understand, please, that the world is superficially in harmony but basically unstable, to some extent deliberately so; it is a world in building, arising out of planetary disaster. We don't know yet where it is going or in which direction stability lies, and the work of Security may be assumed as holding it together until the direction becomes plain. This involves swift decisions, sometimes so swift that the ensuing complications have to be taken on chance for the sake of an immediate result. And so with you; you were unexpected.''

Lindley crowed, ''Forgotten!'' He was becoming raucous: Raft placed a hand on his arm and he shook it off. ''While the world licked its stinking wounds the greatest voyage in history was forgotten!''

''Why not? Who wants the stars? We have no use for them yet and much else to do. That is a measure of the catastrophe. Some knew of you—archivists and astronomers—but in general you were forgotten. The archivists gave notice of your return and some routine preparations were made for receiving you home. Then something else occurred.''

He was not sure he could make the seriousness of this clear to them, but at least he had their attention. ''A whisper began to circulate that an obscure biologist of your era is still alive, though it seems unlikely. Whisper became rumor, springing up in many areas simultaneously; there was something messianic about it, a promise of a better world, but vague. The youngsters seemed impressed, but among them there is always unrest and a readiness to follow smoke dreams. Security was alerted because it bore the earmarks of a planned campaign, but the mystical quality and the absence of definite statement makes it difficult to find a starting point for investigation. Then an archivist discovered his connection with *Columbus*.''

''John.''

''Your Heathcote. Search of old newspapers indicated an element of mystery; it seemed likely that he had been hidden from sight by the Australian government of your time and his name allowed to be forgotten. And it seemed that this resurgence was fomented by a clandestine group for a purpose we can only guess at, so when you contacted us from space we acted quickly. Unwisely perhaps. Confronted with faceless danger you don't always behave competently.''

''Suspicion!'' Lindley again, barking, unappeasable.

''Can you imagine what it means to be the guardians of a world in traumatic fear of its own past? Even Security exists only by sufferance and a record of successful activity; a strong concerted action could destroy us, and what then? If *Columbus* contained clues we wanted them, and at once.''

Matthews laughed in spiteful delight. ''Forty-two years of documents to search! Hundreds of miles of film and computer tape, millions of scribbled words! Poor little black crows!''

''With a corps of trained archivists it was not difficult. We found Commander Raft's remarkable speech in a matter of days. And became more afraid.''

He watched their eyes center on Raft; the Commander appeared thoughtful. Campion had the irrelevant idea that Raft might make an able Security man.

Kulayev stirred in his chair. ''Joachim and I are biologists but we are not professionally blind. We have discussed the implications of cloning; we see that unregulated, or controlled by a power group, it could be used to ruin a civilization and rule the ruins. Given time, that is; it is not an instantaneous process. But it has an advantage over conventional violence in that it would leave the physical world intact for takeover, destroying only its individuality, its genius.''

''So we think. At least some of Heathcote's original clone have survived; there is at least one member in Melbourne Town, Commander, and more are dispersed across the world. We are still searching.''

Lindley said with a new mildness, almost tiredly, ''And so to gaol, children. It's called protective custody.''

Campion snapped, ''We aren't idiots. There will be surveillance which under the circumstances you can hardly object to, but you will be turned loose to live your own lives. We want to see who talks to you, contacts you. Particularly you, Commander. If a conspiracy in fact exists, you could be used as a symbolic rallying point.''

Raft said, ''I would not agree to be so used. I never cared for John's research once I had begun to think deeply about it.''

''Drugs. And other forms of indoctrination. You would agree?''

''We were able to do that sort of thing: perhaps you

can do it better. Stay with me, Jim; I shall need
friends.''

Lindley nodded, a calculating life back in his eyes.

Campion held out his hand, seeing the moment for it.
"You will need me, too. Commander. I am not the enemy.''

Raft hesitated but took it.

—3—

The size of the shuttle's cabin, as a ratio of its overall
dimensions, was greater than Raft had guessed; the motor
must be of awesome efficiency and small size. As he sank
into the couch, whose backrest and footboard shifted to
accommodate him, he fancied that whatever Earth offered
in uneasy social problems there would be a keen technology
to stimulate him.

Taking flight was no more ceremonious than starting an
automobile. A word from Campion, an acknowledgement
from the black-clad pilot, and the shuttle pressed him into
the seat as it moved. A faint resonance sounded in the metal
walls but he could detect no distinct engine roar. Fusion
power? Was that practicable on so small a scale? The required masses of shielding decided him it was not. But with
new methods of shielding, such as magnetic deflection? He
would do better to wait until he met those who could inform
him in technical language.

Meanwhile he pondered the fact that the shuttle held not
the three he had predicted but all the complement of *Columbus* and their baggage, while the second craft had taken
off the Tech guards. Casually, the starship had been left
uninhabited.

Acceleration built rapidly to about 2g. The shuttle nose-
dived towards the limb of atmosphere just visible in the
forward window when he craned his neck. The trip was
swift, powered and controlled every downward mile. Re-
entry was a delight—a single braking half-circuit of the
globe. (No observable heat shield and no rise in internal

temperature!) There was a gliding approach at an impossible landing speed and three tremendous jerks—tail chutes?—before the shuttle grounded, lumbering and bulky but controlled.

So the starmen came home.

Columbus, stripped, dark, empty, flashed through her orbit in a spot roughly over the tip of South Africa.

Twenty-four-hour orbits, close to the fringes of atmosphere in a space more crowded with matter than the outer miles, are notoriously unstable. Sooner or later she would slow, veer, dip and begin the long tumble towards Earth and brilliant dissolution in the upper air.

Raft thought about it and cared.

No one else seemed to. He could hear Streich and the Russians chattering at each other and Matthews being small boy excited; Lindley was bitterly silent. As if, Raft mused, any modern England could ever have been "home" in a meaningful sense. Psychiatric expertise did not bar out emotional unreason.

—4—

With the tail down the nose was raised above the horizon Raft could see only summer sky, hot summer blue, with a wisp of cloud. But there was sound, human sound muffled and meaningless, the sound of voices.

Campion, leaning over the pilot's shoulder for a view of the ground, made a wordless sound of disbelief and remained transfixed.

Matthews called out, "Where the hell are we?"

Campion turned his head slowly, frowning, abstracted. "On a landing field outside Melbourne Town. There's a crowd, a big crowd ... something's happened ..." His voice breathed down into puzzled thought.

"Sure thing. *We've* happened." For an uncomprehending Campion, Matthews ticked off his fingers. "We are the astronauts, the only genuine, original *astro*nauts. We have circled Barnard's Star. We have come home.'' He bellowed, ''You bloody nit, they want to see us!''

''Why?'' The flat enquiry would have silenced fanatics. ''You don't think——?'' He shook his head. ''I explained to you.''

Lindley crooned maliciously, ''Change and decay in all around I see——'' He let it die in a chuckle. ''This is fame!''

Raft sat upright and the chair moved obligingly to help. ''So the space dream is really dead.''

Campion answered roughly, his mind not on them. ''We have observatories and laboratories and a few specialized factories on Luna, communication and weather satellites—useful things.'' He tapped the pilot's shoulder. ''Open up.''

The entry porte slid into the wall cavity and the sound of humanity crashed through it.

It was loud, blatant, continuous, but did not seem very close; it could not compare with the surf-thunder of a football crowd; it was more like the inchoate restlessness of a street mob. It was a noise of shouting, words indistinguishable but not welcoming, a confused, angry but basically *organized* noise; it had meaning and direction. Yet it did not sound like the voice of a throng great enough to give pause to the authoritarian Campion whose dark form filled the opening.

The starmen rose together, stumbling over the politely adjusting chairs. Round Campion's shoulder Raft caught a glimpse of people behind a low, lightly built post and rail fence, perhaps a hundred yards distant from the shuttle, before the Security man thrust him back. ''Keep out of sight until I understand this.''

He was pushed too easily back, reminded that this was Earth, which proposed tricks to be relearned; permanent gravity was a more serious matter than unadventurous muscle toning in *Columbus's* centrifuge. He supposed, beneath a muddled wonder at the brouhaha outside, that he would tire quickly and move clumsily until he regained the habit of weight.

From outside the shuttle a thoroughly Australian voice called, ''Get the blasted steps down, Ian; I want to get in there.''

The pilot touched a control; steps rattled to the ground; the mob yell strengthened. Someone mounted, grunting effort and cursing in terms unchanged in centuries. Campion leaned to help him up and ushered in an apparition.

He was in his sixties and stick-thin, bareheaded and utterly hairless. His skin was a color neither sunburned nor pigmented yet something of both; it was *dis*colored. To Raft a slight thickening of lips and splay of nostrils suggested some aboriginal blood. His faded eyes scanned the starmen briefly, rested a longer instant on Raft, passed to Campion's face and away again.

Matthews breathed, "Shades of the hippies!"

The man wore what appeared to be a single length of cloth, deep blue and decorated with a pattern of red and orange whorls, folded and draped to leave one bony shoulder bare; Raft could not decide whether it resembled most a sari or a toga. From beneath it an advancing foot was shod more familiarly in a point-toed but bright red shoe. One wrist carried a red leather decoration like the forearm section of a driving glove, from whose upper end a primrose handkerchief peeped modishly.

Campion asked, "Dad, what the hell's going on?"

The old man—old spectre, old clothes-horse—swung his gaze back to Raft and said with strength, "I am not his father, but what is he to you?"

Raft settled back into his chair. "Who asks?"

The old eyes flickered approbation. Campion placed a hand behind the bare elbow. "This is my Ombudsman, Mister Stephen Jackson. He is a man of great authority." (Raft fancied a gleam of sardonic amusement in the pale old eyes.) "Commander Raft, you must speak freely with the Ombudsman. What he hears is . . . I have no expression with the right meaning for your time——"

Jackson said, " 'Confessional' is the word, though it is no longer used in that sense. Don't be offended, Mister Matthews; Catholicism is not altogether dead, but the forms have changed. Now, Commander!"

"The Commissioner is not of my clone. Is that what you wanted to hear?"

"Hoped. Can you be sure?"

"Quite sure. Must I explain again?"

"I have heard your tape. I do not accept it fully."

Across Albert's angry reaction Kulayev threw his own little firework. "Nor do I. I believe Albert; he never lies, but he may not realize that he is wrong. The resemblances are too distinct over a gap of two generations."

Matthews grunted. "Likenesses happen."

"In novels. In life most rarely. Put reported resemblances together and the likeness becomes vague. This is nearly twin likeness. Probability suggests a faulty cloning procedure."

Raft muttered, "We'll be back where we started in a moment."

Lindley was harsh. "We're already there. Your certainty was always open to question."

Jackson raised his voice. "Shut up, all of you!"

Campion protested, "I'm damned if I will. Where does all this leave me?"

Only Matthews had an unfeeling answer: "Up shitter's ditch, Commissioner."

Jackson gave him a cracked chuckle. "I haven't heard that said in forty years. Your position is regrettable, Ian, but it will have to rest there a while. This crowd is ugly and we must get away from here."

"I don't know yet what's going on out there."

"Nor in detail do I. The situation has not clarified much. Transport is here, so—out!"

Matthews asked patiently, "Why don't we just fly to another field?"

Campion's irritation yelled at him, "Because we need a booster to get this thing off the ground and it would take hours to get one." He continued more calmly, "Leave the gear here; it can be picked up later."

So the shuttles were not completely self-contained; that explained something of their smallness.

Jackson led the way down the steps. They seemed to have landed at the head of the field for there were buildings clustered there—low, with a prefabricated, temporary air. For the rest Raft saw trees wherever he looked, and felt at last the reality of home.

The crowd was even smaller than he had judged, perhaps no more than a thousand, but rowdy enough for twice the number. Still, it was not his idea of a large and menacing mob, nothing at all to a man who remembered the Energy Crisis riots and the police strikes of the eighties. They were too far from him for detail to be clear but they were certainly a colorfully dressed, humming-bird group and they seemed mostly young. Their noise was meaningless except in its animosity—against whom? Himself? Man, what a homecoming.

Black uniforms loitered here and there on the field side of the fence but they were outnumbered by figures in grey. Civil police, perhaps? They seemed only to stand facing the noise and displaying patience; they took no action.

Between one downward step and the next he recognized the nausea in his stomach; it had been there since the landing but submerged in the pressures of arrival. With it came a conviction of being surrounded by eyes. Not the eyes of the mob but special eyes looking with special intensity. His skin crawled.

He called to Campion, "They're here," and the Commissioner answered, "I wondered."

He tried to ignore the preliminaries of physical sickness.

The transport brought for them resembled a small, low-slung, streamlined bus with no indication of where its motor might be. It would carry about twenty; already the guards from the other shuttle were seated. Campion practically pushed him into the bus and climbed in beside him.

To heightened awareness the menace of the crowd became nervously tangible, infiltrating and reinforcing his body's discomfort. The nearness of clone-members caused the instinctive aversion he might feel for a snake; he tightened his teeth against a need to vomit.

As the bus moved towards a break in the fence Jackson's voice urged, "Speed, man, speed!"

The vehicle picked up pace and there was a corresponding movement in the crowd. With a concerted ripple, a serpentine flow, it heaved together from both sides of the gap; in seconds a hundred bodies crowded the passage through which the bus must move.

The driver slowed and Jackson howled, "Drive through them! They'll shift."

But the driver hesitated and the horde poured through

the gap. As they closed in Raft searched without success
for his own face; they could be anywhere, hidden by numbers.

On either side of the break there came a sudden, orderly
bending of backs and a united effort, and twenty-yard sections of fence were lifted out by the posts and flung flat.
Campion swore, "That was rehearsed." A gun appeared in
his hand; a real gun, not a gas toy.

The mob swept across the field and their target was not
the bus but the men in uniform. It surrounded and engulfed
them in a planned, cold ferocity. Police and Security men
were lifted and tossed by a mass grasping of hands; black
and grey rose momentarily as though squeezed up by the
pressures upon them; then they submerged, clawed, kicked,
beaten in a storm of fury that had seemed only noisy animus a heartbeat before. Taken whole by the unexpected,
they were too slow in defense. They vanished, enfolded and
swallowed by a savagery sprung full-powered from a
merely unruly mob of youngsters.

Campion was right; this had been planned, organized,
rehearsed.

As he saw his men attacked the Commissioner was already half out of the bus, bellowing to his Techs to defend
the starmen. In a flash of prescience Raft tried to stop him.
Campion lashed at him with the gun butt and was off, running.

Raft's premonition was justified; this was what had been
designed.

Like a mouth the crowd opened before Campion and his
check was too late; they closed round him, sucked him in.
Raft saw his gun rise and fall, clubbing, and heard the
sound of shots. The man's whole body was for an instant
visible, heaved on shoulders out of the press, struggling,
shouting; then he was drowned under the weight and the
tearing. Raft saw women there too, screaming in an exultation of violence.

Suddenly, most weirdly, it was over.

The scene slipped into quiet, retarded motion.

Bodies tripped, stumbled, fell. Savagery died.

The gas pistols were at work.

The youngsters still on their feet ran back to and across

the fallen fence, some supporting others, and slowed to a stroll at what they apparently knew to be safe range. Perhaps fifty lay motionless on the field, many of them in grey and black.

Incredulously Raft heard Matthews, hard as nails and unimpressionable, enthusing over the soporific that operated so effectively in open air.

The Techs and police still on their feet were those who had managed to slip small nosegrip masks over their faces. They seemed stunned by the happening, unable to act further; they stared apprehensively after the retreating mob or knelt futilely by the fallen.

Then one, capless, dishevelled, took command and unbelievably Raft recognized Campion's red hair. Through his creeping sickness he heard his own sigh of relief and wondered at it; he had nothing to thank the man for, but he had thought him dead.

Campion marshalled his men into some sort of mobility, set them to first-aid measures and returned to the bus. With torn clothes and bleeding scratches, gasping and red with exertion and sweat, he growled, "Leave them alone till the gas degrades. Only a few minutes." He waved his arm at the crowd in a gesture curiously like a salutation. "They're getting out anyway. It's over."

Peculiarly, the mob was in fact dispersing. Raft found the leaving hard to credit; no one hung around, not even the customary ghouls fascinated by blood. They thinned, faded, went away into the trees, as if the thing to be done had been done and there was nothing to wait for. Yet they seemed to have achieved nothing.

If only, Raft felt, they would go right away, quickly. His nausea increased and the eyes of the mind still watched.

Jackson came out of paralysis. "Radio for ambulances!" Raft supposed somebody did so and Campion croaked, "Get out now. Let the wounded lie for the medics. There's enough there to look after them."

Raft's seizure was becoming unbearable, the urge to vomit mounting. Campion sat in beside him, the bus moved across the shambles of the field, and a new factor entered Raft's revulsion—a deep anger which had nothing to do with what he had seen and everything to do with the presence of ghostly eyes. He grasped at last what had been the point of the riot.

A touch on the wrist startled him, but it was only Campion saying, "All right, Albert?"

Holding down sickness he nodded. "Albert," indeed.

Campion's sweat and dirt opened into a tired smile. He said, as if this day's work meant something which only he had understood, "I think everything will be all right now." His smile was intimate, conspiratorial.

The bus entered a highway, tree-lined, and opened up speed, silent as a bird. Raft swallowed bile to clear his mouth and called out, "Stop! Stop the bus!"

Heads swivelled. He stood up, swaying, bawling, "For Christ's sake stop!"

Jackson muttered; the bus glided to the side of the road. Raft asked, controlling his spasming throat, "Are we safe here?"

Jackson surveyed him pensively. "I think so, Ian?"

"Of course. Are you ill, Albert?"

"I am ill." He called out to Jackson, to all of them, "This thing beside me isn't Campion."

Then he collapsed, put his head between his knees and heaved his stomach on to the floor.

He lifted his congested face to Matthews hugely enjoying the uproar, to the Techs at a puzzled loss, to the star crew gabbling excitement and to Jackson, very thoughtful and self-possessed, gazing at the man who looked like Campion. With a forcing of will to the man himself.

Campion's eyes, voice, hair. Yet he was clone-brother.

And clone-brother was in shock, static, glazed. Something unbelievable, too incredible to assimilate had happened to him and he had withdrawn. Raft's denunciation had shaken him out of sense, as though a fundamental belief had been wrenched about and distorted into a weapon against him. It was possible he neither saw nor heard nor felt.

Raft shouted through his dribbling, "Get another bus."

Matthews raised his sharp-soft drawl: "He means it; he can't stay cooped in with that man."

Jackson said clearly, "Prove to me first that this is not Commissioner Campion."

"If Albert says so, it's right. Get them apart before he becomes a cot case."

The man who was not Campion began to emerge from rigidity, and sighed; a spasm of sound, infinitely wretched. Raft flinched away, crowding the Tech on his other side. Jackson muttered, "I don't know."

The simulacrum's gaze came slowly alive, fastened on Raft with an incredulity which faded into bewildered sadness. Jackson seemed to find expression there which convinced him, perhaps a flicker, a subtlety of line which was not in the Campion register. He opted for immediate action. "Arrest him. For an hour I override."

Whatever that phrase meant, it was effective. The Tech with vertical bars repeated, "One hour," and the six of them came to life. One reached across Raft and slipped his hand inside not-Campion's jacket, brought it out with gun and gas pistol; another called quietly into a radio for more transport. All of them, with their prisoner, climbed out onto the road.

Raft struggled out on the other side of the bus, widening proximity, aching for air. One of the Techs opened a rear compartment, produced a water can and a bunch of waste rag and began impassively to clean the floor.

Not-Campion stood quietly in defeated sadness until without warning, jolting them all into a sense of the alien and the unknown, he lifted his face and screamed to the sky, to the world, to the desolation of his soul, "Why, Albert, why?"

It sounded not so much of misery as of bitter accusation; he had been betrayed where he trusted utterly. No pretence now; it was Raft's voice crying back at him, not Campion's. Jackson at last showed personal feeling, finally sure that he must count his dead. "I override until overruled."

The Senior Tech hesitated a second, evaluating situation and demand and answered reluctantly, "Conceded." Raft could only guess that he was loath to surrender authority but agreed that some special expertise of Jackson's was here required. The agreement was sealed with a touch of fingers to heart. Some local ritual. *Cross my heart and hope to die*, Raft thought erratically.

Removed from close contact he felt marginally better. At least there was only one of them; he was no longer the center of a forest of eyes.

He heard Lindley murmuring, "Limited transfer of authority without argument. Very trusting, very civilized. Or just plain naïve?" Lindley's mood would see no good in anything.

Jackson ordered, "Two of you take the bus back to the field and find Ian. Or his body." His voice quivered. Without discussion two black uniforms separated themselves from the group and in a moment the bus vanished back along the road.

Not-Campion sat down, hard, as if his legs failed, and wept. An unnerving but not a pitiable sight. Jackson walked across to him and spread his feet with care, a suddenly ancient man shuffling for balance, and asked, "Who are you?"

Not-Campion did not seem to hear him.

Jackson turned away. "Doctor Doronin, Doctor Lindley! You are psychiatrists; what do you make of this?"

Lindley offered one word, like a sneer, "*Agape*."

Doronin took it quite seriously. "Probably. And individual influences." Jackson frowned, not seeing their trend. "We cannot commit ourselves without questioning the prisoner, which would be useless at this point."

But Raft understood at least partly and asked savagely, "What's the guess?"

"Wait, Albert; we cannot afford to be wrong. But broadly it may be that you are the variant, not he. You may be the only clone-member with adverse psychopathological reactions. We will have to do something about it or your life will become unendurable."

"I've had enough attention from both of you these past weeks; you haven't been subtle about it."

"We did not intend to be. Now it may all be gone to waste in a single premature contact."

Jackson was testy. "If you can diagnose, we can attend to the rest. Psychiatric treatment is mostly chemistry and electronics."

Kulayev snorted a long cherished triumph. "Eight years ago—forty-two years ago, how you will—I told you so."

Lindley sniped. "Hundred per cent effective of course, Mister Jackson?"

"Of course not. Paranoia and adolescent growing pains are still major problems. Don't try to bait me."

He might have retired into ruffled dignity, but Matthews applied a fresh needle. "Isn't an Ombudsman some sort of protective middleman between authority and the poor sods on the bottom? A sort of honorary post? Ordering Security around seems pretty way up for a man in the middle."

True, Raft thought; the men in black did little but listen, and Jackson's override seemed absolute. Then he noticed the small fiddlings with buttons and lapels and decided that every word and action was being recorded. Here was a check and balance system loaded against incompetence and Jackson would not be able to argue his way out of the consequences of a bad decision. He wondered how well it worked.

Jackson said coldly, "Words change their meanings over the years. I am an adviser. And I am not in lecturing mood." After a while he asked, "How long must we wait?" and a Tech told him twenty minutes or so. His eyes roved the road, pained and impatient, until the search bus returned. Then he was given blunt words, spoken out of anger and shock.

"Two Techs dead and four police," they told him, "but the Commissioner wasn't among them."

Jackson's response was spitefully human; he kicked the clone-brother in the head. The man gasped, shrank, recovered and gazed impassively ahead. The Senior Tech frowned but did not interfere.

"I had thought you might want Commander Raft but you wanted the Commissioner. Why?"

He was not answered.

Lindley, still sneering, said, "That's obvious."

"So?"

"They didn't need Albert; they thought they already had him. *Agape*. The League of the Philadelphi."

"Brotherly love? They depended on that?"

"Depended! You saw his face in betrayal."

"You aren't slow for a man out of his time."

"My time of violence and unrest? Perhaps in your upheavals some commonplaces have been forgotten, even by you who grew up with them."

"Your insight could be valuable, if you are willing to use it."

"Use it for whom? Why should your incomprehensible loyalties be preferable to any other party's?"

"True." Jackson turned his back on him.

The clone-brother had ceased his comfortless weeping; his glance at Lindley was shrewd and assessing, all Raft.

Jackson said to him, "God help you if the Commissioner is dead."

The man spoke. "The clone does not kill."

"With six dead men on the landing field?"

"None killed by the clone. Your kind kill." He grinned as Raft sometimes grinned, roused and ready to snap. "It was your generation, old Ombudsman, that perpetuated useless death in the new world. Just as you killed the old one."

"Where is Campion?"

"I don't know. My business was to *be* Campion, not to guard him."

"But for a miscalculation you might have been him very well. Excellent training. By whom? Never mind; we'll have it out of you later."

Raft complained, "He's clone but he's twin to the wrong man."

"Gene surgery."

Kulayev and Streich spoke together: couldn't be done on a grown man, had to be achieved in sperm or ovum.

"In your day," Jackson said. They looked excited rather than snubbed. Then the bus came from the town and the Techs shoved the clone-brother towards it.

From the step he shouted, "You, Lindley! Englishman! This beloved Ombudsman is the type who killed your England. Lindley Lackland, remember it!"

He was jostled inside and Lindley laughed at Jackson's brooding. "I haven't forgotten it, Mister Authority, nor shall I. But I can wait a little before making decisions."

Jackson grunted.

Kulayev and Streich gabbled gene surgery in Russian, English and German.

Matthews spat.

Raft, dwelling on brotherly love and himself as the variant without it (but how could the original be without it?) was lost.

Lindley touched his arm, saying not too bitterly, almost with wry appreciation, "Oh, brave new world, that has such bastards in it."

Jackson took the rear seat of the bus and called Lindley and Raft to join him. As the vehicle whispered down the road Raft said, "A thousand or so isn't much of a crowd but it hit Campion like a bomb. I've seen Melbourne turn out half a million at carnival time."

"On a public holiday. I remember Moomba processions."

"Then why——?"

"Why a crowd at all? A few sightseers, perhaps, but you are not Gagarin or Glenn in their day; nobody cares except for a few scientists." He mocked, "Am I being unkind?"

"We're getting used to the idea. When we started calling from ten million miles out we got told, 'Get off my bloody band; it's on priority!' When I identified us he asked, 'What the hell's all that about?' When I explained he suggested we try bands 23 to 26; somebody on those might have a clue. Then we had to find out what that meant in megaherz and he didn't know and screamed like a madman for a specialist to tell us and farewelled us with a curse. Yes. we're getting used to it."

"Deflating. He was a Lunar astronomer at Tycho talking down a three-way record of a solar flare with field stations. You spoiled his day."

Lindley insisted, "The crowd; the tiny crowd."

"There should have been no crowd. Ian was rightly concerned."

"And you?"

"I had envisioned a possible attempt to get to you, Commander, but not such organized violence. We have become . . . unaccustomed."

"So a pressure group of sorts has formed around the clone. Its object?"

"We don't know. Revolution, possibly. Security can't grasp that idea except as something from a historical novel. Minority protest they recognize and control, even guide at times, but this is beyond them. I hope their moment of truth has taught them. It might have worked—a substitute controlling a sixth of the world's Security, if only for a few hours, with the Commander built up as a publicity symbol. They could have achieved something, if only a useful confusion."

"And now?"

"First we must have information from the clone-brother." He jerked upright, suddenly urgent. "How did they get Ian away? Did nobody see?"

Lindley suggested that a dozen cars with sirens screaming could have left unnoticed while the brawl lasted.

Jackson lay back again. "There are only twenty-two private cars in all Melbourne Town, no more than two hundred in the entire country. Only special people have them; it is a signal honor. We have cleared the roads of those damned things."

"But a car is possible."

"If an honored man is dishonest."

"A stolen car."

"A private vehicle will start only for its owner."

"With a gun at his head?"

"Ah. Of course." He closed his eyes, sad and tired.

Raft found these apprehensions and arguments valid but remote; he needed some simple, recognizable thing—a petrol bowser or a newsboy—to convince him that this was the world on which he had been born.

He was roused by the unexpectedness of half a dozen kangaroo hopping across the road in front of the wildly braking bus, but the sight was exotic, untrue to memory; kangaroo are not seen so close to a city, to that Melbourne they kept calling Melbourne Town as if it were still Batman's "spot for a village."

The countryside was interminably the green-brown of Australian summer and . . .

"A house!" he said. One house, in fact, with a garden,

in a paddock at the foot of a hill, with a cow. A cow! It was little more, externally, than a roomy box without individuality—the original machine for living in. It was bare, unlovable, but a relief from the surfeit of organizational man, a promise that real people existed still.

They passed more solitary homes, then clusters of them, little different from the first, even to the ubiquitous cow; then side roads appeared and sparse traffic in the form of long, low buses similar to their own. Some of these carried passengers but the majority, enclosed in commercial bodies, he assumed to be freighters; they bore insignia, presumably with meaning for those who used them, but not business names or descriptions. All transport centrally controlled? Logical, given certain circumstances—such as the elimination of monolithic commercial structures.

The first few bicycles did not strike him unfamiliarly; the resurgence of the bike had begun in the seventies. But soon the sheer number of them—single, tandem and parallel—crowding lanes set aside for them, made him exclaim, though it did not need Jackson's sour comment to remind him that what oil remained to the world was too valuable for private use. He was more interested in the riders. He distinguished no specific fashion in clothes; men and women wore trousers, kilts, skirts, wraparounds and a score of personal styles indiscriminate of sex, determinedly brilliant in colors that burned in the sun. The riders confirmed his impression of general youthfulness; few seemed more than thirty. Despite Security and the landing field he was much taken with the idea of a young and colorful world.

Was it all so colorful? He supposed they were at the outskirts of the city but the dispiriting sameness of pattern-cut houses did not change; three or four basic designs and a scatter of personal touches made a depressing show.

Lindley noted with lazy contempt, "Catastrophes take their time about going away; this one hasn't got round to gracious living yet."

Jackson opened an eye. "A matter of definition. We know more than you did about necessity and waste and the meaning of luxury."

Raft estimated the distance of the mountains he could see to the east, recognizing the Dandenongs. "What's happened to Melbourne? We should be near the center by now.''

Jackson said calmly, ''In minutes we shall be. Your Melbourne is gone. There is only Melbourne Town.''

''How? Why? Campion said there wasn't much damage here.''

''If he meant the Five Days, there wasn't. As for Melbourne, we tore it down, along with all the other useless monster cities. We needed a world people could live in.'' In their stunned silence he knew he had chopped the past away more effectively than anything so far in their reception. ''We preserved what we felt had historical or architectural value, and some buildings for what they contained in the way of records because we couldn't waste time or materials on new storage space. The rest we destroyed.''

Lindley was bent on insolence. ''Cultural spite? Couldn't you just build elsewhere?''

Jackson cut him down bluntly. ''By 2012, just two years after your departure, we had little transport, no petrol, no electricity and only what food we could grow for ourselves. The factory civilization was dead and you can't live in a city whose facilities have ceased to operate unless you like the purlieus of plague and the stink of ordure. Though it's surprising how fast you get used to the smell of shit. At first we moved away from the cities to grow food; then, as we got the transport back into operation we needed the city sites because of their road complexes and railways and airports; we didn't have the manpower to rebuild those things and still pursue livable lives. We didn't need the cities themselves; we couldn't service such huge complexes; but we did need the bricks and timber and steel and copper and waterpipes and bathtubs and glass and fittings. So we built the core of Melbourne Town out of the guts of old Melbourne. We didn't knock the place down overnight with mauls and pickaxes; it took time to repair bulldozers and manufacture gelignite. In fact large part of it is still untouched, simply falling into ruin, but we don't use those areas; they stay overgrown and out of sight until we are ready to attack them. There's no hurry for that; Melbourne Town is big enough now.''

''How big?''

"About eighty thousand people."

Raft asked, predicting the answer, "What happened to the rest of the three million?"

"They died. Plague loves cities."

"Honest plague or bacteriological warfare?"

Jackson's eyes snapped. "Yes, that also happened. I know you have no love for biologists, Commander, and neither have I. Most of them now work behind barbed wire; but the wire is for their protection, not to keep the secrets in but to keep the long knives out. 'Molecular biology' is a dirty phrase in many countries. Things are not so drastic here yet; the government keeps them under reasonable control. But your Heathcote, dead or alive, may change that."

Streich and Kulayev, Raft thought, might find their new knowledge a chilly gift.

Lindley, silently weeping for England, asked, "What is world population?"

"About four hundred million. Excluding China. We don't know much about what happens there."

"Closed frontiers?"

"After a fashion. China asked for privacy, a time of withdrawal; she wanted no part of our rebuilding programs. There are hints of a resurgence of old philosophies—Mencius, Confucius and the rest—and the emergence of a culture based on art, but I have my doubts. However, the world respects their privacy."

"That," Lindley said, "is the most astounding thing I have heard yet. Do you mean to tell me the world's yahoos aren't trying to prise the country open and exploit it?"

"They might, if Security let them. The China Branch of Security is the only group with real knowledge, and it doesn't talk."

"In heaven's name, is Security the voice of God or the ultimate nursemaid, or what?"

"Call it according to your point of view—an interfering clutch of do-gooders—the candlestick of the political seesaw—the protectors of the ruled against their rulers and of the rulers against the ruled—or a force of intelligent young men dedicated to maintaining the *status quo* until humanity works out some sensible procedure for cultural stability. We Ombudsmen created them but they no longer need us; we're on our way out; they'll let us die and that will have been that. Eventually they'll rule the world. Then the world will have to get rid of them for its own good; meanwhile it must preserve them for its own good. The classic dilemmas of history haven't changed.''

Jackson's answers were only the stuff of further questions, and he had his own problems. ''You mentioned brotherly love; Doctor Doronin understood you but I'm not sure I do.''

''We were discussing a theory, in verbal shorthand if you like. I threw out a line of investigation which Ivan approved. That was all.''

''And the line?''

''I told you I have not chosen a loyalty. My ideas remain mine.''

Jackson sucked his lips. ''We can drug the answer out of you in minutes. This is done only in cases of special need—such as this.''

''You would get only theory, untested.''

''I am not threatening at this stage, only warning you not to carry natural spite too far, for you can refuse nothing the administration needs. Think with your head rather than your heart.''

''Just another damned police state.''

''Already you know better than that.''

Raft said, ''Nevertheless, Mister Jackson, you are not really a nice, fatherly old gent, are you?''

Jackson stared at him. ''Is there anything you would die for, Commander?''

Raft replied slowly, ''I think so. One or two things.''

''Then you will realize that I find it simple to be any required type of infamous old bastard in defense of the world it is my life's meaning to preserve.''

''I heard you accused of destroying a world.''

''You heard my generation accused. It was your generation also; remember it. Some rewriting of history has been done for that clone-brother's education.'' He thought, shrugged, said, ''Still, there is truth in it; it isn't a simple thing . . ." Perhaps the thought continued in his mind.

The bus, traveling now through a built-up area of the same dreary houses interspersed with small shops whose designs were little more diverse, swept up a hill. From the crest they looked down a wide, straight, tree-lined road whose other extremity rose another hill on whose summit two miles away, an old familiarity rose like a lump in the throat.

Raft cried out, "For God's sake, we're in St. Kilda Road! That's the old Shrine. That one was a bit too solid even for bulldozers, eh, Mister Jackson?"

Jackson smiled wanly. "Throughout the world we have preserved the more immense war memorials—to remind us that there are two sides to glory and that the builders commemorated the wrong one. Our young people have never experienced war as we knew it; why should they have to?"

The huge neo-Grecian temple grew as they raced towards it: the bus sped round the base of the hill and the heart of the new city was displayed before them, not where the old one had been but on the nearer side of the river.

To Raft it looked like a country town, with a few four- or five-story buildings at its center and the rest a spread of low structures among trees and gardens. The sight neither depressed nor pleased; it was simply another place. His mind did not yet really comprehend that a great city had disappeared.

The bus curved off the road into a courtyard. The block surrounding it on three sides was five floors tall but had the same air of swift-built impermanence as every other structure he had seen.

Jackson told them, "A Security Headquarters building. A barrack."

Plain, ugly, efficient and temporary, it was uncompromisingly an administrative block. Like the rest, like this entire civilization if he understood Jackson correctly, it was there only to serve a passing purpose and be torn down. It symbolized with repellent neatness a world with an immutable past and a hopefully solid future but only a ramshackle, disposable present.

Jackson's office was large, gadgeted and bleak, a place fit
only to work in. Raft admired a three-meter TV screen—
stereo, 3D and supercolor, no doubt—and three smaller
screens which might belong to closed-circuit systems. Various types of recorders formed a bank around the central
desk and one of them, he decided, could only be a voice-
operated typewriter. He wondered if it spelled phonetically;
perhaps everybody did by now; a sensible idea and one
repulsive to every person with a feeling for language. The
office was uniformly functional, lending a modicum of austere, charmless technician's beauty.

The wide front window looked across to the mass of the
Shrine, its heavy harmonies brooding grotesquely over the
angular geometry of the town. On impulse he asked, "Are
the Botanical Gardens still there, behind that hill?"

He seemed to have jolted a dormant connection in Jackson's memory. "They *were* there, weren't they? I think that
during the crisis years they were sown with vegetables.
There's not much left for nostalgia. Will you all please sit
down?"

Chairs ringed the walls, each with writing arm, pad and
ball-point pencil; it was conference room as well as office.

Not Jackson but the two-bar Security man began without
preamble. "I know these people need massive briefing but
immediate business comes first, whether they follow it or not.
What's your reading of the significance of Ian's abduction?"

"Probably what it seemed, an attempt to place a proxy
in a key post. They may want him also, if he is alive, for
deep questioning on Security's reactions and opinions so
far. He had hoped to discover their aims without overt
clash; that is no longer advisable. We need urgently to
know what they want."

"Power!" Lindley said. "What's up with you, Mister
Ombudsman? Has memory gone to seed? What does violence want but change and power? They've decided that
Security is on the way out and some other form of brute-
powered sweetness and light is coming in."

In 1210, Raft thought, he would have been told to mind
his own business, but the Security man followed him with

angry interest and appealed to Jackson. "Is that possible? Why can't they put a case to Experimental Life Style? What can seizure gain them? Is a totally paranoid group a possibility?"

"Yes." Lindley again, enjoying ruthlessness, salving private wounds. "We remember totally paranoid *nations*. You babies in your nursery world! If you don't want your toys broken and your picturebooks torn up you'd better act fast. So help me, you didn't even make an arrest at the landing field."

"Unnecessary," Jackson said. "Those uniforms are walking cameras. Every person within range was photographed and can be taken at need." He asked the Security man, "What have you done about Ian?"

"I've set up an A-grade emergency network; I don't think they can get him out of the country. You have some advice, sir?"

"Yes. You won't like it." He swiveled his radiation-ruined head. "Will he, Doctor Lindley?"

"I couldn't care less about your primitive politics. He means, Sergeant or whatever you are, that you've got to get off your arse and be violent. The new order changes, giving place to old. Apologies to Tennyson. Chaos is come again to the nursery floor and we star children bring not peace but a sword. End of quotes. You're going to be hit where it hurts and the Ombudsman, who still remembers how to savage up a gutter brawl, is about to tell you to get your blow in first, low and dirty. And I am about to laugh my head off while you make a ham-handed mess of it."

The Tech matched his contempt. "We don't think much of your period and its methods either. As for violence, that's already decided. The clone-dummy is in deep question; every person at the landing field will be questioned and every clone-member we can locate in this country. Or any other. World Security has been alerted for that. We will place the Commander under shadow watch—and Doctor Lindley also, since his bias is hostile; they will be guarded, bugged and scrutinized every second until this crisis is resolved. Does that cover it, Mister Jackson?"

"Well enough for the moment."

"Then can we assume your override as cancelled?"

Jackson nodded. "It was justified while we suffered personal confusion and for that Security thanks you. Doctor Lindley's diagnosis of our organizational attitudes and shortcomings is to the point, but there will be no more hesitation. Will you make the preliminary governmental report, sir? It will save us time."

"I will report directly to the Prime Minister. At this stage I will recommend that Security handle the affair alone."

"Thank you." He made the rapid, sketchy hand-to-heart gesture and left.

Raft asked. "Does he carry higher rank than I imagine? He assumes wide powers."

Jackson answered absently, thinking of other things. "He's the man on the spot, so he acts. The Security definition of authority is very fluid."

The integrity involved in such a system was awe-inspiring; in Raft's experience a committee running a children's picnic could not have operated so.

Jackson said abruptly, "I must see the PM. People have been made available to look after you."

As simply as that he left them.

From behind them a voice—female, low cool, impersonal—said, "My name is Alice White."

They swung in their chairs so swiftly, so intently, that she left the introduction afloat in silence, disconcerted and only with difficulty realizing the effect she had created.

They saw a woman of perhaps twenty-five, moderately good-looking, moderately well-shaped, not clothed in the peacock colors of the world outside but in a workingdress blouse and skirt.

The Old Adam in them, eight years sleeping (restlessly), bypassed facts to see a beautiful girl, youthfully radiant, full colored and fine figured, nostalgically clothed as one he might have yesterday farewelled on Earth.

Under silent fire she said hesitantly, "I am Ombudsman Jackson's private secretary."

The scraping of chairs was the sound of the manners of an earlier civilization, of gentlemen rising at the entrance of a lady. Not understanding, she drew back a pace, startled.

Matthews advanced on her grinning, preening, splashing words. "I'm sure we're all very pleased to meet you, Miss

White.'' His hand stabbed, groping in an absurd hurry to be first to touch her.

She drew further back, no longer startled but upset by a reaction that should have been predicted and had not been. Matthews froze, realizing three things simultaneously:

That, leaning against the wall behind her, a Security Tech watched with undisguised amusement—

That he felt a damned fool alone in mid-floor, dithering in a half-gesture that would never be completed—

And that he was behaving like a brash teenager who might earn a social lesson for his pains.

The laugh that diverted attention from him was only part salvation. It was Lindley's, derisive, unfriendly and piercing. He alone was still seated, eaten with his savageries, uninterested in the more obvious aspects of Miss White.

"Forgive the boys for being boys, but eight years is a long time in the company of imperfect suppressive techniques." The jibe was crude, the tone open insult. "It looks as though present needs must be satisfied before the massive briefing will be appreciated."

The tone generated in her a control apology might have shaken. She asked, secretarially, "Shall I regard that as an official request?"

"Why not? If the procedure hasn't vanished into history I suppose it's still a matter of demand and supply."

She smiled at last, and it was a warning. "To a degree, Doctor—Lindley, I think? There is the question of the willingness of partners; there could be difficulties about the provision of complaisant therapeutic meat. It isn't as though you are famous people who can pick and choose among admirers."

The Security man said, "Forget it, Alice. If that's what they need, it can be arranged."

Lindley, undaunted, jeered at him. "Pimping still a sideline of international politics?"

The Tech said tranquilly, "On your performance so far, Doctor, it's hard to think of anyone who'd put up with you. You can masturbate without my arranging it."

It got a moment's quiet, enough for Raft to say, "You asked for it, Jim," and ask the girl, "What were you going to tell us?"

She was reservedly official now. "Only that quarters have been prepared for you in this building where you can bathe and eat and rest. Clothing will be made available. You will have questions and we will obtain expert reference for you. Or you may wish to see Melbourne Town; if so, Security will provide guides. If you have immediate questions I will try to answer them."

"Money," Raft said at once. "Can we get some and if so, where?"

For the second time she was disconcerted by a question that should have been foreseen. "The Ombudsman has a small emergency fund which can be drawn on. I could authorize immediate expenses, I think."

"And then?"

"I don't know, Commander. It will be a question of employment and the manner of life you decide on."

"And you don't use secondhand astronauts. When we left Earth trust funds were set up which guaranteed each of us a solid income for life. Will all records of this have vanished along with the memory of us? During the Five Days, whatever they were?"

She answered crisply, assuming official armor to make the telling easier. "Your own personal documents have been recovered, Commander, from Canberra Archives. Those belonging to you other gentlemen will possibly be in your own countries, if they exist at all. But they will mean nothing. Not only the funds disappeared but the entire financial system which supported them; the web of money and exchange and economics had to be recreated. Arrangements made before the Collapse have no meaning."

"All right; we're broke. It was predictable but I wanted it spelled out. Now I would like a bath and the change of clothes you mentioned; by then I may have worked out some fundamental questions to ask. Homecoming as a key man in a political farce makes for tangled thinking."

"Farce?" The Security man was not amused.

"What else? Politics was always a joke—lavatory wall standard."

CHAPTER THREE

THE FIRST NIGHT

Never ending, still beginning,
Fighting still, and still destroying:
If the world be worth thy winning,
Think, O think it worth enjoying.

John Dryden: *Alexander's Feast*

—1—

Jackson's instinct was to keep the whole matter under cover until a recognizable shape of events emerged, but he struck immediate trouble with the Prime Minister over the question of the public right to knowledge; instinct is no argument to put to a politician. When the PM's own Ombudsman joined the discussion Jackson was forced to retreat; Ombudsmen did not conduct policy arguments before a third party and the PM's man made it plain that he supported his principal and there would be no private consultation. He was made to face the fact that clone-members had been located in other countries and that their existence and appearance were already newscast knowledge; discovery of Raft as clone-father was only a matter of time; he had to agree to limited publicity designed to ease the public into the situation gently as facts became known. But no melodrama; they agreed with him on that.

The best he could achieve was a separation of events into two unconnected items. The fracas at the airfield was to be played down into an item of purely local interest, with no mention of official suspicion that hypno-drugs had been used; the whole affair was to be glossed as an unexpected interest of juvenile groups in the returning starmen, with an overtone of excitement spilling into mass hysteria and an unfortunate reaction by the civil police. (Parker, the Police Controller, would seethe with suppressed fires at being required to shoulder blame, but as a public servant he would shoulder it.)

At least they all agreed that the abduction of Campion remain secret for the time being, if only because overt action against Security was close to unthinkable, predictably traumatic in its public effect.

In the end the newscast of the homing of the starmen became a peculiar construct which only the self-absorbed character of the time could have permitted. The men themselves were not presented (all in good health but resting) and the throwaway nature of the coverage even allowed a playing down of the interesting but not important fact that the clone-members being sought world wide for biological investigation were budded—if that was the word, ha-ha—from the starship's Commander, making a piquant link with the pre-Collapse world. Then on quickly to the subject of real interest, the monopole whose nature and activation had been lost to science in the Collapse: archival research was proceeding apace and areas of industrial and national application were being examined by intercontinental groups . . .

Jackson felt that a secrecy blanket would have made more sense; evasions never held together more than a day or two. The youngsters from the airfield would probably keep quiet from sheer uneasiness until the net hauled them in for questioning—and a fair number would have been rounded up by now—and after that would keep quiet because they had been told to. The student underground newspapers were the real problem, they tended to anti-authority too often just for the hell of it, but he was firmly against taking repressive action against those valuable safety valves.

Then the silliness of the newscast wrangle vanished from his mind as he re-entered the barrack to be told that Campion had been found—on a roadside, unconscious, badly injured and abandoned. His gush of relief stung unashamed eyes; Campion was the nearest approach to a son he could ever know and confirmation of the Commissioner's death would have broken what remained of his heart.

In the shudder of emotion his mind ground still on procedure and method; the successful oracle inevitably becomes a calculating machine, feelings scheduled to non-interference. It became urgent that Raft be orientated, updated as far as possible on world conditions; he could be more easily milked of strictly relevant knowledge if he knew the background. His scientist crew might as well be repatriated to whatever remained of their home areas and so kept out of the dust of trouble; there would be an unholy outcry about lost knowledge if one of them was accidentally killed in local rioting.

Senior Tech Colley, deputizing for the Commissioner, saw to it that Jackson was not told of Campion's singular remark when he had regained consciousness for a moment as they man-handled him on to a stretcher. He had said, quite clearly—four shocked Techs had heard him and not really believed it—"The old man's right; we're rotten beneath." And, very loudly, "The fucking ethic!" Then he had muttered words nobody could catch as he drifted back to sleep.

As Colley pointed out, the words of a man in bone-broken agony should not be taken at surface value; there would be no point in worrying the old man with them.

Nor, because he had in a quiet fashion a strong personal devotion to Campion, did he include them in his report to International Headquarters.

—2—

The bath and fresh clothes could wait; Raft needed rest. A too-present gravity tugged at every move now that he could not step through the centrifuge door into null-weight; his body was arguing him into tiredness. He hoped acclimatization would not take long.

In the small room, plain as a cheap hotel room—a gadgety hotel room with disappearing furniture and magic-eye light fixtures and windows which opaqued themselves with a pressure on the frame—he removed his clothes and stood before the full-length mirror.

Some of the old revulsion stirred because a foreboding from the old world had come viciously true in the new, but it was a muted revulsion. Lindley had worked with precision in a short time, excising resentments, scattering sublimations before the comfort of fact.

He thought about Lindley, about debts of gratitude and how far the most necessary interference could be tolerated, then put on the dressing-gown they had provided, stepped into the passage and knocked on Lindley's door.

The psychiatrist's brassiness was no welcome. "Come to tan my arse, Commander?"

Raft tried the light touch. "Remember Kulayev? Does your subconscious desire punishment?"

"It desires a corner to curl in and lick its wounds. It desires neither comment nor friendly warning; it is aware of its offensiveness and doesn't give a damn. Go away, Albert."

"But it will have to compromise; we shouldn't court dislike."

"You feel you need to fit in here? Then do it. But they took England away, burned it to death and declared a national park on its grave."

"Does it matter?"

"Are you raving?"

"No; it's not so different for the rest of us. This isn't home simply because it fits a certain spot on the Earth's surface. There is no Australia here for me just as there will be no America for Ewan or Russia for Ivan or Germany——"

"Slop."

"It isn't, Jim. While we were gone our world went away. We only expected to be out of date and ignorant, but we're foreigners."

Lindley shrugged. "So rationalize until you've constructed a snuggery. I was too disaffected, too intellectual to be chauvinist or even a mouth patriot. I didn't realize I cared and now I'm hit where self-knowledge doesn't reach. Leave me alone."

Raft returned to his room, refusing to worry further over Lindley. Emotional storms tend to cure themselves and individual human beings simply did not touch him strongly at sub-surface levels.

Yet Campion—out of his depth, angry, flailing, puzzled dedicated—had touched him deeply. But that, he thought as he stretched on the bed, was a different matter. He had a fairly coherent idea who Campion might be, almost must be, in relation to himself, but the mechanics and timing of birth did not make easy sense. Unless—

He was relaxing, muscle by muscle, in the total rest routine. The "unless" was fantasy at the edge of sleep, when the mind wanders at will and at risk. There was only one womb from which Campion could have sprung. The face of Jeannette flickered briefly, very young and long ago . . .

He slept.

The sleep was indolence born of Earthly gravity, but it was dark when he woke. From the window he welcomed soft stars in familiar constellations, in clear air lovelier than the diamond dust fields of space. He had slept for two hours.

He hunted briefly for towel and soap (these people had a mania for putting every damned thing out of sight) and went to the shower cubicle. More problems here, for they also had a mania for setting controls flush with the walls; there were no knobs or handles. He discovered hot and cold water controlled by a sliding thumb-strip and approved an intelligent design; anyone slipping or falling under the shower would not bruise himself or crack his head on protruding metalwork. Excellent for old people.

What old people?

The only person he had seen of more than middle age was Jackson. He had good recall when he chose to force it, and in recollection he charted his progress through the Security building, from the bus to Jackson's office to this apartment, through corridors busy with civilian employees as well as black uniforms. All youthful.

And they had without exception scrutinized the *Colum-*

bus party with that politely veiled curiosity which impinges like the dart of needles. Why? The starmen were not celebrities; that had been ground into them. Could the curiosity have been for six men, in a group, all plainly between forty and fifty years of age? It seemed a grotesque question but needed an answer.

The room had been visited while he showered. (How many had pass keys? Even surveillance-for-your-own-good should offer a pretence of privacy.) On the bed lay a pile of black clothing with a note: "Security thinks these more suitable than civilian clothes. The uniform may afford a measure of protection under presently unpredictable circumstances and will open many doors should you find yourself in need of help. A. White."

His upsurge of irritation was irrational; a second thought—of Campion twisting and plunging head-high above the storm—welcomed protection.

The uniform was a one-piece overall, zippered from crotch to throat, gold piped at all seams and lettered "IS" in gold on shoulders and breast-pocket flap. A heavy leather belt went with it, with holster clips but no holster; he was protected but not given *self*-protection. The black buckle featured a golden hand grasping what might be a golden olive branch. It was gaudier than the silver piped uniforms he had so far seen and was probably a dress overall. It looked too small for him but that was illusion caused by the exactness of the fit. Closing the zipper he was encased with contour closeness.

Suspiciously he struggled out of the sleeves, dropped the top and craned to see the inside of the collar. In the traditional place was a small cloth insert lettered "I. Campion." He might have known. Yet the fit was too good; they were not clone-brothers.

He pondered again what they might be, considering possibilities little to his taste; Heathcote, with all his old-maidishness, had been capable of a frustrating cold-bloodedness when research dictated.

The wall buzzed at him. He had been briefed on use of the intercom, and spoke to the air. "Raft. Who is it?"

"Jackson. Have you eaten?"

"Not yet."

"There's a dining-room on the ground floor. Meet me there right away." There was a short silence. "Should say please, I suppose, but I've a head full of other things."

"I'll come now."

"Good." Jackson added roughly, not covering the break in his voice, "They've brought Ian back."

"Campion? Is he all right?"

"No. And somebody will pay for it."

Ralf said distinctly, "I have been thinking about him. Exacting payment may be my business."

Jackson snorted. "No heroics! You aren't in your home backyard."

The wall buzzed again; Jackson had cut him off. Heroics? He had none in mind; all he had was a generalized sense of responsibility for Campion, not fully rationalized.

He zipped up the suit again. The black shoes also fitted, which was unlikely; he had noted that Campion's hands and feet were neater. They might have been matched against his own by the quartermaster. There was headgear too, like an oldtime service forage cap which could be unfolded to be worn with earflaps against cold. He stuffed it into the buttock-pocket of the overall and casually destroyed the line of the tightly fitting dress uniform by cramming the pockets with a balled-up handkerchief, a couple of notebooks and other oddments. Lindley had removed his preoccupying repulsion but had not been able so quickly to replace it with a positive feeling for appearance.

Jackson waited for him at the dining-room door, now wearing a garment like a belted caftan. With, of all damned things, a sporran.

"I've ordered steak. The staff's finished and we aren't popular."

"Suits me."

The dining-room might have seated two hundred. At a table by the service entry they were waited on by a youngster in green silk kneepants, a scarlet cummerbund and soft scarlet shoes and nothing else, who served them with professional rapidity and total lack of ceremony. Fatherly Ombudsmen were apparently nothing in his young life though he had a covertly appraising glance for Raft.

"That the lot?"

Jackson said, "Thanks, Joe; nothing else. We'll clear up for ourselves." The boy hovered. "What is it, Joe?"

"Just—" He flushed and asked Raft, "What's Barnard's Star like, Commander?"

Raft smiled and said deliberately, "Like dark red thunder, brooding."

The boy's eyes lit. They might not want the stars but they could still itch to romance.

Jackson said, "Since your ear is surely tuned to the underground, tell me what rumor says of Commissioner Campion these days."

Joe looked uncomfortable but answered, "They say he's been in some sort of accident."

"Who say?"

"No one specially; you know how word goes round." Jackson made a disgusted sound. "Is it true?"

"Yes. Piss off now; we've got all we want."

Joe vanished. No cross-my-heart stuff there, Raft noted; Joe might be worth cultivating for additional points of view.

Jackson sighed, "So much for cover-up; the story will be all round the Town by now."

They ate in silence, one ruminative and the other impatient, until Raft asked, "Now what?"

Campion lay still, immobilized by multiple fractures. They had taken the pain away and would not let it return but they could not smother the hellfire in his mind. Only the psychlinicians could do that and he had no intention of allowing their dampings and erasures; this experience, however shattering and traumatic, must be preserved, scanned, dissected, until he understood every moment and meaning of it. As yet he could only cry out in distress as belief and trusts withered.

He saw the faces of the youngsters with a clarity beyond true recall, with the clarity of insight, not only their howling, murderous faces but the minds behind them; he felt still not only the bruising and wrenching but the impact of focused hate.

They were the youngsters to whom he and a whole generation dedicated their lives, for whom they groomed and sleeked the world, and they had turned on him like jungle beasts. They had meant to kill him. Not cleanly, but with their hands and feet.

Training had held through shock and pain and he had known that the youngsters were hypno-drugged; almost he could smell the stuff in their crowding sweat. He had known, too, that some others were protecting him in their fashion, big men who fought off the mob and carried him out of the press, men with his own face lightly disguised.

At first he clung to hatred for those who had drugged and perverted the youngsters he had been raised to love and guard. Later he faced the truth that drugs and hypnosis can only arouse what already exists.

They had *wanted* to kill him.

He needed Jackson now, now, now, with wisdom and answers.

"Now this first, I think," the old man said. "Who was Jeannette Campion?"

As an opening round it fizzled. Raft chewed impassively, swallowed and said, "Was? Is she dead?"

"Yes."

"She was my daughter; Campion was her mother's name. I thought of her when I realized Ian's likeness to me."

"He is her son."

"By whom?"

"We don't know. You've come home a grandad." This was not necessarily the answer and Jackson nibbled at it obliquely. "Ian was afraid he was a clone from you. Is that correct phrasing, or is clone a collective noun?"

"It is. He isn't."

"As you say. Still, we had to trace his birth. He was raised as a state ward, like thousands more; he didn't know his parents. He was born in '18 when confusion was still rampant and records a matter of chance. My secretary located a sort of birth certificate—just a book entry really, carrying the mother's name. Father unknown."

"And the father must have looked a lot like me, eh? But I didn't leave any son to fill in with a little incest. When did she die?"

"Also in '18."

"Ah." It was a peculiarly blank sound even from so phlegmatic a man. "I saw her only once. I didn't know she existed until just before we left Earth; her mother brought her because the kid had asked to see me. Daddy in the sky, pie in the sky, who knows a kid?" He chopped angrily at his steak, hating what he had to say and determined to say it, rejecting and suffering guilt in the one process. "I had no feeling for the girl. How could I? Somebody you've almost forgotten shows up at a time of maximum involvement, shoves a sixteen-year-old under your nose and says she's all yours! Her mother and I weren't married; we weren't even lovers; we were just a couple of brats who had a stray shag at a party—teenagers—and copped it unlucky." Jackson revelled quietly in colloquialisms as dead as their era. "Our parents fixed it up; or mine did, they were the ones with the money, and we didn't see each other again. There was no reason we should; it was just a fun thing that went sour. Then they had to turn up at the last wrong moment, all enthusiastic about Dad chuffing off to the stars, and it was embarrassing because I couldn't respond with an interest in them. Only when they'd gone I felt something of what they must have felt and recognized what my reaction should have been, but sometimes I think all the affectionate facets were bred out of me. I respond so little."

But you would like to, excluded little boy. Impertinently Jackson prodded, "Ian?" and was smugly pleased to catch Raft off balance.

The starman said sharply, "I am interested in him, but the circumstances are unusual; I can't identify the interest in emotional terms. How did Jeannette die?"

Jackson laid down his knife and fork. "Of starvation," he said.

Raft grimaced. "The Five Days?"

"Their aftermath. I'll try to explain the background to you but you'll have to read and to see the tapes to get the feeling of it. It wasn't a war; it was multiple disaster."

Working in smock and plastic gloves, Alice White prepared the envelope with Lindley's name on it, typed because he would be familiar with Raft's handwriting.

She brushed the envelope lightly with fluid from the first of the tiny bottles they had provided. In a trusting world they had had no trouble getting them to her. The youth—completely unwitting, hypnoed to the gills but not too obviously unless you were looking for it—had asked for her at the desk and she had told the clerk to send him to her office when he used the agreed form of request for her recognition. She had blanked the recorders and listened while he spoke his little piece, gave her the bottles and walked out.

She wondered could it have been done so easily in the old world. There the transaction might have involved all sorts of evasions of security measures. ''Security'' seemed to have had a different meaning then; mutual trust had been nonexistent. How had such a civilization persisted so long? If no trust, how progress in a maelstrom of secrets?

That she was herself engaged in deception did not color her thinking. The knowledge loitered somewhere in the recesses of thought, but obscurely; another knowledge, firm and incontrovertible, assured her that what she did was for a great and necessary purpose.

She stripped off her smock and gloves and painted her hands from the second bottle, the protective fluid, which would be precaution enough once there was no danger of splashing. The liquids were on the Relegated List, naturally, and though as Jackson's secretary she had known of their existence she could not have obtained them for herself. The Gangoil people were everywhere, had access to everything it seemed. Yet there were not so many of them; the use of hypnoed dupes gave the illusion of numbers.

The envelope dried more slowly than she had hoped, and Jackson and Raft would not stay in the dining-room for ever.

Best to act immediately.

''Multiple? A sort of general collapse? Civilization turning the neurotic corner and crashing?''

''That corner was turned before you and I were born. All we needed was a push and we got it. What is your memory of the planet you left?''

Raft said readily, "Wars—small, bloody, hot wars between small nations and large, confined cold wars between big nations. Knife-edge politics. Art sterilizing itself in revolt without vision. Protest, disillusionment, starvation and grinding poverty."

"Hopeless?"

"Appalling but not hopeless."

"Details?"

"What do you want? That I condemn my world before you begin?"

"I want you to prepare yourself for the facts. Forget politics, economics, art; those are transitional states. Talk about final things."

Raft considered somberly. "Ecology. Over-population. The plundered planet. Arable land was falling to ruin; with super-fertilization we could have fed ten billions, they said, save that the rains leached the nitrates out of the soil and dumped them in the rivers and poisoned the water supplies and the ecology became still more lopsided. We had been afraid of fishing out the sea but instead we were killing it; back in the sixties Nasser's dam spoiled the Nile delta and the Mediterranean fisheries. Fresh water itself was in short supply in Europe and North America; industry used too much, but throttling industry back meant increased poverty, increased starvation. Ecology was too complex for effective foresight. There were plans, but damage had reached the point where centuries of natural processes were needed to re-establish balance. We knew that no matter what we did our children might starve. And their children."

"There were plans for population control."

"How could they work, with half the world refusing to admit what had happened to it and the rest putting its silly faith in God? In any case, it wasn't stabilization that was needed but an active cutting-back."

"And there were other things."

"Heat pollution, for one. And weather control was becoming a major industry, with no explanation of how to put desired weather in one place without stealing it from another. The problems of scientists became power struggles between politics and money."

"A wrong division of responsibilities coupled with blind self-seeking. Hopeless."

"We didn't think so. There would be bad times but not ultimate disaster. But there was disaster. What caused it?"

"Specifically, starvation and bio-chemistry. And fear. Don't you remember the fear?"

"I don't think so. Or do you mean subliminal anxieties? It was a neurotic civilization."

"Psychotic. Never a day without war in centuries of history; little flares and big flares, in our time desperately contained by terror of a final flare."

"The Five Days?"

"That was a by-product. There was no final flare; we are still here." Jackson looked sick and he looked—with a leaping suspicion Raft identified the emotion behind the eyes—terrified. "That is, some of us are here. Nothing happened as predicted, but the end was little better for that." His hands shook, remembering, and he could not eat "Starvation and bio-chemistry. And someone's attempt to rule the ruins."

Raft laughed shortly. "Oh, no! Not a world conqueror. Ming the Merciless?"

"Napoleon and Hitler had dwindled to names in books but what is so new about a man who wants everything?"

"Nothing, I suppose. The melodrama shook me."

"History is mostly melodrama."

"I'm not fighting you. Who was it?"

"We don't know. Perhaps that's hard to believe but the fact is that we may never know, though the answer is probably somewhere in the millions of still unlooked-at documents of the time. If we find out we'll probably suppress the knowledge; the results are beyond revenge. The final war had already begun before you left Earth; it was several years old but we didn't know it, didn't recognize it for what it was. There had been degenerative mutation among staple crops."

"That? I recall speculation about long term radiation effects; the background level was rising."

"But not to that extent. Then came foot and mouth disease, mutating from season to season, with medicine always a step behind new forms. Herds dwindled. Then mutating cholera and mutating measles. You were two years on your way before the pattern became clear; somewhere biochemists were at work and probably genetic surgeons. Somebody had a final solution: tear the world down and what's left is ours. It was only what some of the stupider dropouts of our day wanted, wasn't it?''

She rapped, and Lindley's muffled voice told her to go to hell. She had to hope he was only exhausted, not totally unapproachable; this time she pressed the com button and spoke into the grille: ''It's Alice White. I have a message for you.'' Silence. ''I think it might be urgent.''

The door opened violently. ''The sex symbol! What's your message, or are you touting?''

His contempt terrified her. She felt momentarily that she was in fact contemptible, that what she did transgressed and buried other manner of behavior. But conviction held.

She offered the envelope. He did not take it.

''From whom?''

''Commander Raft.''

''Tell commiserating Jesus I can do without tender sympathy.''

She floundered. ''But he was—'' and thought again quickly. ''He has been taken away; he said you ought to know.''

''Taken where?''

''I haven't been told. Perhaps the note will say.''

Grudgingly he took the envelope, and was lost. ''It's damp.''

''It was like that when he gave it to me.''

He tore it open sullenly and the stuff was on both hands. ''It's empty!''

''How extraordinary!'' It would take only seconds now.

''What's all this about?''

''How should I know? He said—''

His face changed slightly, relaxing, still puzzled but with resistance ebbing.

She said firmly. ''I'm coming in now.''

There was only a flicker of bewilderment, which passed. She pushed by him into the room.

*   *   *

Jackson's ruined face worked as his words fell. "It is just possible to imagine that somewhere, someone felt that humanity could be saved by doing for it what it would not do to itself. Too many people, too much psychic erosion, too much of everything bad! So put a stop to it, a complete stop! Imagine the fanatical lover of humanity, father confessor and master of forgiveness, paranoid to the steps of the throne of God, inflicting enormity in the intention of salvation. Perhaps it was like that; perhaps it was only the loosing of the demon beneath the skin. We don't know.

"By '92 the plagues had reached genocidal proportions. The condition of the world is beyond telling; we don't know the extent of it. But I know the shock when the rumor spread that these monstrous happenings were the outcome of deliberate planning, and how we reacted with panic when it became certain that this was true. What sparked final insanity was the realization that there were parts of the world only minimally affected by scourge. Some whole countries were islands of life, suffering but not being murdered. Fortune or design? Australia was one, and was that the luck of isolation or the self-protection of guilt?"

He fell silent.

"No," Raft said. "We didn't. We didn't do that."

"Somebody did. Why not we?"

"No."

"My country right and incorruptible? Perhaps mere geography saved the worst of it. We didn't suffer enough to quite destroy us. And it no longer matters. I mean that. To think now in terms of good and evil and blame and vengeance is only wasteful; it doesn't matter now who was responsible or how it came about. All our science and politics and literature stank of the tensions and the Collapse was inevitable; only the date and the manner were to be determined."

"Or is that simple unwillingness to say, 'If I did it I don't want to know?'"

"No one today will listen to that; they're too much appreciative of their second chance. We taught them that— we, the Ombudsmen—" and here Raft could not miss the note of defiance "—and we made it stick. The first generation born after the crash runs the world and the second is being groomed to run it better. They are too busy for old hatreds.''

"Someone isn't,'' Raft said, but cut the defense short "Let philosophy rot. What was the Five Days?''

Jackson said instantly, in words prepared. "A vast incident, and only that. I suppose violence had to have its day; the big powers—with their people dying in millions, industry rumbling to silence, communication failing—saw intrigue and menace everywhere. Or perhaps, like you, they needed someone to blame, and so there had to be a crisis of hysteria. They fought in sullen and crude fashion, like men badgered into a fight and unable to back out of it, mostly with what we called conventional weapons. Nuclear weapons were used but not with the blind freedom that might have been expected; the atom was still a symbol of terror to user as well as used-upon. It was a short week of vast airstrikes, and whole cities dissolved in dust and fire.'' He grinned crookedly, making a mask of his burned-out face, and stabbed the air. "Can you guess what stopped it, why it simply petered out? Just that there was nobody willing to carry on. Famine had reached the stage where individuals killed only to stay alive, to steal another's food.'' He paused, pinning Raft with snake's eyes, defiant again. "I know; I did it.''

Raft offered no reaction; the old devil must find his own soft spots to land on. Jackson, deprived of shock effect, reverted to an offended, lecturing tone.

"The Five Days was Earth's last scream of mobilized hate; it ran out of breath. There was no fuel for the planes and no one to service them or fly them. No one would supply a parasitic armed service, and the servicemen deserted rather than starve. And starved anyway. The aim of the godlet was achieved; the world clattered to a halt. I suppose the godlet, if he existed, perished in his own cataclysm; at any rate he never stepped forward to claim his prize. What a prize! We were reduced to two necessities— food and shelter. Back to the Stone Age, to caves and scavenging. You might be surprised at how many found it a relief from civilized bedlam.''

"I might have been one of them.'' Raft thought, *He's had forty years to grow a shell but I must be like an ice-*

pick in his gut. And so he meant to be; he didn't enjoy making the old brute dredge recollection of guilt, but he needed it all. "It sounds as if half the world died."

"More, much more. The strong survived but in the western world, as we called it—and few today would know what you meant by it—medicine and technology had made it possible for the unfit to survive in their millions, so now they died in their millions. It was the price of borrowed life in an artificial environment. In that same western world, psychotic to the core, the family unit had degraded itself into a phrase, so when the starvation became acute there was little desperation on the part of the young to save their parents and grandparents, whom they tended to blame for the mess anyway. It was very elemental; the old died. Procreation went on—apace, you might say—in the absence of TV, liquor and electric light, but most of the results died of malnutrition, neglect or sheer unfitness in a toughened world. In the oriental areas where starvation had always been a commonplace and family solidarity had more meaning there was probably less psychic degradation but sheer congestion bred disease—not just the created plagues, which turned out to have a genetically induced obsolescence factor—but the old-fashioned diseases of dirt and propinquity, cholera, typhus, bubonic. And of course malaria as insect control disappeared. The VDs ravaged everywhere; there's nothing like unfettered morality and a dead pharmacopoeia to spread infection. Do you think I'm cynical about it?"

"It probably helps; you need a defense."

"You bastard." It was a flat, indifferent curse; Jackson was scratching his sores with something like satisfaction. "Well, there you have it; communication vanished save by word of mouth and the whole structure was in fragments."

They had warned of a period of shock and something close to withdrawal but she was unprepared for the reality.

He staggered as she pushed past him, reeling until the bed took him behind the knees and he sat, hard, like a drunk, his head cracking against the wall. He did not seem to feel it but stared at her, or at the space where she was while sweat gathered and ran.

He would be unaware of her during this time but, unable simply to watch and wait, she dabbed at his forehead with a damp towel, her nerve rocking to failure point. He looked abominably ill.

The fast-working preparation was very different from the gentler, subtler drug used on the kids who had carried out the useless uproar at the landing field. Their enslavement had been effected in full daylight, in public, with finesse and no onlooker the wiser. But here time was a prime consideration, though the stuff was potentially lethal. It would not alter eventual outcomes if he died, but The Lady had demanded him and she must deliver alive if she could.

When his irises rolled upward and he became rigid and slug-white she wanted to scream, but could only wait in nerveless quiet.

Raft prodded, "What next? The old science fiction post-holocaust, with tight little groups fighting off marauding bands?"

"You aren't that kind of fool, Commander. There was some of that, of course, but not too much; there were needs that made gangsterism dangerous for gangsters. In fact those with access to weapons were often service personnel with firm organizational backgrounds, and very soon there appeared islands of comparative calm; what emerged was a tremendous desire to regain what had been lost, if only because we had become people who could not imagine fulfillment without our pamperings. And there was more in our favor than prophets of doom had allowed for. For one thing, the day of the unskilled laborer was over, in the west, at any rate, and even the shriveled remainder of the population was a vast reservoir of knowledge and technical skills; and in those patches of Earth which had not suffered ultimate violence they held out better against famine and disease and recovered faster. It was in those that the reconstruction began, and Australia was one of them."

"Hail the unconquerable spirit of Man!"

"Balls to that, and you know it. Survival first, then the need to regain the lost."

"Not even the deathless, pioneering urge to conquer nature?"

"Little, frightened, deprived but educated men and women who remembered their newspapers and central heating and supermarkets and wanted them back."

"And you really rebuilt the world on fright and pettiness?"

"On resentment and nostalgia; would heroism have done a better job? You jibe too easily; what could we have done with heroic mouthfuls of 'upwards and onwards'? We had scientists, tradesmen and organizers, out of work and needing a place to work in; to give it to them we had knowledge and intelligence and people who wanted their vanished lives back again. We had the huge rubbish heap of the world to ransack for usable artifacts and disassemble for usable materials. We had tremendous libraries that had survived partially and often totally and we had surviving machines to serve for blueprints. We had enormous advantages."

"Even so—"

"Shut up and listen. My own story is the pattern of thousands. I was in mild burn range of one of the few nuclear warheads to hit this country and you see the result. I lived because we had a few medical supplies still, and survived because I was an amateur anthropologist with an interest in the aboriginal branch of my family tree. I had studied the tribal methods of survival in one of the world's harshest lands—I had been writing a book!—and the knowledge was invaluable. I had suffered a few years in the army and knew something of organization, administration and discipline. In a smallish group, only a hundred or so at the start, I became a leader. Like scores of other groups we had two immediate aims, to produce food and to start up a communication system. Both agriculture and radio I could teach. A few salvaged tools, some scrap-heap generators, fuel from old dumps and steampower when need be, and we were in business. Not in years, Commander, but in months.

"I think that flying start saved us from apathy. A competent leader could bully out results, and once we began to reduce isolation progress was fast. Government began, not by politicians but by practicing human beings working from grass-root necessities and not much hampered by recollection of old systems few of them had properly understood;

amateur politicians, playing the game for its own sake, tended to have short lives. Life ceased to be sacred unless it was also useful and that made for willingness and a failure of the grosser hypocrisies; relationships were basic. So you see we had enough to build a sort of backyard civilization at high speed. People like myself became not kings or presidents but something like arbitrators; by quirk of language we became after a few years the Corps of Ombudsmen, centers of advice and memory all over the world, linked first by radio and pretty soon by physical transport. We were able to feed ourselves, communicate and govern ourselves by one system or another—and there were dozens of systems. After five or six years we could say we were on our way back.''

He stopped, conscious of climax. Raft nodded without applause. ''Back to what? Only to what had been lost?''

''Not only. Probably the most useful single thing that Corps did was to turn the world into a network of teachers. Preserving knowledge was no difficulty; it was everywhere, needing only digging out. Spreading it was what mattered because we hadn't the material to spare for the printing of millions of books and the creation of technological universities, and we didn't want to revert to a purely agricultural stage because the road back from that could have been millennia long. So we turned every suitable brain into a teaching mechanism that spent a fair part of its time teaching the young to take over. We developed instructional systems that would have left the last century paralyzed with awe, though all the basic techniques were known then. That was a stupidity of our time—the things we knew and didn't use. By the turn of the millennium we were producing responsible adults at fifteen. Today a kid may take a degree at eleven or twelve and even the backward can be dependable technicians in early teens. In the seventies it was known this could be done. We did it.''

''And when are they children? Where has youth gone? When does the sap rise in these pre-aged saplings?''

Jackson heard dreariness and thought he detected hunger in a man who had never been young. ''We take nothing away. Who wants to interfere with puberty and the energies of growing? I spoke only of the inculcation of factual knowledge and logical ability. Social responsibility, sexual philosophy, the purely humanist stabilities can only develop with time and the individual. Discipline of our young is in some ways stricter but of a different order from the old day; mental maturity comes a little earlier but social usefulness much earlier. I can promise you the kids are happy; we may have killed Santa Claus but the private worlds remain and we have learned a great deal about muting the root causes of teenage discontent. You see, this is a social world; God knows how many systems are in operation across the planet, but every one of them is acknowledged as experimental, and anyone can leave his society and choose another without let. But it is also a technological world, and that part of it is most strictly administered. We don't want a return to yesterday's excesses.''

"You mean controlled research?"

"Only in that inapplicable or unwanted lines of research are discouraged."

"What is inapplicable? Sidelines often provide the answers."

"Just as the slowed metabolism procedure sprang from research on a useless problem?"

"Useless or dangerous?"

"Both. For what is cloning of humans useful?"

Raft's animus against the whole business of cloning had never considered a favorable argument but he made an uncertain attempt: "Preservation of unique talents?"

"Are there any strictly unique talents?"

"Maybe not; I suppose that any talent, once understood can be duplicated by teaching techniques. But there could be multiplication of talents in high demand but short supply—physical talents."

"Such as ambidextrous factory workers? Or highperformance physical specimens—" Raft winced "—to turn into ditch diggers or soldiers? Who needs them? Our civilization, yours and mine, would have used them; this one can't." Untrue, untrue; but not so much as the possibility must be allowed to thrive.

Raft protested, "On the intellectual side . . ."

*   *   *

Rising panic was pierced, bringing an irrational calm, by contemplation of Lindley's fair hair and pale skin against the black uniform, as in one of those old museum portraits where faces glowed out of mysterious chiaroscuro. The thought surfaced that he was an attractive man. Or, at any rate, that he had been, for he was old enough to be her father.

Would age have yet affected his mental and physical powers? Her generation had seen little of middle age, practically nothing of old age—one did not think of the ancient Ombudsmen as being human in quite the same sense as one's contemporaries—and her ideas about the debilitations of time were vague and mostly inaccurate. Nevertheless he looked appealing and lost, for all that it was only the effect of color contrast.

Color! She had known that Lindley had been provided with a Security uniform, as had Raft, had herself signed the notes explaining the provision, but had not until now appreciated its bearing on her actions.

The uniform was a technician's masterpiece of miniaturized cameras and transceivers; every word spoken here was being recorded in the cellar libraries and would include routine scrutiny in the morning. In twelve hours it would be known what she had done and the hounds of surveillance would be in full cry. She had made herself an exile.

She had not realized what commitment could mean and could not understand how it had escaped her; she had envisioned, when she visualized at all, some gentle interpretation of philosophies in which the plans of The Lady became somehow the spiritual guidance of Earth.

In the instant of truth she was homeless and lost, and must remain so until The Lady reigned. Until. She perceived the menacing uncertainty of pie in the sky.

But she was no fool and the education of her generation had been psychologically strengthening; she suppressed new panic by concentrating on the matter in hand, shutting out all else.

Lindley assisted her by coming out of shock as quickly as he had succumbed. A few heavy breaths, a rubbing at his eyes, and he said in nearly normal tones, "That was a nasty turn." He felt his skull. "Did I hit my head?"

"Yes. You frightened me."

"Frightened myself. Can't think what caused it."

She offered cautiously, though caution should not now be necessary, "Reaction. You've had an unusual day."

"I'd better be examined. That should have been done for all of us as soon as we landed."

He was too normal for her comfort, showing none of the signs which betrayed hypno-drugs to the informed eye. She was terrified that the thing might have passed climax and failed. Gathering courage she said firmly, "That can wait till morning."

His reply was so slow that she despaired but he said, in a puzzled agreement, "Yes, the morning will do."

"We've no time for it now."

"No time? Why not?"

There should be no resistance; almost her drummed-up determination died. She almost shouted, "Because I say so."

That was a test with a vengeance; she had been warned that it was dangerous to be unreasonable, but she was afraid and unpracticed.

His smile held. "OK."

She exhaled a long relief and said, "Now we're going out."

"We are?"

The persisting puzzlement shook her badly; he should acquiesce and nothing more. She had no idea how long the effect lasted, but surely more than minutes. She tried, with forcefulness struggling through fear, "Yes, now! You said you wanted to see our world."

Persist in planting affirmative ideas, they had told her.

"I did?" His frown cleared. "Of course. And who more pleasant to see it with?"

The sudden sociability was almost too good, but that was the eeriness of the drug, that the victim concocted instant mental background to justify the role forced on him.

"Now slick down your hair and do up your collar and get your cap."

He followed the orders precisely but not with a robot-like activity; he did it jauntily, a man taking in good part the sassiness of a bossy woman. In the depths of his mind the drug was forcing his brain to lie to him, to invent circumstances and attitudes to make sense of what he did. It was abominable, she thought, who had never doubted before.

It was too late for doubt; her road had vanished behind her; there was no way back.

"Come on, Jim."

He followed obediently to the lift, answering easily and lightly while she chattered with alarm and tension. She regained confidence as he played smoothly to every cue and she began to think ahead. Most importantly, the uniform must be defused and she must prepare herself to do it. This was mainly a matter of choosing the right time; he must disappear from electronic view only when pursuit would be too late to catch up with him.

She knew roughly when the time should be.

She set herself to natural behavior as they emerged into the main lounge on the ground floor. In other circumstances she might have felt distinction in his escort, despite his age, for he had presence and wore the uniform without self-consciousness. They swept through the lounge with flair.

A solitary Tech by the door saluted with a mild wolf whistle. "Stepping out, Alice?"

"On the town, no less, to show a starman the sights of Earth."

Lindley tucked her arm in his. "First night in port. It's traditional."

The Tech looked at him without enthusiasm but said "And good luck to you, starman."

At the front door the electronic sentry buzzed and snapped and demanded to know who was wearing a uniform that did not belong to him. Alice talked to it, explaining to a grille in the wall while her escort watched with amusement.

As they crossed the courtyard she was powerfully aware of the light in the dining-room, like heat on her back. But whatever Jackson and Raft discussed there would not matter much longer. She was visited again by the odd distress, the sensation of wrongdoing at variance with truth. What she did was *right*.

But she needed reassurance.

*   *   *

"What intellectual side? More and faster research? With eternity ahead of us do we have to rush fences? In our day the ability to interfere had outstripped the philosophical recognition of need to modify the performance; now we need time to strike a balance. We want to know why a thing is worth doing, if at all, and to have some forecast of the consequences."

"No more research for the state-of-the-art's sake?"

Jackson spread his hands. "Who can stop a scientist in full cry? Knowledge increases exponentially and oozes round every clamp; what we can do is guard against unfettered use. In 2010 biology was on the edge of the ability to remake the human race and as a by-product helped to destroy the greater part of it; today's biologists *could* remake it—if we let them. That's one reason they and some others work under close control. Science must remain a tool and nothing more until we discover what we are and where we are going. Stability first, then the big leap forward can have its way. In the meantime no robotic clones, no superstimulated intellects, no headlong rush into tomorrow."

"As Jim might put it: don't move, don't breathe, don't think."

"And don't exaggerate. If we're wrong, God help us, but for the first time humanity is looking at itself as a unit with a common destiny. We have learned by our mistakes to be bloody careful what we do next."

"But in fact you're at full throttle—the shuttles, those multi-recording uniforms, the references to deep question— and all in forty years from a standing start."

"I've told you it wasn't a standing start. Today's kids begin research while ours were still fumbling with their first erections, and they do it untrammelled by historical attitudes of thought and procedure. There is no private knowledge, no duplication by teams working in ignorance of each other's programs. When a particular result is considered necessary we set up the project, define its parameters and give the kids their heads. They have drive, enthusiasm, initiative and a minimum of bureaucratic leash. Side issue discoveries are noted and promoted or filed for future investigation. The desired end is all."

''The drawbacks are obvious, but they must be remarkable kids.''

''Just kids with their potential let loose.''

''And what about the old people?''

Jackson stiffened as if he had been struck; Raft decided that he had been and pressed the point. ''Where do the old folk fit in? The ageing and the aged, lost in a world where youngsters run it all—how do they see it?''

''There aren't many of those.''

''It's noticeable. Where are the people over forty-five? There's yourself and, I presume, the rest of the Corps of Ombudsmen, but who else?''

Jackson's answer came with the difficulty of a man exercising care when it is too late. ''In the famine years, they died like flies. Only the fit survived.''

''Fit? Such as the Ombudsmen, the Old Men of the tribe, the founts of wisdom and experience? That makes some sense. But the others can't have starved, not all of them. Where are they?''

''They died.''

''All?''

Jackson's face opened and shut like a badly articulated mask. ''We let them die.''

Raft said nothing; he wanted the whole answer spoken aloud. Jackson spoke rapidly, as if speed could gloss. ''It was monstrous but we did it. They were wrecked by hunger and disease and they carried the old ideas with them like poison; they were a dead weight on an emerging world they consumed and they contributed nothing. Their instinct was only for the world they knew, the one that killed itself, whereas we needed to build something new.''

His justification ground to silence.

''So they lay down and died? Of simple neglect? Your whole holier-than-thou world of youngsters threw off the burden of responsibility in a surge of bright-eyed dedication? Love and duty vanished in a sunburst of practical common sense? Try again. I'll find out eventually, you know.''

Jackson muttered, ''Don't blame the kids. Not much in the way of families existed by then; subsistence groups but not families. The kids had their backs to the wall.''

"So, in world-wide agreement . . . ?"

"It was essential. For survival. To free the kids for the things they needed to do." His hand fluttered once, hopelessly. "We—the Corps of Ombudsmen—advised it." His eyes pleaded for an impossible pity.

At the time, Raft thought, they had probably believed in what they did; should a man be punished for actions committed in desperation and hysteria? But can an abominable precedent pass unscathed? After forty years the damage was irreversible and what a homing starman thought would stir no ripples in a society wherein he was only a curiosity. He said, because something must be said before the disgraceful question was set aside, "I'm glad I'm not one of the benevolent and beloved Corps of Old Killers. How, just how, do you stay alive?" No answer to that. "I suppose you created Security too? After a cool, idealistic act of genocide you'd have to, wouldn't you? To keep the world, all of it, flat out busy creating paradise to justify what you had caused it to do."

Jackson nodded tightly, with some anger returning.

"And when your usefulness ends, when your ability to advise on ancient problems runs out, will they just let you die? Because they can't afford you any longer, old carcase?"

"Yes."

"How right, but too late. I don't know what you have created out of murder but I hope for the peace of your soul that it's good."

Jackson produced defiance. "What else do you think drives us to keep on? But what's this world to you, Commander? More to the point, what are you to it? What use are you? Who needs star pilots? Nobody, *nobody*, battens on the public weal."

Raft laughed at him. "I'm safe. You need me, mister; you didn't bring me here for history and a friendly steak."

"Not entirely, but it was better for you to get the history from me in a beastly lump than pick it up in fragments. My version is more accurate than most you'll get. I *am* history."

"And you wanted what else?"

"To tell you what I know of the situation with the clone

and whatever inspires it. Ian wanted no action taken against
the few we detected, but there was one in Melbourne Town,
so I had him questioned. That was against Security instruction and I will have to answer for it, and what I obtained
was not much. First, Heathcote is alive. How old would he
be?''

So! That need not be a laudable survival, though he loved
the man in his fashion. ''Touching the century.''

''I thought as much, and a man that age would stand out
like a beacon. So he has been in hiding for some forty
years; the clone doesn't know where, geographically, only
that the place is called Gangoil. There is no such place
name in computer records.'' He was taken aback by Raft's
shout of laughter. ''Have I made a joke?''

''No, but old John has. Nearly two centuries ago a nov-
elist named Trollope visited Australia and wrote novella
about the country called *Harry Heathcote Of Gangoil,* and
John's second name is Harold. He doted on Trollope and
he was that sort of gentle old bird who fancies little literary jokes and mild mysteries, so when anyone asked
where he lived he would tell them Gangoil. And it was
true, because Gangoil was the name of his farm, his laboratory, three houses at different times and anything else he
felt like labeling, like a hen roost or a kennel. Wherever he
is, is Gangoil. You might as well have been told, 'Out
there somewhere.' ''

Jackson was disgusted. ''Your gentle old bird is avian
dynamite. But was he so gentle? How did he respond when
you argued against his experiments?''

''Not at all. He believed in the essential niceness of man
and a planetful of evidence never dented his trust. Did you
know what his farm was? A sanctuary for sick and
wounded animals, to be cared for and released. He talked
to kangaroos and swore they understood him. He was a
history changer.''

''Then someone else has him and his work. Our clone
specimen knows practically nothing. What we got from him
was a semi-religious garble of brotherhood and understanding; start a philosophy of togetherness, bring the world together in a unity and love will find a way. He knew nothing
of the project to replace Ian, which smells of secrets within

secrets; he knew of the landing field gathering but seemed to think it was a clone welcome for you.'' He had a moment's satisfaction from Raft's exasperation. ''You should hear the rest from Ian.''

''How is he?''

''Arms, nose, one leg and five ribs broken. Kidneys bruised. It's a wonder he wasn't killed. Have you finished eating? We'll go to him.''

''After all that can he be visited?''

''Why not? He's had anti-shock treatment and a hypnotherapist is handling the pain; it's too generalized for acupuncture.''

The gate sentry, informed of the minor paradox of an identified uniform on an unidentified but vouched-for body, counted them out and murmured, ''Goodnight, sir and madam.'' Lindley snickered. They turned left on the footpath, towards the center of the town.

It was a clear night, the trailing edge of a hot day which had scarcely registered in Lindley's mind as the new Earth closed round him. He looked expectantly about, enjoying what had become a rarity in the old cities, an avenue sheltered by trees. His mind was at peace yet a worm gnawed in the dark; it was too warm for the uniform but there had been some insistence that he wear it because a danger threatened and it could protect him. He stopped, seeking the danger.

''I shouldn't be out.''

Alice White—he was not sure what he was doing in her company—said, ''Don't be foolish,'' and tugged his arm.

In the summer night was a sound of voices, unintelligibly massed, not far away and rising and approaching.

''They said . . .'' They hadn't actually said anything, but this uniform had a significance and he fancied menace in the nearing voices.

''It doesn't matter what they said.''

She spoke always in that hectoring fashion as though he was resisting her, which he was not. He did not like it, but if she said the voices didn't matter, that was that. But he resented her thoroughly and would cheerfully have told her to get to hell away from him had he been able to—to what? Raise the initiative? It was easier to be led.

The noise took on personality. Along the footpath towards them came a crowd of youngsters, gay with color and incredibly noisy and boisterous, like drunks in full throat before the downbeat struck. He thought they were not drunk, however, and there were others on the far side of the road. Old memories warned of violence snuffling after a focus of rage.

"What's this lot up to?"

Her hand tightened on his sleeve. "Kids on the spree, enjoying themselves."

She was lying, inexpertly and inefficiently, but he could do nothing about that; he could resent but could not act upon the resentment; an incomprehensible inhibition restrained him. He said uneasily, "A mob of kids like them used to mean get inside and stay there till they go."

The sound became more intelligible as they approached and what he heard spurred his unease. Not words troubled him for there were no words, only an emotional slur of throats chanting. Slogans? Ritual? In any case, dangerous. "This mob's nasty."

"Just young and lusty."

The contradiction released him a little. "No! This is anger and bad business."

The fool girl said, "Of course not." Then, with that dogmatic, blustering tactic, "They're happy sounds."

"Don't be so damned stupid."

Had he been watching her he would have seen her panic as she realized her incompetence. Never, the instruction had been, say anything that contradicts the evidence of the senses. He heard her gasp of distress but was intent on what lay ahead. He watched their advance, absorbed the zombie litany with no meaning beyond the stiffening of intent, and recalled the dreadful teenagers of the final generation of protest. Then Alice took charge in that grating voice, overriding instinct with command.

"We'll walk straight through them. They won't touch us I know more about this than you do. They won't see us."

So she knew more. He believed because he had to and was bizarrely aware that he had to, as though there were two of him, and one walked aside and watched. But which?

"Walk!" she ordered, and he walked.

The wave of bawling boys and screaming girls rolled upon them, incantation and threat view-hallooing ahead of them. Alice's hand trembled on his arm and this contradiction of her certainty opened a slit window in his mind; his sense of divided personality rose as fear and he would have stopped her if her voice had not overruled him.

"They won't harm us. Keep going!"

He did because he must; the window closed.

And the wave divided to let them through.

Shrieking, bellowing, it split with robot precision. Robot! There was the word. Things with a purpose, ignoring all else. He took in distorted faces and staring eyes and knew what was the matter. Then the sound rolled away from them as if a freak storm had broken and passed.

"They're drugged!"

"Of co—" About to say, "Of course not," she changed it to a snapped, "Forget about it."

That order was not easily obeyed but he did his best by forcing his mind to other things. But matters were not right in his thought and his puzzlement grew as a conviction broke surface that he was behaving like a fool. No, in a manner uncharacteristic of James Lindley. And yet . . .

She said, "There's a spot on your uniform. Wait."

She rubbed at the cloth, laughing, and he laughed with her, not knowing why but helplessly following the cue to create the scene and did not feel the gentle tug under the lapel as she defused the overall.

"That's better. Come on."

"Where are we going?"

She answered with a gasp of recklessness, "To Gangoil."

"What's that?"

Her voice cracked with relief as she told him, "The land of dreams come true."

Behind and above them something roared dully in the night.

"Aircraft?"

"A dragonfly. Like your hovercars but better."

They walked on and she was quiet, thinking of the dragonfly which would pick them up when its work was done, and of what that work was and that she had got him out of the building only narrowly in time. And that at any moment Raft would be dead, if not already. And, disturbingly, that she was doing something she should not, as though her mind played her tricks.

In the warmth the dining-room windows were open. While they talked there had been small sounds in the night, a footstep or two, an occasional voice, a sough of wind in the courtyard trees. Jackson, facing the window, had noticed with a fraction of his attention Alice White go out on the arm of some Tech he did not recognize from the back. Raft had his back to them.

Now there began, quietly borne, a distant sound, a human sound, swelling, forming a rough pattern as it approached— a river of feet on pavement. Jackson frowned. Raft, alert to danger in an unpredictable era, watched his face.

As if a signal had been given, voices were raised, many voices, all at once yelling. It was the noise of a mob, a wordless enmity both had heard earlier in the day, and it was close at hand.

Jackson pushed back his chair, grunting an old man's anger, seeming less apprehensive than furious. Raft by-passed inessentials to ask, "Is the barrack guarded?"

"A few civil police in the yards and store areas. Token only. Security doesn't do guard duties."

The bloody élite preferred to sweat the lower orders, Raft thought as both of them went to the nearest window. The sound of the mob grew shattering and came from no one direction; the building was being converged on.

Jackson said through his teeth, "We have never needed sentries," then asked, "Clone?"

"No. None near here."

Two grey police uniforms appeared running in the lighted courtyard and Jackson screamed at them to take cover. They raced for the walls, tugging at their guns, and disappeared in tree shadow as a surge of figures swept to the wide gates. And halted. Like a chorus line mid-stage, poised for the entrance of the star, they halted.

Raft, uneasy but phlegmatic, observed them curiously. They were all young, very young; teenagers. Dressed in a medley of styles and colors—peacocks, hummingbirds. *And baboons' arses*, he thought in revulsion against omnipresent, cynical fancy dress.

Within the gates they yelled. Few words, only undifferentiated sounds. He noticed that though they bellowed and shrieked from still positions their eyes swept the courtyard, seeking . . . objective? resistance? victim?

Gazes focused on the window and arms pointed. They were recognized and named, no doubt of it, but there was no move forward. The taint of rehearsal was heavy over it all. Someone taught violence to the peaceful, making a sick joke of an idealist's world.

Tearing the night with uproar they waited. For what?

He knew soon enough.

Something rushed out of distant darkness and hovered overhead with a purring of engines. Jackson put his head through the window and muttered, "Dragonfly," and withdrew sharply as brilliant light flooded down. The two policemen had been joined by others and stood stark as gallows-meat in the glare. The youngsters moved as they had moved at the airfield, to both sides as more poured in behind them; the grouping was choreographed, stagily unreal. The alarmed police began shooting, and not with gas. They might have done better to use gas; Raft knew them for certainty to be dead men.

He heard Jackson, his voice breaking, "Hypnotics! They're loaded with them."

Then the scene vanished.

Nothing changed within the dining-room, but outside the window light, mob, courtyard, even the stars winked out of existence and the uproar ceased in mid-note. The eerie cessation of sound was terrifying more than the darkness outside; beyond the window ledge no universe existed; they stood unprotected at the edge of ultimate space.

"Blinded!" It was a disgusted sound; the old man exhibited a spectrum of emotions but fear was not among them. He had probably earned his disastrous leadership.

"What?"

"Back from the window! We've been blinded. An energy-damping curtain." He grumbled, gnawing at his problems, "That takes a lot of power." He walked, muttering, to the hall entrance and opened it on blackness, and again to the kitchen. "Just a circle round this room. It's you they want."

"Why not you?"

"What use would I be? They might make something of you now the Campion move has failed. And all this diversion! They must want you alive."

Raft was not so sure of that. "What can we do?"

"We, nothing. The place is full of Techs on duty call; they'll start something very quickly. But those bastards out there will have to be fast, too; they can't maintain a long blind with only a mobile generator."

They waited, chilled by the knowledge of indetectable movement all round them. Raft asked the central question, "Who knows we are in this room?"

"The waiter."

"No, this wasn't organized in the short time since he left us. Whom did you tell we *would* be here?"

Their voices dropped flatly in the baffled air.

"Only my sec—" He stopped, devastated. "No!"

"The White girl? Why not? Treachery can only come from within: only a friend can harm you."

He thought. "*The clone does not kill!*" but no clone-members were out there and he had thought of a reason why he might be wanted dead.

The proof came unexpectedly.

A hand emerged weirdly from the blackness, detached, fluttering, feeling along the window ledge, locating itself. It stopped, rested; it had groped an eerie passage through the blind and now knew where it was. A face showed briefly like a mask with no head behind it, swept dull, drugged eyes over him and vanished. The hand flickered and a small object, whizzing in flight, came through the window and skidded on the floor.

It was a plain white card. Together they bent over it to read the printing in large black capitals: COMMANDER ALBERT RAFT.

"Threat? Ultimatum? Or just a valentine?" Raft stooped to it and Jackson prevented him.

"Paper can be treated with skin-absorbent hypnotics. There's a simple test; put some salt in a glass of water."

Raft went back to their table, reaching for the cruet, and for a moment was sheltered behind Jackson as the Ombudsman covered his hand with a handkerchief and took up the card.

The air cracked apart with the sound. The explosion, incredible from so light a wafer, blew the old man in two.

Raft, drenched in Jackson's blood and spattered with his flesh, was flung across the table and on to the floor beyond it. Reflexes spared no time in thought. He was on his feet and running for the door while his ears still reverberated with the blast.

Expecting death he plunged at full speed into the darkness and cannoned painfully into a body. He kicked sweepingly and successfully at its legs and stamped on its collapsing bulk. Someone touched him from the side; he felt, found an arm and broke it.

In this terrible place without sound or direction he turned to his right, towards what he hoped was the interior of the building, found the wall and felt his way along it, ready to fight at a touch.

Abruptly the blind lifted and the air racketed noise. He glimpsed colorful clothing grouped round the dining-room door and two heaps on the floor, one still, one moaning. He ran. Round the first corner and across an empty lounge that filled as he ran. From doors and passageways Security men poured, in uniform and undress and practically no dress at all, guns already firing past him.

A black-clad arm brought him to unwilling halt. "All right, Commander. We can deal with it."

Full of the reason he should be wanted dead Raft gasped, "The Commissioner! Campion! I've got to see him at once."

The Security man—it was the Senior Tech from *Columbus*—steadied him. "Take it easy. We can look after this lot."

Briefly there were guns in the outside night while he panted and cursed restraint. Then quiet.

"This lot! They don't matter." He took breath and said with all his force, "What's in the balance is your whole simple-minded world. Take me to Campion!" The Tech hesitated still. "Now! Now!"

—3—

Sick wards had changed little; more color but the same essential bareness and the same aura of stillness and anti-sepsis.

"Blood! You're soaked in it!"

It was Campion's voice, straining through battered lips, and Campion was an unholy sight, unrecognizable under bandages, both arms and a leg in plaster, the visible flesh blackened and swollen; even the patch of red hair flaunting from the crown was a ragged flag.

"Not mine." Raft knew he must look like a slaughtered beast; the old man had come literally to pieces, *spraying* over him. He found now that he was bruised and aching; he had been flung about six feet and was lucky to have escaped broken bones.

"What has happened? The noise?" Campion's lips fumbled but his tone was lively and concerned.

"Another mob of kids. They wanted to kill me."

The lips, twisting, may have smiled. Or may not. "No luck, I see."

"No." The words defied him to speak them; he heard Campion calling the man "Dad" and saw Jackson's battened-down affection and his mouth rebelled.

Behind him the Senior Tech said, "Tell him. He isn't in shock. He has to know."

Cautious phrases would not do. "They got Jackson." Long silence became unbearable. Whatever the Ombudsman had been and done, his dream had been genuine, worth an epitaph. "The people he lived for killed him. He was trying to protect me."

Campion cried helplessly in his mummy wrappings. With a feeling different from anything in his experience

Raft took out his crumpled handkerchief and wiped the anguished eyes. Campion shook his head weakly and Raft said, "I have the right to help," and found himself mumbling more than he had intended in a random attempt to divert, perhaps to replace loss. "I'm probably your grandfather, you know."

The lips made a meaningless sound. Raft hadn't meant to say it so soon; said, at this moment, it seemed trivial.

"Is that possible?" Campion's voice was under control, cooled by training and dedication.

"Yes. We'll work it out later. There are more urgent things."

"Tell me about Dad."

He told briefly. "But he was mistaken; they wanted me dead."

"Why?"

He heard the Senior Tech move slightly in his position by the door.

"For the present this should be for your ears only."

"No; I'm out of commission. Senior Colley will listen and act for me. Come here, Laurie."

Colley took the chair at the other side of the bed.

"Now, then."

"It depends on something I'm not sure of. Have you been told about the substitute Commissioner?" Campion had. "I think my rejection of him could be known to the clone. Possible?"

Colley was sure of it. "He wore Security uniform; every word spoken would have been picked up until we defused him."

"Defused." As though they realized such gadgetry had the potential of a psychological bomb. He hoped they did.

Campion's lips slurred, "That's why they dumped me; the abduction was pointless."

Colley added, "They dropped him by the roadside; just dropped him and left."

To Raft it made sense. "They don't know why I rejected their man; to them it's unthinkable—or so we see it. If they regard the clone as literally indivisible, my reaction becomes wilful treachery. They thought I could be milked at leisure once non-Campion was installed, and I have knowledge they want.''

"What's that?"

"How to run *Columbus*. They would have expected me to run the ship for them."

Their blankness made nothing of that. He continued, "I think it would have been a last resort, but they needed to have control of a major threat."

Campion asked, "Threat?" Colley seemed lost.

It seemed so obvious to Raft. "Who controls *Columbus* can control the world. She is—can be—the ultimate weapon. And I am the only pilot."

His climax fell flat; they reacted not at all. He told them angrily, "You've left her out there empty, unguarded; a shuttle and a cutting torch and she's anybody's. In a few days any good engineer could work out the control system in essence. They may even have the plans; there were scores of copies. Now, as an enemy they want me dead; they'll take *Columbus* the hard way."

He ran down, beaten by silence. At last Colley said, "You seem to mean that the ship can be used to blackmail authority into submission."

"Yes."

"How? It isn't armed."

"She *is* a weapon. The range of the monopole extends for thousands of miles; *Columbus* can stand off in space and suck the air off the planet."

They were startled but not convinced. At length Campion murmured, "No. She would crash herself doing it. Almost at once.'

"Not in reverse." He scrabbled for the notebook he had stuffed into a pocket. "It's like this—" He sketched rapidly. "The hull is only a web; the real structure is a complex of magnetic forces; dozens of small monopoles shape the direction of the plasma after intake. To reverse, we don't somersault or invert the intake, we simply change the focusing monopole bearings to direct the intake on to baffles for deceleration. I tell you she can sit in space and strip Earth down to strangulation.''

But Colley had been figuring times in his head. "We could take the ship out with homing missiles before she did much damage." He speculated, "There could be some hellish storms for an hour or so."

Colley was no man's fool and Raft knew he had gone too far too fast; he couldn't panic them. He said quickly, "But the ionosphere could be cut to ribbons in minutes. It's very thin; from an oblique angle great strips could be torn out of it and tossed into space. It would take months to close over and solar radiation would fry the Earth. The Van Allen belts could be disorganized in the same way and God only knows what the results of that would be."

Campion rolled enquiring eyes at Colley, who nodded. "Sounds possible. Disruption of the belts would be catastrophic. Hard radiation flooding in . . . a sterilized planet, at the least."

Campion asked, "And if the plans no longer exist?"

"As an engineer I'd back myself to elucidate the system from scratch, and each clone-member is presumably as good as I am."

"Would they know of the possibility?"

"Who can tell? But Heathcote would. You people would have realized it for yourselves eventually."

Campion said tersely, "Blow the thing out of the sky."

That was too much; Raft howled, "No!"

"Your baby? Your beloved? *Our world!*"

"I'm not just sentimental. A weapon for them is a weapon for us, too. And she can do other things." He sought the other things and found an outrageous one. "Pinpoint their headquarters and I can sit her down on them tail first, spitting plasma at twenty thousand degrees."

He heard himself with amazement, knowing he would not do it and not honestly sure he could control her so finely near a planetary surface, but desperate to save his ship. And this world which had deferred the stars might need them sooner than they imagined; but they would not believe that yet.

Colley said, "We don't need to answer barbarity in its own terms, but the ship should be preserved if possible. We need the monopole and probably other things that have dropped out of current knowledge."

"If possible. But can we?" Campion's eyes flickered at

Raft, unreadably, probably hiding speculation under the bandages. "You have some advice, Commander?"

The question was a triumph for Raft, offering what he would have not dared broach for himself, marking a first rung on the ladder of position, stature, responsibility. He was ready for it. "Put a Security guard aboard, armed to repel boarders. Then let it be known that you have her and what she can do. That should keep them well away."

"Laurie?"

"Yes, of course. Better still if they are too scared to make the attempt. No methods of combat have been worked out for such conditions."

Raft said, "Nobody ever did fight in space that I know of. The opposition will also have to think it out. I have some ideas."

He was needed; he would see to it that they continued to need him, at least until this viciousness was over.

Campion's head moved sharply. "See to it, Laurie. To-night."

Colley started for the door. "A dozen men, Commander?"

"Should be enough."

Campion called painfully, "Not to go yourself. I need you here."

At the door Colley paused; "Commander!" He placed his hand over his heart, seriously, not in the usual sketchy fashion, said, "You think ahead of us," and left them.

Campion gave a stiff-lipped grunt of a laugh. "Laurie's your man!"

"What does it mean?"

"Salute for an Ombudsman; he shouldn't have done it, but we need an adviser with experience of violence." *Do they think our streets ran round the clock with blood?* "I can't make you an Ombudsman; nobody can; there'll be no more of them. But you can advise me." He added quickly, "No power of override."

"I wouldn't want it."

Campion brought him bluntly to earth. "Wouldn't you? Don't you want power? Then why do you offer loyalty?

Lindley left the decision open and he was right. How do you justify loyalty?''

Raft risked a long shot, making it forceful. ''Who harms mine, harms me.''

Campion said calmly, ''We don't make much of blood relationships. Am I in fact your grandson?''

Did a smile hide there, or a cat-and-mouse grin? Raft wished he knew. ''Perhaps I was too definite, but we'll know certainly when you get Heathcote. He has to be found.''

''Yes.'' Campion's voice remained bland. ''The idea of you takes getting used to. Oh, I'm impressed; we'll get along with or without a bloodline. You're a sort of honorary Dad now that Stephen's gone. But not Grandad; not yet.''

''I'm sorry I jumped the gun there.''

''Did what? What does that mean? Stay and talk; tell me about the old world, the old slang speech, the—oh, anything. I never got much out of Stephen.''

Campion's request was as much political as friendly, as much an attempt to gloss inept beginnings as to recognize a possible blood tie. Yet he was more taken with the idea of relationship than his caution admitted.

A Security man's training began in extreme youth. Its procedures, designed to replace and obscure the emotional complex of family environment, could scarcely avoid creating alternative areas of extreme vulnerability, and one of these had been struck a considerable blow. He was tantalized, a little excited by the possible family closeness, which he and his kind knew only as a prerogative of those they served.

The flip style of the youngsters had it that Security was in the world but not of it, and the saying had its core of fact. Campion was before all things a Security man and his most urgent thinking circulated in areas beyond personality and pleasure. Raft the man was a part of his calculation of events; Raft the putative forebear was a relaxation.

And must remain so.

Because outside, in Melbourne Town, that tiny echo of a resounding city, dead policemen were being taken away. In the streets, in the gardens, in the houses, drug-sodden

youngsters were being rounded up before the stare faded
from their hypnoed eyes, and Campion was sick at heart.
His kids had been used like herded beasts. His very bruises
ached to stamp and destroy.

Only half his mind listened to Raft speaking of the chaotic, deadly past and he was asleep when Colley brought
the starman a fresh uniform.

The dragonfly cruised with windows blacked out. The big
man in shorts and shirt, wrapped in quiet reticence as if he
were not a guard, was a Raft simulacrum but less than a
perfect image. He was a shade more slender over-all, which
might signify immediate vagaries of physical condition, but
his face was differently lined, printing an expression Lindley could not fit to Raft as he knew him—something of the
fanatic, something of the saint—and he moved more relax-
edly. So the clone resemblance could be muted by factors
of environment and training; it was to be expected.

This was a professionally automatic observation; Lindley's deeper attention was inward, towards his frightening
mental condition. Memory recorded all he had said and
done since Alice appeared at his room door, and self-
knowledge was derided by facts; he seemed to be watching
a peculiar and shocking case of schizophrenia from the inside but intellect, slowly taking hold, insisted that he had
acted both voluntarily and against his will. This could only
mean duress of a special kind.

He said over the muffled roar of the dragonfly, ''I've
been drugged!''

Alice recoiled from his anger but whispered, ''Yes.''
Then, as if in release, she became babblingly appeasing.
''But it can't harm you. A short term hypnotic. And it
won't harm you. I know it won't——'' She broke off,
ashamed, and said drearily, ''It must be wearing off.''

He thought it was. He concentrated on visualizing a complex geometrical figure in three dimensions, a calming exercise he had devised long ago. It helped.

He contradicted her, calmly because information took precedence over anger. "Not a hypnotic. I was fully aware and always basically hostile. A sapper of initiative; something new in the pharmacopoeia. Why was it done?"

"The Lady sent for you."

"What lady?"

The girl frowned. "I don't know who she is." The fact appeared to puzzle herself, a point he held for future consideration.

The clone-brother broke silence to talk nonsense in a matter-of-fact tone. "She is the soul of the remaking, the promise of tomorrow, the symbol of the world."

It was the ancient profession of faith in a charismatic phantom, familiar and contemptible down the years. But the man was sincere. The real Raft could not have said it; his occasional enthusiasms were never blurred or mystical.

"What does she want with me?"

Alice answered uncertainly, "I think it is John Heathcote who really wants you."

So he lived. "Why?"

She had no idea. The clone-brother spoke again and it could have been Albert's voice, softened and smoothed. "He feels you may be able to explain Albert."

Speaking the name seemed to depress him.

"Why not take Albert and let him explain himself?"

Alice said shakily, "Commander Raft is dead. He was dead before the dragonfly picked us up."

The mob; the screaming mob. At the edges of his shock he saw that the clone-brother also was stunned by the news.

"Killed? Murdered?" She nodded fearfully. "Why?"

"Perhaps he was dangerous."

"How?"

"I don't know." Again the flash of wretchedness at her own ignorance.

Lindley snarled at the clone-brother, "Whose responsibility?"

"I do not know that—yet. I did not know what the drugged children were to do." The Raft face darkened with menace. "But I shall know; *we* shall know." Threat gave way to slow thoughtfulness. "I did not feel him die. If he were half the world away I should have felt the vanishing.

He was different in his fashion—but so different?"

Alice suggested timidly, "Perhaps the blind interfered with your perception."

He shot her a grin of contempt and spoke to Lindley. "We know you for his friend, Doctor, and you might have been ours. Will you now be an enemy?"

The poor thing was too naïve for credibility. Lindley mocked, "The clone does not kill."

"Do you doubt us?"

"If not the clone, then who?"

"Other agents."

"So you do not kill but 'do not strive officiously to keep alive'?"

The brother said primly—and "primly" was the word for it—"What others do is not our responsibility."

"And your hands and your souls are thereby clean?"

"Clean."

"Dear Jesus!" He contemplated with grudging awe the monstrous conditioning that could produce such a rationalization in a group of—"How many of you are there?"

"Throughout the world there are eighty-three units."

"Eighty-three robots?"

The thing said stiffly, "We are highly individualized."

"Yes? I bet you can even tell each other apart. Or can you?" He turned to Alice. "Now, little traitress, tell me where we are going."

"Don't abuse me; I am loyal to a belief, not to a social system." But she hadn't much spirit left for defiance.

"The final refuge of the thoroughly confused. Where are we going?"

"I told you, to Gangoil."

He knew of Heathcote's little private joke; he had earned a gusher of scrambled reminiscence aboard *Columbus* once the Raft ice had broken. (Raft gone and himself alone among strangers? Irrational need clung to the small fact that the brother had not felt him die.)

"Is it far?"

The brother reverted to apostleship. "Not far in distance, infinitely far in meaning."

It was not worth pursuing; fanatics are as determinedly obscurantist as they are potentially dangerous.

Alice's nerves were strung beyond restraint. She prattled, "Gangoil isn't an Australian name. We have old native names like Croajingalong and Tallangatta—" through the gabble Lindley began to make tentative deductions concerning her condition—"and Caddibarrawirracanna"—her cluttered tongue barely compassed that one—"but Gangoil sounds wrong."

Lindley said, "Trollope had an affection for the Irish," mystifying her completely. She was a woefully ignorant conspirator. So, for that matter, was the clone-brother.

—5—

Raft woke to the voice of the doorcom. "Who is it?"

"Senior Colley."

"Wait on." He shuffled into a bathrobe and pressed the window sash. Summer rushed into the room with a shout of gold light and blue glazed sky and the promise of heat; it was the Australian special, blazing and bruising as soon as the sun cleared the horizon. It brought the sensation of homing all things had so far lacked.

He admitted a Colley who had probably slept little and that little in his overall. "What's up?"

"A lot. I'm to keep you up to date on everything."

Ombudsman Raft, Acting, Unpaid. It was time they cut away their umbilical dependence on outdated experience, but for the time being it could be a useful status prop.

"Sit down, Senior."

"I've ordered breakfast sent up. Eggs and coffee all right?"

"Anything. I suppose the dining-room is wreckage?"

"Not too bad. It will be mostly a matter of replacing panels—prefabricated stuff." He did not mention blood and shredded flesh. "I want some private conversation—conference—while we sort out what matters and what doesn't, so I've had your room bugs blanked."

"Bugs?"

"We have to keep an eye on you after what's happened."

"Yes, but every move and word!" He stopped because Colley seemed surprised at the protest and because in an environment so sophisticated in the apparatus of watchfulness he might need all the protective surveillance they could offer.

Colley said, "It shouldn't be for long. Where's your overall? It's broadcasting, so we'd better defuse it for the moment. Like this—tab under the lapel."

Raft pitched it on the bed. "When's the funeral?"

"The what?"

"I'd like to attend Jackson's funeral."

Colley was rueful. "You keep taking me back to things I've only read about. We don't have funerals. That was a grisly business, holding a sort of social gathering round a dead host. We just cremate; the remains of the Ombudsman were burned hours ago."

Eminently practical and dauntingly cold. With usefulness finished, toss it into the incinerator. Would no one want to farewell Jackson except himself? Or was he indulging sentimental crap, letting blue funk pay its offering to luck?

He could not help asking, "Do you people believe in an afterlife?"

"You mean as though the psyche or some such doesn't knock off with the body? I've never thought about it; I enjoy life too much to worry. A couple of religious sects among the aesthetic groups are based on ideas like that— where a soul, whatever that is, keeps going indefinitely. Do you have those ideas?"

"Damned if I know. Many did. It was always one of those things it was comfortable to believe if you could see any reason for believing. Even if you couldn't."

He realized that Colley was being polite within his limits to an elderly citizen from the temporal sticks and that he was relieved when the arrival of breakfast allowed the subject to wither. Then the Senior said, "Alice White disappeared during the night."

"Expected. She just about had to be the go-between."

"Yes, but Lindley went with her."

Raft's utensils clattered on the plate. "Christ!"

"Must be a shock. But why Lindley?"

"Willingly or kidnapped?"

"Kidnapped, we think. Certainly drugged; the contact item was left behind in his room."

"Clumsy."

"Perhaps they didn't care. Their actions have all stunk of confidence."

"Are the others all right?"

"Your crew? I suppose so. With Lindley gone we decided that having them concentrated here was tantamount to endangering them, so we've shipped them back to their own areas. 'Countries,' I suppose you'd say." Eyes on his plate, he did not see Raft's expression. "In any case their governments were all claiming them; in fact Moscow asked for Kulayev as soon as the first newscast went out."

Raft hadn't known about the newscast but that was unimportant beside the immediate shock. "In the middle of the bloody night!"

Colley stared. "Why not? What difference, night or day? The thing was to get them away, so they've been airborne a few hours now."

Raft was all at once completely, furiously alone, stripped of every familiar thing. "You could have let me know before they went! For God's sake, man, we've been together for years!"

Colley complained like one who had breached an unfamiliar code, "But you can contact them whenever you want." His expression took on sudden inquisitiveness. "Or has so much propinquity magnified emotional attachments?"

Whatever he envisioned, he was honestly interested. Raft spluttered coffee and recovered. "Senior, have you any close friends?"

"Of course. The Commissioner, for one; we entered Security together."

"And if he were seconded to the other side of the Earth you wouldn't feel any interest in saying goodbye to him?"

" 'Goodbye' implies for ever, doesn't it? We don't use it much. Where could anyone go that computercom couldn't locate him in minutes?"

(But Colley had an uneasy inkling of what Raft meant. His face gave no unnecessary information—that was a lifetime's practice—but his thought fluttered about the words

Campion had pushed through bruised lips only minutes ago, when the Senior had reported to him the re-nationalization of the starmen: "Hope hard they stay safe, Laurie; we should have kept them here." He had pandered to the Commissioner's upset condition, pointing out that he could not have refused the national demands, little as he liked the systems of some of the areas involved. Non-interference . . . Campion's mask had said, "Ah, the ethic!" as though he spat. There was no need to report a sick man's reaction. Nor would he tell Raft who, if he didn't know, couldn't talk out of turn.)

Raft gave up, appreciating the logic but wishing there were less of it. *But we made a habit of sentiment instead of sense and look where it got us.* Still, a little empathy would have been welcome even to his cool self-sufficiency; he had never before been beleaguered on a hostile planet.

Colley returned to essentials. "Lindley and Alice were picked up from an open square on the edge of the town center, probably by the same dragonfly that covered the raid here. A dozen people saw them but there's nothing unusual about a dragonfly pickup."

"No chance of tracking them?"

"None; his suit's defused. But what do they want of him? Who wants a used-up, out-of-date psychiatrist?"

So much for twentieth-century pride. "Heathcote does." He said it without thinking, then saw that it was true. "He wants the one psychiatrist who knows me backwards and forwards and who may be able to suggest how a rogue mind may occur in a clone."

"Reasonable, but why should he have you killed if he wants to investigate? Sounds like cross purposes somewhere." Raft had no suggestion; Colley passed on. "There's another item. Some of the kids picked up last night were deep questioned before they were out of hypno. That's a touchy technique but sometimes it brings up fringe stuff that might be missed. They have a saying in common, a sort of recognition phrase, perhaps—'Peace and love through The Lady.' Suggest anything?"

"The Virgin Mary?"

Colley was contemptuous. "A religion of peace? By blood to the holy throne?"

"You should read up on Christianity; it wouldn't be the first time."

"Mass paranoia?"

"Why not? A historical commonplace. Your reconstruction program isn't changing human nature, only keeping it busy."

"You really mean this?"

"Really and deadly."

Colley placed the idea on mental file, though doubtfully, and raised another aspect. "The thing turns on the hypno-drugs. They're all on the Relegated List—unobtainable save by laboratory people and then checked to the last grain. How in hell did they get them?"

"A criminal mind will find a way to get any damned thing."

"But where are the criminals?"

Raft said tiredly, "I refuse to believe you haven't any."

"Very few. The criminal mentality is mostly detectable in adolescence, even infancy. Psychologists of your own period did the statistical work, correlating physical and mental traits, and ours took it from there. For twenty years we've been picking them up in their teens and re-directing the drives. It isn't foolproof, but there's little major crime."

Raft's stomach contracted as he extrapolated the statement. A mind loaded with incidental reading recalled Eysenck's work on the criminal personality and wondered if that had been the genesis of this potentially murderous program. The permissive, superficially easygoing world possessed every weapon needed to turn it into a concentration camp.

"I suppose potentially criminal types don't get into positions of trust."

"Generally not."

"But one touch of a hypno-drug . . . ?"

"That brings us full circle. Where does it come from?"

"Honest fools can be manipulated by criminals and highly responsible IQs can be pathetically foolish outside their specialities. Surely you have manipulative psychologists?"

"A criminal psych? The therapy system—"

"Shit to the system. Somebody must get missed, if only

by bureaucratic error—somebody kept in hiding, like the clone. Run a check on those located and see what your data banks know about them; the information system should have noted the existence of a unique group and it could be that no one has ever asked the question which would reveal it.''

Colley was on his way before Raft had finished.

The computers spanned the planet in superfast linkage, but the examination took a maddening hour of homing in on the most useful questions. The answers set Colley bellowing, ''The clone doesn't exist. It doesn't bloody well exist!''

Raft said with pleasure, ''You run such a tight club you think everybody must be a member. Now you know a few never joined in the first place; the clone never signed the register.''

''Have you a criminal mind? Your ideas hit the nails.''

''I wouldn't know; try me.''

''How could such a group exist without physical detection? Where, on an integrated planet?''

''In dispersion almost anywhere; never causing comment by never being seen together. You don't need me to think of that for you. But there would have to be group contacts, so how about uninhabited areas? There must be plenty aside from deserts, mountains, jungles and England.''

''Movement in and out of the areas would be noticed and queried if no relocation permits had been filed.''

''So they were filed; with suitable excuses. Give a computer system the right kind of pat on the head and it purrs as contentedly as any cat. The Ombudsmen created your problems because they were in a hurry. So they set up systems—good, workable systems, too. But any system is vulnerable at every seam and it inhibits the user from thinking outside it. After a generation of goodwill and cooperation you've forgotten dissent; the clone is your warning that peaceful brotherhood is on the way out. You'll have to start thinking in terms of your own weaknesses.''

If Campion attacked foundations, Campion was a *beau ideal* and above criticism; Raft attacking them was little better than an enemy. Colley asked with controlled fury,

"And where shall we look for our weaknesses?"

"Gangoil, for a start." Rapport with Colley had vanished: Raft imagined the Senior repressed an urge to hit him. It was unfortunate but there was worse to come. "I mean it. It's a lead of a sort and it can be followed, but I'll need help."

"You will get it."

What Raft wanted was insult and he knew it, but it was what he must have. "Not from Security but from the civil police. Crime isn't your real business and it is theirs; if there is expertise available, they'll have it."

There was a malignant pause. Then Colley set about arranging liaison with the police, with set face and without the ritual touch of the heart.

—6—

Just before dawn the jet lifted from the airfield, and the plane held Kulayev's interest nearly as much as the attitude—official, incurious, remote—of the Russian crew. He knew its lines, the complex calculus of its airfoils and the narrow-vent designs of the double-rotored nacelles; it was a troop transport of a type introduced only a year or so before he left Earth. He was intrigued by the implication that some technological areas had stagnated while others flourished. To be expected, perhaps . . .

As to the crew members, he guessed that they did not know how they should react to him, any more than he did to them. Nevertheless, remembering old Russia, he was suitably wary.

When at last one of the crew came from the forward cabins to keep him company he was careful to contain surprise, for the man wore a clerical collar Kulayev was sure had not been about his neck minutes earlier. But the slightly Tatar face was friendly in its reserved fashion and the scientist broke silence on a neutral subject which could scarcely involve him in political traps.

"Could I perhaps have a glass of water?"

The broad face turned full on him. "Before prayer?" There followed a silent space of mutual calculation. "But yours was a Godless era and you would be of no belief."

This was true; Kulayev had not concerned himself greatly with religion, though belief had no longer been a matter for state suspicion as in his youth. But, like any man who had lived through periods of purge and permissiveness and witnessed bland and brutal reversals of power, he knew the smell of authoritarianism; old habits of adaptation returned with speed and force.

He said at once, avoiding the ingratiating tone which might invite suspicion, "You are mistaken; I am a believer. No doubt forms changed during the years of chaos, but I think the essence remains."

The dark eyes did not relax. "Belief is all-powerful and waxes greater still. The State *is* belief." Kulayev relived the half-forgotten feeling of an intense scrutiny waiting for the most miniscular error, and he met it blandly. "Through they years and the light years, did you pray?"

"Daily." If a reasonable God existed he would not record the lie.

"In what form?"

"The basic prayers, of course." Surely "basic" must always be safe. "The Lord's Prayer and the twenty-third psalm were my constant invocations." God alone could help him if he were required to recite the psalm. *The Lord is my shepherd*, and then what?

"Primitive!" It was contemptuous irritation. "So animals could pray, babbling memory. Prayer is the *art* of Russia." He dropped to his knees, dragging Kulayev in a grip of surprising strength. "We shall pray. I shall speak the prayer; you will listen. To the glory of God!"

After ten minutes on his knees, with the plane riding a shattering series of airpockets, Kulayev knew the meaning of prayer as an art form. The young man poured out a torrent of language whose magnificence sprang directly from Holy Writ and an appalling arrogance of brazen humility; for Kulayev it rang with the naked threat of a new and fanatically austere totalitarianism.

When at last he was permitted to rise he had to lever himself up with hands flat on the deck.

"I think you are not accustomed to kneeling."

"It is full gravity to which I am not accustomed."

"Ah." It was the unsatisfied acceptance of the bigot. "I will get your water." He walked towards the rear of the plane but stopped to say, "And then I will question you about the clone," and Kulayev heard the voice of the police state interrogator.

He said, knowing already that he wasted breath, "I know practically nothing about the clone."

The young man removed his collar with one hand and the man of God had no fount of prayer left in his expression. "After so long a time you must surely know a great deal. The Kremlin insists on information."

In terror Kulayev thought, *I am going to die for my ignorance.*

Unfortunately for himself he was wrong about that.

At the airfield Doronin persisted in asking why he had been separated from Kulayev, then stopped as the bleak familiarity of uninterested expressions carried him back to a style of handling which in the Russia of the ageing century had begun to disappear. The lack of reaction meant "we are doing our job," "we don't know and dare not care" and "you have ceased to be a person until certain requirements are satisfied." If pity lurked there he could not be allowed to know it.

Only the two nurses, one male, one female, spoke to him and he noticed that their syntax halted occasionally, as though Russian was not their first language. Straining his ears when the pilot and navigator passed near him at the plane ramp he heard them speak Polish to each other.

In fear he swung about for aid, but the Security escort was gone into the darkness beyond the edge of the airfield. He turned back to the woman, to the man, and saw only the anonymity of wardens who guarded with indifference to person.

The man said suddenly, "Telepathy!" and made it sound like an order.

"I don't understand. What about telepathy?"

"Think about it."

"To what end?"

"All the way to Warsaw you will talk about telepathy to recording instruments."

Doronin shouted in terror and incomprehension, "But I must go to Moscow! My superiors——"

"Are dust. And Moscow is not your home place. Think of telepathy."

"I know nothing of telepathy."

The man thrust his face close and shouted, "Telepathy!"

On the other side the girl cried piercingly in his ear, "Telepathy!"

"Telepathy!" yelled the man and "Telepathy!" the girl echoed.

The word bounced side to side across his skull, again and again. He flinched at the jab of a hypodermic and soon there was a short period of nausea while the senseless word still riddled his head. Nausea passed and with it his puzzlements and fears, superseded by a grey, muddy, walking sleep wherein his mind churned up all it knew about the word driven crudely but effectively into it.

He would not have been helped by knowing that the Security escort was disapprovingly aware of his probable treatment, though the references to telepathy would have meant nothing to them. He was not their affair; he was in the hands of his own people and the ethic of self-determination did not permit interference unless the person illtreated demanded it.

If Doronin had screamed, that would have been another matter, prima facie evidence of rights invaded. But in Doronin's day screaming at that juncture would not have helped; it had not occurred to him.

Matthews may well have been the last of the homeward bound starmen to realize that four decades had brought about changes he might not have credited in four centuries.

His plane was no outdated military craft or modern version of the jet, but a silver bullet following a trajectory rather than a course in the outer wisps of atmosphere, up and over and round the swell of the world. He was quietly proud that in the shattered planet his country still created new technology, and if the country seemed to be called New York rather than the United States, that would sort itself out. Home was anywhere in those three million square miles between the oceans.

His company were young men with familiar accents and a tremendous interest in his voyaging. So much for Security and its contempt of space. They questioned him, fell over him like puppies, joshed and gagged and laughed and couldn't fit in questions enough. And if it seemed a little self-conscious, well, they were doing their best to make him welcome back and he loved every minute of it.

And if much of what they said seemed to have meanings he didn't catch, how much would a man of 1950 have understood on Broadway of 1990?

But the insistent questioning became irritating, and the air seemed to tighten a little when he cried off, "Later, fellers, later," with his grin beginning to strain. Then they would quieten, but soon it would begin again, as if curiosity was uncontainable.

They were over the eastern Pacific when the pieces he had failed to understand commenced to fall together into a pattern, and when they saw that he understood they watched him with the same curiosity which had infused their questioning. But they were silent now, avid for his reaction.

"The States! Communist! I don't . . . no!"

"Yes," said one, and Matthews became aware of a sameness of attitude, as if it did not matter which one spoke; they would all say the same thing in much the same words. "*Your* group is the New York Soviet."

None of them misread the outrage in his eyes; for the first time their possession of guns became obvious.

Matthews said with the extreme care of strain, "I believe I may choose my own country of residence."

"True. You simply make application to the local Security office."

"I shall do that."

A purring note now, "Why not? But you should become acquainted with your country first. A fair trial, eh? Say for a year or so. Then perhaps something could be arranged. If you still wish it."

The speaker smiled. Matthews took his meaning perfectly.

"Meanwhile you have interesting things to tell us. In particular we are interested in the telepathic abilities of Commander Raft."

At once the situation was ridiculous; Matthews laughed his head off while the dead stares waited. "All this, for something that doesn't exist!"

"We think differently."

"Then I don't know a damned thing about it."

"Perhaps, but there will be significant details not ordered in your mind—the things you don't know you know. We need those from you."

"For Christ's sake! I can't——"

Interruption—savage, forceful, overbearing. "You will!"

Matthew's black belt was more than an academic qualification and the ethical considerations which hedged it about were annulled by the situation; also, karate was unknown in the new world, where even boxing was a crude sport constructed from old and faulty memories. He killed four of them before a fool found a target for his slow, astonished gun.

The bullet took Matthews between the eyes.

There was a dreadful, frightened silence while the doctor came aft to examine the wound and confirm that resurrection was out of the question, that the brain was ruined.

The silence turned on the man who had killed New York Soviet's entry to the new secrets, and closed round him while the fool put the barrel in his mouth, shuddered twice in fear of the unknown and blew the back of his head out.

Nobody ever did find out what happened to Streich.

CHAPTER FOUR

HEATHCOTE'S GANGOIL

> . . . all that lies ahead is our image of the future, which means our collective image of how our collective actions are going to work out.
>
> Brian W. Aldiss:
> *The Shape of Further Things*

—1—

The room was a concrete cell in a concrete hive, but reasonably furnished and warm with unobtrusive diffused heating.

The young man with the touched-up blond hair and plucked eyebrows and formidable muscles said, "Underground? Where else would a sub-social organization be? Joke? No? One can but try. Actually we're inside a mountain and half-way up it."

Flippancy, Lindley judged, would be second nature to Francis, who carried mild homosexual excesses without the self-consciousness which could make them irritating and otherwise was probably just an ebullient young man in a young man's enchantment with gaiety.

"*We* didn't build it." Shrug to disclaim responsibility for austere ambience. "It's an old hidey-hole, a sort of super-bomb-shelter, though it's hard to imagine it being efficient against anyone who meant business." Pensive pursing of lips for ancestral foolishness. "But it's hard to imagine you being only eight years younger at the time it was built, too." Quizzical eyebrow.

Alice sat apart, inattentive, immersed in misery. Lind-

149

ley's instinct was to attempt comfort but as yet he could only guess at what troubled her. He concentrated on Francis.

"What was it? A parliamentary refuge?" By 2000 every major government had some such bolt-hole, as though a bureaucracy might persist unscathed though its country crumbled around it.

"No, no; it was for old John. John Heathcote—you know about him? Then you know that he was terribly important because of his discoveries so when things blew up, or even before, they shifted him and his work underground—that is the government did—and kept him out of sight. So when the world fell to pieces here was old John like a grub in a tunnel, carrying on regardless. They had food and what-have-you for years."

And that was the simple fact of Heathcote's retirement out of humanity and into history. "Where is 'here'?"

Eyebrows arched at heaven. "Ask me another; *I* don't know. I suppose the pilots and The Lady and a couple of higher-ups all know, but the rest of us come and go in sealed transport; we're quite clueless. All part of the big hush-hush of course; I'd bet even the pilots have hypnoblocks that will stop anything short of synaptic surgery. When you think about it secrecy is terribly simple."

The speech decoration was just that—decoration. Behind it was bleak watchfulness.

"In my day you wouldn't have lasted a month. Your secrecy is built on worldwide naïvety. That's my whole impression of this age so far; naïvety equipped with dangerous playthings."

The eyebrows, essential to communication, bent in distaste. "All complex and suspicious, weren't you? Think of this as a new adolescence, growing from first principles, and don't use down-putting descriptions."

"Naïvety," Lindley repeated, "and it will destroy you all, here and outside."

"Well, perhaps we'll need a touch of your old-fashioned deviousness before we're through. You're the one who wouldn't take sides for old Jackson, aren't you? You'll be able to make up your mind here. At least some of us know what we're about, which is more than you can say for the mess outside. That should appeal to you.''

''Albert's murder doesn't appeal.''

The shapely but very capable hands caressed the folds of the scarlet sarong and the lips curled slightly. ''You placed a tremendous value on human life, didn't you? Protected the individual like mad while you slaughtered whole populations. We've put an end to that sort of hypocrisy. Does it matter if an individual lives or dies? We like living, but everybody's replaceable. It's the race that matters.''

''Clone philosophy?''

''Them!'' He made it sound like spitting, then added grudgingly, ''But they do point up the unimportance of unit survival.''

''Heil Hitler!''

''Eh?''

''An invocation to an old god. He'd have loved you.''

Alice broke out of silence, crying, ''They shouldn't have killed him! They didn't have to.''

''Safety precaution, darling. Or so they tell me.''

She muttered, ''It was wrong,'' then burst out loudly, ''I wish I'd never had anything to do with this. Never!''

Francis inspected her keenly. ''You sound as though your conditioning has broken. Never mind, duckie, the therapists will fix you up.''

She wilted to near collapse, whispering, ''Conditioning! Oh, no!''

'' 'Fraid, yes! It's always a bit of a shock when you find out. But the boys will tidy you up, never fear.''

Anguish and the after-terror of violation closed round her; she shrank.

Despite pity, Lindley found himself speculating on possible techniques ''they'' might use in shoring-up a personality which now might easily tip into paranoia or fall all the way down into catatonia. Some suppression of memory would be needed. Could they do that? Or would they go about it the crude way, directed by a computer, reconstructing personality so that the new dominant would regard the old emotions as ill-generated and inefficient? Either method would be vulnerable to deep synaptic linkages . . .

A muted chime sounded in the ceiling and a voice spoke: "Francis."

"Here, sweetheart."

The voice asked disgustedly, "Don't you ever let up? The Lady is ready for Lindley."

"Better an honest queen than stud to that decrepit bag," Francis said and smiled serenely as the ceiling breathed anger. "Mister Lindley, the old girl's waiting for you. Miss White, you stay here and I'll arrange for your therapy."

She cried out of a face contorted in despair, "I want to die!"

Perhaps she really meant the idiot cry for death; at any rate Francis patted her shoulder and gave what may have been his version of compassion. "Don't be a silly girl. You can't carry on with your insides all of a mucky dither. This way, Doctor Lindley. Or is it Professor or some such?"

A long corridor split the center of the complex, severe in enclosing concrete, but in this section austerity vanished with an exotic flourish. Deep, lush, crimson pile ran a hundred yards into the mountainside between walls covered with paintings and between stands and display cases of ornaments and figurines.

Not quite believing what he saw, Lindley reached to take up a fat vase in black and red ochres, then withdrew it with the realization that if it was indeed what it seemed it was twenty-five centuries old and infinitely precious.

Francis surveyed him lazily. "You can touch if you like; we've quite a few of them. There's a big old museum down the road a bit from the Security barrack in Melbourne Town and the old bitch had a lot of stuff brought in here during the crack-up period. Greek, that one's supposed to be."

"It is."

"You sound all awestruck, like The Lady when she's having one of her culture fits."

Lifting his eyes, Lindley tried to take in the extent of the treasure on the walls that were packed rather than hung with paintings. His grasp of the history of the Collapse was minimal, but on this evidence there must have been a lengthy time when the country could be ransacked at will by those with the transport and fuel. Just reach and grab—and how many collections of splendor were pilfered, broken up, defaced by amateurs or totally destroyed? If The Lady with cultural fits had saved a little, then praise to her.

Then he saw that not only the country had been ratted, but the world. The terrifying last of Van Gogh's self-portraits brought him up standing.

Francis cocked his head. "You like?"

"*Like?* Are you mad? Surely not the original?"

"Why not? This stuff comes from all over the place." The face—powerful, valiant in the knowledge of insanity, poised against swirling blue flame-shapes of fear and illusion—wavered in his amazement while Francis chattered amicably on. "A bit out of touch, that one, wouldn't you say? Not my idea of art, but what the hell? There hasn't been much incitement to develop an artistic philosophy since the Collapse, now has there? Come on; you can look later."

Lindley's eyes roamed in wonder. *Olympia—The Bridge At Arles*—two Rembrandt self-portraits and the *Man In A Golden Helmet*—the *Blue Boy*—an obvious Canaletto he could not place . . . It was enough to blind all sense.

Taste? No, no taste, but a jackdaw collection of works safely known as critically impeccable.

"Now, she really loves these." Francis flicked an incredulous finger at two colorful portraits painted with an almost caricaturist dwelling on characteristics. "Some forgotten politician—and I think the old dear in this one made cosmetics. Pretty bloody, aren't they?"

"No; they're very fine."

"Oh? Well, I give up."

Helena Rubenstein and Sir Robert Menzies might have sneered at their retreating backs, but Lindley thought that if Dobell's astringent visions represented The Lady's attitudes and appreciations he might expect arrogance and egoism and much theatricality, the commonplaces of corrupt power. And not to forget her attraction to Van Gogh in the flower of decay.

They came to a door set in a small alcove with benches round its walls. "Nobody waiting," Francis said. "Sometimes they pack the place like flies." He put his head round the door and called out, "Here's your psycho-boy, sweetie.

He's nice in his disagreeable way and he likes the art-work.''

An impatient female voice spat from within, "I don't need a court jester every hour of the day. Send him in and get out.''

Francis withdrew, unruffled. "She's got a shitty on. In you go, but watch it, duckie—she's the last of the red-hot man-eaters.''

Her voice told him more than Francis's warning; as the door closed behind him he was able to assure himself in an encompassing glance that he was taking part in someone's personal delusion.

Forewarned and seeking a technique, he deliberately failed to see the preposterous figure on the couch. With calculated insolence, designed at least in part to cover his uncertainties, he concentrated on the other contents of the room.

It was another art gallery, furnished as a luxurious salon, with as central feature Tiepolo's enormous canvas of *Cleopatra's Banquet*—one of great art's greater vulgarities, voluptuous, relaxed with a contemptuous power, attractive to a specific type of mind.

On a small table before the couch was laid a silver tea service of some antiquity; a faint thread of steam curled from the spout of the teapot. Tea, freshly made; so erratically homely. What might he do to earn a taste of it? He could not identify the china but it was delicate stuff, porcelain and heavily gilt.

"Do you appreciate a fine service? It is two centuries old.''

He did not answer or look at her but contemplated the two husky men leaning against the farther wall, dressed in brilliant kilts. They were clone-brothers of Raft.

A personal attendance of decorative beefcake? A preference for oddities as older autocrats had collected dwarfs and idiots? A self-indulgent flaunting of possessions and quaintery?

"You're damned rude," she said, sounding interested rather than insulted.

He allowed himself another survey of the walls (how

the devil had they managed to get the Tiepolo through the doors?) before he answered, "You don't seem to have the *Mona Lisa*."

"I never liked it." Throwaway line: *I could have had it if I wished*.

He looked straight at her. The Lady who collected art and had been able to pillage the centuries while humanity clung to the shreds of existence was unhealthily overweight; she was not gross, but that would come. For the present she was pink and white rolling flesh with great unsupported breasts; she wore a humorously tiny cache-sexe mostly for display of a diamond placed with the infallible bad taste of the unrestrainedly opulent, and lolled on the Recamier couch like a baroque courtesan. Rubens would have delighted in her though not she perhaps in Rubens, for he could not remember that master of the peaches and cream school of femininity in the corridor gallery. She flaunted nudity. Sexual defiance or sexual frustration? Lindley was alert to the viciousness possible in a mind attempting to outface physical decay.

She would be, he thought, about forty, then revised his estimate to a superbly preserved fifty. Then, studying her face, all estimates fell apart; he could only imagine her as one who had reached a final decadent bloom and there put a stop to time. The bio-surgeons had been at work.

"Don't gape like a hayseed. Sit down."

He sat carefully on a frail-looking chair (Queen Anne? He was not "up" on furniture) and asked; "And who the hell might you be?"

She chuckled. "Sassy, eh? They call me The Lady."

"I suppose you have a given name?"

"That's my damned business. They call me 'old bitch' and 'fat tart' but to my face—and to you—I am The Lady." Her eyes picked at him with a matching of his own insolence. "You're a skinny piece for a hero of far stars, aren't you? Are you fit for female company after forty years of male monasticism? Or did you comfort each other?"

"We didn't." In fact he was less than sure of two of them but had not considered it his business to meddle with the inevitable.

"No? Then don't let your hot gaze play over me; you're not my type."

He could risk a little contempt for a sexual guttersnipe; he hadn't been brought so far to be chopped down for entertainment. Already he doubted her leadership, was unable to see her as more than a possible figurehead, of what use he could not imagine; nothing of her could command loyalty or admiration. She was simply a mannerless trollop with an unbridled tongue.

He said, "Nor you mine. I don't take to vulgar bitches."

It won him only a heaving of outsize breasts in brassy laughter. "The Lady is socially above insult and she doesn't react to a psychiatrist's pinprick. Would you like tea?"

And perhaps the boys will join us for a hand of bridge? "I would like it."

"You can say little things like 'thank you' without straining your integrity."

"Thank you."

She rose to pour, handling her bulk with elastic ease; she was almost attractive in her ageless, overblown way. His nose told him this was China tea; so she could reach into that supposedly closed area. He must not let the surface of aggressive stupidity betray him into underestimating her potential.

"What do you want of me?"

"I, nothing. John wants you."

"Heathcote?"

"So you know who he is?"

"Only that he's a remnant of the scientific past."

"Marvelous description! I *like* it. Remnant!" She quivered, rippling this time with real laughter, unforced, and he fancied she could laugh at miseries and cripples. "You'll understand when you meet him. He thinks you may be able to explain Albert's disturbing behavior. After all, a rogue clone-brother is a contradiction in terms."

"With a little thought he could explain it himself." The eyes of the—serfs? wardens? bodyguards?—were fixed on him expectantly but he saw no need to supply them with gratuitous information.

The Lady, with her back to them, did not appear aware

of their possible interest. She rippled again, gasping a little. "Poor John isn't quite himself, you might say, when it comes to explaining things." Then she did recall her attendants and looked to them for applause of her wit. They smiled dutifully but plainly did not appreciate humor which concealed a double edge. "For myself," she said, "I was just curious to have a look at you."

"To decide my possible usefulness?"

"If any."

"Forget it."

"A manipulative psychiatrist with already some experience of our capabilities should realize that the decision doesn't rest with him."

A feral point to her. No argument was possible, but he must seek information where he could, and attack might gain more from her than questions. Casual attack. Like so: "Regarding decisions, it was a mistake to have Albert killed."

The effect was stupefying.

Behind The Lady the clone-brothers attained the faces of fiends as their fine bodies tightened in an instantaneous petrification. And as suddenly relaxed. The demonic expressions vanished. They crossed glances with communicative vividness and with accord turned on the woman's back matching smiles of contempt overlying a stabbing anger.

Her reaction was both restrained and total. Shock was powerful but contained, diverted almost unnoticed into a flowing setting down of her teacup; her eyes widened enormously and were at once veiled by lids. Her attention was not on Lindley's monstrous impudence but on the men behind her; she dared not betray fear by turning but strained as if for psychic knowledge. She was most intensely frightened.

It came to Lindley only belatedly that he had announced to the brothers that the woman, to whom it seemed they owed devotion, had planned and ordered the killing of their . . . How would they regard him? Father?

"I had no hand in that!" Her voice snapped without quiver; self-command was absolute; there was more power in her than he had granted.

Perhaps she told truth—it had been random firing on his

part—but he had seen her terror and did not believe her. Nor, he saw, did the brothers, whose reactions evaded reason until painfully he sorted and thought he understood them. Plainly the news of Albert's death had not reached this pair—he thought of them, a little shamefacedly, as units, not quite as persons, certainly not as individuals—until he spoke; then initial shock had at once been killed by the realization that they had not, as that other one had said, "felt" him die. The accusation of her responsibility even for an attempt was what fed their animus. Whatever the nature of their loyalty they believed her capable of it.

Fearful or not, she was swinging at once into attack, demanding, "What could I gain by his death?"

He did not know but was sure he had her measure. "Your idiot intrigues aren't my affair, but I know you ordered him dead." He invented rapidly, over a corrosive wonder what this impudence might later cost him, "I was there when they came for him. I was struggling through that mob of drugged kids with murder on their minds and your name in their mouths. They killed for The Lady and they yelled it aloud. By now the whole city knows it." (He had not absorbed what they yelled—something about a "traitor brother"—but he was committed to maintaining pressure.)

The rapt faces of the brothers accepted the lie. The relationships here were too complex for his guessing, but he had succeeded in creating enemies for her.

(Something unsleeping in him heard England a little avenged. It did not matter who paid so long as there was payment. Continually.)

Yet now she surprised him. With extreme speed of decision she assumed equanimity, accepted exposure, determined her course of action, raised her teacup as a symbol of suavity and said, "It was necessary."

The admission was surely courageous while she dared not risk a revealing glance behind her. The brothers smiled at—probably—their secret knowledge. Lindley repeated contemptuously, "Necessary!"

"Yes!" To question her decision was presumption. Defeat was temporary; she remained The Lady.

"Are you sure you succeeded? The thing on the plane seemed to have doubts."

The spontaneous pejorative was unforgivable and she picked him up for immediate discipline. "Don't derogate the clone. That is a warning." She paused, cold-eyed, for him to consider and remember. "As for certainty—" She gestured over her shoulder. "*They* know."

Her head whipped round to assess their feeling; he had given her the opportunity and she had seized it. She saw only instant sadness on faces of suffering reserve. They knew her and had been ready for her, and with silence lied to her.

She repeated, gently, coaxingly, "Necessary, brothers. He was spoiled, not truly one of you."

They bowed their heads, accepting. Only Lindley saw the return of malice when she turned back to him and he asked her, out of his genuine ignorance, "Why?"

She watched him over the rim of her cup, satisfied that a menace had been averted by swift thinking, talking between sips. "Grand-daddy Jackson just happened to be with him, so he's dead too," sip; "that was accident, but the Raft man had ruined a beautifully planned action." A long sip and the beginning of a threat: "You had best not attempt interference of any kind." Sip and the end of the threat: "If you do I shall have you killed."

The brothers concurred in minute headshakes. He need not fear her. He protested, "But what is all this drugging and killing about? What do you want?"

"The world," she said. "Have you finished your tea?"

He had not and his hand shook too much for him to risk the fragile cup; he strove to manage his voice. "In all history no revolution ever succeeded as the revolutionaries planned. They tended to die in their own victory fires."

"History has no rules. If it had, they could be changed. The superior human understands that." Her expression changed to secretive cunning. "You might say that I specialize in superior humanity."

He did not understand. Perhaps she meant the clone. Before he could ask, she made lightning transformation into gracious hostess dismissing boring guest. "Now you really must go and see John. The poor dear gave me no peace until I sent for you. Francis is out there; he'll show you where to go.''

He took up his cup, still half full, and her brittle mood broke. ''You don't have to finish that! I'm sick of you!'' Reasonless spite followed him to the door. ''You're a boor and a bore. Get out! Go on, get out!''

As he left her, with his dignity in rags, he saw that the two clone-brothers moved quietly behind a curtain and vanished. He suspected that The Lady was now more alone than she knew.

—2—

Francis was sympathetic. ''Bored it up you, did she? A very difficult woman; it took years to learn what I could get away with.''

''She's mad.''

''Don't bet on it. Unpredictable, but not mad. She has a keen intellect.'' He was serious, not playing satirist.

''That's common enough in specific types of insanity.''

Francis looked as if he might argue, but reverted to fairy floss. ''You're the doctor, duckie. I wouldn't have a clue about psychobatics.''

''You're no intellectual butterfly either.''

Fleeting bleakness peered from the careless eyes. ''I try to keep it light. Being bred in a concrete box isn't all uplift and gaiety. Come on, now; John's waiting.''

''Now? At one in the morning?''

''Night and day are interchangeable in the termitary; the metabolic clock gives up chiming after a while.''

They turned into yet another corridor of paintings. Lindley's dazed recognition lingered over familiar canvases from a dozen countries until he forced himself back to the need for information.

''Are there no other women in Gangoil?''

The answer came with a snicker. ''Lots, but not in this area. *She* won't have women around her; there is no competition in her sector.''

"A closed market?"

Francis turned on him a brilliant smile. "Duckie, I could tell a tale or two! But she seems to feel my kind don't count, and if she's happy with the setup who am I to wave the facts of life at her?"

They continued in silence until Francis opened a door and cursed quietly at an empty room. "The bloody old relic's not quite with us most of the time. Wait here while I find him."

He vanished through a curtained arch presumably leading deeper into what must be a private suite.

Lindley found himself alone in a Victorian gentleman's spacious den—library, office and lounge in one—and he examined it with amused appreciation. The lack of windows increased the air of snugness; it was a nineteenth-century illustration faithfully copied, with the addition of concealed lighting and a television set. But the lighting was for convenience only; atmosphere was preserved by splendid brass and porcelain kerosene lamps, and the television simpered a little in a William Morrisish cabinet equipped with a veiling curtain. Such details were marginally funny but in fact fitted without incongruity; this was no vulgarity in the style of The Lady's brazen display.

The floor was a halcyon sea of pile, subdued blue and green flowing over slumbrous red and brown, Persian-patterned; furniture, lustrous in mahogany and rosewood, floated like polished rafts. A vast roll-topped desk in stained cedar squatted commonsensibly in a corner. Two grandfathers of all fireside chairs, winged and high-backed, guarded an immense fireplace with a laid fire which surely never was lit. Opposite stood a monstrous buffet displaying crystal goblets within and crystal decanters without its curving glass doors.

Heathcote, praise be, did not go in for old masters but there were clusters of old English sporting prints, genuine and breathtakingly precious, and a drum-shaped tumbler rack of Australian washes and drawings from colonial days.

Paranoia behind and schizophrenia coming up. A blindingly good bio-chemist with a soul in the 1850s backed by an escapee from a surrealist harem. And these two oddities are out to capture a planet!

The huge bookcase covered an entire wall. Carlyle, Ruskin, Mayhew, Gibbon, Darwin, Thackeray (whom Trollope had rated above the otherwise quite excellent Mister Dickens) Tennyson, Byron (a mite daring, perhaps), George Eliot and that promising young buck, Meredith. Expectably, there was a complete Trollope, every one of the sixty-and-odd volumes showing, even on the bindings, signs of constant handling.

Dedication! Does he identify with the Duke of Omnium? Or would it be that nice Doctor Thorne?

From an adjoining room an elderly attempt at choler achieved only cracked peevishness. "And tell her not to send her beastly freaks on errands to me!"

The bang of an inner door was probably Francis's answer.

The man who entered belonged to the room. He was short and thin and bony where his wrists protruded from the sleeves of a deep purple, velvet smoking-jacket. His white shirt glittered with laundered purity; his pearl-grey trousers, uncreased, were strapped under glacé kid slippers. It was a creditable attempt at the private *déshabillé* of a Victorian gentleman.

He came towards Lindley with the gentle shuffle of age, smiling with a hint of querulousness on his fleshless, fine, transparent face, his whole being redolent of a forgotten gentility.

He could not have been more than twenty years old.

Lindley caught at floundering credulity, disbelieving his eyes while his mind backed away to the point where it might believe anything at all.

The young gnome said in his frail old-gentleman's voice, "I can't stand them, you know. One admits their existence and their right to existence, but one should not be required to *mix*."

He came further into the room with a suddenly youthful step, as though for an instant he had forgotten his age. "I regret having kept you waiting, Doctor Lindley, but there is much to be done and frankly—" His head darted forward, returning to an old man's birdlike motion. "Frankness is best, I feel. Do you not?"

Lindley's bemusement contrived a whispered, "Yes,

sir.'' He could not help the ''sir''; it felt right—in period.

''The truth is that I am presently in a peculiar mental condition. Please do not think I have called you here for professional consultation; my problem is not psychiatric, save perhaps in a contingent sense.'' He smiled on a Lindley who understood not a word, then fluttered, literally fluttered, as he recalled the requirements of hospitality. ''But please be seated, Doctor. Here, here; this is an excellent chair.''

It really was an excellent chair and Lindley sat with gratitude while he hoped his stare was not of glazed idiocy.

Lunacy followed. ''There are moments of considerable confusion when the memories conflict. And of course there are still gaps; the gaps are most disturbing.''

Lindley's scalp crawled. He managed to ask, ''Who are you?''

The young man was taken with an old man's dim surprise. ''I am Doctor Heathcote. Whom did you expect?''

''Forgive me; I was prepared to meet a very old man.''

''And so I am, so I am.'' Suddenly he understood Lindley's situation and erupted in senile temper. ''That Francis! That laboratory assistant's catamite! It would fit his conception of humor to have you confront me without prior knowledge. I can't credit that woman's fascination with the type.''

Lindley took a deep breath and suggested that a taste for the outré and the grotesque was a common accompaniment of the dictatorial personality.

''Is it indeed? Well, well, I am no psychologist. You would perhaps care for a drink? Scotch, gin, rum? I'm a brandy man myself.''

Brandy, port, cigars and a hot toddy nightcap. Taking a grip he said, ''Scotch, thank you. I'm a later generation.''

The young man snickered appreciation but poured with a steady hand. ''Now, explanation without further delay.'' If he closed his eyes Lindley could picture him as the Heathcote of his fancy—snow-white hair, deep lines, quivering shanks—from whom the slow sentences dropped in that utterly un-Australian accent from Dublin, reputed to have been the purest English in the world. ''You must realize that I became senile and quite useless, quite beyond geriatric techniques as they were then, some twenty or so years ago. So I arranged to be cloned. Make no mistake, I am still John Heathcote.'' He chuckled. ''Twice over, one might say.''

Absurdist theater, Lindley decided, presented with unbecoming realism, for this ambiguous ancient was real. He grappled with his straight man role to ask, ''And the . . . other . . . the remainder?'' In God's name, what would be the correct word?

''You mean the template body?''

How coldbloodedly right. He nodded.

''Ah, there was a use for that!'' The insupportable archness of second childhood. ''The old body was needed for the memory transfer process. It was placed in metabolic retardation to the point where awareness ceased but cellular degradation was inhibited; then the necessary organs were macerated for assimilation.''

Lindley supposed that what he heard was actually being said. Then unreality scattered before a notable fact, that the ''old man'' voice had, in a couple of sentences, slipped into the faster, more precise tones of youth. He was listening now to the reborn biologist, the man who had with his assistants created a new and original dilemma for mankind: an old man and a young man who were (was?) both the same man and mentally confused as to which was who at any given moment. Not funny.

Young Heathcote continued rapidly, compressing horrific concepts into non-technical language which even a superseded psychiatrist could follow.

''Memory, you must understand, is much more than a matter of the contents of the brain, which may be thought of as operative memories. There are deeper forces, the great basic urges of procreation and self-preservation, the intuitions of danger and apprehensions of the metaphysical, the primal memories from which actions stem and which have their roothold in all the body's cells. Perhaps in the RNA chains, though I think not; they may belong to more basic combinings not yet observed. As a weak analogy think of the 'memory' of still water, retaining in its molecules the recoverable volition of its last direction of flow. I postulate a residual memory of some such type. Factually we know only that the brain is not enough, that practically the whole of the visceral and procreative systems are involved. The Russians had worked it out long before you started on your voyage but they were keeping it to themselves.'' (Drink-loosened Albert shouting it at them during that revelatory session—and here it was, alive, talking.) ''Starting from the planarian worm experiments they did marvelously well, and we were able to recover most of their records to establish the basic approach.''

Lindley nearly choked on his whiskey, thinking of the planarian worms fed to each other to establish the learning-memory chains. ''Are you saying you ate him?''

Heathcote sniggered. ''Ate myself? If only it were so simple. Cannibalism is too severe in a sophisticated organism; the essential molecules will not survive our complex digestion. Much of the material was incorporated in the clone nutrient, so a form of feeding was involved, but most was injected after the brain was fully formed. Then there were long periods during childhood of chemical stimulants—amplifiers you might call them—and endless sessions with hypnotherapists seeking the basic memories and coaxing them into operation, seeking out triggering synaptic junctions to release whole areas of recollection. Those are still continuing. I have a considerable mass of the original John's memory; I recovered his scientific work intact before I was ten. But much of the personal material remains dormant. *They* think the private memories unimportant to their purpose, which is simply research, but the gaps leave me with comfortless moments of indecision and blankness.''

''Who are *they?*''

''Scientists. The older ones may have been my youngest assistants, but I am not told; the younger ones were born here in the hive, raised and educated to carry on the work Gangoil was built for. I feel alone in their presence, and it is most confusing to be a battleground of warring instincts of age and youth, of experience and urgent desire. But one day I shall be whole.''

Lindley's professional sense of order was revolted. Unable to comment on affairs so far outside his range he asked, ''Are there no others of you?''

"Only myself, I was far past the cellular climactic of maturity when the operation was decided upon and most of my regenerative faculty was already lost, so it was necessary to initiate a large number of buds. They lost all but one. And, as the young fellows so succinctly put it, there has been no need to bottle another batch while the memory transmission proceeds so successfully."

The true end of John Heathcote: guinea-pig to his own techniques, reliving by virtue of the assistants who recreated him, one more experiment in the laboratory tunneled to hide him under a mountain. It was as curious a destiny as might be imagined.

"At times I have wished others had survived, when I see the emotional closeness of Albert's clone. But I also realize that they may be unique in their empathetic sense; also they are impenetrable, caring for no one but each other. They care for me in their cool fashion, but it is veneration for a father-symbol, not for the man. They are not what Albert was." Without warning his voice reversed ages, taking on hardness and certainty. "And Albert, it seems, is not at one with his clone. That is why you are here, to tell me of Albert."

Lindley had decided his course. "Does it matter? You must have heard the news of Albert."

"That Security has him? That is nothing."

"That he is dead."

Brandy splashed on the carpet; the balloon glass bounced and rang faintly and did not break. The ancient voice made sounds before it found a word. "No!"

"He is dead."

His face contorted and he wept. "How? How?"

"The Lady did it. The old bitch had him murdered. She had him blown apart with a bomb."

The sobbing ceased abruptly. "She?"

"I think she feared him. I don't know why."

"*She!*"

Rage and hatred shaped themselves clearly in the voice of desolation. "For forty-two years I have waited for my boy to return. That memory they gave me early, one comfort alight in suppression and dimness. Albert was my boy, never theirs. They were useless to him."

Some other "they"? "His parents?"

"His progenitors! Mere bodies for the spawning of a marvelous child, never parents."

Plain curiosity asked, "What were they like?"

Heathcote stared blindly. "So little memory. There is a gap full of glimpses, of feelings, but no memory. I know they nearly ruined him with neglect and selfishness, but it is knowledge in a void, part of a pattern not released. To these new ones it is inessential to their purposes."

A long, comfortless silence was broken once by an explosive, "*She!*"

He groped for the fallen glass and placed it on the mantel. With firm, old-world and wholly successful dignity he said in the misplaced tone of youth, "Please pardon my disturbance, Doctor Lindley; remember that at times I am an old man and always a divided one. I am not fit to talk further now. The Francis-thing will be waiting for you outside."

—3—

Francis levered himself from the wall. "After all the fuss about getting you here that didn't take long."

"Why conceal Albert's death from him?"

"Didn't he know? I suppose nobody thought to tell him. He doesn't bother with the newsbands and we don't bother much with him. Silly old nit; he's not much more than an experimental animal these days, after all. Did he perform? He had this big thing about Albert Raft—oh, purely paternal, I'm sure—but he'll get over it. Where to now? Couldn't you just go to bed?"

"Are you supposed to look after me?"

"Yes, for my sins."

"Then please arrange for me, and the sooner the better, which means now if possible, a summary history of the last forty years. I may get some idea what your nonsensical politics and violence are about."

Francis exhibited a genuine emotion, cool dislike in an

appraising glance. "I'm assigned to you because that's my specialty period. Shall we go to your room?"

The room, limited to the provision of essentials, was comfortable in its sparse fashion; Francis appropriated the only chair without apology. Lindley stretched on the bed and discovered himself being lectured with a clarity and precision much at variance with the bored jester personality.

"You would have had no chance to observe it, but your civilization was under final attack when you left Earth. Before you were a light year on your way to that useless star the planet was a shambles . . ."

Lindley listened without question or comment. The botanic-genetic approach to warfare had been an old forecast by the eighties and had, like all future discomforts, received the fat cats' Cassandra treatment; nothing new there. The rise of a youthful intelligentsia came as no surprise; his generation of psychologists and educationists had been fully alive to the possibilities. Only the rapid evolution of the Ombudsmen from organizers to neoshaman status was a fresh twist to a gaggle of old tales. The swift resurgence of technology was less remarkable than gratifying in its justification of his own ideas; he had never believed in the likelihood of final blackout or reversion to a primitive dark age.

The coldblooded removal of the old and unfit was revolting in its completeness but told him nothing of human nature that a reasoning man could not have anticipated, however it was here that his attention became concentrated on the emotional overtones of Francis's voice and phrasing. He listened for bias, for the questionable, if unintentional, misdirections.

". . . that the Ombudsmen were primarily responsible for the murder of a generation is pretty well established. They *advised* it; that much we are sure of. When you consider the influence they wielded as mature men among troubled and fearful kids, their advice was tantamount to an instruction. They weave and dodge when they are reminded of it, but their true role was patriarch, authority unquestioned. The moral problem lies not so much in responsibility for mass murder as in the reasons for it. The Ombudsmen can claim that they freed the young from an intolerable burden of the physically useless and this has the advantage of being perfectly true. But it is not *the* truth. In fact the Ombudsmen were embarrassed by those peers in age and experience who could oppose them on an equal footing; their authority could be and probably was called in question, so they had to secure themselves and their vision of the new world or become one with the whole generation that was to be pushed to the wall. I suppose that in any emotional framework the way they chose was monstrous, but it was effective and we don't feel it our business to be eternally bowed down because we owe our chance in tomorrow to a guilt we had no hand in . . .''

At the end of half an hour Lindley felt that, discounting bias, he had a reasonable idea of the world's convulsion. Most notably Francis's attack on the Ombudsmen, a series of believable inferences with little adduction of verifiable fact, struck him as being the philosophical basis of the Gangoil group, as the act of faith on which action was founded.

Of course they might be right. At any rate he agreed that the dead should bury their dead and that the verdict of history should wait on history; what mattered now were the happenings of now.

He said, ''It's a fascinating world conception, wholly experimental societies trying out social formulas in something like laboratory conditions. But is it really the ultimate aim to examine all these isms and ologies like modern Pericleans and select one as the world model?''

''I doubt whether there is any ultimate aim. How likely is it that one social formula will satisfy everybody, or even anybody? Give them a generation or two and there'll be wars and tyrannies and empires and slavery. Security had to be invented to keep the groups' hands off each other's throats; half the Ombudsmen aren't on speaking terms. What is the viability of such a mess?''

''Much the same as it always was; should be worth watching for a few decades. But you and yours don't intend it to last. You won't give them the chance.''

Francis eyed him with speculation and indecision. ''Order,'' he said sullenly, like a last-ditch invocation, ''order and the rebirth of man.''

Lindley thought about it and translated, "A single social system, whether they like it or not, and the bio-sciences for ever! Now there's a program!"

"You haven't seen enough to risk a sneer."

"But have I got it right?"

Grudgingly, "More or less."

"What system?"

"Something like what you called socialism."

"State ownership of resources?"

"*Common* ownership."

As with The Lady's art gallery? He suppressed a sharp remark on the confusion of words with the things they represented. "And the new man will be built in the bio-labs? Heathcotian man? Healthier, better designed, more intelligent?"

"We can do it."

"With co-operation and determination we could have done it ourselves; however we saw disadvantages."

"You had no dream, only self-seeking and mutual distrust. We have John's men to design the beautiful children who will come after us and," his voice changed perceptibly, "design and guide the new world that will belong to *their* children."

Lindley took his risk cheerfully, giving it the throwaway technique: "It's an insane vision, you know."

Francis colored. "The difference between insanity and a freed vision was something your mind-butchers never detected."

Lindley laughed and opened up the insult. "Oh, we had LSD."

Francis stood. "I'll leave you before I am tempted to beat your gutter-bred mouth into blood."

Alone, Lindley would have laughed at absurdity, but there was no profit in mere philosophic superiority over a group which had plucked him from Security as neatly as a pea from a pod. Pondering what might yet be his fate as grist in a mill of nonsense he suffered a period of panic and emerged from it unnerved.

He discarded thought of escape. The camouflaged entrances to Gangoil were only porticoes for the series of doorways whose masses were unguessable tons of steel and concrete, cell beyond cell, built to survive everything but the direct impact of a nuclear blast. No doubt huge air ducts existed and no doubt they were as impassably structured as the entrances, all baffles and filters and deflectors. Useless even if he knew where they were or possessed the fortitude for the undertaking, with its probability of ending sliced in the blades of a roaring circulation fan . . .

He tried the door and it opened. They had no fear of his movements or, consequently, of his escape; his name already printed on the door panel implied extended residence.

This corridor was uncarpeted and undecorated, possibly part of a little-used area, a bird-of-passage section. There were names on other doors hiding unguessable people and it was no surprise to discover Alice White's.

It was late but he did not imagine her feverish mind would be sleeping. He knocked. She was still dressed, in the simple fashion reminiscent of his lost time, and stony calm had followed disintegration. She did not speak but indifferently swung the door wide.

He entered a duplicate of his own functional room and joked that cheap hotels had changed not at all. His wit fell as flat as it deserved; he tried again with "You're feeling better?" as a matter of starting somewhere.

"Better?" Her tone judged him mad.

"Well, coming to terms with realities."

"Submitting," she corrected. "Waiting."

He sat on the end of the bed, pushing familiarity an inch or two. "You haven't seen a therapist yet?"

"No."

"Haven't they even offered a sleeping pill?"

"Yes. I'll take them later. I've been trying to think."

"What have you thought?"

"Nothing."

He suggested cautiously, "We're allies now."

"Until morning and therapy."

"Yes. I've been under strain, as you have; perhaps we can observe each other more impartially now."

She said listlessly, "I suppose you're all right. It doesn't matter; I'll be traitor Alice again in a few hours."

"How is it done?"

"Oh, various ways. Drugs and post-suggestion for short projects; they rope in bunches of kids by having them handle impregnated surfaces, as I did you. And simply tell them what they are to do."

Like all effective activities it was blatant and simple and a cold-blooded misuse of knowledge. With such intellectual sheep, innocent with dreams, to work on, misuse was inevitable, if not by The Lady then somebody else. If a thing can be done, it will be.

He offered empathy as a beginning of comfort. "I knew what I did when you took me, and couldn't refuse; now I feel degraded. But how must the kids feel when they wake up to the knowledge of murder?"

"They have post-commands. Forgetfulness."

"So The Lady has some pity for her puppets."

Something like emotion was roused in her. "Tactics! Self-preservation! I think she has no pity."

"What is she like?"

"I thought you saw her."

"Only for a few minutes."

She pondered. "Perhaps she is a very great woman, but she is not wholly human."

"She's insane."

It seemed not to have occurred to her. She admitted doubtfully, "I've never seen her, but I suppose anyone with an overriding idea is not normal. Not to be judged. Like your Christ or our Ombudsmen."

That juxtaposition was no more unlikely than Gangoil itself, and Alice's was probably the prototype rationalization of The Lady's followers.

"How do you feel about the use of the youngsters?" She shuddered and could not speak. "Yet all the time you abet these plans with revulsion in your mind."

"No, no, I have nothing to do with the drugging. There is a sense in which I know about it but it passes me by. How can I explain? As if I have knowledge but cannot react to it. But my business is with the clubs where the kids discuss the systems of the world." *Poor bloody kids, playing at competitive ideology for their sport.* "It helps fit them for choice if later they want to try some other way of life. We move among them and listen and fasten on the ones with malleable ideas; that's how they found me, years ago. We guide them toward dissatisfaction and protest until they are ready for indoctrination; then we use hypnosis to strengthen selected modes of thought and suppress doubts.''

''And always it seems that you are doing right?''

''Yes.''

Hypnotic suggestion alone could never have achieved her. He guessed it was hypnotism used to open doors to areas of the mind where other manipulative techniques could be brought to bear, obtaining brute distortions impossible with a functioning consciousness.

Her empty voice continued, ''The youngsters don't know what is being done to them; they become part of a subgroup within society, primed for revolt, thinking it all springs from their own desires. By then perhaps it does. Some of the promising ones, moving like me into responsible positions become agents, part of the machine.'' Noisily, unexpectedly, she cried out, thrusting away guilt. ''But not the violence. We didn't do that. She has others for that.''

It would be necessary, he thought, for God to devise a special hell for The Lady and her advisers.

''And we work willingly. That's the dreadfulness—that it is willing.''

''Until something disturbs your conditioning.''

''Perhaps.'' She puzzled at it. ''I haven't heard of this happening before.''

''What broke yours?''

''How can I be sure? I began to have terrible feelings of being two people at once, of doing things I should not do while one of me looked on and doubted but did nothing to stop me. Then the killing . . . the killing frightened me.''

Activities against her basic instincts and possibly a less than wholly competent practitioner monitoring her. ''Maybe your revolutionary feeling was more intellectual than emotional.''

She agreed bleakly. ''The young are arrogant and easy to trap.''

''The organization must be immense.''

''I don't know. I don't think so. They take people up and use them and put them down again.''

Yes; with memory-flushing you could do that.

There seemed no more to say and in the long silence her dreary self-possession broke and she wept remorse and shame at psychic rape.

He comforted her, at first professionally and later with an awakening warmth of pity.

Later still the thought arose that these were damned peculiar circumstances under which to be making love. *But that was why I knocked on her door, wasn't it? All the rest was window dressing.* In the attempt to feel less like a dead bastard taking advantage of Poor Blind Nell, he ruminated that this was a more tender therapy than she would face in the morning.

—4—

Lindley awoke to a voice. He had meant to return to his room, playing the lecher tiptoeing off with the dawn, but full gravity and an exhausting day had clubbed him to sleep while Alice, overwhelmed at last by conflict, slept before him.

The voice complained, "So *there* you are! I've looked everywhere and never thought—But you've been on hand feeding all these years, haven't you, and I suppose the real thing—Ah, well, it's your business, but you did have me worried."

Francis had elected to face the day in sandals and a bottle green ingenuity almost too attenuated to be a jockstrap; whatever it intended was barely achieved. The rest of him was decorated at strategic points with designs in green and yellow adhesive speckling. On his muscular figure the effect was neither laughable nor wildly camp, merely odd.

"What the hell do you want, Francis?"

The thinned-out eyebrows stirred. "I am *not* Francis. My name is Arthur."

"A twin. Sorry."

Arthur sat himself on the end of the bed, searched out the shape of Alice's leg under the sheet and shook her ankle. "Wake up, love; time for breakfast. And I am not just a twin because there are six of us."

"A clone?"

Alice woke, glanced incuriously at both of them and remained quietly within herself, totally alone.

"That's right. Arthur, Bertrand, Charles, Donald, Eric and Francis. You tell us by our color schemes; I'm green and yellow. Now please get up and dress; breakfast in ten minutes."

Alice did not move. Lindley suggested, "Perhaps Miss White should not eat. I believe she is to have treatment this morning."

"Not that I know of. Why should she?"

"Something to do with conditioning. Francis said—"

"So *that* was what the row was about! Davey and the Old Bitch shrieking the shit out of each other at four o'clock in the morning about us pretties acting outside our province, and Francis looking as if he had his hand caught in the jam jar. He should have more sense; he did six months as an assistant in the drug labs and thinks he's a bio-psych on the strength of it, always wanting to rearrange people. There's nothing planned for Miss White. Or you either."

"Then why are we here?"

"Really, hasn't anybody told you anything? I don't know about Alice-girl; I think she's just an accident that got tagged on to you." He offered a pensive parenthesis, "Sometimes I think the organization here is positively childish and sometimes I think there just isn't any. Where was I? The Old Bitch had you brought for her Johnny, the youngest geriatric in captivity, but he's probably forgotten what he wanted by now."

"I met him last night."

"Then you'll understand. The Old Bitch gets sentimental fits, so what Johnny wants, Johnny gets. There's a story that they used to have it off together back in the dark ages but we really don't know and I'm not one to point the finger."

"And who is the Old Bitch?"

Arthur shrugged elaborately, setting his decorations in suggestive movement. "Who knows? Big mystique business. But I'd say that's all shot now; her latest antics have been too upsetting and killing Albert was disgraceful.''

"How old is she?"

"What a question! If you ask me she was probably around for the building of the pyramids but I can't prove it. Now, please, we have to be strict about meal times.''

"One more question.''

Arthur raised pleading eyes to heaven. "Give me strength! But I suppose Barnard's Star *is* a bit out of touch.''

But Gangoil, by all signs, was not. "Does your clone-group have strong empathetic bonds, awareness of each other?"

Arthur stood up, bridling. "You mean like that Albert-pack of simultaneous dancers? No, duckie, we're normal. Is that a joke, I think? We were cloned for a specific purpose.''

"What purpose?"

"Checking a possible heredity factor in homosexuality. Six husky little darlings, each with what was suspected of being a homo-influencing gene combination built in and all raised separately under widely differing circumstances. Well, it seems the heredity factor exists, at least in some cases, though Eric did his best to bugger the results with some slut in Hormone Research. Much good the knowledge will do anybody.''

"It could be of vital importance.''

"If you say so, but we can't stay tattling. Back in ten minutes and if you aren't ready you don't eat.''

He went out.

"Does food attract?"

Alice turned her face as to a stranger and said with little interest, "I can eat.''

There was running water in the room and a towel. They shared them, she slowly and remotely, he with a vitality rising to the fantasies of Gangoil. She surprised him by saying, "I'm glad they aren't going to recondition me.''

He discarded a dozen replies and selected, "It will be hard going at first. Major readjustments aren't easy. You will suffer.''

"At least I will know who is suffering.''

He applauded silently and after a while she asked inconsequentially, "How old are you, James?"

Under the disinterested scrutiny he felt centenarian. "Forty-six."

She smiled, in comment rather than amusement. "You don't behave like an old man."

Almost it took away his appetite.

When Arthur returned Lindley remembered a question he should have asked earlier. "Who is the Davey you said quarreled with The Lady?"

"Doctor David? He's the head of the biology faction. I suppose you'll see him around."

"You said 'faction.' "

"And, duckie, I meant it. The place is a worms' nest, and it seems you started an extra writhe last night when you let the clone know it was the Old Bitch that ordered Albert killed. Did you know what you were doing?"

"No."

"Well, her boys have deserted her for trying to kill their clone-daddy. Allegiance strictly to dithering Johnny now. That makes her a faction of about one."

"And to whom is your allegiance?"

Arthur's reply did nothing to restore semblance of order to the internal affairs of Gangoil. His old-fashioned leer was horrendous. "I try to be all things to all men."

They were given eggs and bacon (both fresh, which set Lindley puzzling) and coffee (also fresh but faintly ersatz) in a huge communal dining-room where several scores of people—dressed in laboratory coats, overalls, informal clothes or personal freakeries—ate cafeteria style.

Arthur showed them where to go and what to do and left them to it; he had his own brand of tact. No one else paid attention; they might have been familiar faces there for years past. Alternatively, Lindley felt, they might be unimportant to the point of invisibility. The idea of fresh faces arousing no curiosity among the members of a presumably secret organization was no odder than anything else in the past twelve hours, but it was most isolating.

He began to mention it to Alice and let the sentence die because she did not hear him. She stared at her untouched

food, not seeing it. He considered approaches; since they
had been thrown together he must, if only professionally,
make some move against her misery.

While he watched the tears came, easily, with no twisting
of features and, he imagined, without much realization on
her part. He settled for sympathy and placed his hand over
hers.

She jerked from the touch. "Leave me alone! For good."

"Don't be bloody stupid; that was sympathy, not sex."

"Sympathy!" The little shock had been sufficient to
stem the tears. "What good is that?"

He answered casually through a mouthful of food. "I
don't know. Probably none. Wipe your eyes; you look
forty." The word made her jump; braced against assault,
she was vulnerable to the mild jab. Technique; cheap stuff,
but effective. "I can tell fortunes."

"Don't try to amuse me."

"I'm being professional. Shall I prophesy?"

"That if I don't take a grip on myself I'll deteriorate into
schizophrenia or depression? Save it."

"Balls. You won't deteriorate into anything and you
don't need treatment; you certainly wouldn't benefit from
coddling by memory erasure or reinforced suggestion.
There's nothing wrong with you that a few good crying
sessions won't make bearable and when you've had those
I'll start teaching you the difference between right and
wrong, voluntary and involuntary; it's time somebody did.
You've had a psychic shock but after a while you'll stop
shaking. For immediate purposes that's all there is to it.
Dammit, girl, you aren't stupid. Or are you?"

"I'm not stupid."

"So give over the drama and eat your breakfast."

She was not offended. Her chaotic needs evaporated as
fast as they arose. Obediently she picked at her food and
eventually ate most of it.

CHAPTER FIVE

QUALITY OF LIFE

I must Create a System, or be enslav'd by another Man's. I will not Reason and Compare; my business is to Create.

William Blake: *Jerusalem*

—1—

The Controller of Civil Police of Melbourne Town was no more than thirty, probably nearer twenty-five. The neat grey uniform might have been worn by a conservative hotel porter of the eighties but the face had been worn by the law through centuries—polite, helpful, uninformative and tough, tough, tough. Colley's account of the era's criminal therapies became, before that predator's gaze, the wish-dream of an idealist or the evasion of a politician.

Parker disliked Security and made no secret of it, nor was he impressed by Raft; his official politeness was not quite insulting.

"Organized crime? No. The psychoclinicians have the major tendencies under fair control but they miss badly on individual proclivities. That's why Security is on its virtuous arse over this business. They'd have done better to hand it to us right away but old Jackson was lost in dreams of sweet reason and he convinced the Prime Minister differently. And the PM's not much better."

Politics, Raft mused, might be rough and tumble when a senior public servant could be so outspoken; being PM to many like Parker could be a dog's life. He said, "I suppose you're right."

"You wouldn't know."

179

"I know your kind; you could belong to my time." Parker was not amused. "It was meant as a compliment."

The Controller grunted. "Bright boy Colley says you have ideas."

Raft was unpleasantly conscious that the office was masked by an energy blind; the absence of outside noise was tomblike but it seemed the only efficient protection on a Paul Pry planet, and that he should warrant one indicated that this young thug took him seriously. Three other blank, tough young men sat at desks within hearing but did not move or speak unless required. It was dialogue among dummies.

He began, "We've a few things to go on. First, the Gangoil organization has to be pretty big."

Parker was ahead of him. "Not necessarily. We've dug a few scraps out of the kids under deep question and they're recruited for a single job—hypnoed, post-suggested and dumped. And some bastard will pay for that."

"It has to be big enough to run a first-class biological team and in Heathcote's work that involves engineers, electronicists, computer technicians, maintenance staff, psychologists and a clone of unknown size. And why only one clone? There has also to be a planning and executive group to control and co-ordinate them and to design these aggressive operations; also field operatives to drum up mobs as needed, including some smart hypnoing legerdemain. And they have to be fed, which means transport and service staff. Put it down as an HQ of several hundreds."

Parker was impressed, as if he saw solidity emerging from fog, but not overwhelmed. "Dispersion. Why in one place?"

"Communications. Could they communicate effectively by radio or other systems without being detected? My bet is that all communications are thoroughly monitored; the Security setup stinks of it."

"No, they couldn't. Open voice would be noticed at once and code would stand out like dog's balls. Point to you, Commander." Sour, but honest.

"So, a large HQ."

Parker ruminated: "It would have to be a complex—laboratories, recreation facilities, transport sheds. It's almost out of the question; the country's mapped to the millimeter; every building is known and plotted. Where could it be?''

"The depopulated areas?"

"Mapped. Anything that moved, in or out . . ."

"Then underground."

"Caverns?"

"Lord, no; something thoroughly designed and structured."

"Couldn't be built undetected."

"No? Pretend it could."

Parker eyed him stonily, said unwillingly, "Very well, I'll play. It couldn't remain undetected. For one thing there would be heat loss; the area would radiate a degree or so above the surrounding country because of energy losses and the survey satellites would pick it up. The computers would squawk until it was investigated and explained."

"Heat can be shielded, drained, diverted, re-used."

Parker jerked his head at the wax-museum pieces. "Possible?"

"Difficult," said one, "but possible."

"You're doing well, Commander. Go on."

"Consider the scale of the thing. Say three hundred personnel, and that's conservative. How big a place?"

"About a city block."

"You're not a scientist. Much bigger. Question: how was it built and when?"

"Not in the last twenty years; we'd have known. And before that the heavy equipment would not have been available."

"So it was built before the Collapse. Back in my day."

Parker's young men eyed each other, questioning. One said, "I've never heard of such complexes in Australia." The three heads shook and were still.

"There was at least one. The federal government built an invasion retreat in the late nineties; where was not known, but its existence was an open secret—"

"If the records exist they can be found."

"—but that isn't the place I have in mind. Heathcote had become so important that the only credit he ever got for his *Columbus* work was an accidental mention on a censored newscast; so important that the government pushed him out of sight and isolated his laboratory. Nobody could get near him.''

''You did, on your final leave. I've seen the *Columbus* file.''

''I was a guinea-pig, as highly classified and incommunicado as he; I could get to him.''

Parker breathed out hard; the three policemen fixed Raft with eyes set to pierce. ''And what did he tell you?''

''Nothing, because he knew nothing. In social relations he was a gentle old ass. Nobody ever told him a secret, even about himself, because he couldn't get to a phone fast enough to share it with fifty confidential friends. But if you had in your keeping a man who was set to rebuild the human race—that is, if you were sitting on a secret so big that every nation in the world would tear your country apart to get it—and if the world was in a vicious state of armed anger, ready to erupt, where would you put him?''

Parker nodded. ''It could have been done in the couple of years after you left, before everything fell to pieces. It wouldn't have needed to be a secret; they could have called it a defense project of some sort.'' His young men engaged in a swivelling of heads, rolling the idea round their circle. ''But where? *That* would be restricted information and it could take months to locate a single classified folder— which might have been in the mountains of stuff destroyed before we started saving everything.''

''They have to get supplies in from outside. How?''

The silent colloquy rippled, subsided. A policeman said, ''Truck or dragonfly.'' Another disagreed. ''Not trucks; they'd have to break journey and that would be detected at their home base. Dragonflies, I think.''

Raft asked, ''Are some of those privately owned? I know you have practically banned private surface transport, but the air?''

''Hundreds of them. Private. Not checked coming and going. Freedom of the citizen.''

Was that a straightfaced joke? Other times, other conceptions indeed. ''So if you could detect dragonflies in quantity landing and taking off in some area where there's no plain reason for such numbers . . . ?''

Parker brooded on him with something like approval. To Raft the suggestion had been obvious but it was one which might have taken Parker time to arrive at for himself; his experience did not include the large-scale activities of an organized opposition. But when Parker said simply, "See to it," and the dummies took up their caps and left without further instruction he thought, *A bloody efficient force*, and shuddered. He said, "I hope they get quick results. I'm concerned for Jim."

"Lindley? I suppose so."

The offhand tone made the starmen's positions brutally clear. "You don't give a damn, do you? To you we're just bloody trouble-bringers."

Parker's face cleared subtly; the policeman vanished momentarily. The man was capable of pity. "Perhaps we care less about individuals than you did. Try to see that to us the past is hell, that all this Gangoil business is a resurgence of devils. You won't understand this time until you realize that to the general population yours was an age of terror where individualism reigned and there were no great goals. Our goals mean more to us than the single bodies and souls."

The face, trained to impassivity, looked as though nothing could terrify it, but the voice was racked; its sincerity pierced Raft's obsession with his personal problems. The half-familiar humanities of this world were deceptions; beneath them lay modes of thought as unapprehended as the ideas of a new race. In the emerging century he was more alone than he had dreamed.

—2—

It had been dumbfoundingly easy to make an enemy of the friendly Colley. Raft's blunt approach to the necessity of police co-operation had been touchy but still had underestimated the nature of the relations between Security and the very junior police service. When police were needed for minor cleaning up, Security *told* Parker what he must do. That Parker's men might possess individual and group superiorities had never been considered; they were tools, not rivals.

The elevation of Parker to full partnership had bruised Colley's pride of service to the point of active dislike of Raft; Campion also had for a moment looked with less than favor on his presumptive ancestor. But Campion was an amalgam of men; the bureaucrat in him tasted gall but the politician recognized the value of the move and began to consider fresh relationships between the two forces.

However, when Raft came to him after two days with a request that had been inevitable from the beginning the starman found himself referred to Colley on the ground that the Senior Tech was Acting Commissioner and must be treated as such. Raft was to eat his peck of dirt.

With a setting of teeth he presented himself before Colley who said, without looking up, "Sit down, Commander," and continued writing. Raft, recalling *Columbus*, had the grace for an inward smile, but the smile itched.

When he was ready Colley laid down his pen, looked straight at him and waited, unforgiving.

Raft said, "You're a hard man to get to, Senior." He should have given the man his courtesy title, but he thought of Campion as Commissioner and did not at once realize the unintended slight.

Colley snapped, "Probably. I haven't time for—" and bit back words in the interest of dignity.

Raft lost grip of good intentions. "For minor irritations? Sorry if I've become one but I think I've done no harm and possibly some good."

"Like a well-meant kick in the teeth. You have tacitly criticized my service as inefficient and given the police opportunity to crow over us publicly."

Security's monstrous pride would not be soothed, but Raft suggested, "Use them for the legwork; that was always the copper's forte. Security must make the final moves and crucial decisions."

"Regaining face isn't the point. It chokes me to admit"—and he looked as if it did—"that you are the only useful adviser Security has in a situation outside its expertise. And you have achieved something; Ian and I have made reports, objective reports we hope, to World HQ about your points of view and it may satisfy you to know that the whole philosophic background of Security is in question. Given an unfamiliar circumstance we have handled it ineptly and a man from a civilization we have been bred to despise is showing us what to do. Security doesn't love you, Commander.''

Raft said coldly, ''Commissioner Campion seems to have recovered his sense of values, however.''

Colley shrugged. ''But then, he's some sort of a Raft, isn't he?''

''He has the family appreciation of facts without self-pity.''

''I think we can do without open insult.''

''Yes. I'm sorry.'' Point to Colley. Raft said as lightly as he could manage, ''I am, you know, because I've come to beg help,'' and knew he sounded only impertinent.

''To charm the opposition, put him in a position of doing you a favor?''

''Something like that.''

''And it will be something I can't risk refusing?''

''I don't know that. It concerns the clone-brothers in the police cells. Or anywhere else for that matter, but the closer they are the worse it is.''

''You feel them, a mile away?''

''Acutely. They inhabit my food, my sleep, my thinking. I am in a sweat of conscious self-control the whole time; it's a nagging sickness without let-up and I want to be freed of it.''

Colley told him with practicality, ''Your awareness is vitally useful and may continue to be so, but we might think in terms of a hypno-therapy that can be reversed at will.''

''No. I'm not going to spend the rest of my life in a haze of drugs and suggestion.''

''It could come to that. Your problem is one psychology knows nothing about.''

''I'm not so sure. Jim Lindley had some ideas and I'd like them tested. Under deep question.''

''The hell you would!'' Colley found nothing intrinsically frightening in deep question but he had never heard anyone actually request the experience; that Raft should do so conveyed something to him of the insupportable nature of the affliction. But need came before sympathy. ''I'll talk to Ian about it. Controller Parker may have need of your—talent—also.''

''I've asked both. They say, go ahead.'' And so, of course, he had offended again.

Colley asked coldly, ''Then why come to me?''

''Ian insisted that you are the operative officer.''

If Colley was mollified he did not show it. ''The therapists are worked to their limits with several hundred hypnoed kids in various states of residual shock as their post-commands are negated under question. Fitting you in could be difficult. I'll let you know.''

''Don't call us; we'll call you.''

''Eh?''

''Ignore it; it was meant as a joke.''

''And the point?''

Damnation! And, oh, to hell with it. ''It was a twentieth-century way of giving a brush-off.''

Colley stood, enraged. ''We live on the fruits of twentieth-century stupidity and they're bitter. To us, Commander, you are a barbarian—intelligent, even housebroken, but a barbarian. And I don't care to have a barbarian challenge my good intentions. You will have your appointment tomorrow, even if it means setting urgent work aside and upsetting curricula to pacify your vanity. Time to be fixed. I repeat, I will let you know.''

Raft took his dismissal. From the door he said, ''Thanks for the good intentions, but it's as well to remember that civilization is a comparative condition and that this barbarian thinks yours has a strong smell of decay, for all its extreme youth.''

Colley's inclination was to go back on his given word, to let the bastard stew in his nauseous awareness. But he was a man of some quality, not given to letting anger rule sense; and sense, reviewing the exchange of humiliations, reminded him that this trusted adviser had displayed no uncertain animosity against the world he advised. It might be well to know more about Raft's attitudes, and his request for question offered a perfect opportunity.

He called Psychlinic and arranged, over the venomous protests of harassed personnel, for Raft to be placed under deep question on the following morning. To his description of the awareness problem they listened stone-faced, knowing already more about it than he ever would though still not enough for the construction of better than cloudy theories. In his list of specific questions to which he needed answers they recognized familiar ground; the Acting Commissioner was more concerned with Raft's mental processes than the state of his empathetic guts.

Cutting the connection, Colley went immediately to Campion, half expecting Raft there before him giving his version of the dialogue, but the starman had apparently not thought it worth while to seek tactical advantage with power. That Campion accepted his account as a display of temper-tantrum, better forgotten by grown men (although Campion would not himself forget it), soured him further.

Then Campion surprised him. He wished to be present, behind the one-way screen and unknown to Raft—bandages, immobility and all—to listen to the questioning.

Colley found such sessions irredeemably boring; what scuttled from under the turned-over stones in the backyards of men's minds was mostly cliché. Campion, he concluded, might add questions of his own to the catalogue; he might desire to learn more of his antecedents, although few concerned themselves with such unproductive queries in an era when half the world had only doubtful knowledge of its parentage. For himself, he would be satisfied to receive his required information, neatly interpreted and summarized by a questioner who knew his job.

—3—

"Just sixty hours home, if that's the word for the place; and frustrated already into journal-writing. Officially dead, I can't leave this damned barrack, but am beginning to wonder if this 'dead' business fools anyone. Must speak to Ian about it.

"In the meantime, what I have asked to have done tomorrow has me half-stupid with revulsion, but I must have treatment or live on the edge of physical and mental debility and unremitting nausea. I face it with gritted teeth and black resentment.

"I have said something of this to Ian, but he is a man of his time and can't share the feeling; that I feel as I do seems to him all the more reason for therapy.

"His attitude emphasizes change and alienation. Today's men don't understand the reactions of an outmoded, impractical, emotion-guided intellect (the starship selectors should hear that, poor ghosts). I don't suppose I understand theirs; I only suffer them.

"The deep question business underlines the clash of attitudes.

"It is certainly to be preferred to depth interrogation as we knew it—blood and bestialism. I am told that an expert questioner, properly briefed and knowing precisely the areas he wishes to plumb, can arrive at most of his material in a matter of minutes, asking exactly the right questions and framing them with the precision of meaning used in programing a computer.

" 'Invasion of privacy' is meaningless to these people. I have put it to a few in the barrack and they feel that the concept does not apply to such interrogation. They can understand that it applied in my day, but we were barbarians who wrecked our/their world (it's a marvel hearing them wriggle round saying this outright to my face) and *they* are different. The poor bastards actually think they have in some way become basically different.

"They explain, as to an idiot child, that the practice is ultimately therapeutic although it has political aspects for both individual and state. But Security records are as sacrosanct as the old-time confessional—which shows how much they know of what could be done to the sanctity of the confessional. Not even a government, they tell me, can demand Security records because Security works outside governments, not for them.

"I cover my cynicism because it rouses their resentment and their contempt for my barbarian conceptions, but I only wish their fantasy of love and goodwill had a chance of working. The Ombudsmen have had their day; they know it themselves. A new kind of preceptor is needed, one with more facts at command and fewer dreams to roll in. *Then* their Reconstruction can begin.

"It seems that, after all, there is work for me here."

He re-read the last line with a stirring of doubt. It was not the considered ending of his thought but more like an odd comment which had slipped to the page while his mental back was turned—a most odd comment from a mind whose immediate concern was simply to stay alert and alive.

He ran his pen through the line but did not forget it; he knew that the mind does not produce inconsequential oddities, that there is always a connection.

—4—

They took Campion, bed and all, to the basement Psychlinic and installed him in the "snoop-room" with an earphone to relay sound and a throat microphone in case of need.

He felt no disloyalty or indecency in prying into the personality of one whose blood he believed he shared; he felt it logical to take the opportunity of discovering what this possible grandfather might be behind his stoic face. For him there were two Rafts, one a human figure whom he wished to like and respect, the other a puppet manipulated by circumstance and necessity. Deep question was for the puppet; his thought did not connect it with the man.

Campion could not have conceived that he suffered the eternal dichotomy of the dedicated, that Campion and the Commissioner were different people.

Raft's expressed revulsion to the therapy he found irrational, and he felt to the man as he might to a child—protective and what he supposed the world called "fatherly," which was a reversal of roles but seemed to fit the case. *The men won't hurt you, Son; remember, Daddy knows best.*

In thinking so he was visited by a doubt, a generalized uncertainty, calling infallibility into question. For an instant

of total clarity, involving all his senses, he was enclosed
again in the tearing and screaming ambience of youngsters
who would kill him while men with his own face struggled
to preserve his life. All the decades of indoctrination could
not explain or contain that event. It tilted his whole environment to display unfamiliar, contradictory vistas.

He wondered, with an odd feeling that this was not the
first time he had wondered, if it was possible for quite literally *everything* a man believed to be wrong, for his whole
life and ethic to be based on an unstable platform which
could tumble him into unsuspected realities.

Through the snoop-glass he saw Raft enter and he steadied himself to observe and interpret. Certainties closed in.
Days of inaction were disturbing and unsettling him; it was
nothing more than that.

He knew it was much more than that.

On his way through the Psychlinic complex Raft was
given an unintended glimpse into a waiting-room.

There were a dozen or so teenagers in there, and no
dozen youngsters wait in silence, even if they are strangers
to each other. These sat in dumb anguish, each one alone.
A girl cried quietly, one boy shivered in psychic cold, two
hid faces in hands, most stared ahead of them.

He knew who they must be, kids whose post-commands
had been vitiated under question and who now knew what
they had done on the landing field and in the barrack courtyard. They sat like the prematurely aged, horrified by un-
earned guilt, unable to accept what had been done to them,
mentally unequipped against ruthlessness.

Psychlinic would clean them up, steady them. Psychlinic,
Raft thought with an access of irritation, would wipe their
noses and clean their dribbly chins; how like these sentimentally harsh idealists to set about returning the kids to
the pattern without stopping to wonder if a few scars were
not a necessary adjunct to maturity.

None of them took notice as he paused in the doorway,
but his guide's arm reached across him to pull the door to
and urge him on.

At his own examination point he saw that laboratories
throughout time and space are probably archetypal—at

once functional and cluttered, austere and worked-in.

Two men waited for him, traditionally white-coated, one in his mid-twenties with an assistant of about nineteen. Their youth roused his innate distrust; all his outdated experience doubted young expertise.

He spoke resentfully to the older man. "Doctor Grierson?"

The "assistant" said, "I am Doctor Grierson and this is my assistant, Tech Playfair," and discomfited him completely.

He muttered, "Sorry," and the boy grinned at him, understanding perfectly the prejudice and rejection. "Sit down, Commander. In that one."

Raft sat, curiously taking in the apparatus around him; only the rear-projection screen at eye level five feet before his face was a familiar item.

Grierson hoised himself on to a bench, swinging his feet, very young and very sure of himself. "I know the general nature of your trouble and it could be largely psychosomatic. Your men Lindley and Doronin were not explicit about their ideas in any record we have but I can guess roughly at their conclusions. Perhaps they told them to you?"

"No, but like you I can guess."

"Guess for me." Then, blinking like a schoolboy who realizes dereliction of good manners, "Please."

"Well . . . the condition exists throughout the clone, so there is probably a physical basis. Genetic, I suppose."

"I can think of other possibilities. If it is wholly genetic we are up against some very special considerations of your role in the cloning experiment. Have you thought of that?"

"Of course."

"And?"

"Insufficient data."

"Try."

"Forget telepathy. There's simply a knowledge of the presence of the clone-brothers."

"Empathy?"

"None. Evidence says the others have a powerful brotherly bond while I have at least as powerful an antipathy to them. The rogue in the brood."

"Not necessarily. It could be the same faculty expressed in different form, conditioned by special experience. You had a basic experience denied the rest of the clone: you were involved in their first-consciousness trauma, but as an outsider.''

"Yes."

"You were adult, complicated by experience and intelligence, not a bundle of receptors seeking emotional warmth. The clone-awareness may have pre-empted the role of the missing mother for them but have no such meaning for you. It's an interesting speculation. Anyway, you reacted violently."

"With physical nausea."

"And self-loathing?"

(Campion thought that would not be easy to confess to, and a restless time passed before Raft managed an unwilling nod.)

"Why, Commander?"

"I don't know."

"But you do, you do." (Campion recognized the beginning of dominance, of Grierson concentrating on himself the man's emotional as well as intellectual attention.) "Since Doctor Lindley succeeded in overcoming your symbolic physical self-rejection, you must have recognized what he said as true."

Raft said with difficulty, "He said I blamed myself for being——" But he could not use the word without feeling a posturing idiot. And the Doctor-boy was hugely amused about it.

"For being beautiful, Commander. For being a magnificent animal. And because you were still more impressive in the springtime aura of youth, Professor Heathcote fell clinically in love with you as the progenitor of the perfect clone. He wasn't in fact homo, was he?"

"No."

"And you thought the experiment abominable?"

"It was exciting at first, but later I began to think of the implications."

"And that was when self-loathing began?"

"I think so."

"Guilt for willingly involving yourself in a perversion of nature, with overtones of psychic rape? Manhood assaulted and misdirected?"

"Something like that."

"And the other thing?"

"What? Oh, I see. Some resentment of the circumstances of my upbringing; a feeling of being unfit to be the—father—of a new humanity."

"Most would be proud."

Raft breathed deeply, wringing truth out of himself. "I am cold at heart; I don't love, don't warm much to a friend. Sex with a woman, yes, but no love, no affection. I had a daughter and never gave her a thought; when finally I met her she was an irritation to be put up with. I supposed the clone would be the same, monstrous inside."

Grierson shook his head. "Cloning is emphatically a physical process; the simulacra would start out with identical psychological bases but would meet with various traumatic experiences in the formative years and shed many manifestations while acquiring others. Which is probably what happened and why you, not sharing their group experiences, are the odd man out. Did Lindley take you further than that?"

"No."

"Sure?"

"Quite sure. What more is there?"

Grierson whistled softly. "Then he's a bloody good practitioner and I salute him. He broke your fixation by sheer argument without presenting the real basis. He's good."

"Very."

Grierson's style changed abruptly. "And he was compassionate. He did it the difficult way rather than rouse further ghosts." A professional hardness—assumed, not yet grown into his personality—flattened his voice. "I am not compassionate. I am faced with a problem and the additional information is necessary. What lies behind your conviction that you are incapable of love or close friendship?"

"Simple reality."

"Despite all the evidence to the contrary?"

"What evidence?"

"You know perfectly well but you won't face the reality of your condition; there would be confusions you don't want to encounter. Commander, we are about to dig truth out of you and a whole lifetime of repression working round the clock will not prevent us.''

''No?'' Anger expressed itself as contempt. ''If I decide to walk out, do you feel you could stop me?''

''Easily.''

He was already standing when Grierson said, ''Sit down, Commander.''

He sat. Surprise held him a moment before he began again to surge to his feet.

Grierson's command came without special emphasis, almost with boredom: ''Sit down and don't get up again.''

Raft sat, unable to summon the needed movement, able to do anything but stand up.

''I believe you've seen something of the range of hypnodrugs; now you're meeting one. It is in the chair seat, volatilized by body warmth and taken in directly through the pores. This is normal clinical procedure and clients expect it, but the sensation of being under command while nominally in control of all faculties can be schizophrenic unless explained to the patient. Now you needn't worry further about it. We'll go into the question of why you consider yourself a cold man.''

Raft watched him sullenly. Grierson nodded over his head to Playfair, enmeshed behind him in unidentifiable leads and panels and machines.

A buzz, a click, and the projection screen blazed with immediately riveting color. Geometrical shapes leapt in a coruscation of alternate green and red, green receding to some central emerald infinity, red leaping from the screen to assault. Brilliance shocked his retinae; vision petrified, then commenced agonizingly to move in unpracticed directions. The squares shook, split, reformed in interlocking triangles which moved even more confusingly to and away, simultaneity defying sight to fix the action.

His wrists were caressed and he glanced down—with a distinct wrenching of the gaze—to see his forearms locked to the chair.

''Look up!'' His head jerked. ''You must not look away from the screen.''

Thereafter he could not.

The patterns changed continually, hypnotic in a soporific

sense other than the effect of the drug. He heard his voice remark from position above and outside his level of interest, "We called this op art. It was out of date."

"The hell it was!"

Playfair spoke for the first time. "This one, I think." "This one" was a marvel of orange and indigo pentacles, interacting most absorbingly in a complication of relationships he could not determine. It was necessary to solve the pattern if only to rest his painful, tearfilled eyes.

Grierson, alongside but in another continuum, said, "You may blink."

He blinked furiously; vision cleared a little; pain eased; the pentacles related mockingly as he failed to analyze the pattern.

"Did you love your father?"

Something in him chuckled, *Not old Oedipus!* and forgot it at once because consciousness was pinned ferociously to color and line. He said what he said thereafter, not knowing and not remembering.

"No."

"Did he love you?"

"No."

"Did he hate you?"

"No."

"What did he feel for you? Be explicit."

Very nearly he understood the pattern when, most unfairly, it changed and he had to begin again. His voice chattered about its own affairs.

"No feeling. Annie wanted a son; Annie got a son. Her husband could afford it, so why not? Or a swimming pool or a new lounge suite? As long as it didn't bother him. He was busy. He proposed a system for recognizing prime numbers of any magnitude; give him a fifty-digit number and he could tell you in a couple of seconds. You have to be busy to do that sort of thing."

"What was your feeling for him?"

High, contemptuous laugh. "He wasn't there."

"Do you mean your parents were not——" Grierson was uncertain of the old marital terms "——did not live together?"

"No, no. For me he wasn't there. Like furniture; you don't notice it."

Grierson said, not sure he made sense in the terms of a lost era, "So, effectively, you had no father."

"Oh, I did, I did."

"Explain that."

"John was my father. When I was ten John became my father."

"Who was John?"

"Doctor Heathcote."

"He loved you like a father?" What, he wondered, did loving like a father involve? He supposed he would find out some day.

"I think so." A correction. "I thought so."

"Aren't you sure?"

"He changed."

"He stopped being father?"

A strange, muddled sound. Wrong question, Grierson decided; too many possible meanings. He substituted, "Did he stop loving you?"

"No. Yes."

Grierson said aloud, "Wrong question again. What can he mean? Um—when did he stop loving you?"

"He didn't stop. He changed." Something down in the dark seemed to have sorted itself out.

"When did he change?"

"When I grew beautiful."

The ill-made face was worth a smile. "Why did he change?"

"He just wanted me for his work. He wasn't father."

Grierson exclaimed to Playfair, "The bastard's crying! Little boy all lost and alone. You loved him very much, didn't you?"

"Yes."

"But you stopped loving him when he stopped being father, is that it?"

"Yes. No."

"Damn! Did you feel the same as before?"

"No."

"Tell me how you felt?"

Raft's voice became lighter, younger. "I went cold."

With a slight whine of resentment he corrected himself. "I went hard." His face worked; childish petulance surfaced more clearly. "I stopped inside. I stopped."

Grierson doubted if he would get that much more clearly; Raft was regressing and taking clarity of expression with him, becoming limited to the verbal ability of the remembered age.

"Do you mean you stopped feeling?" Meaningless stuttering told him he had fumbled again; with inspiration he asked, "Do you mean you *made* yourself stop?"

"Yes."

"Why?"

"So as not to get hurt."

"But deep down did you love him just the same, underneath the part where you stopped?"

Raft pouted and twisted his neck but seemed unable to answer. Perhaps the question, involving abstract visualization, did not chime with the child's equivalent abstraction. He tried more directly, "Did you still think of him as father?"

"Yes."

The single word dripped in the laboratory air, infinitely alone and dreary. Grierson let out a breath. "First signpost. There's room here for a split loyalty."

Playfair said, "Poor little bugger."

Grierson cried out from his own depths, "Why pity him? How many of us knew our parents? Do we have to be self-pitying slobs?"

Playfair's voice swirled in Raft's ears without touching his brain. "He wanted what all kids had in his day but it went rotten on him. That's worse than never having."

Grierson spat savagely, "I know, I know," furious at the betrayal of a self he had not known existed.

(Disturbed, Campion pondered the little scene. He had never imagined himself essentially deprived by the lack of known parents, yet he felt an obscure but definite pleasure in the idea of possessing a visible, touchable grandparent, a representative of an existence extending beyond the self. It was a feeling not for on-the-spot assimilation. It occurred to him, with a fresh warning of instability in the universe, that all Security men of operational status—those who actually participated in manipulation of public affairs, not laboratory or clerical Techs like Playfair—were group-raised. It might have a bearing on facets of Security psychology. It was a disquieting thought, that there actually might be special facets of Security psychology making them not completely as other men are.)

Grierson asked, "Did you love your mother?"

Raft screamed.

Grierson muttered, "Whee-oo, man! Now there was a kick." He asked, "Didn't she love you?"

The answer came half-strangled, "She hated me."

But Annie had wanted——"Was her name Annie?"

"Yes."

"But she wanted a baby."

"Only a little one. One to play with. Not to grow up."

"So when you became big she turned against you. Is that what happened?"

Raft reverted completely. It was a sight against which the clinicians never became fully hardened. It chilled.

His face cleared, relaxed, miraculously erased lines and took on false, bright smoothness; his expression faded to the vacuity of repose, of youthfulness before character was imprinted. His quivering mouth produced a shrill discord as adult vocal cords screeched at the vanished treble of the child.

"She hated me she didn't want me she hit me always!"

Large, trembling tears.

Playfair's mouth wrinkled in distaste for a woman of a dead era but Grierson asked in unbroken continuity, "And did you hate her?"

The face transformed itself from within, dredging darkness until adult evil peered out. The cracked voice shrieked and bellowed together, "I'll kill the bitch!"

Grierson nodded. "Forty-two years too late. It's a wonder he never did it, with all that pre-teenage buildup. Perhaps he did, symbolically, but there's no point in chasing it; we've got enough. At least we know why Commander Raft is lonely and his women are good for a slap of sex and nothing more. I suppose part of it is guilt for hating his parents; kids of that day had to love their parents whether the so-and-sos were worth it or not. Well, here we go: One, self-hate stemming from family conflict and aggravated by a fancied rejection by Heathcote when he became too interested in his work to keep on playing Daddy to a grown man. And finally unloaded on the clone as being the alternative selves for whom Heathcote rejected him. If that rejection ever occurred outside Raft's mind. Two, most of this awareness trouble is psychosomatic; there's probably a real physical basis, which we don't know how to touch, but it's magnified by the self-hate syndrome which led to the revulsion he felt at the first-consciousness contact. Three, removing the reactions should be no problem but the fundamental awareness will remain, probably without the upsetting side effects. How does that sound, Tech?''

"Reasonable," Playfair agreed, "from what we have. But we'd better get on with Colley's questions first; we don't want to take out anything bearing on that area."

"I almost forgot his dreary list." He fumbled in his pocket for Colley's memo. "Commander Raft, why do you seek to assist Security with its problems when you despise the civilization it works for?"

The change of question provenance snapped Raft back to the present as if a switch had closed. "Not despise. I don't like it, I don't understand it properly, but I don't despise it." Some remnant of old training emerged in sententiousness: "It is never safe to despise anything or any person."

"Safety hints for star travelers. Serves me right for clumsiness; I presented two subjects at once and he took the second. Commander, are you willing to help Security as an adviser?"

"Yes."

"Why?"

"To help Ian."

"Ian Campion?"

"Yes."

"Why?"

Raft had a surprise for him, delivered in a soft, yearning tone so uncharacteristic as to be caricature.

"Because he is my beloved son in whom I am well pleased."

And having said it he laughed like a maniac.

Grierson groaned, "Here we go again, down into the worms' nest."

Playfair interrupted, "That's a quotation from somewhere. I've heard it before. Cultists, I think."

"Trace it through the library."

Campion's voice issued from the wall speaker. "Tell them to check the New Testament; Gospel of St. Matthew, I think, but don't hold me to it. The meaning's fairly plain but you'd better get a gloss for symbolic undertones." And if they wondered was he privately a cultist—a most un-Security-like activity—then let them; he had read through most of the New Testament with curiosity, bafflement and some retention of marvelous phrases.

The Central Library produced a cultist who could gloss from memory and did so in considerable and frustrating detail, leaving an ocean of possible interpretations. Grierson and Playfair handed their puzzlement to the one-way screen.

"No," Campion said. "I have my ideas but *you* tell me."

Grierson said carefully, "The word 'son' doesn't have to be taken literally; it is probably a general reference to consanguinity."

"Agreed."

"So the importance is not in the quotation but in the background circumstances."

"Go on."

"To be loved by an omnipotent god may be flattering but there's the reverse consideration: who may suffer his wrath? At the moment it would be anyone who attempted to injure you, which means whoever is behind this Heathcote business, since they have already tried. Full marks to Colley's intuition; the man is a latent bomb."

"But he's our bomb, or mine if you like."

Grierson pondered. "Canberra located his pre-*Columbus* file and there's no history of incipient paranoia, so we can take it that was an eruption from pretty deep levels. We could go down after it but it would take time and preparation and a higher level specialist than myself."

"Not now, but we'll keep it in mind. Do you think he really imagines he's God or a god?"

"We all do, but on those levels of the pre-conscious it doesn't do much harm. Harm begins when other functions of the mind become pre-empted."

"Then there's no point in fiddling with drama, is there?" The rest was not difficult, merely time consuming.

An angry Campion confronted Grierson from his bed in the private ward.

"Did you have to go at him like a butcher? Was it necessary to rip him up with your bare hands?"

Grierson had his own anger to purge and no fear of Campion; he was not a Security doctor but responsible only to the Psychiatric Board. "If I'd had my way the session would not have been held, but Colley leaned on me in the name of political urgency and I gave way in the name of smooth relations. Another time I'll lean back. Between you both you put me in the position of having to dig like an amateur, and I don't like it."

Under the mask of bandage Campion's eyes could still snap with his voice. "Are you blaming Security?"

"Who else? Raft demanded an excision job that fortunately turned out to be simple but could have been beyond the limits of our knowledge, and in a fit of pity you let him have it when it wouldn't have mattered a curse if his guts had churned for another week or two while we sifted evidence. Colley's questions were pressured by personal malice as much as necessity and the answers will help nobody significantly. Don't you people realize that it's bad practice, bloody near unethical, to probe personality factors without prior investigation and discussion? Oh, you know, but it's always a 'special case.' All you've got for your rush tactics is an obscure quotation and a badly disturbed man."

"Disturbed?" Campion was harsh. "What do you mean?"

Grierson's aggression retreated in an onset of unease; he was, after all, a very young man in the presence of a very powerful one. He admitted, "I don't know, but there may be personality changes."

"Serious?"

"Too early to say; it may amount to very little. The thing is that we were working without preparation and in the area of family relations, where we haven't enough practical experience—how many old-type families do you know of—to appreciate the danger points. A couple of routine gambits went right to the gates of his personal hells and you might have noticed I didn't stay there a second longer than I had to. So there may be side effects.''

"How so? People have no recall after question.''

Grierson regarded him pensively. "So we say and it's mostly true, but there's a whole region of investigation here which we're still only opening up. We theorize that in a case like Raft's, where the questions moved into sensitive areas without cushioning, there can be a sort of pre-conscious shock. Pre-conscious material is forced into higher levels of consciousness; repressed characteristics are released; the ego alters its attitudes in accordance with the new material and perhaps a personality shift occurs. I can't give a prognosis; we don't know enough. You'll just have to keep an eye on him. What comes up from the cellars isn't normally pretty.''

He felt like adding, "And serves the lot of you bloody well right for insisting when we wanted no part of it.'' But Campion could report him to the Board for insolence and he had enough trouble on his plate with more depressed kids coming to light each day.

Raft woke in bed. Playfair sat at the foot, packing miniature instruments into a pouch. "Awake? Good. I can't detect any physical hangover. Let me know if you suffer headaches or stomach upset in the next couple of days.''

"My eyes ache.''

"To be expected. That will pass.''

Raft sat up. "Operation successful?''

"Only you know that.''

"I can hardly feel them.''

"Excellent. No nausea?''

"None; hardly any reaction. It's something like an activity barely noticed at the corners of vision.''

"That's more or less what we aimed for. Lindley's diagnosis of mainly psychosomatic was correct. The rest was easy.''

Raft swung his feet to the floor. "Was it? How easy?''

"Suppression of selected synaptic pathways and some drug-magnified hypno-suggestion; non-reaction to the clone should be habitual by the time the suggestion fades. We can't do anything about the residual feeling; it seems to be physically based and isn't our line. I dare say the bio-clinics will winkle it out in time. Maybe a mutant gene; probably recessive, most mutes are. Anything else?''

Raft was wriggling into his overalls. "Yes. A record of the questioning.''

"Why should you want that?''

"Because I don't know what I said down there; I was glued to that damned screen.'' He might have known the request would not make sense to the Tech.

"The screen was the wedge to separate the strata of the mind. Better than scop or the other drugs.''

"But it blanks memory.''

"That could be recovered if it became necessary, but why should it? Why lay yourself open to unpleasantness? True confession isn't necessarily good for the psyche.''

Anger would not help to present a point of view Playfair was not programed to appreciate—and "programed" was the description of Jackson's vaunted instructional system. He persisted, pulling viciously at zippers, "I'd like to know, just the same.''

"Believe me, Commander, you wouldn't.''

That could be true; no man honestly wants his personal illusions stripped stark naked. What ground against the grain was the implication that Sonny wasn't old enough for really straight talk from his elders.

Still rankling, he visited Campion and unloosed ill-humor on him. Campion's good-tempered resistance roused him to undignified yelling. "All right, Ian! I observe a fact and understand it but I don't have to bloody well like it. I object to a psychiatric record being preserved in the public domain.''

"The Personnel Section of Archives is not public domain.''

"Then it's Security domain. Preserved.''

"Of course. No hospital or doctor destroys a patient's records until he dies. And not always then.''

The equation of Security with healing organizations—quasi-medical-psychiatric-political—Raft did not pause over; he was becoming habituated to filing minor queries for later resolution. He said, "That's worse. It means Security has purely private psychiatric and factual information on people which can be used to manipulate them or keep them in line.''

Campion seemed shocked. "That would be an extreme use; only exceptional circumstances could warrant it.''

"Power corrupts. Who would decide on the exceptional nature of the circumstances?''

"Whoever was in charge of the relevant project.''

"Too much freedom of decision. That makes a large number of people with opportunity for blackmail or extortion.''

Campion's temper barely took the strain. "I wish you'd forget your twentieth-century terrors. Self-seeking is not part of a Security man's makeup; his indoctrination over-rides it. Privacy of the individual is observed to the point where the individual himself forfeits the right.''

Raft was caught by Campion's utter trust in his own words. Could it be possible that fallible humanity lived with and genuinely employed such moderation and selflessness? His whole life experience derided the idea as powerfully as Campion's faith embraced it.

He said heavily and clumsily, "I hope you never learn that even a safety razor can cut you.''

Campion, brought up to the use of depilatories, fumbled for the meaning and, finding it, dismissed it as fuzzy metaphor.

Raft abandoned the subject.

—5—

Columbus carried no weapons. Raft had said, "A shuttle and a cutting torch and she's anybody's.''

Training and philosophy led Colley to think first in purely defensive terms. He saw an attack on the starship as an affair of hand-over-hand approach along tielines, of spacesuited figures wielding cutting torches on the ship's thin skin and of Security issuing forth to repel boarders.

Not until he fell to thinking how he himself might launch the attack did he begin to think realistically. The method was obvious and simple. He would fit magnetic tackle to his shuttle and clamp directly to the ship's skin, laser a five-centimeter hole directly into the crew quarters, insert a flexible tube and pump in a liter or so of hypno-form III. With a rehearsed gang this would take about three minutes and Security in all its glory would need a miracle to prevent it happening.

So enemy transport must be stood off or put out of action. This might involve killing, and even defensive killing was not lightly authorized. Life might not be sacred but neither was it wantonly expendable, and the inevitable courts of enquiry might not easily excuse Security failure to attempt less drastic methods.

He could mount cannon on the hull but they would shatter on any attempt to fire them in space, though shielding and heating could be devised—if he had a few days to spare. So cannon were impracticable. Which was just as well; he might have been tempted to use them.

Lasers could be a possibility, but most were too small for the swift and powerful work required or too cumbersomely mounted and powered to be modified for the job in less than two or three days. What he had was several hours.

Finally he recalled that a few heavy-duty, flexibly mounted lasers did exist. The Melbourne Town Reclamation Authority used them in its program for clearing the sites of tall buildings; the prestressed concrete in their lateral members exploded like bombs as stresses were released in demolition, and chopping from a distance was essential. Against a chorus of Town Council outrage he requisitioned them. Something else he would have to answer for later.

So it happened that a squad of quietly complaining Techs found themselves carrying out old-fashioned sentry duty in space suits, one to each of the four lasers mounted on the web of *Columbus* and sited to cover the bulge of the hull, and one lone wight contemplating Earth, Moon and stars from the dead ground of the tail vent.

Use of the lasers might entail deaths, but the decision was Colley's and he was expected to make it without fuss. And possibly pay for it later. He must be stern for the immediate necessity. He noted grimly, *I'm thinking like a soldier*; all his life he had heard that word only in contempt.

When, on the morning of their fourth day as sentries,

Columbus's radar signaled the approach of three shuttles which ignored the ID request, the reaction of the Techs was unbelief settling only slowly into acceptance of aggression as a reality. Once they had accepted it there was nothing slow or undetermined about their operations.

If Colley had bludgeoned his preconceptions into an appreciation of elementary strategy, the Tech commanding *Columbus* had improved on his superior by devising simple but thoughtful tactics for dealing with an unprecedented situation.

If the shuttles had come in from several directions he would have been reduced to flailing at opportunity targets and somebody would surely have been hurt, but in his strategic simplicity he had imagined them converging in a group on the hull at a point near the entrance lock and out of vision of the blister porte. Since the raiders did not know of the lasers, and a few projections on the web would be meaningless to men gaining their first view of the starship, they had no reason to approach in any but this practical fashion. Being as inexperienced as the Techs, that is what they did.

The Techs, who knew the design of the shuttles as well as each other's faces, used the lasers in their secondary capacity as welding torches to melt and distort the propulsion vents, immobilizing them where they lay magnetically clutched to the hull. With swift touches they then sealed the airlocks and by radio pointed out that the crews could, if it suited them, stay inside until starved or asphyxiated; alternatively they could extrude their weapons through the waste disposal tubes, after which Security would bring them inboard as prisoners.

There were no weapons; if the plan had gone as intended there would have been no need of them.

And, as the Tech commander noted in a marginal addition to his report, "A clone-bunch of eighteen is an unnerving sight."

Not so much unnerving as unreal, the display of an illusionist—eighteen striking physical specimens with eighteen strikingly ugly faces, alike as prints from a single negative.

A bizarre tableau, Campion conceded, himself not quite making the nineteenth now his head bandages had been removed. He was not sure what he hoped to gain from this confrontation, but any random eruption might be paydirt.

He had had Colley bring them all to the barrack and here they were in the main briefing hall, ringed by guards but unconcerned, unapprehensive of harm. Their love-in-a-mist philosophy, confounding in its confident impracticality, was an armor against truth.

He had placed himself in a corner; he could move his head freely but was otherwise immobile in the chair. The clone gave him a cursory glance and that was all; Commissioners held no terrors for their spiritual cohesion. As for his family resemblance, Campion supposed that an imperfect product was not worth comment. Oneness was all; you either were or you weren't.

He had them facing him so that Albert should enter from the side, be unexpectedly among them. An unguarded exclamation might provide a clue questioners had missed by not knowing what questions to ask. They sat in silence, he waiting for Raft, they simply waiting.

Out of stillness a stir passed through them; it was barely definable but he felt that something had occurred. The clone-brother nearest him turned to look him fully in the face and said, "I speak for the clone."

It was mind-shaking. In that tiny stir a voice had been selected and a communication decided upon. Telepathy, after all? He would not have it; it was not an inevitable deduction. A powerful empathy. Or perhaps the group sensitivity that made a flock of birds act in concert, wheel, scatter and reform without apparent leadership.

He said, "Go on."

"You—Security—have lied. Albert was not killed. We have known this almost from the moment of the lie. There is a brother, unaccounted for, in this building. He is Albert."

Campion did not answer. He had been caught by an obvious capacity overlooked in the sheer unfamiliarity of the thing.

The clone-brother continued slowly, with great emphasis, purposefully declaiming. "Security claims to protect, but protects only the dream of Security. Security sometimes kills. Who then is safe? Security lies and lies and claims it lies for the general good. Is truth then evil? Security is a falsehood wrapped around the world. Albert's death was not even a necessary lie; that someone thought it so is a measure of spiritual weakness. Albert knows. He is here. He will tell you so.''

And Raft was there, in the doorway, stone-faced, listening, quietly inimical in Security black, a founding-father disgusted by his posterity.

The eyes of the clone turned to him. Their identical faces smiled the welcome of utter understanding, embarrassing Campion with the naked emotion of the silent greeting; it resembled too much a public display of lovers.

Raft's gaze slid along the mirror of figures; his mouth relaxed in ungentle humor. " 'As others see us.' I'm not flattered.'' The mirror faces cleared of welcome, remained still. "But it's the internal likeness that counts, and that's not so good, is it? And there's your problem.''

The nearest image of him rose to its feet, on the far side of the room from the one who had spoken to Campion. "I speak for the clone. Why hate your flesh? You are the father-flesh, the master-brother; why hate?''

The sense of ritual was overpowering, compacted in a mode of speech stripped down to insistent simplicity. Rejecting it, Raft schooled his words to flatness. "I don't hate you. Once I did, in self-protection because you made me physically ill.'' He decided against further clarification of that; let them worry at it. "But I don't like you and I won't like you. Nor do I appreciate myself repeated in a gaggle of puppets. You *are* puppets. Manipulated.''

The spokesman smiled briefly. "So you feel and so say, but you are of us and in the end must come to us.''

"Forget it. You're John Heathcote's stagnant spillage from a rack of bottles. Multiplication of a gene pattern is reversal of evolutionary requirement. You are only a biologist's mistakes; repeated, you would become a bad habit. The race can't progress down a hall of mirrors.''

A stir, a ripple, an instant of unrest fluttered and died. Only the spokesman moved appreciably, turning his head slightly to take in them all in a swift glance. The sense of communication was as inescapable as it was incomprehensible.

"We are the fathers of the new race, but you are the real begetter of the new world."

The spell broke upon the comic vision of himself spawning endlessly across the globe in a riot of reproduction. *In a generation or two they'd be calling me God*. With that the laughter vanished in a complex of feelings coming uncalled from depths simple consciousness could not visit, agglomerating unidentified about an irrelevant notion that to be God was a terrifying and ennobling responsibility.

Disoriented by the meaningless sequence, he had to return his mind forcibly to the point of departure, to lay about him with energetic contempt. "Rubbish! The sooner you recognize yourselves as an aborted effort the better. Nor do I think your revered Lady sees me as the universal father; she tried to kill me."

It was as if a shadow passed over the clone; lips twitched and the spokesman made a tiny gesture of severing, breaking off. "Thereby she lost us. We are now John's men only. The Lady is insane."

A rift in the party? The rest was hardly news; mass leaders in nonsense tend to paranoia and hallucination. He asked, "Who is she, anyway?"

"We do not know." That was of a piece with all the nonanswers arrived at since the moment of homecoming. "Perhaps John knows. We think she may be from the old world."

And why not? Conquest was a typically old-fashioned dream this day and age. "An old woman?"

"Who can tell? Who commands Gangoil's resources need not age."

Some laboratory beauty surviving as an ageless virago? He asked, "Where is Gangoil?"

"We do not know."

It was laughable but undoubtedly true; who would lie when a touch of a needle would spill truth? He supposed them taken in and out under blindfold or hypnosis; it could be as simple as that.

The spokesman offered, as if he wished he could help, "It is a mountain."

Tired laughter for that; the eastern coastal range is more than two thousand miles long.

Unexpectedly he was asked a question, "Why did you pretend death, Albert?"

The yearning, the lover's complaint, had returned to the image's voice; he was glad of Campion's interruption.

"That was my order. The first play against me failed. If your leaders felt the second had succeeded they might be tempted into further action. They were and you are here." He added to Raft, "You were right in thinking they wouldn't need you to run the ship; they had blueprints and wiring diagrams." He smiled wryly. "And each of them has your intellectual capacity and presumably your engineering talent."

"If they're no longer operating for this pestilential Lady, why want the ship at all?"

"Well, spokesman, why?"

Campion got then more than he bargained for. "So that you and your kind might not possess the ultimate weapon. It is not The Lady who is the enemy of the world. She is a poor mad woman dreaming psychotic dreams; *you* are the enemy. Security is the disease which eats mankind."

Campion managed an irritable laugh that sank in troubled contradictions. And Raft—adviser, grandfather, barbarian from the concrete jungles—was staring at him in cool challenge, as if he might advise: "They could be right, Commissioner." Down somewhere in darkness was the Raft-God calling him to judgment?

But if God were present he had concerns more pressing than purgation and celestial law. Raft asked, "What has happened to Doctor Lindley?"

"Nothing. We understand he takes great interest in all he sees. He is not our concern."

"Why was he taken?"

"I said it was not our business. We are not certain. John asked for him but we think it was David who really wanted him."

A new name. "Who is David?"

"Doctor David is a genetic surgeon. He controls the biolab section."

"Under John?"

"Oh, yes! All Gangoil is John's."

Raft looked helplessly to Campion, who picked up his own lines of enquiry and in a frustrating hour obtained nothing that mattered. The clone was worse than ignorant of what took place around it; it was uninterested in anything but evangelical philosophy. Had he not known the begetter Campion might have written it off as a collection of saintly idiots.

The brothers did not know or care where the shuttles in which they had assailed *Columbus* had come from and were only mildly intrigued when Campion told them the machines had been pirated from repair docks. But they were suitably shocked and grieving when informed that the non-clone pilots were dead, post-hypnoed into suicide via pellets concealed in tooth cavities as soon as questioning commenced.

In Raft's era it would not have happened; the pellets would have been found long before crisis. To Campion it seemed an unpleasant but original and effective idea, but Campion and Security were in their way as innocent as the clone.

—6—

The clone-brothers were quartered, under guard, in a travelers' hostel. Gaol was out of the question; bizarrely dangerous they undoubtedly were in a narrowly defined area but not criminal in the eyes of Security. There was argument about the limits of self-determination of minorities and non-interference until Raft decided he no longer knew what a crime was.

Campion was severely shaken by the clone. Techniques of conditioning and persuasion were commonplaces on which much of the drive towards social stability was based; only by careful, selective use of them were the world's educationists able to prune inessentials and channel the drives of the urgent, brilliant generations. He was alert to the possibilities of misuse, for there had been errors enough in refining the processes to their present accuracy, but he had never until this morning's interview seen what monstrousness was achievable.

The clone was effectively mindless. Whatever intelligence resided in the individuals—it was not easy to remember that each of these parrots was another Albert—the corporate body was unthinking, robotic.

He badly needed historical information on mass indoctrination and manipulation but could not yet manage his fingers delicately enough to handle the chair's button controls with certainty, though full recovery would be a matter of days only now that electro-stimulation had been initiated. So he made Hunter, his bored Tech attendant, push him to the Twentieth-Century Room of the Research Section.

Hunter spun catalogues on the index strip and flashed the selected items on display screens. When from the corner of his eye Campion saw Raft come in he said, "That'll do for a while." Hunter blanked the screens and the index strip vanished smartly under a clicking cover. "I've been researching the information-gathering groups of your period, Albert; there seems to have been no end to them. The CIA, the KGB, the MIs and all their little imitators are understandable; among suspicious nations defensive catalogues must have been vital. But the others, the industrial data banks and the outright muckraking of the private information services are hard to credit."

"The rotten result of a rotten system." *Of an* uncontrolled *system*, Campion thought, and found himself under attack. "Why do *you* need files from the cradle to the grave?"

There was an easy answer, the only one he had, but a dozen incidents had undermined his confidence in it. "Statistics. All information goes to Central Studies in the capital cities for analysis and the analyses are cross-correlated through Security computer libraries throughout the world. For every crisis we have some relevant statistical analysis to help us deal with it. Plague, earthquake, fire, flood, city planning, traffic control, population movements or what you will—we have information that covers masses as well as individuals and analyses that probe down to effects on typical and atypical citizens. Can you disapprove?"

"While it's all in disinterested hands, no."

"But you can't believe in disinterest?"

Raft circled the room, peering at titles, poking at unfamiliar machinery; Campion recognized the Commander's instinctive misdirection while he prepared assault. "I begin to believe in it but anyone born in my battleground of history, where the only good friend was a dead enemy, would find it hard to believe in acute intelligence backed by primal innocence. However well-intentioned you are, it takes only one bent man to misuse the dedication of nations. And what can be usually will be, sooner or later. We can't see eye to eye; we live in different parameters."

Campion watched Hunter observing Raft with a stony curiosity, as though he talked rubbish. *Only days ago I also . . .* Deliberately he pushed the point. "As with the clone?"

"Why not, 'As with Security'?"

He had asked for it; he was not hurt. But Hunter's disciplined stolidity was pierced by signs of anger and argument; there would be peculiar talk in his mess today. He hoped it might do some good, in some measure prepare them for the ideas troubling their Commissioner.

Without warning Raft dismissed the subject and came to his own business. "The clone knows I'm alive, so Gangoil knows. Hiding's lost its point, so I want to get outside, to see and talk to people who don't wear uniforms."

"Why not?" He had anticipated and thought about it. "It may help adjust your ideas."

Neither of them believed that.

"I'll need civilian clothes."

"The Audit Section will let you draw on the Ombudsman's emergency account."

"Thank you. Another thing: I want to talk to my crew. They were rushed out of the country without so much as kiss-my-arse and I want to know how they're getting on. I'm told that people anywhere in the world can be located easily."

"As a rule. Arrange it, please, Hunter. Put the charges on a COM 2b for Mister Colley's signature."

"COM 2b! Some things never change."

Campion and Hunter smiled slightly but Raft could not

fully appreciate his own irony; the calls on a COM 2a would not have been monitored.

When Raft had gone Campion called Colley and gave him his instructions, and Colley complained furiously of the drain on his complement; arranging the bugging of civilian clothes at the point of purchase called for precision, speed and squandering of manpower. Campion insisted; it would not be possible to install a personal network as sophisticated as the equipment of the black uniform, but he did not want Raft out of surveillance at any time.

Raft, loose in the streets, apparently unguarded, might be sufficient bait to rouse whatever capacity for action remained in Gangoil.

Raft would be safe enough, he considered, with the protection an alerted Security could give him, and Gangoil must be tempted into action if it were to be located without an inch by inch search of three million square miles of territory. He would as coolly have staked himself out as a tethered goat had the circumstances required it; he would have hated and feared the requirement, but he would have done it.

He knew Raft worried in his cool fashion over Lindley, but nothing could be done there until Gangoil was located.

As if he were not embroiled in complexities enough, another came to him with the urgency of fate, the one which was finally to strip a lifetime's blinkers from his brain.

He had not given thought to Raft's crew. He had done what seemed best for them and removed his attention; now the placement of Raft's international calls brought them to the center of his fermenting mind.

None of the calls could be placed; nobody in their countries knew where the starmen were. Or nobody would admit to knowing.

"Information!" he bellowed at a protesting Colley. "Hunt, dig, coerce, buy, but find out!"

That four men should disappear from Security's sight was an insult but could be dealt with. What pierced him was a consideration of their homeland systems and the reasons which might lie behind disappearance. And the political ethic which would prevent him acting.

While Security Communications began a manhunt in four countries, his mind surveyed what he knew of those countries. Never before in his life had he found himself in the position of observing his world from the viewpoint of one who dwelt in it. Security dealt in masses and movements, watched from the eagle's eyrie and never saw from ground level; the new perspective shamed and frightened him and finally stripped him naked.

—7—

Lindley's cardinal error with Alice White had been his assurance that a night's hysterical intimacy preluded an easy liaison. She repulsed him impassively. When he protested (and was horrified to hear himself protesting) she told him she liked him well enough but preferred for a while to set emotion aside until her internal warfare found peace.

She talked without much animation on neutral subjects and turned conversation away from herself, but at least she talked. She smiled at his humor but did not try to cap it. She was an intelligent companion when he sought her out, but she did not seek him.

Violent persuasion, which startled him as it slid into his mind, was outside his civilized range and the sexual urge, which had been small problem while opportunity lacked, became an irritation.

Trying to scrape acquaintance in the corridors, the dining-room, the community lounges, he discovered that everyone knew who he was and wanted nothing to do with him beyond the exchange of common politenesses. He was, he decided, under tabu. As a useless eruption he was unwanted and possibly resented in the inturned and tight-mouthed community; perhaps the word had gone out that he be socially neutralized until a role had been decided for him.

The clone was little in evidence and seemed to preserve an unpopular apartheid.

Heathcote might have forgotten his existence.

Then his position was rationalized, after a fashion, at a moment when he was not seeking it. It happened on a day when he could not know that in Melbourne Town Raft was relinquishing his uniform while Campion agonized between new insights and old conditionings, and the whole planet's *status quo* shifted imperceptibly under the gathering thrust of small incidents and private thoughts.

It was his third visit to the corridors around The Lady's quarters—or museum or bordello or pleasure dome or whatever. Having no taste for poverty-stricken delusions, he hoped not to see her. He wanted to view the paintings, to wallow and luxuriate and bow before them. Before canvas and ceramic, marble and bronze he dissolved in wonder.

There were four long corridors flaunting the rape of nations and centuries. Conquerors had always looted the art of the vanquished but this garbage-wife had ravaged the heritage of the crippled and dying.

After the surfeit of staring, consuming, absorbing, came the anger. That she should have dared! No right, no right . . . If Jesus himself returned to ransack the world of the only real glories it contained they should be wrested from him; though these corridors contained only a fraction of the planet's whole, they were worth a season in hell.

Then he played a sequence of his mental calming game because he saw he was not alone.

A man in a laboratory coat had entered his absorption and stood a few feet from him, not looking at him but observing him. He appeared to gaze at the huge painting in front of him but did not; the Pollock *Blue Poles*, its enmeshed surface streaming across the wall, carried eyes and head helplessly in patterns of observation; Lindley's observer was too still to be seeing what was before him.

Middle-aged—if that had meaning in bio-fantasy land—tall, dark, slim and unhandsome, almost chinless, he looked like somebody's lab assistant stealing a moment for his hobby. Under Lindley's gaze he ceased pretending and waved a hand to take in the entire display.

"Well?"

Was gushing appreciation required, breathless admiration? Lindley snapped, "The accumulated tastelessness of a clown."

"Indeed!" Oh my, oh my, oh sacrilege! "I would have thought—This is a collection of the world's *great* paintings——" The chinless amateur ran down, ruminated and tried again. "You mean, perhaps, that no definite line of taste is exhibited? A hodge-podge?"

"Magnificence can't be called that, but the collection brands its collector a tasteless magpie."

Extremely pale eyes—probably weak, Lindley noted automatically—surveyed him as though they might blaze to burn holes in defences. "You are Lindley, the psychiatrist who wasted his time and talent on Barnard's Star. What do the corridors tell you about the—um—clown?"

Lindley decided to enjoy himself; opportunities were rare. "There's nothing here that wasn't reproduced in cheap print so often that any illiterate could know it was supposed to be great art—Murillo beggar boys and a clutch of Rembrandt self-portraits, Van Gogh grainfields and pairs of boots, Turner sunsets and Canaletto pink palaces—everything that has been cheapened by over-exposure and the yammerings of suburban aesthetes. A safe player, the clown; everybody says it's good, so we'll have it. But what about the stuff that *isn't* here? In four hundred yards of splendor do you see a single woman, except as a member of a group? Oh, yes, the Duchess of Southampton hung opposite her door, probably because there's a faint facial resemblance. But do you see a religious group or triptych among all the rat-pickings of Europe? A Pietà, an Annunciation or a Descent From The Cross or a Madonna And Child? About half of the great art preserved in the world was religious, but our clown isn't religious, so the whole lot is disregarded because she has no taste and no appreciation, only preference. 'I just know what I like,' says the clown—and chooses what everybody else likes. No women, notice, but plenty of naked studs, all the big muscles where Lautrec's acrobats limber up, and even Goya's figure of Panic! It's a wonder she didn't have them strip the Sistine ceiling for Michaelangelo's athletes. Perhaps they didn't know how. And do you see any Dürer or Brueghel or Bosch or any of the great reminders of mortality?

She's been rejuvenated to the eyeballs and beyond, but she's scared of death.''

His listener was entranced, whether by the performance or the content he could not tell; he took a breath and carried on. ''She picked this lot out of catalogs and art magazines and coffee-table books. Ticked 'em off with a pencil—I'll have that an' that an' that an' that . . . Do you know something? Every damned one of them is from a museum; none from private collections or small unpublicized galleries. The art lover knows where every last worthwhile picture in the world belongs and I can tell you where every inch of canvas on these walls was stolen from, and I hope some day they'll go back where they belong instead of hanging here like a harlot's payroll, under a floorboard where the snoopers won't get at it.''

The laboratory man clapped his hands in sudden pleasure but Lindley tiraded across him, gesturing at the Pollock. ''Canberra, that one, and a whole pile of canvases from Melbourne in her brothel-boudoir.'' He tugged the other after him down the corridor, chanting a litany of pillage. ''The Munich Pinakothetek, the Uffizi, the Louvre, the Musée d'Art Moderne, the Prado, the Berlin Museum, the Rijksmuseum. Name it and she's had the packrats in. But nothing from America; must have struck trouble there. Competition, maybe?'' But his throat refused to cry out that her plunderers had been afraid also to enter poor, deadly Britain. ''The only one missing from the scouring of Europe is the Hermitage.''

''I've heard her speak of it. It was in old Russia, I think.''

Lindley swung on him. ''Was?''

The mouth pursed, indifferently apologetic. ''The Five Days. It was—uh—indiscriminate.''

''Jesus!''

''A shattered gallery disturbs you so much?''

''The shattering of that one is a tragedy for civilization.''

''Oh, be sensible, man!'' The sudden contempt would have split glass. ''The world has a million generations of art ahead of it. By the time the end comes these will be no more regarded than the cave paintings of our louse-infested ancestors.''

"The cave paintings were highly regarded and will be again."

"Very well; I'll not quarrel. Art isn't my subject, but I'm damned if I see that much of it matters. That Blue Poles arrangement for instance . . ."

"And if you don't see it, there can be nothing to see?"

"Touché." But he did not mean it; he had had his entertainment and was losing interest in the subject. "You'd better come to my office, Doctor Lindley. I'll have to talk to you sooner or later."

"And who are you?"

"I am Doctor David. You could say I run this place. If anybody runs it."

David's office belonged to no era or any era, containing a table-desk with voice-operated typewriter, closed-circuit communication, straight-backed chairs against the walls for the discomfort of bores, filing cabinets deep enough to swallow the secrets of nations and, for decoration and color, a blaze of incomprehensible charts. David had come to seniority's dead end, science forsaken against the need for administration of scientists.

Lindley sat without waiting for invitation. Assumption of equality might pay a dividend against an uncertain player. David might be that, slumped in his swivel chair—genuinely antique, genuinely comfortless—half-turned from Lindley and for the moment oblivious of him. His lips were closed but the muscles of his face flexed minutely; hints and flickers of expression made a classical exhibition of self-communion.

He settled his mind and opened a drawer, made rapid one-handed adjustments Lindley could not see from the far side—and Raft's voice spoke from a point somewhere on the edge of the desk: "It is never safe to despise anything or any person."

Lindley's nerves screamed once and quietened to alertness. David looked smug.

An unfamiliar voice, young and amused, spoke, but to whom? "Safety hints for star travelers. Serves me right for clumsiness; I presented two subjects at once and he took the second." Then he plainly addressed Raft—but who else was there, wherever ''there'' was? ''Commander, are you willing to help Security as an adviser?''

''Yes.'' No hesitation; decision already made. What was going on?

''Why?'' Indeed, why?

''To help Ian.''

''Ian Campion?''

''Yes.''

''Why?''

Raft said in an implausible, sentimental tone Lindley could not associate with him in any mood, ''Because he is my beloved son in whom I am well pleased.''

Having said it he yelled with laughter as uncharacteristic as the inane quotation.

David's hand moved. Click. No more speech.

''Why 'son,' Doctor Lindley? My information is that he claims to be Campion's grandfather. But it's a cultist quotation, isn't it?''

''In biblical speech the word doesn't necessarily imply a blood relationship. Son of God? In Christianity so are we all.''

The acceptance of that breathtaking statement made him sure of David's ignorance.

''A universal family, with all the implications? Little wonder the creed slumped.'' He asked sharply, ''Your analysis of the laughter?''

Play along? Why not, until direction showed? ''Mockery, contempt and something like surprise at an unexpected fact discovered. But it's guesswork.''

''But who is mocked?''

''So Albert was not killed?''

David insisted, ''Who is mocked?''

Very well, questions afterwards; but if Albert lived, David's question was possibly booby-trapped. Lindley had some ideas about Raft's bizarre pronouncement and liked none of them. So, a diversion, and quickly. ''God is mocked.''

David's face doubted, rejected, reconsidered. ''Has he a religious—what used you to call it?—denomination?''

''He is agnostic.''

''Stupid; neither one thing nor the other. Such a man

might mock God to calm his fear of God's existence, eh? However, starship commanders are not stupid; I had thought of self-mockery."

"Albert never mocks Albert; he is the only person he takes seriously."

"Ah."

If Albert's psychology was a matter for concern, the less discussion the better until Lindley knew why. He leaned forward, all puzzlement and enquiry to bypass the subject. "But how the devil did you get that recording? Surely Security can't be bugged?"

"If by 'bugged' you mean counter-wired, it can't. Not without swift discovery. But we receive duplicate tapes of things worth attention. Miss White was not the only innocent agent in the barrack; with epidermal drugs the possibilities of control are limitless."

And, Lindley thought, *freedom of action is impossible . . . so progress eats its young and civilization becomes monolithic—and freezes . . . and I have come home in time to see the end begin.*

He suggested, feeling his way, "Yet substitution and murder both failed."

"And last night," David informed him expressionlessly, "the clone failed again in an attempt to seize control of *Columbus.* We needed the ship as a—a bargaining factor. You know its capacities for good and evil."

"But they failed, you say."

"We think Raft predicted the move." He paused for reaction, received none and explained patiently, "Security knows little about violence because it has never been attacked on equal terms; it thinks only of giving orders on an ethical basis and seeing them obeyed on a culturally conditioned one. Security, meaning Campion in this country, can't think in real terms, so we think your Albert is thinking for him."

Lindley prodded ironically, "So you are about to offer me a job. The enemy has an unfair tactical advantage, so you feel the need of an adviser who knows how Albert thinks. But I see no reason to tie myself to you rather than another." David merely closed his eyes, prepared to wait. "First I want some answers. Was Albert hurt?"

"Untouched. Jackson died."

"The old Ombudsman? Pity; he was good in his way."

"What way? Do you mean that stupidity is not culpable?"

"Point taken. Still, I'm sorry he died because of us. Why the hell did she do it?"

David opened his eyes. "I don't know what she had in mind—if anything, I think it was idiot revenge and nothing else. She had lost self-control. It was John who raised the clone and conditioned them and taught them his naïve philosophy, and unfortunately he taught them to revere her. You see, he was once her lover, thought his present version doesn't know that yet and she isn't interested in reminding him. Then he became senile and incapable and we decided to clone him and attempt the memory transfer procedures; he was of no other use as he was. It was only when she emerged as controller of the clone that mania showed its shape. We didn't take her seriously; who the devil would imagine a raving nymphomaniac trying to undermine the world system with a brotherly love campaign? When she graduated to universal love via violence and drugs it was time to stop her. But how?"

Lindley said disgustedly, "Shoot her."

"With what?"

"Are you saying you have no weapons?"

"Why should we? This is a biological laboratory complex and was never meant for anything else."

Lindley laughed till he wept. The situation was beyond rational credence; he stopped when breath failed and he doubled in pain. David was furiously unamused but he could not transmit to him the monstrous humor of a memory-snarled scientist's ex-popsy planning world revolution without weapons and a mystically befuddled clone for insurgent army.

David said sharply, "Straighten your ideas. She's mad but she's not a fool; she got weapons when she needed them. Not here, because the clone wouldn't stand for it; they were raised to believe they could conquer the planet with soft words and a gentle smile. But they didn't feel called upon to interfere with the violence of others. Those men have had forty years of conditioning from The Lady's manipulative experts—your type, Lindley—and they can believe black's white without blinking.''

Frighteningly, it was a practical psychological paradox. Lindley murmured restlessly, ''Six impossible things before breakfast,'' and saw David's incomprehension. ''Forget it; go on.''

''When she opened the hypno-drug offensive the clone became recruiting agents; it was all for the eventual good of the people, you see. So, if she wanted something done she could arrange for outsiders to do it; the clone drugged them as temporary recruits and their ethic didn't even quiver. She built the thing into an octopus of a group, tentacles everywhere—people like Alice White, believing they were revolutionaries, absorbing all manner of bizarre dogma and doing dirty work the precious clone couldn't bring itself to touch. The short-term hypno-raids when *Columbus* arrived were sheer impudence; perhaps she thought they would reinforce confusion but she also thought she had the game in her hands. She damned nearly did.''

''I don't see it.''

''If it hadn't been for Raft's rogue-conditioning the attempt to replace Campion would have worked.''

''Even so, one man!''

''The right one. Within hours he would have neutralized Security by dispersing operative Techs all over the country on fake alerts from the hypno-groups, who at the same time would have caused diversions enough to tie up the city police, the only other source of weapons. Simple then to arrest the Prime Minister and announce a *pro tem* government on public TV. Add the clone, coming into the open, preaching The Lady's revolution and creating a hypno-puppet every time a wafer touched bare skin. The fifteen to twenty-five age group constitutes a third of the responsible population and their elders will as often as not do what the kids want because the ethic is that tomorrow is for the young—that *pro tem* cabinet would roll into office on sheer enthusiasm. If you suspected half what I know about adolescent restlessness you'd see that it could have succeeded on simple hysteria.''

''And in the morning Security would have come home with blood in its eye and upturned the whole works again.''

"How? With public backing of the new cabinet, Security couldn't touch the situation. It would be an internal quarrel, a family affair."

"Dear Jesus!"

"Ethics as the philosopher's bastion and the bandit's weapon! With the Melbourne Town youngsters on top and enough TV noise and hypno wafers, the country rolls over paralyzed while the new order moves into gear."

"And tomorrow the world?"

"Why not? But your Albert buggered the play in a manner nobody could have foreseen."

"So she decided to kill him, and only succeeded in bringing Albert down on the side of Security. What now, with every play blocked?"

David made a brushing-off gesture. "The clone reacted with something like a mass neurosis when you let it out that she had tried to have their template murdered; they hadn't been directly involved in that and hadn't known the purpose. So she lost her entire operating force in a matter of seconds. She's finished."

"And you?"

"The clone is loyal to John and I think the new John will see reason. He's been out of the thing during the re-growth period, if he was ever really in it, and doesn't know much about these events."

"Don't you want to be emperor of the Earth?"

"Either you're mad or you think I am. I want to stay alive."

"Who threatens?"

"Security."

Lindley shook his head. "Why? You don't seem to have been willingly involved. Duress. They'll be rescuing you."

David's smile came from the heart of winter. "Revolutionary Gangoil may be a joke, but Gangoil itself is not. This complex was built to take secrets literally underground, by a government that fell to pieces and vanished. They hoped Gangoil would survive bombing but it survived the entire Collapse and the secrets are still here." He added thoughtfully, "They aren't quite the secrets they buried; we've had forty years or so to work on them. If Security smells out what is in the basement laboratories they'll close us down and destroy our records." His smile shook a little. "And probably find excuse to kill the lot of us."

Lindley stood, stretched, said, "Then you're as good as dead. Now they know Gangoil exists, they'll find you."

"Yes."

"This, I think, brings us back to the job you are offering me."

David's uncontrollable face jerked; he was frightened and desperate but what he wanted seemed to Lindley a reasonable need in the circumstances. "Raft has great influence with Campion if he cares to exercise it; I need it on the side of Gangoil. You in turn can influence Raft where I doubt if anyone else could. Given his backing we might survive."

Lindley was sure of himself now. "What's in the basement?"

"The future."

"Heathcotian man?"

David attempted impassivity but his face was a nervous tic. Lindley sat on the edge of his desk, grinning down as he called the play.

"You offer me the job of courier between two disorganized rabbit warrens. Why should I work for you? What can you offer that Security can't top? What have you that can buy my loyalty? The future? You haven't even a decent present to build in. Take me to the basement. If I like your future . . ."

He let it hang.

David fumbled in a drawer, shut it, put his hand to his mouth and swallowed. Lindley realized belatedly that the man fought physical exhaustion; he must have been laboring nonstop to obtain an orderly decision in this shattered complex of faction and failure.

CHAPTER SIX

IDEALISTS AT WORK

As dynastic Chinese worshipped their ancestors, so the present dynasties of the West are inclining towards descendant-worship . . . Rightly, we begin to fear about the sort of world we are bequeathing our grandsons.

Brian W. Aldiss:
The Shape of Further Things

—1—

Raft insisted on going alone into Town Center. He preferred not to be professionally told what he looked at, but to observe and enjoy and casually stop the passer-by for information.

Since Campion had confirmed, over protest, that the man must not feel himself observed, this created perplexities for his guardians, requiring far too many men in civilian dress for a simple surveillance behind and before, carefully unnoticeable, passing him from hand to hand.

Still in black overalls he stepped into summer sunlight out of an enamel sky; summer at least had not changed. He needed a gesture, a raising of hands to smooth the light over face and shoulders; if others had not been coming and going he might have done it. But in St. Kilda Road, with its island lawns and quadruple avenue of trees, excitement took him. He walked in a state close to hallucination, breathing air remembered from paradise, wondering at grass and flowers grown from dreamstuff, tempted to return the laughter when a kookaburra derided the world from overhead.

When had anyone last heard a kookaburra laugh in the city? Chalk it up to the new men that they had brought back something of the real world.

Like a boy he had energy begging release. He broke into a run, regardless of stares, until sweat and breathlessness and the drag of Earth slowed and halted him. He sat on the grass verge, feet in the gutter, red-faced, panting and full of life.

Some kids in early teens galloped over the grass strip in the middle of the road, playing a game involving the passing, on the run, of red and white balls in a rapid crossfire pattern he would have thought too complex for spontaneous sport. Their faces were intent and calculating; perhaps it was not so spontaneous.

They stopped when they saw him. He supposed that an insane Security Tech snorting like a grampus in the gutter made a break in a routine day, but he was not prepared for one boy to cross the traffic lane and approach him with grave courtesy to ask, "Are you all right, sir?"

Sir, indeed! The archaic courtesy made him uncomfortable, but though the boy might have been thirteen his expression was formidably adult, with nothing soap-opera cute about the grownupness. Jackson had said that the kids still had a childhood, and that energetic game had seemed some sort of evidence; but they had a forced life as well and the sign of it peered from this cool face. He felt constricted, unable to be outgoing, to smile; he was too conscious of appraising stares and of the pre-packaged adulthood in all of them.

He said as amiably as he could that he was all right and the boy replied with his intolerably perfect manners, "I hope I don't sound foolish, offering advice to a Security officer, but I think you should lie on your back and follow through a relaxation procedure."

It was blackly funny but Raft dared not laugh. "It's nothing; I just haven't got my g-legs back yet."

The boy caught on at once. "You're that one? I am honored to meet you." But he wasn't really surprised or impressed, merely polite. "Was it horribly boring out there?"

"No; not really." And they had nothing more to say to each other.

Jackson, you lied. The kids have been short-changed. Or is it possible you believed the nonsense you told me?

The encounter bled some splendor from the day; he walked to the edge of Town Center through a sweaty Melbourne summer, dissatisfied and depressed, until he came to the river and a memory preserved—Princes Bridge.

It was little changed—the disused tram tracks remained sunk in the surface though the overhead power lines had gone—nearly two centuries old but at last empty of packed, sounding, stinking traffic. A few bicycles crossed it, a few transport vans, a few pedestrians. When he looked over the water, to the far bank where the city towers had heaved and crowded, he wondered that anyone crossed it at all.

The new Melbourne Town had been built on the near bank, stretching south on his left over what had been a factory area. The fortress-like National Gallery still stood at its border, stark without the needle spire which had been razed for its ribs and priceless copper sheathing. The grey building brooded over the spreading, low-built heart of a lively country town.

On the other side of St. Kilda Road the complex of Domain gardens still reached down the river bank and up the hill, changed from his memory of it, replanted and redesigned, but part of his past.

Across the river—

They had destroyed it, smashed it down, taken what they wanted and left the rest in rubble, forty city blocks of shapeless and heartless trash heaps of brick and concrete, plaster and tile and splintered glass. Vaguely he had expected that the area would have been cleared, but there had been too few people and all of them too busy for the gigantic garbage operation; they had not had leisure for disposal of millions of tons of rubbish and possibly nowhere to put it. There is little to be done with a dismantled city save leave it to time.

Perhaps it was intended some day to attack the vast eyesore, for a single clear street had been left through the ruins, keeping open the road to Sydney on the north side. And two buildings remained intact; at the far end of the bridge the twin spires of St. Paul's Cathedral kept Gothic dignity, and further away the saucer dome of the Public Library

crouched like an old sea monster on the skyline. Some remembering Ombudsman had insisted that not all the past
be destroyed, that something must remain to speak of origins, and they had allowed him these.

Raft had known, as all his generation had known, that
their gluttonous, ravaging world must end, and soon, but
the cold shame of the garbage pile was more than he could
stand. There would be no crossing of the bridge to wander
amongst memories. They had seen to that.

He turned left into the new town, the little, bustling,
growing, self-satisfied country center.

He had no trouble locating the shops named on his
purchase orders and did not know that he was served by
plainclothes Security men cursing secondment as counter-
jumpers, or that everything he bought passed through a third
pair of hands which inserted what might have been fine
lengths of metallic thread invisibly into seams. He did not
yet appreciate how completely microphones and transmit-
ters—and even cameras and electronic weapons—could be
miniaturized in almost any form by technicians with access
to a force-fed, information-hunting technology.

He was unsure of the conventions governing the startling
personal tastes around him and settled for familiar grey
shirt and shorts for immediate wear. Then they packed up
his uniform and the rest of his purchases for delivery to the
barrack and left him to wander.

In the street he was lonely; he needed someone sharing
common attitudes. His submerged worry for Lindley surfaced briefly, but you don't kidnap in order to kill out of
hand, and in this day torture had been superseded. The concern languished because it could not lead to action, but it
troubled his depths.

What could teach him most in the shortest time? The
man who had lived eight years without knowledge of the
world took minutes to recall a simple fact of life, the newspaper. He had not seen one in the barrack; it was a typical
arrogance that Security, with its sophisticated information
sources, paid little heed to a public press it assumed could
only be less well informed than itself.

Where to get it? In this main street, shop-lined and
busy with bicycles and pedestrians, he had not seen a rec-

ognizable news agency or a newsboy or a news stall. He was a hick from the stars who did not know civilized usage.

Covertly he scanned people, as if one face might tolerate his ignorance more than another, and realized what had been subliminal before—that most of them recognized him. He had been photographed by what he had assumed to be news cameras on the day of arrival, and forgotten it, and these people were conscious of him—or perhaps they merely noted the remarkable likeness to a known public figure; in any case they neither stared nor flicked glances but with universal politeness left him his privacy. It did nothing to soothe his diffidence; he was still the new boy at school, fearful of unknown codes.

Gathering bravado he fixed on the oldest man in sight, still younger than himself. And was stopped by a familiar voice. "Lost something, Commander?"

It was the waiter from the barrack dining-room, dressed today in simple white shirt and kilt, Joe who had shown a flash of curiosity on the night Jackson died and thereafter remained the self-effacing steward, Joe unexpectedly friendly with his smile and touch on the shoulder.

Raft was instantly alert, perhaps unreasonably—and perhaps reasonably in the land of smooth surfaces and jagged depths. He said, "I think it's me I've lost somewhere in the last forty years."

He guessed Joe would be seventeen, like dozens of those hallucinated kids questioned after the raid. He had heard that the boy studied as a major subject something not quite graspable in the application of cryogenics to molecular information storage; his work in the barrack was a scholar-duty which helped pay for (or perhaps simply justify, in the hair-fine ethical reasoning of the day) his tutoring. Physically he was tallish and muscular, which seemed typical of the youngsters; the second generation had not starved, and Raft felt that their physical well-being had been cherished with dedication.

He saw, with a sense of discovery, that the new generation was a special entity and recognized as such, almost a separate species. No one spoke of kids or youngsters but of *the* kids and *the* youngsters, referring to a defined group within the body of society but also beyond it. He recognized the force of the unspoken consensus that tomorrow belonged to the new generation; the first cobbled together a basic world for the second to shape and develop. Even self-contemplating Security understood that; it was too well understood to require emphasis and until this moment had not touched his mind.

Joe was saying, "That's too much to lose; can I help you look?"

And if the new generation had been raised in the knowledge that they were the heirs not of the past but of the future . . . why, there would not be a generation gap, that familiar cleavage of all history, but a monstrous gulf between an old species and its created new . . .

No, not that . . . between the royal children and their wet-nurse adult servants.

"What's up, Commander?"

Adrift in thought he had lost sight of the object thought upon. "It just hit me for the twentieth time that everything that seems familiar isn't." Lie. It had hit him for the first time that his days in the new world had been spent among its expendable builders; for understanding of who and what and where he would have to move among tomorrow's world owners. Such as Joe; such as those polite and forbidding children. "Tell me where I can buy a newspaper."

"What's that? Perhaps we call it something else."

"The printed news of the day."

"That! It's called the daysheet."

He seemed to have amused Joe, who for a moment looked-happily cunning.

"Over here, Commander." He tripped a lever and a folded paper dropped from a wall slot. "Fresh edition morning and evening." He presented it to Raft with exaggerated ceremony. "If that's the sort of thing you want.

"How would I know? No charge? Government printed?"

"Is that bad?"

"Do you think so, Joe?"

"Of course it is. In your day, with a free press——"

"Balls. What would you know? Competitively produced

news is not necessarily more accurate than censored news, only more detailed. And mostly slanted, with owners playing politics.''

He had upset the boy. ''We've thought the commercial press to be one of the good things you had.''

''Who's 'we'?''

Perhaps Joe really did not hear the question. He said carefully, ''You'll find what's printed there completely truthful—but not complete.''

''News is suppressed?''

''I wouldn't put it like that, but the administration has ideas about what matters and what doesn't and some of us have other ideas.''

''I care about ideas. Where do I get both sides?''

He had asked an absolutely right question; the boy's reaction was fleeting but unmistakable. ''From the letter sheets. Of course you have to pay for those.''

Raft laughed. ''*Samisdat!*''

''What?''

''Secret press.''

But he had misunderstood; twentieth-century modes and associations had no precise counterparts here. ''There's nothing secret about it. People in a position to pick up more information than the daysheet gives, put out their own info-sheets. I suppose their version isn't always right either but at least you get a broader picture.''

''Can you get me some of those letter sheets?''

''Of course.''

''So, if I read this first—what did you call it?''

''We call it the shit sheet.''

''Who do?'' But Joe had stepped away saying, ''I'll get some for you; won't be long,'' and joined the crowd while Raft stared after him. The meeting had not been fortuitous; his attention had been caught and directed to a specific aspect of daily life and he had, perhaps, been alerted. But to what?

At least he had made contact with the inheritors of the Earth. Or they with him? Or—stretching it further—was he now in touch with whatever Gangoil might have become now that the mysterious Lady's day was done?

Meanwhile he could read the paper.

*   *   *

There were seats under trees, islands in grass, garden strips and spaces between buildings. The trees were young, planted with love for a long tomorrow; new Melbourne Town was designed to be green through generations. But so had the old. *Good luck to your dreams*, he thought without great confidence and chose a blazing jacaranda for shade while he discovered what constituted news in a quiet country town where drugged teenagers murdered and abducted and the forces of law and order discussed the ethical problems involved.

The daysheet reminded him of an army bulletin, though marginally more straightforward in style. As for the contents——

He sought mention of Gangoil, but there was no mention of Gangoil, or of The Lady or of the attempt on *Columbus*.

It took him some time to locate anything at all in the nature of news of actual physical happenings; the front page contained a verbatim account of caucus discussion of a request from the PM's Ombudsman for reconsideration of certain provisions of the Universal Superannuation Bill. An editorial tailpiece argued vigorously that some system of evaluating and recompensing the more productive lives be sought. Perhaps the debate was hot news among the lizard-blooded survivors of plague and disaster.

The headlines featured nothing sensational in the terms of his own day but on an inside page he came on a column of brief references to ongoing events, and there found three items, widely separated, with no indication that they were related: eighteen more members of the Raft clone had been located and were being questioned regarding their origin. The Controller of Police had offered evidence (Raft imagined Parker's stone-faced irony as he offered it) that the computer-census system was imperfectly programmed. Teenagers involved in the recent hypno-drug riots were still being treated and sources of drug supply were being tightly scrutinized.

That such a story could be played down into a few passing references told him more of the conditions—and conditioning—of this era than any amount of journalistic outburst. As for the morality of news suppression . . . well, they saw things differently, and he could scarcely grasp their point of view at all.

Curiously, he searched for reports of crime. He did not believe they had crime tied up to the point where human nature rested content. Did the Jacksons and Parkers imagine that new descriptive terms erased the facts?

They didn't; not quite. Search located another short column of notices about individuals; he read, in order, of a minor theft, some evasion of duties whose significance eluded him, two suicides (both teenagers, he noted) and seven—he counted again—seven cases of violence involving serious bodily harm, *all* initiated by teenagers.

All that in one quite brief column, with the duty evasions receiving most attention. The suicides and assaults were dismissed in minimum wordage, little more than announcements that so-and-so was dead by his own hand and someone else had run amok. The lack of emphasis intrigued him, together with the absence of indication that seven cases of extreme violence in one day in so small a community was unusual.

His view of the new world shifted for the nth time as he considered violence among the people who looked forward to the Earthly paradise, and felt it might shift more drastically yet when he talked again with Joe——

—whose voice spoke cheerfully in his ear. "Wasn't long, was I? There's a spider on your neck. Hold still; I'll get it."

Fingers moved round his shoulder, fiddling with the shirt collar, and a second pair of hands plucked at the seams from the other side. He turned his head to see Joe's face. The boy winked and brushed a finger lightly against the starman's lips.

"Got it, Peter?"

"Yes; only a little one but quite a flycatcher in its way."

Peter's voice hinted at sub-text, second meaning. Joe wrote rapidly on a pad while he said, "This is Peter Shand. He wants to talk about Barnard's Star, which ought to make you happy because nobody else does."

Raft nodded perfunctorily, his eyes on the pad. Peter said that his field was electronics but he was developing an interest in astronomy as a sideline; there were questions regarding the orbit of the two major companions of the star . . .

Raft answered him genially while he read: "Peter is a miniaturization expert. Did you know your new clothes are bugged?"

He shook his head, furious, but not halting his exposition of orbital peculiarities. The note continued, "Probably only a trace."

He grabbed the pad and wrote, "No. I'm probably decoy." It had occurred to him immediately and he was disgusted by Colley's deviousness; it had to be Colley.

But while Peter talked amiably, Joe wrote, "Campion wouldn't do that to you."

Raft said aloud, "Oh yes, he would." And let electronic ears make what they could of that. He was thinking that no matter how the daysheet separated cause and effect, Joe knew his facts and implications. But Joe possibly had special opportunities.

And Joe was scribbling, "But he's your family."

So there were those who knew what the word meant. Just the same—He snatched the pad and wrote, "Where did you hear that?" He grabbed the boy by the wrist and closed the grip until the boy panted with pain, unable to find words which would pass the filter of the microphone.

And Peter talked with strident clarity. "Then there's the matter of interface. Is there a true definition between solid surface and atmosphere?" He bent close, projecting meaning. "There would seem to be a sphere of indecision, where you might say matter hadn't made up its mind what it should be."

Raft evaluated honesty. The youngsters wanted from him something that was less than loyalty to Security's *status quo*. And Peter—or somebody behind Peter—had read him with formidable insight. He nodded and released Joe who massaged his wrist, sore but not otherwise upset.

Raft said, "A state of flux, perhaps, like a man unsure what attitude he should adopt." It seemed obvious, but spur of the moment double-talk was not easy; he covered, clumsily it seemed to him: "But let's not anthropomorphize too much; there's no place for man on a gas giant. It's like this new age of yours—I see interfaces everywhere but I'm damned if I understand them."

Peter was quick. "Social interfaces?"

"Between Security and police, between services and civilians, between the generations. Even, I think, between childhood and youth."

Joe stopped rubbing his wrist. "Natural divisions; they always were, weren't they?"

"Here they're more like rifts."

Peter said with heavy irony, "This is the era of organized rifts. Each man has his place, his assured progress and a more or less ordained end. Society runs on sets of parallel tracks, exchanging signals but not visiting crosstrack. The rifts are ethical; one just does not impress himself on what another does."

"If the other does wrong?"

"Who decides right and wrong?"

"So, if another country were determined on your destruction you could not ethically do a thing about it?"

"Oh, we keep a service staff to look after that sort of nonsense. You know—Security."

He hoped somewhere a listening ear burned. If open ridicule was passable, what would secure action? "What if people don't agree with Security's handling of a problem?"

"They make a fuss and sometimes Security gets told by World Council to go stuff itself."

"Often?"

Peter said regretfully, "No. The truth is that Security, within its charter, is pretty good."

Joe broke in on him. "That bloody charter! We can't learn by mistakes because we aren't allowed to have the problems. International affairs are governed by an international ethic enforced by an armed Security. It works, and that's what's wrong. It makes life good for anybody who doesn't give a damn so long as he is left alone. We're guided; we don't evolve."

Raft felt Peter's hand at his nape, pressing the shirt collar firmly against his flesh while the boy spoke quickly. "I have the mike muffled. Some of us want to talk to you privately, to tell you things nobody else will. And we need help. If you agree nod your head, and Joe will arrange a meeting later.''

His hand dropped away; he stood back, smiling; a watcher might have thought he had told a joke.

It was sudden but not altogether unexpected. Raft remembered that young enthusiasms could spill over into violent and dangerous nonsense; there could be risk. But he was being offered knowledge, the unrefusable bait. With brain and muscle and the backing of Security, he thought, he could disengage at any time.

He nodded.

Peter, without visible reaction, led talk back to Barnard's Star while Raft wrote: ''Who said we were family?''

They bent over it, making public play of discussion, and Joe scratched quickly, ''Ears everywhere even in barrack.''

It was evasion, but if his suspicions were facts the whole answer would be complicated and they couldn't play for ever at exchanging technical diagrams in public.

Joe's mode of delivering a private message proved mildly breathtaking. During dinner at the barrack he made opportunity to stop by Raft's table and said, ''That old place on Princes Highway is still there so the bus drivers say. You want to have a look at it in the morning?''

Impudent, naïve, or just a matter of knowing what he could get away with? ''Yes, I'd like to see what's left of it.''

''All of it; that area hasn't been axed yet. I'll pick you up after breakfast.''

''OK.'' Joe moved off. The two Techs eating at the table looked politely interested. One asked, ''Nostalgia trip?''

''A place where I lived as a child.''

It was enough answer.

But there were not yet answers enough for Raft. He fancied Gangoil behind the two boys, using them in its fashion of remote control to ease him gently out of Security's clasp. It was not wholly fantasy or wilful stretching of coincidence; John would be reaching for him now that the power of The Lady was broken away from the clone.

—2—

Colley put together a hasty report on the reasons why the crew of *Columbus* could not be reached. Some of these experimental societies, he thought, showed barely civilized aspects; one could only hope they would fail.

Campion could show only facial expression still. What he felt as he read the barbaric account demanded the nervous capability of his whole body—confined, he felt that he loosened, sundered, collapsed inwardly. The staggering run downhill which had begun when Jackson asked, "Do you think your world is so different?" was completed in a repellent vision of the societies he lived to perpetuate. His stirring consciousness of a life of programed naïvety perceived with dread what Raft would demand—and which imprinted honesty insisted—he should do.

Colley, expecting bursting anger, did not understand the signs of despair; he took back the report from the eye-level reading rack, asking, "What now?"

Campion's eyes followed the disgusting paper. "I'll tell him. Somebody must. That report makes the thing worldwide; World Security Council will have to move."

He knew it would not as certainly as he was convinced that it should. If it did so, he could believe again.

Colley cut down the faint hope. "No. I queried it with the Gen Sec; no country has lodged complaint, so the ethic stands."

"That!"

His tone set Colley's training and dedication reacting visibly to internal alarms, and he unleashed the angry grin that identified him so closely with Raft. Colley would be tested much farther before he reached the end of this insight and tumult. "What will you say if I suggest that the ethic is outmoded, narrow and unpliable and may yet be the destruction of us all?"

Colley's hesitation stretched interminably but it was at last the trained, unshockable operator who answered "That such a doubt should be referred to the Ombudsman."

"Who is dead and will not be replaced, even for the preservation of training-manual psychology. And to jolt your wonderment, it was Jackson who implanted the thought I offered you. Now what?"

Colley sweated; Campion had not thought the man would be so easily reduced. The answer when it came was predictable: "That you are a sick man and should not have insisted on retaining control. You should rest." His eyes were hunted. "Rest completely."

There would be little rest, and fate could be tempted now as well as later. "Why then, you should report me to Psychlinic."

Colley dropped his eyes, spread his hands, made a naïve and monstrous business of his acute discomfort and said a thing Campion could never have dreamed of hearing from him. "No. I have always had a special loyalty to you—a private loyalty as well as duty." He shook his head as if incomprehensions might fly off in drops. "You must rest. Get over this."

He left abruptly. Campion repressed an impulse to call him back, to talk endlessly about the explosion in his mind. Colley's declaration amounted to upheaval and outburst. Security men rarely made friends of Security men; they existed together in a wholeness of comprehension which contained much of dependence, even admiration, but little of love; they were brought up together, taught together, guided together to share the ideal that could make them as merciless to each other as to an enemy when the ethic demanded. Yet there must be other Colleys whose efficient exteriors disguised the fact that they were men as well as——

As what?

Robots?

Yes—robots. A good word for all of us.

A disorganized Colley had forgotten to retrieve his report. It lay on the side table, shredding and eroding the ethic which had dictated it, its content forcing Campion at last beyond simple acceptance of his orderly world.

While he felt, through the frustration and anger, that his mind had been liberated he knew that technically, as Psychlinic would see it, his indoctrination had broken. He floated at a stress point of conflicting emotions, facts and duties.

So he was momentarily stampeded by the entrance of a Raft all smiling evil over cold rage—an enemy. But he was not a frightenable man and the reflections of the past hours had called upon powerful moral courage, and when Raft towered over him, a big man enlarged by anger, he had a swift thought: *Is this me also, terrifying people with fury?* Another part of his conception of the man Campion was cracked and dislodged.

Raft put his back to the door; no one was coming in until he had finished. He stated rather than asked, "You've seen the report!" in a voice challenging Campion to comment on his own damnation. "Your shopkeepers must have been bloody expert to bug the stuff as fast as I ordered it."

He had not been prepared for this minor item and could not take it seriously, but if the bugs had been detected honesty would cost nothing. "How did you find out?"

"I was told."

That was no minor item. Campion thought distractedly of renegade Techs, of Security penetrated by Gangoil. "By whom?"

He expected refusal to answer but not the question that came instead.

"Do you care?"

It collapsed him back to contemplation of loyalty and double dealing and the unanswerable questions of honesty and intention. He said dully, "Yes, I care, but not in the way I did. Or not about the same things." He gazed blankly at Raft. "I think that's it."

Raft's paternal feelings, indistinct at best, were in recess; a little of the waiting anger was released in jeering. "Do you care that I am probably to be kidnapped tomorrow?" Campion's head jerked. "You should. Wasn't it the sort of play you let me loose for? Well, it will be with my connivance and how does that fit you?"

Campion replied automatically, "You'll be protected; I'll not have you endangered." The rest reached him slowly. "*Your* connivance? You want it?" He shed his surprise, knowing why Raft wanted it. The starman had seen one side of the contest; now he wanted to see the other side, and choose. Campion also would like to see, without the blinkers of a lifetime, if it were not too late for that to be possible. But whatever he saw, he was not in a position to choose . . .

Was he not? It was an extraordinary and terrifying question, postulating nothing less than the rejection of Security and his whole past life. It was a fantasy question, of course.

But was it, was it?

Meanwhile Raft stared at him as at an idiot and he must make some effort.

"How do you know about this? There was nothing in the surveillance report."

"The setup was put to me this afternoon right under your microphone's listening ear."

Somebody had been clever or somebody in Security had been stupid. But, of course—"The two boys! Trust the kids to come up with something impudent." Almost he admired them, but he asked anxiously, "Were they under hypno?"

"Not so far as I could tell."

"At close quarters you couldn't miss it—but they're only little fish who'll know no more than that useless clone. And remember that Gangoil wanted you dead."

"Not Gangoil, only The Lady. And fancy you remembering, after you sent me out bugged to the eyebrows as Albert the Bait."

"Nobody will kill you; there will be protection every minute."

Raft used contempt as a hammer. "When a death is decided upon there is no protection. And why must it be Gangoil? There are other subversive elements on your ethical chessboard—such as the *samisdat* kids."

"The what?"

"The kind who run underground newspapers because official versions don't match the truth, or supposedly 'uninteresting' items go unreported, or properly ethical explanations of bashings and criminality don't satisfy some inquiring minds."

"The kids are always cutting up, but that's an internal government matter; we can't take an interest." And with that the matter of unrest among the youngsters fell into place with all the seething pieces of inner questioning; theirs was one of the points of view he must pursue more deeply than the cant phrase "generation gap" allowed.

What did they see that his training barred from his view?

"You should." Raft jeering again. "They're asking information about the ideas this kindergarten planet has forgotten, the facts and ideas your well-intentioned Ombudsmen censored out of sight so that only pretty thoughts should flower. They need a referee of their own, someone who wasn't here for the rule-making and sees the game more clearly than the players can."

Referee Albert? It was the sort of thing bright and pushing kids might dream up. Campion said, "You could be right," while his thinking stretched a long arm into speculation on problems of right and wrong, indoctrination and uncertainty . . . until Raft bent over him, asking, "What's up with you? You aren't with me."

His anger had ebbed but Campion did not doubt it was at hand if required; Raft was that sort of player. And there was a note of inquiry under his jeering. "Have I got through at last? Has love-in-a-mist realized that you can't run a world like a schoolroom?" Campion looked at him through rising emotional exhaustion and the eyes inches from his own seemed at last to grasp something of his mental condition. Raft asked, roughly but reasonably, "What's wrong?"

It was Campion's moment to take a step in the dark but he did not know the way. He wanted to make clear his deep trouble but had never learned how to make appeals of any kind. In ignorance, feeling desperate and ashamed, he took the one course that could succeed, and said very simply because he knew no better, "Help me, Grandad."

Raft's face receded as he stood to full height, looking down at him with calculation and dawning approval and distrust and some other indefinable intensity, all kaleidoscopic and unhidden. He took Campion's chin in his fingers and raised the immobilized Commissioner's face to the light. "All right, son. If I can."

It was unsentimental, a concession, not a capitulation.

Campion knew he was still on trial. He had achieved something intangible that he did not know how to use. He was unreasonably certain that Raft was uniquely placed to be his confidant, but—Why should consanguinity (and the sharing of blood was a damned silly distortion of fact) constitute a bond?

And Raft was watching him quizzically, in the half-jovial fashion himself might offer to some youngster making a youthful mountain out of some molehill trouble. Offended pride saw it as Raft's attitude not only to him but to his whole struggling era.

"You continually question our values." He heard and resented the slight whine in his voice. "Now I'm having to question them also."

From a man of his training that was a bombshell admission; reaction should have been instant and powerful; less had come close to breaking Colley. Raft only scratched ruminatively at an ear, leaving him speechless with the great clog of ideas and events to be sorted before they could cross his tongue. He needed help even to explain himself.

Raft asked, "Something has happened? Today?"

"Not only today; it began before that." He explained painfully what Jackson had asked him of his certainties of this best of all possible worlds.

Raft commented unfeelingly, "It didn't take much to set you rocking."

"From an Ombudsman—a world-builder throwing doubt on his creation—it shook me badly." He frowned as another aspect appeared. "Particularly because it was Jackson. I suppose there must have been——" he had to search for unaccustomed words precisely fitting "——affection. A bond."

"They really did a job of training on you, didn't they?"

He had not expected so swift a plunge through inessentials; he went on eagerly, "Did you know that all the operative Techs, the decision makers, are all orphans, parents unknown or dead? We—I didn't realize it but our training started when we were five or six and we grew up unquestioningly as a Security group." The frown reappeared briefly. "But I have no feeling of being apart from the rest of life. Should I?"

"There was a saying attributed to the Jesuit priesthood: 'Give us the child at six and he's ours for life.' Or something like that."

"They may have been better at it, but my conditioning

has been pierced and I'm lost." From a religious man the tone of the final word would have meant "damned."

Raft leaned forward, projecting authority. "Or found. We don't have to mumble it over like half-wits, so talk about today. What happened?"

Grandad was not interested in confessional, only in results. Grandad would make a good Tech, who would reward training by boring at the beams and joists until the structure of Security collapsed. And why not? No, no . . . too far, too fast. He said quickly, "Your transworld calls failed. You'll get none of them."

Bluntness earned only a shadow movement, a heightening of attention. And one word. "Why?"

"Many reasons. For instance, Doctor Kulayev——"

"Pete. What about him?"

"The Kremlin has him."

"Kremlin? Wasn't it destroyed, during the Five Days?"

Yes, of course; it had been the name of a palace or fortress or some such. "The Kremlin is the Central Russian Committee of Political Interdependence. Most of European Russia split into a loose union of areas with the central district round old Moscow having a sort of spiritual hegemony."

"Communism was given to eating its children. What has it done to Pete?"

"Not communism. The centers of communism are America in hard politics and, we think, China in an idealistic form. Russia returned to the cultist simplicity which was so strong before her revolution." He added uneasily, "The rest of the world isn't much taken with Christianity, but you'll know how intransigent a religious community can be."

"Meaning, how brutal."

"Yes. And that it tends to be centralist, all-powerful. The Kremlin controls everything within the state, including most strongly the sciences. They think Kulayev may have knowledge of the cloning procedure."

"He hasn't."

"But they suspect, and with them that makes it fact until proven otherwise. And cloning is a crime—an intrusion upon the prerogatives of God. Kulayev has been under question.''

''His ignorance would show up at once.''

Campion licked drying lips. ''Not every country is technically advanced to the same level in the same direction. How could they be? The Kremlin's psychology is—primitive.''

A frozen voice told him, ''Go on.''

''Doctor Kulayev collapsed under question; he is insane.''

''Ah.'' A stillness. At last, ''Can you get him out and cure him?''

''Security cannot interfere on behalf of an individual unless he claims sanctuary.''

The unbelieving stare crucified Campion and all his organization. Raft stepped back until a chair caught his legs, and sat heavily. ''Tell me, did an Ombudsman set up that region?''

''No Ombudsman ever set up any region; his function is only to guide for the best what is already there. Ombudsmen are human; they come in all colors of genius and error.''

''They should be got rid of!'' Campion could only be silent before the sound of his own emerging belief, but Raft was not waiting on reply. ''Ivan, then. Is he also under the protection of the Lord?''

''His area is not under Kremlin hegemony. The message received is that he does not wish to speak to you, that after forty-two years there is nothing left to say.''

''I don't believe that.''

''Nor do we, but we have not been able to discover much. His home area has become allied with what once was Poland, and I think the Poles had some enmity against the Kremlin in your day. Does this make sense?''

''Yes.''

''They reacted vengefully against communism at the Collapse. And it seems Doctor Doronin was a staunch Marxist. I'm not sure what that meant——''

''I am. Go on.''

''Aside from any digging for suspected knowledge of the cloning procedures, we suspect he is being re-educated.''

"Brainwashed."

"Was that your word? It's expressive. The Poles are technically better at such things than the Kremlin; they are not hampered by the conviction that they know the will of God, and that leaves room for compassion. When Doronin reappears he will be unharmed but changed in his views."

"Induced changes were never permanent."

"Techniques have changed. He will conform or die."

"And you benevolent watchdogs can't interfere. Christ, but what use are you!"

Campion dared not answer that; he was no longer sure his organization had ever had a use. And Raft was leaping ahead of him. "And you let commie-hating Ewan Matthews go back to communist America!"

Campion shuddered. "New York Soviet claimed him and their right was legal."

"So long as it's an internal matter any pack of bastards can do as they please!"

Campion heard himself uttering the indoctrinated litany: "People make their political choice and the ethic is non-interference unless mass right is infringed."

"*Shit!* Stop it! What happened to Ewan?"

"He left on a New Yorker plane. The story is that over the Pacific he discovered he was going to a communist state and became violent and was shot for the safety of the crew and passengers. He was dead on arrival. It might be true."

"Or?"

"He may be alive, being questioned about cloning. All of them will be intensely questioned about that."

"They know nothing. That leaves little Joe. What happened to him? Fell under a truck? Was eaten by lions?"

Campion answered wearily, "They say Streich was kidnapped by persons and nationality unknown. As a biologist who lived so long with you he will be considered valuable property for any government."

Raft spoke like a man leaping. "You can act on that. Violation of private rights."

"We are searching, but we think the kidnapping was a cover story, a devious beginning to keeping him out of sight. But the important matter remains here, with us." He burst out, "It was our own stupidity that let the cloning story on to the world's newscasts. We didn't anticipate the hunger in them all—the need to have the process for themselves. What do they want? Imperial power?" He said miserably, "I suppose Stephen would have prevented it, covered it up, but he never had the chance. We've been very innocent, haven't we, trusting to an ethic to overcome the savagery of men?"

"What do you think the great religions were all about? Your Security is just another goddamned religious failure because you poor bastards were never given the chance to realize anything but your own holier-than-thou destinies. It doesn't matter what you do now because the cloning process is a fact; discovered once it can and will be discovered again. You're helpless."

At last Campion was on surer ground. "Not if we locate Gangoil before Parker does. Bringing him in was a blunder, but it's done now. If Security holds the process then Security can have it declared a prohibited activity and police it. And believe me we can police effectively when we have a free hand. If Parker finds them first, then the PM has it and we can do nothing until some connected activity infringes the rights of other nations."

Raft's contempt was a snarl. "What could your PM do with the knowledge? Create supermen? That's what all these scrambling kidnappers and questioners have in mind—superman and super-specialized man. John, damn his stupidity, approached his work with reverence; he also meant to create supermen, but he was ready to stand aside and see the new race take over. These political power grabbers will think they can build the new race in the laboratory and then control it. Tiger riders!"

That was the crux of the matter. Campion began to see what must be done for the best and it appalled him. He was afraid of what was needed and called on anger to force him towards it. "Save the prophecies! What is happening is happening now!"

The answer snapped back as if this moment had been awaited, as if Raft with his disruptions had been grooming him for it.

"Security can preserve the *status quo* or let it evolve. It has the weaponry to take over the world and perhaps the prestige to make the move acceptable—for a while; that way it could control everything it feared and the sheep would love it. But there are wolves in the forest and they'll chew your bones in the end. Alternatively, Security can dissolve itself and let the world go its way in blood and brutality and whatever beauty it can salvage when Nanny stops telling it what to like and dislike. And that's probably what it wants when its conditioning wears thin."

"Back to the twentieth century!"

"Further back. Because you've changed nothing, only confined the smell. Evolution doesn't mean the survival of the nicest or the most moral or the prettiest—only the most adaptable. Man won't kill himself off; his first try has failed but put the fear of holy hell into him. A little barbarism may be next in line—a Dark Age of high technology and moral ruin."

"Yes."

Raft studied him. "I think you mean that."

"I do."

"But Security——" He shook his head. "You people are too firmly settled; you won't budge until the world destroys you."

Campion chafed against his immobility; he needed gesture, emphasis, as he said, "This world can go to its useless end. But the youngsters, Albert, the kids . . ."

He began to talk of the ideas weltering in his mind and Raft listened with an incredulity that the man could have come so far in his perception in so short a time. He talked mainly of new powers newly directed to new beginnings until there seemed no end to his urge to clear and reshape and rebuild.

Suddenly it became too much. Raft, with all his pinprickings come to a head, had more than enthusiasm on his hands; it was an outpouring of dammed-up fanaticism.

"Ian, boy, I don't want you dead! They'll rack and burn you! Easy, easy, until you see clearly."

Campion did not argue; Raft had said, "my beloved son," and he saw the meaning fully. He did not care if he were for a time a little mad; there is a place for that too.

But Raft persisted; he had wanted to sow ideas, not to inaugurate a crusade.

Why then, Raft would have to stand by the results of his urgings. His mind was made up and he did not want to listen to reason just yet. He was glad when an interruption put an end to their talk.

The wall speaker announced Controller Parker downstairs, wishing to speak with Commander Raft.

"Perhaps he's found Gangoil."

Campion's eyes sparkled. "It doesn't matter now."

"It matters. Everything matters. Get the stars out of your eyes, boy! Our family doesn't have the stuff that makes evangelists."

No? Raft would learn.

—3—

Heathcote possessed a gun. This unlikely property was probably the only lethal weapon in Gangoil, if one discounted the Bitch's collection of romantically jeweled daggers filched from round the world.

He kept the abominable thing because it was connected vaguely with Albert, belonging to a memory sequence not yet restored, one of the sequences of no importance to David and his mind-fornicators; all they wanted was the detail, down to the last flush of thought, of his experimental and theoretical work so that no nuance should go unexplored in their basement of miracles. That he, old and young and incomplete, wanted his life returned was of no moment

The gun must once have belonged to Albert, he supposed, to wrong-headed, loved and angry Albert. And now dead Albert. For whose killer hell would gape.

Old John opened the drawer occasionally but he never touched the gun.

Young John, however, was not settled into prejudice and aged fastidiousness. He took it out occasionally, appreciating it for a beautiful thing in its repellent way. His imperfect memory could not recall any weapon like it in what he thought of as the "Albert period" of earlier life (and did not too often think of because Old John would obtrude doddering emotionalism) but the connection with Albert dated it.

It was not an ordinary gun. It was long-barrelled, like the Mausers which he did remember, and had a blade fore-sight and a ring rearsight but, inexplicably, no range slide. It was much thicker in the barrel than the fifteen-millimeter bore required. Set in the circle of the muzzle was an an-nulus of what seemed to be soft iron, but the main portion was, he felt sure, aluminum. Which was ridiculous. And the bore was unrifled, which was more ridiculous still.

So, possessing as it did a bulbous but hand-fitting butt, the thing was grossly unbalanced; such a weapon must be nearly recoilless if it were to hit anything aimed at, but he had never tested it, any more than he had fiddled with the unusual group of thumbcatches set in the butt.

He was innately scared of weapons. At most he would lift the little monster from its drawer, using both hands in cradle, and deposit it carefully on the writing slide of his rolltop desk—and look at it, admiring beautiful workman-ship and revolted by the implications of murder.

He did not wish to know its secrets. If he learned how, he would undoubtedly kill Her; he, most civilized of men, would join the brutes.

He extended a finger, pushing it round to view it from another angle, mourning and wondering how it had come to him and what was its connection with dead Albert . . .

. . . when a voice spoke behind him, "Fancy you keeping that all this time."

His hands flew to his mouth in an old man's gesture of shock and the breath drew sharply in his suddenly old throat.

Lindley—the starman bringer of death news—reached past him, took up the little monster in his right hand, cra-dling the barrel on his left forearm, applying his eye to the ring-sight, saying, "It's a sweet thing, the last word in side-arms," laying it down again, smiling with a wolf's happi-ness, saying, "A breath of yesterday; something from home."

Old Heathcote whimpered, "What are you doing here? It was unmannerly to enter unannounced."

The wolf said, "I didn't want to be announced. This call is private."

"You are no gentleman! Sir, to invade———" He could not go on; he was dimly terrified that the gun's existence must now become public knowledge.

The wolf took him by the shoulders, shaking, shaking. "Come to your senses! Bring the young John forward!"

Old John could only gape in anger and fear.

"Listen, if there's a brain in your mixture of heads. Albert is not dead. The news was premature. He is alive."

Old John fainted.

Heathcote's split-personality problem, Lindley mused as he applied the conventional slapping of cheeks and rubbing of wrists, lay in thinking that he was still himself, which was at least a sprightly variation on the classic definitions. Complicated by an ingrown identification with Victoriana it presented a case which might make a famous monograph despite modern computerized psychology. After all, he could bring to it a background authenticity unique in this century . . .

Young John pushed him away and sat up. "Sorry I made a fool of myself; you shocked me while personality confusion was ascendant." He stood, dusting himself finically, still primly precise in his youthful version. "It is difficult to realize always that I am not John Heathcote but only contain him. Or much of him, not all. Are you sure?"

"Of Albert? Quite sure. David should have told you."

Heathcote turned suspicious. "Have you talked with David? He is an evil man. And tells me nothing. I am only a memory-transfer experiment, a guinea-pig caged and fed. Not talked to."

With his eyes on the gun Lindley said, "He's not so bad. Too dedicated perhaps, but at least he's not out to rule the world and he has some protective feeling for his staff."

Young Heathcote snapped, "Who would wish to rule the idiotic planet? Even the Bitch did not really want that; she wanted the forms—adulation and wealth and choice of men; ruling would have bored her and exposed her incompetence."

"She tried to take over Melbourne Town and through it Australia."

Heathcote waved a dismissive hand. "She's pathologically romantic. The Francis catamite has told me something of the Melbourne Town matter." He made a furious parenthesis, "I am reduced to such informants for the most everyday news!" and returned to the subject: "Someone formed the foolish plan and she embraced it as she would the plot of a romantic novel, seeing herself as Semiramis or Joan of Arc. Vanity engulfs her."

"It could have succeeded."

"What an extraordinary idea! But she taught the clone their insane philosophy which is beyond my power to reverse——"

"No. You did."

Heathcote gabbled, inarticulate in refusal and reproach, stammering down to a breathless, pleading, "No!"

Lindley wondered if these lapses into aged helplessness were not a useful diversion the personalities had worked out between them. "The clone say you taught them; I've spoken with some here though they are not very willing to talk. To them you are the god who created and taught them."

Heathcote gazed silently, stricken.

"But it occurs to me that you've been some twenty years a-growing and had become senile before that, so the clone you taught were at best teenagers. I think that you brought the kids up in your own tradition of goodwill and human-kindness and that the rest—the inability to recognize right from wrong, the clone arrogance and assumption of inherent superiority—were taught them later. Possibly by The Lady, serving her own cloudy ends. Or even that the boys, left without your guidance and influenced by their own uniqueness, created these ideas logically from their misunderstanding of what you taught, and credited them to you. Gods get blamed for everything, you know."

Heathcote groaned—like a Trollope hero, Lindley guessed between amusement and irritation, "I hope you are right, Doctor Lindley; God grant you are right."

Lindley wondered who was speaking. Possibly the War-den of Barchester. A change of pace was called for; he asked, "Who is The Lady, anyhow?"

Like every other whom he had asked, Heathcote shook his head. "She seems always to have been here. That memory is somewhere in my head, waiting for related information to trigger it. My brain does not contain all the synaptic cross-references of the old Heathcote's; many connections are made only by chance."

Trigger, Lindley thought; he should try a random shot. Had she created the legend of namelessness herself, guarded by the invaluable clone from being disposed of as an unproductive nuisance?

"They say you were once her lover."

The target certainly rattled. Heathcote squealed protest. "No! No! No no no! She is repellent! Vile! Who says it, Lindley? Who says it?"

"David."

"That man!" But his contempt was uncertain; the name troubled him. David was of the older brood who might have heard rumor while it was still truth.

"He doesn't strike me as a liar; at any rate, not a scandal-mongering liar."

Heathcote said mutinously, "I loathe the woman; she tried to murder Albert."

"But did you always loathe her?"

The confused eyes did not know, and Heathcote was Victorianly rigid in the habit of truth. "It could have been so. Her physical type . . . I am attracted by——" He drew his face tightly together, finding the dignified phrase, "——well-fleshed women."

From him the statement was positive pornography, with Lindley trying unsuccessfully to visualize a prim, aseptic sexual encounter. "But your memory doesn't stir?" And, if it did, a gentleman of the old school simply doesn't discuss . . .

"That will require patience. Hours pass, sleep intervenes, associations work in their own time, like dreams. Perhaps tomorrow I shall have gathered recollection from your nodal facts. And perhaps not. But tell me about Albert; those are memories I urgently wish to recover."

"He was thought dead, and lives. That's all I know."

Heathcote became imperious, not ridiculously but like a man who could call on power. "He must be brought here."

"How?"

"The clone, the clone! In concert they can achieve anything, no matter how prepared Security may be. They will *want* Albert, their clone-father. His rejection of them was traumatic."

The damned clone! "Have you spoken with them in the last few days? Has no one told you?"

"What?"

"That the clone is a spent force. Security has eighteen of them and is alive to their ideas and capabilities. And Albert works for Security, circumventing them." He said gently, "All the dreams are over. That stupid and vicious woman precipitated disaster. There is nothing left to do but bargain for terms from Security; David knows better than to trust the national politicians."

Heathcote accepted that with surprising equanimity; Lindley could not decide how much he really appreciated the crumbled situation of Gangoil, but the man frowned into his drink and said, "There were too many dreams, all vague and I suppose mostly foolish."

It was an epitaphal comment.

"What was your dream? Just Heathcotian man?"

Heathcote smiled his tired old-man smile. "Albert has many unusual capacities. His reflexes are abnormally fast and accurate—his audial and visual ranges are unusually wide—he has a natural measure of control of some autonomic functions—and his learning capacity is incredible."

Some of this Lindley had been aware of. Physical control—he had been fascinated by a pianistic ability displaying a staggering exactness of fingering and control and an equally staggering lack of musical understanding. Streich had once described him as a man who could play the Minute Waltz in thirty seconds and might as well spend the time playing scales.

Memory—exact repetition of conversation heard weeks before.

Assimilation—retirement to the library to con an area of interest, and emergence with an avalanche of facts and yet a basic indifference and no deep grasp.

Inertia—no action taken until further inaction would be destructive, the action sudden and efficient . . . and cold. As when Lindley had pointed out a degenerating situation and within days Albert had become *commander* of the ship.

Albert played with minor art forms—mini-sculpture and slapdash painting—but only played. What did he want to do? Lindley did not know. What did he want of life? He did not know that either.

The tantalizing quotation cut across his musing: "My beloved son . . ." He sensed a clue but it was too plainly a clue to mental imbalance.

Heathcote still talked—old Heathcote, it seemed, "I sent him away, Lindley. To Barnard's Star. Political blackmail—but that is an old, dead story. I did not want him here as a focus of hate when my work was finally revealed, because the father of the coming race might well be the murder object of those afraid of being supplanted. The people have no scientific vision. It was, in simple terms, a matter of isolating and strengthening genetic components, and a large experimental body was needed. Hence the clone, though eighty-three was perhaps excessive, like one's young enthusiasms. Still, if public anti-reaction occurred there would be a good chance of saving a useful number of them, and Albert's characteristics would be preserved."

Lindley considered hopelessly the contradictions possible to the human mind. Albert, love figure, must be saved even at the ends of the universe but all the other Alberts could be thrown to the dogs though each of them was in fact the first Albert. Or was he? Upbringing, environment . . .

He asked, "Are the clone only experiments to you? After all this time, un-people?"

Heathcote's forehead creased. "Intellect tells me they are human beings; to all others they are human beings, but to me . . . You see, I *know*. I made them. *Made* them, Lindley. They are simulacra, facsimiles, laboratory animals. As I am also, yet I have not the feeling for them one has for one's kind. They are works of art. If one dies, I grieve, as I might grieve for a perfect figurine dropped and broken. But I cannot love them, or care."

"But you care that the work goes on, that Heathcotian man is still in preparation."

"Is he? I don't know that. David and his brilliant young men surpassed me long ago; I have not been in the laboratories in this body except as an object of study. I don't know what new dreams they follow." He swung to childishness. "Nobody tells me anything!"

Rest ignorant a while longer. You'll know soon enough the dreams I've seen crying on their beds in the basement.

Heathcote continued crisply, assuming youth. "Albert was against my work. He held that society obeys evolutionary laws, that the varieties of man are interdependent forming a psycho-ecological web, and that interference would be disastrous. He feared for my safety much as I feared for his, but he had no alternate *Columbus* to ship out on."

Lindley picked up the monopole gun. "Is that why he gave you this? For self-protection?"

"Did he?" Heathcote's face worked; he placed his head in his hands. "I cannot force memory; there is a closing of random circuits until one gives a result. How do you know he gave it to me?"

"He told me. There was time for talk aboard the ship, we knew a lot about each other."

He hefted the gun reminiscently. It glittered, darkly murderous in the apartment's subdued light. "Only a few of these were made. Prototypes. They probably never reached production stage." He spun it and caught it. "This is the finest hand weapon ever made; powered by a tiny battery in the butt."

Heathcote stared, revolted. "A battery—after forty years?"

"It will work, now and in another hundred years. The muzzle ring is monopole iron. Squeezing the trigger powers the monopole and fires the round, which travels in the channel of a rotating monopole field. No trajectory; straight as a beam of light. Sight it and you can't miss, but I've seen Albert pepper a target from the hip at five hundred yards."

Without warning he tossed the gun to Heathcote, who put out his hands too late and fumbled it. Flushing, he bent to retrieve it gingerly in both hands.

" 'This is my beloved son,' " Lindley said. "Does that mean anything to you?"

Heathcote peered at him. "Mark, nine, seven," he said with seminary precision, "also Matthew, three, seventeen. Two separate occasions. I do not know if the repetition is coincidental or simply a matter of confusion in the disciples' memories. I doubt it is exegetically important." He put the gun on the desk. "Do you feel it might be?"

With restraint Lindley said, "Albert used the words about Ian Campion."

Heathcote pursed his lips, disapproving. "It was unlike Albert to quote scripture. He was being sardonic, of course." To Lindley's interrogative sounds he explained, "Well, he must have guessed at once who Campion is. The extreme physical duplication modified only by his daughter's auburn hair and blue eyes would have alerted him."

"A grandson?"

"With such replication? Both son and grandson. An interesting legal relationship, when you think of it." He did not seem aware of outrage.

"Are you telling me that Albert had Campion by his own daughter?"

Heathcote packed the gun deliberately into the drawer. "He knew nothing about it; he had been gone about seven years when I decided to use his sperm-bank cartridge. It was necessary, you know; she had powerful characteristics from her mother which it would have been a crime to lose from the line. The combination turned out magnificent. Raft's dominants, mated with a girl properly selected for complementary recessives, guaranteed a remarkable child." He pushed the drawer gently closed, as if the gun might snap at him. "It is a pity she died in the early years. Things were very bad, you know; even in Australia people died as the land sickened. In that chaos who would want to leave Gangoil? Yet she did; she developed great animus because she had not been informed of the mating given her. One does not give such information prematurely to a young mind still astir with prejudice and clouded viewpoint. She stole the boy—and, mother or not, it was stealing—and ran away. When eventually we located him Security already had him in the Youth Barrack and she was dead. And I was past original research. But we have always kept an eye on him, and he has done quite well in worldly terms, hasn't he?''

He felt the weight of the starman's silence and complained, ''You are not disturbed by the incest factor, surely? It is always necessary to breed back occasionally to preserve specific strains, particularly rare recessives. If you had ever bred show dogs you would know.''

Between incredulity and sick-joke laughter Lindley said, ''I'll bet the Security Commissioner will love that comparison. Psychiatric practice taught me long ago that the sentimentalist, in matters where his selfish emotions are not involved, can be depended on for solid intellectual intransigence and no mercy or care for those outside his personal circle of slop.''

Heathcote was not and never had been the gentle old dear of Raft's description; Raft, swaddled in his adolescent problems of rejection and dependence, had never been able to see him clearly and had left Earth at the time of disagreement when he might have begun to observe facts. Where his work, his personal drive was concerned, Heathcote was as capable of monstrosity as he probably was incapable of realizing it.

His reaction now was resentful disbelief, refusal to accept what he had heard, inability to combat what could not conceivably be true.

What his final response might have been Lindley never discovered because their dialogue was scattered and dissolved in a fresh sound and fury.

They scarcely heard her coming because she was barefooted, had barely a slither of warning before her bursting entrance. She came as a breaking storm, scarlet-faced and screaming, ''You miserable bastard! Give me back my boys!''

She was surely a little drunk. She was also stark naked, which seemed to be her normal condition. She carried her bulk easily, chin raised in an attitude of formidable and furious dignity, all ruined by staring eyes and distorted mouth and disordered hair. Lindley thought briefly of a regal fishwife.

''You've taken them from me and I want them! Why am

I not attended?'' She dropped, not at all contemptibly, into a crouch of dangerous aggression. "What have you told them? What lies? They are The Lady's minions. Mine, mine!''

She made preposterous noise in the confined space and Heathcote was practically liquefied with terror of her. He retreated until he was backed against the desk, bleating while she advanced on him, a screaming eagle at a rabbit. She certainly would have attacked him with her bare hands if Lindley had not spoken sharply and close to her ear.

"You're making an undignified exhibition of yourself.''

Totally concentrated, she had been unaware of him, but "undignified" caught at self-love. She paused to survey him with annihilating contempt but her hands went to her hair, poking and patting, and grotesquely over her hips to smooth an invisible gown.

"I am The Lady! Never forget it, skinny psychiatrist.''

Running feet sounded outside and two identical figures jostled through the door—Francis and Eric, if Lindley understood the color coding correctly. They flung themselves on her, one to each arm, but trying to handle her gently. She treated gentleness with unfeminine ferocity, dragging them with her as her taloned fingers reached for Heathcote.

The scientist was sure of death if she reached him and his fright burst in panic. He scrambled at the desk, dragged out the monopole gun, incontinently dropped it and groped on the floor for it, distraught and gasping. From his knees he leveled it at her, clutched ridiculously in both shaking hands, bawling in an aged cackle of despair, "Kill you, Bitch, kill you!''

The scene froze. At sight of the gun she became utterly still and terror of death broke out of her like a sweat. All her living, her unguessable years rose up to reject ending. She did not try to run or plead but stared, hypnotized, into the monopole circle.

The enemies confronted each other in abject mutual cowardice.

Francis found speech, tension squeezing from him the tones of an enraged schoolmistress. "Do put that thing down, John; you know perfectly well you won't use it. Oh, for pity's sake, Doctor Lindley, don't just stand there! Take it from him." He and his brother urged The Lady backwards to the door and a note of relieved spitefulness entered his voice. "Come on, duckie, and we'll dish up a lovely meal of tranquillizers. Enough for a week."

She went without resistance, probably not hearing him, her mind fixed on death.

Lindley took the weapon by the barrel and twitched it from Heathcote's fingers. "To fire it you must first remove the safety catch and press the battery stud." He tossed it into the drawer so casually that Heathcote cowered again in wait for an explosion.

As they shepherded The Lady out, Eric said—or it could have been Francis—over his shoulder, "The service staff really has to overwork its sense of humor round here. And even so, who's laughing?" They vanished, coaxing the dreadful woman who must be obscenely old and who had dwelt too long in an erosive haze of gratification and power.

Doctor David's face appeared in the doorway. "Some excitement? She's a thoroughgoing nuisance now she can't get her own way by calling the clone."

"Who is she?"

"I don't know. Nobody here knows. Her identity is lost in chaos and she won't tell." He did not seem happy with the subject and changed it quickly. "Forget her now; we leave for Melbourne Town in an hour; I want to be there and concealed before first light. The information is that we can pick Raft up about nine-thirty in the morning."

"Albert!" Heathcote screamed the name. "You're bringing him here?"

"If he'll come, and we think he will. He was quite a friend of yours in, um, other circumstances, wasn't he? The new look will surprise him, don't you think?"

Lindley said. "Skip the petty cruelties. I must go, Doctor Heathcote; I'll talk to you when I get back." He reached into the desk drawer, snapped down the lid of the guncase and lifted it out. "You won't need this and I just might."

Heathcote made no objection; he had retired into aggrieved sulkiness.

Lindley made no bones about hustling David out ahead of him and in the corridor said, "You've been lying, of course. You know who she is. If you didn't, sheer curiosity would have set you searching Heathcote's memory patterns until it showed.''

David ignored the accusation, asked. ''What's in that case?''

''A gun.''

David's pace slowed. The idea troubled him but after a moment he said, ''I suppose we have to accept weaponry as part of your philosophy, but don't let the clone know you have it. Where did it come from?''

''Tell me, who is The Lady?''

David hurried again, throwing over his shoulder, ''Very well, I know, but I'm not telling. You are armed, and with her so am I.''

''Armed against whom?''

David walked faster. ''Don't be impatient. She'll be more useful if she comes as a surprise.''

''To whom? Security? The government?''

But he got nothing more from the biologist.

—4—

The grey-uniformed constable said the Controller waited outside, in the car.

''Why couldn't he come in?''

The constable smiled frostily. ''He probably wishes to speak privately.''

The implication of inter-service distrust was most likely justified.

The vehicle was the first small car of its type Raft had seen, something like the sedans of the eighties but with the same blunt-ended, disconcertingly engineless appearance as the large freight and passenger buses. He knew now of the flattened rotary engines and compact storage batteries of fantastic charge but still marveled at miniature perfection.

The constable ushered him into the front seat alongside Parker, who had the wheel, and himself sat in the back. Raft, trusting Parker not at all, saw reason in the arrangement and prepared for the unexpected and unpleasant.

"Civilian clothes," Parker noted, without greeting. "Sensible of you not to opt for extreme fashion; it wouldn't suit you."

"First steps with care. Always."

"Bugged to the neck, I suppose."

"Yes." And for once glad of it.

Parker chuckled, not nicely. "Not inside this car, Commander. You have just vanished from the listening tapes. A damper field."

"Perhaps," Raft said, testing the limits of his position, "I should leave now."

Parker flicked the gear lever and the car moved into silent passage. "You should, but if you try Constable Smith will put bullets into both your shoulders."

Down, Rover! But at least an exploratory yap: "Security would not approve of that."

"I don't give a damn about Security."

That was as menacing a statement as Raft could imagine, but he conjured a wraith of politeness to ask, "So where to now?"

Parker did not answer. The car continued straight down St. Kilda Road to Princes Bridge, where Raft had stood that afternoon and in his fashion mourned the desolation of a city, and there stopped.

The moon had not risen. On the far bank of the river a huge darkness brooded, save where the cathedral soared amazingly bathed in light. Against the night its floodlit yellow-grey stone floated in radiance, antique and warm, the three spires making their eternal demand of heaven. It was breathtaking rather than beautiful, more dramatic than reverent. And it seemed irrelevant to the time.

There he was wrong. Parker said, "Believers are spread thin these days but they preserve their church in such state as can be managed. Are you a Christian?" He made the question important.

"Probably not. I don't reject God, but is he a necessity? You can be a good man without following a metaphysical creed."

"Goodness *is* a metaphysical creed. I am a Christian. I believe in God."

The simplicity compelled belief, but was no paradox involved in Christianity linked with craft, threat, deviousness and latent cruelty? How many hecatombs had burned and screamed to the glory of God?

Parker would have had no difficulty following his thoughts. He said, "I am also a patriot—of my world as well as of my country." He turned his face to Raft; smiling. "That means I can kill without scruple." Raft did not move or speak. "I'll have truth out of you tonight, Commander, if I have to put you to limit question. Which is illegal. And then I may have to kill you. Fair warning?"

If only to bolster his shocked courage, Raft matched the smile. "Warning, at any rate."

"Then, to business. Are you a telepath?"

The question he had thought dealt with and forgotten rocked Raft's control. Parker's tenacity was lethal.

"No." He was not telepathic; he was sure of that.

Parker contemplated the yellow ember of the cathedral. Inquiring of his bloody-minded God? "I hope you are not. And a telepath probably would not have been trapped into the car. But there could be limitations of perception only you could know of—proximity, damping substances, electromagnetic interference and so on. For your sake I hope you are telling the truth. You *will* tell it."

Persistent denial would mean nothing to Parker hounding down a fear. And Parker had worse in his armory.

"But if you are not, why did you kill Doctor Fraser?"

This was so unlooked for that thought ran like a mad thing. Sooner or later it had had to come, but not from Parker. The instinctive thought of escape he dismissed instantly; he could not outrun Smith's gun and would only advertise guilt.

And Parker was saying equably, "You must keep talking, Commander. Do you know that the voice is affected by psychological fluctuations and that the most level tone includes microvariations imposed by changes in blood pressure, nervous tension, muscle flexure and so on? Or that the little thread-transceiver which seems to be somewhere round the back of your neck functions therefore as an efficient lie detector for Constable Smith's hand monitor? Not one hundred per cent reliable; these things never are; but generally dependable. So, for your life, keep talking."

Parker's gadgetry worried Raft less than the man's murderous attitude; he had only a doubtful card to play. "Kill me," he said, "and lose everything you hope to gain."

Unexpectedly Smith supported him. "He means that. Comes up very steady."

Parker studied Raft with dislike. "What a coldblooded bastard you must be. So I can't afford to kill you. Yet."

Raft allowed him no time to think it over. "Why do you imagine I killed Fraser?"

"Do you have to be convinced that I know? Security brought him down, metabolic bath and all, and handed it to us for post-mortem because big brother Security doesn't waste its ethical time on side issues; it calls on the locals, which this time meant me and mine. Which goes to show that even gentlemen should do their own dirty work. That bath preserves perfectly, and the blood was still liquid, which proved to be an important point. Now, why should so healthy a physique as Fraser's take heart failure? And such a gentle failure; not even a facial rictus. It didn't take an imaginative man long to locate what your crew friends' superficial examination could not get at—as you hoped and as it happened—a massive embolism which had not actually reached the right auricle. A very special embolism, not a clot but a big bubble of air. It must have had artificial origin; that is, it must have been injected. Why? As a murder weapon—and it just could have been one—it was too chancy; long odds against it proving fatal. But if it had been injected by one of those fascinating hypodermics which snake in and out of the bath walls, then some other required dosage must have been omitted. Right?"

With Smith watching the monitor and holding a gun, Raft conceded, "Your man seems to have gone straight to it."

"Why not? Full instructions concerning the bath were in the ship's computers and blueprints in the library. It wasn't difficult to decide that the missing dosage was an adrenaline injection, obviously crucial, at about the midpoint of the revivification process. Fraser died of total metabolic failure for lack of essential stimulation, because a needle failed to pick up its dose and injected a bolus of air which just might have served to divert attention from the real cause of death.

But Commander Raft, the ship's engineer, who knew all about the baths because he helped to design and build them, found no mechanical failure. He also checked the drug levels of the reservoirs and found them correct, no doubt saw to it that they were correct. And so complete mystery, even if Doronin and Lindley had found the bubble. But they didn't open the corpse; they wanted it preserved intact. Perhaps they gambled that by 2032 some mode of resuscitation might be available.''

"It was mentioned."

"By Commander Raft, in the interest of a quiet voyage? But you knew the truth must come to light back on Earth."

"It would have been dealt with on a level where murder could be a matter for congratulation."

He heard Smith shifting uneasily and Parker's distaste was a force in the small space. "One of your stinking political affairs! Knew too much, did he? About what? Telepathy?"

Raft searched his feeling about Fraser and found no remorse; the man had been a fool and a bloody unpleasant fool. He said tiredly, "Then was nothing for him to know about telepathy."

Parker snorted, unbelieving. Smith's indifferent voice reported, "I think it's true."

"Then why, Commander?"

"He menaced the social balance of the ship, perhaps the ship itself. One man off-center in a closed community——"

"Understood. Be specific."

"Even in training we weren't friendly. He would call me 'dinkum cobber Albert,' smiling to pretend it wasn't a sneer. Made jokes about how Australians had come up fast from the boomerang. Then in space there was an initial period when everybody suspected everybody else of political espionage; you'd be hard put to believe how tightly wound international suspicions were at that time. But Fraser went over the odds, insulting the Russians especially with innuendo about corrective asylums and straitjacket philosophy. Then he started a line of hints about my lack of academic standing, building a theory of political log-rolling behind my appointment——"

"Which there was?"

Remembering Smith and his gadget, "Yes, there was."

"And he was on to it?"

"He was guessing, but it disturbed the others, and his needling might eventually have driven me to some incaution. Because I did have a secret; you know that."

"After all your command training?"

"Six months' confinement with the same faces develops cracks in the personality; our psychiatrists were good but they hadn't enough fingers to plug every hole in the dyke. Fraser worried them; they'll corroborate that."

"If we ever see them again."

"Read their bloody tapes; it's all there." He said with renewed violence, "The bastard had to go! He wouldn't take a warning. Splitting the personnel, undermining discipline, undermining *me!*"

Parker said, "Smith!"

"True, I think, sir. I mean he thinks it's all true, but a man tends to exaggerate arguments in his favor, not meaning to."

"Meaning, whatever the monitor says you don't believe him."

"It doesn't seem enough to kill a man for, but perhaps it seemed enough to him. Under strain . . ."

"Thank you, constable. How does it seem in retrospect Commander?"

"As it did then! *Columbus* cost more than a hundred billion dollars, if you know any longer what that sort of money means; you don't build in space for the price of breakfast food. All that at risk for one man? I removed him. Without fuss."

Stridency and congestion warned him his anger had spilled over. He let his body loosen, his mind shift to neutral visions, but it was too late to care what signal danced on Smith's instrument. Worse was the revelation of anger present after years; speaking of Fraser had tapped stored hatred.

Parker turned his eyes on Smith's face as he agreed with the constable, "But it didn't make a reason for murder."

"Stuff your ethics! As commander I saw it differently."

Smith answered Parker's gaze: "He believes it all right."

Parker asked, ''Do you often lose your temper, Commander?''

''Rarely.'' The tone was controlled, wooden. ''I practice restraint but like any man I can be pushed too hard.''

Parker extended a hand and Smith placed in it a black oblong the size of a matchbox from which a fine cable led to whatever apparatus snuggled in the back seat. Staring at the detector, he said, ''Back to telepathy,'' nodded at a small flicker and continued, ''The thing you were afraid of Fraser discovering was that your appointment was a direct result of Heathcote's cloning experiment. Yes?''

''Yes.''

''Yet you announced it yourself eventually.''

''Psychological pressures and some alcohol. It was too late for it to matter much and there was no troublemaker to magnify it.''

''But you didn't mention telepathy, except to deny it.''

''You're a persistent bastard.''

''And the needle wavers each time the word is mentioned.''

Raft sighed, ''If you had heard that guess made as often as I have! Even John used to talk as if the clone awareness was the beginning of some disgusting breakthrough. He was excited by it, but the idea frightens me as much as it does you. I am no telepath, nor is the clone telepathic.''

Parker tossed the detector back to Smith. ''It could be true.'' He was exhausted, a man who had barked too long up a wrong tree. ''But I don't believe Heathcote blackmailed your way to the stars for the reasons shown in your journal; they aren't enough, and there's a margin note in Jackson's handwriting to say he didn't believe it either. If you quarreled with Heathcote over the general direction of his work, you must have had words over his telepathy ideas also.''

''We did.''

''So that the lad he had loved like a father was becoming a damned nuisance. He wanted you out of the way, but not permanently; he wasn't a killer.''

Facing the blaze of resentment Parker thought, *He is more arrogant and inturned than any of us have guessed*, but he was at a dead end and had obtained nothing. ''Very well, telepathy is not involved." He started the car. "I'll drop you back to the barrack."

As the cathedral glowed across the windows, then vanished behind them, Raft reflected that, believe or scoff, religion remained the most central of historical forces, even for such a complex of faith and brutality as the grey beast driving him home. In irritation he planted a barb. "You've done some thinking about the effect of telepathy in a second-rate, spying, lying, self-righteous world of sniveling patriots."

Parker did not rise to the insult, but said soberly, "It would mean the end of civilization."

"So little? Think further. With only honesty left it would mean the end of humanity. After what you people have done with your second chance, would it matter?"

"Don't look down, Commander, but your spite is showing."

"But you don't need telepathy; the damage is already done. Drugs, hypnotism, spy gadgets, computer records and Security ready to spring on any individuality that doesn't toe the ethical line! You've got the lot. Telepathy would be only a refinement. You're already in position to turn each other into mindless yea-sayers, and one of the true things history teaches is that what can be done, will be. Only the incredible ethic and the dumb devotion of Security has permitted rags of privacy to endure, and when privacy at last goes out—and it will—individuality goes with it. How is the world going to live with itself when the dam bursts and all the ethics go down the drain? It takes a strong mind to live naked. Could you?"

As the car rolled through the barrack gates the courtyard lights flashed in Parker's face, limning him stark as peeled bone structure, and Raft saw that he had misjudged his man utterly. The man suffered! Raft cursed his clumsiness as he realized one thing after another: that Parker was an *honest* policeman, that he was a fully competent individual in a rapidly standardizing world, and that the whole bitter speech had been wasted because Parker already knew it all and was deeply troubled for his world.

The words could not be recalled; in anger and intellectual

arrogance he had further alienated the one man he should have tried to snare for a friend.

As though the speech had never been made, Parker said "I want you to give Campion a message. Now. Even if you have to wake him. And it is to go to nobody else."

"Understood."

"This is the message: I know where Gangoil is, and have not told the PM."

Raft gripped the door handle, silent, stunned, until Parker said, "Tell him!"

"How long have you known?"

"For several hours. He will want to see me; I will wait for his authority to enter the barrack."

Raft went, running, barely able to credit this turn of fortune; he understood these people, he realized, not at all.

Constable Smith watched him vanish across the courtyard. "I wouldn't want that temper loosed on me. You should have seen the detector when he talked about that Fraser; the needle hit the stop and the line went nearly off the gauge. Yet he didn't show all that much to the eye."

"Repression. He *practices* control; you heard him say so. He killed Fraser for insulting him, laughing at him. Nobody laughs at Albert or contradicts him or demeans him. Albert sees no need for God, he says, and we now know why."

Smith began tentatively, "This telepathy business—"

"Is not finished with. Mention it outside this car and I personally will kill you."

—5—

Alice did not ask him in. "I'm going to bed, Jim."

"And I'm going to Melbourne Town."

"Tomorrow?"

"Now."

Her moment of disturbance was gratifying; she needed him, if only as a tetherstone. The door opened wider. "What is it? What's happened?"

He followed her in. "A meeting has been set up with Albert: we hope to bring him here, to show him Gangoil." This had no meaning for her; he had to explain, "A good word from him will be important; he has influence with Security."

"Influence with Ian? Nobody has; I don't believe it."

"It seems Albert is his father. It's a complex story."

"Ian isn't old enough for that." She smiled with the crookedness which had invested all her reactions, not contempt but a wry acceptance. "But who can know what's what any more? Stephen called biology the accursed science. And why should Raft save Gangoil? Because of this Heathcote?"

She had not met John and did not wish to; on Lindley's description she had judged him a psychic cripple and a physical freak.

"We have to present Gangoil in a fashion which will prevent its destruction."

"Prevent!" She was incredulous. "They should bomb the mountain to dust, and everything in it. Myself included. When they know what is here——"

He grasped her wrists and sat her forcibly on the bed. "*You* don't know what is here. I do and it is far more than your imagination can scratch at. Wrongly handled it may mean the end of everything we ever thought we knew about human beings; rightly handled it may be able to save them—may."

"Then let them destroy the beastly place."

"Knowledge doesn't die. We have to absorb disasters, not pretend they haven't happened."

"Let go." He was still holding her arms and began confusedly apologizing. "Oh, shut up, Jim. I have to trust you to be right but I don't really know what you are talking about. Are you coming back with Raft?"

"Probably." He realized that now she had taken his hand.

"I don't want to be alone. Nobody here talks to us."

"They will from now on; David has put the word round. They need us now, so they'll be nice; you'll see in the morning."

"Just the same, come back."

But if he had expected a kiss of farewell he was mistaken; she let go his hand and stepped away. He was reminded, however unintentionally, that despite an incident of weakness and ungallantry he was a father figure. At forty-six, in her universe he was old, old, old.

—6—

It did not begin as a friendly meeting. Security man and policeman refrained from glaring and clawing but the aura of mutual dislike smoked in the cool light of the ward.

As for Raft, he had changed, in the seconds needed for Parker's message to shake out into meaning, from a man dealing with circumstances as they arose into one moving to a seen end. He had arrived where he had presciently visualized himself when, days earlier, Campion first asked his advice. Now he could begin to shape events. This was a greater matter than simple star voyaging because he would be doing; the crossing to Barnard's Star had been a thing done to him, but now he would do.

This new role was heady, needing study before he took the stage. He listened to the cautious opening dialogue of the featured players.

"Where is Gangoil?" Campion was winter cold, affronted by the existence of an organization better equipped for certain operations than his own.

"Not yet. That's not the important thing." Parker glanced at Raft. "Didn't you give the message correctly?"

"I did. Ian, he hasn't told the Prime Minister. That's the thing."

"I understand that and am impressed. But he'll tell me and damned fast. This is the lion's den, Parker."

"Miaow," said Parker. "I've taken the usual precautions—sealed envelope to the PM in the morning if I am not there to withhold it. You wouldn't dare try to prevent that."

Campion, brought down from soaring ideals to the realities of human encounter, capitulated without grace. "What do you want?"

"To know your mind about Gangoil. What will you do with it?"

"Study it."

"Ah." Parker was pleased. "To what end?"

Campion was silent.

"Come on, man! You must have some intention."

"None. That's your answer. So far. Now you owe me one. Why have you come to me rather than the PM?"

Parker answered hurriedly, as if the words must be spoken before regret set in. "Because the world matters more than Australia. Because the Prime Minister is by his appointment committed to Australia rather than the world and is open to political pressures—and politicians regard your damnable ethic as something to be circumvented wherever possible. Because you are an honest man though your service is a dangerous anachronism."

"All that granted, including the last," here Parker started visibly, "what is your problem?"

Raft stood at the window, where the huge Shrine of Remembrance took on a dim glow under the rising moon. They had preserved it as a warning, had they? While Parker hesitated a second too long in his need for exact phrases, Raft-from-the-past took the future into his care and spoke for him.

"The same as yours, Ian."

The pseudo-Grecian mass squeezed down on the hill rather than surmounted it—the Pericleans would have been bored by its weight and lack of color—but its sheer grinding bulk accorded with his sense of encroaching destiny, touching and reinforcing him as the cathedral had sparked grim exaltation in Parker. Knowing he had their attention he turned and spoke between rather than at them, a little flatly as if he dealt with facts needing no discussion.

"You and the Ombudsmen have left national communities to govern themselves, keep their secrets, develop their affairs, and you've got your reward in nationalism, brutality and the greed for power. I suppose it couldn't have been otherwise." He did not expect applause for platitudes, but they listened. "So Security was invented to keep the peace while the apostles and avatars worked something out. To men in a hurry it must have seemed a good idea, most idealistic, a sort of voice-from-a-cloud mystique. They trained operatives from childhood in ethical idealism. Did you know that, Controller?''

''Suspected.''

''Gave them every power except the power to intervene; left them able to deal only with international problems— an umbrella over the world with all the old bitcheries running loose beneath it. You both knew it but didn't want to see, until Gangoil whipped it under your noses and Security was immobilized by its own ethic. Security was born useless but too powerful to be knocked out except by its own will. It requires boring from within.''

Campion's eyes burned over a faint smile; Parker hunched forward, vulpine, to attack or defend.

''Ian has decided that Security must be destroyed.'' He stopped; verbal bombshells should be brief.

Parker, artist in defusing, asked simply, ''How?''

Campion came in as if cued. ''Contact the youngster groups, using the Gangoil contacts. Then resign my commission, publicly, on the newscasts, and take up where the clone left off. Without the violence.''

''Preaching sweetness and light? You?'' Parker began to laugh but in the corner of his vision caught Raft's fingers brushing at his lips and stopped.

Campion said mildly, ''The kids seem to have liked it from the clone's hypnoed agents. Albert has told me of the youngster groups of his day. Curious names———''

''Dropouts, hipsters, bikies,'' Raft recited, staring at Parker. ''And Jesus freaks.''

''Freaks!''

''Don't choke; it meant enthusiasts, more or less. Ian is saying that the youngsters are ready for change—revolution, if you like—and you must know it's true. The current sheet———'' Parker's eye was speculative ''———daysheet— lists seven cases of physical violence, serious violence, in twenty-four hours. All by youngsters. Repression bursting.

Parker shrugged. ''That's not abnormal. There would be plenty more unreported. The kids always fight amongst themselves.''

''And you think my era was cruel and violent! So it was, but that figure in a town this size would have represented psychiatric epidemic. But you've grown up with it; you no longer know what 'abnormal' is. Your kids are in ferment superficially bound by the ethic and the promise of pie in the sky but rebelling against restriction every minute. It can't hold for ever and Ian plans to catch it before it snaps. A new promise of something they can *do* will carry them as nothing else will because you've turned them all into child prodigies before they've discovered what their brains are for. And the twentieth-century experience is that what carried the kids today carries the world tomorrow. So what will you promise—a world for dropouts or a world for guerilla fighters? I suggest Jesus freaks, and I'm not joking."

Parker had listened intently; now he grunted, "Brotherly love isn't enough. I believe in it, and I know."

"Of course not. There has to be struggle."

Parker wore a shoulder holster under his jacket and his production of the gun was drill fast. He let the muzzle watch a spot between them. "If," he said, "you propose to let the kids loose in a bloodbath, it can begin here and now. Speak cogently and to the point."

(He seemed, to himself, to have been threatening all night. In fact he had never killed a human being; he thought he could but did not wish to find out.)

Raft protested, "We aren't mad, you know."

"Of you I have reservations."

That was unexpected and unfair and blindly angering, but it was as well to know the nature of the enemy. Again, Parker was a devious man who sprouted suspicions like thorns; also this could be a simple goading tactic, to be ignored.

He said evenly, trying not to sound as though he spoke through a polar frost, "We—Ian and I—offer something new: an intellectual enemy which cannot be destroyed but only out-thought—the problem of how to exist in a world where privacy is dead."

Parker rested the gun on his knee. "A world," he suggested, "where deep question, however hedged with ethic and regulation, threatens the end of self-determination, and limit question can almost lift the soul intact from the body?

Where epidermal hypno-drugs can enslave as fast as gloved hands can touch?''

Raft was exultant but Campion's service pride still smarted. ''What do you know about epidermals?''

''That not only Gangoil has them; that Security's questioners use them also.'' He waited until Campion nodded grudging admission. ''I came here to be honest, Commissioner. No doubt you keep ears in the PM's offices; I do. I also listen in this barrack.''

''Prove that!''

Parker spoke straight into his eyes. ''My beloved son, in whom I am well pleased.''

Campion's breath hissed. Raft looked interrogative, but Campion was intent on Parker; he had to ask, ''What's that about, Ian?''

Campion told him softly, ''A reference to an investigation which involved religious belief. The Controller is telling the truth about his surveillance ability, but perhaps it doesn't matter much now. What matters is that we agree that the world will shortly become an impossible place for a free mind to dwell in.''

They were doing splendidly, Raft thought, coming of their free will to the crux designed for them. Then his self-satisfaction took a beating as Parker said, ''I feel the Commander should leave us now.''

Campion's eyes narrowed and Raft's stillness was too patently a brake on fury at the insult.

''For his own sake,'' Parker continued coolly. ''You and I, Commissioner, must speak openly from now on. We are fairly safe from question by virtue of position; the Commander is not. It would be unreasonable to burden him with knowledge that any fool with a nose for a secret could relieve him of.''

''More accurately,'' Raft said, ''you have your own reasons for distrusting me and wish to discuss them with the Commissioner.''

''Yes, but I thought you'd have more brains than to make an issue of it. Why feel insulted by facts?''

''Ian!''

Campion said, ''You'd better go, Albert. We can't build anything on a clash of personalities.''

Two men struggled in him, one volcanically resentful of treacherous dismissal, one sanely observing Campion's as the only possible decision. Those two did not yet see him as a key figure, *the* key figure, only themselves as arbitrators and designers and finally activators of the new Earth.

Yet, irretrievably tainted with the conceptions of their time, they could not succeed alone. They would need him. Parker would resist necessity (and from some corner of darkness squeaked the thought that Parker must some day be discarded) but Ian would come to him . . .

Best to leave with such good face as he might. He would have liked to know the location of Gangoil, but Ian would tell him later. And it was very likely that Peter or Joe would tell him in the morning.

He said goodnight but felt they scarcely noticed; they were already absorbed in revaluation of each other. From the door he made them notice him.

"Never underestimate God as a publicity gimmick. Mysticism always looks like a gate to greener pastures."

Despite Parker's open contempt for a deliberate vulgarity he was sure that both of them would absorb the suggestion.

Parker, never satisfied that human beings would do what was expected of them, waited a quarter of a minute before he checked that Raft was not listening from the corridor.

Then, "Beloved son," he said. It was a question.

"I don't know. Some joke-reference so deeply buried it could emerge only under question. His sense of humor is mordant. Perhaps a sneer at biology; he detests biologists."

"I also. Is he your father? The likeness is too close for a grandson; it would be a one in a million chance."

"In any sane probability it's too close for a son. The million to one chance has come off. His 'grandfather' is only a guess, perhaps no more than an expression of his need for contact in an alien world."

"He doesn't strike me as one who needs people so long as he has Albert."

"Prejudice."

Parker said bluntly, "He's a psychopath."

"That has begun to show since the therapy session, but it can be ironed out when the clinic has time; it isn't urgent while they treat the kids Gangoil has maimed. And 'psychopath' doesn't mean 'mad'; in fact he's been very useful to me in clearing my thinking."

"You like him well." The tone of reproof inferred that Campion had no right to the attachment.

"Why not? You like people in spite of their deficiencies; you admire perfections but you don't love them."

Parker wondered did he know about the murder of Fraser, but this was not the time for wrangling. He could not refrain from sniffing, "I am not a sentimental man."

Campion, who equated religious dedication with sentiment and in any case found Parker's religiosity something of a jesting paradox, kept his smile to himself. "Albert has served a purpose; we can forget him for the time being."

Parker would not forget Albert, and he intended to seek methods of removing a man capable of paranoid murder, but it would pay now to consolidate this improbable alliance. He had no illusion what they were about; he had forced this meeting for the plotting of treason on an ultimately global scale, and Campion was willing. So, to business.

"Gangoil is an excavation in the heart of Mount Bogong, built by the last of the old federal governments to house Heathcote and his research teams. Canberra is gutting Archives for clues, but nothing has come up yet. We have picked up some of their men, drivers and fly pilots. Under question they know nothing useful; they're simply used and kept under control. Some of them have reached a point where reality and post-hypno orders are moving into a double-vision view of the world which they accept because both visions seem rational—schizophrenics with realities successfully merged. The clinics will love sorting that lot out."

"Unfortunately they will love it; too many of us live for our jobs and never look at the jobs from an outside standpoint."

"You've been looking at yours?"

"For some days. Go on."

"We still don't know what the place was built to hide."

"Heathcote's clone?"

Parker snarled impatience. "Was that important? Do you believe it?"

"No. I know it wasn't so. I've had a man combing the scientific literature of the time. In 2010 cloning was not a confidential research; the possibility had been a commonplace for some years and a dozen research groups were racing to be first to clone a human being. Heathcote won, apparently by accident as much as intention; he seems to have been regarded as a mediocre talent with luck and a first-class team No, it wasn't the clone."

"So?"

Their eyes fenced. Campion said, "I'll trade my idiot guess for yours."

Parker replied instantly, "Telepathy."

"No trade. We agree."

"Raft says not, and I believe he *thinks* not."

"So do I."

"There's no real evidence, only that sensitivity of the clone, but what else can it mean?"

Campion eased his whole body minutely, stretching muscles in their casts, twisting his frame where he could in his comfortless chair. He said with a gasp of pain and relief, "I've had a couple of clone-brothers under question." Parker cocked his head. "*Limit* question."

"Illegal."

"Towards whom? According to the census printout they don't exist." He paused, but Parker was not touched by cynicism. "Do you know it took me half a day of mental wrestling to break the ethic and order it? Once it was done I felt I could break every convention we live by, just for the devil of it."

Parker knew the exaltation; he had crashed through that hedge of thorns years before. He commented, "You and I are already on our way to being the kind of people the world will have to protect itself against. What did you get out of them?"

"Nothing. They don't believe in telepathy either. Perhaps it's rudimentary and they don't know what they are doing, but if you could sit with a crowd of them and hear one suddenly speak for all . . .''

In the silence of agreement they contemplated a human possibility whose implications reduced all their gadgetry to scrap.

CHAPTER SEVEN

THE BASEMENT OF GANGOIL

I the heir of all the ages, in the foremost files of time.

Tennyson: *Locksley Hall*

—1—

In the terrain of strong visual dreams, with submerged truths shouting where the mouth would not whisper . . .

. . . he addressed a vast crowd in a vast space. It was not clear who they were, or where, but only the voice mattered, *his* voice . . .

". . . in a life where all privacy is void, where thought itself prints sparkling on a spool——"

"Sparkling" was beautiful. It meant—oh, the meaning was to be felt rather than understood.

"——where nothing of you stirs but is recorded——"

Now a change of rhythm; hard prose. And he seemed to be speaking of something else. No matter.

"Ombudsmen promised a new heaven and a new earth, but where did they hide them while the ethic dreamed?" The sigh of raw breathing was his hold on them made manifest. "The ethic protected killers while they killed my friends. *My* friends!" He gathered his superb anger to shout, "I am a jealous God!"

Ian's face swam in the mass. With simple will he flooded the boy with light and turned all enslaved eyes to see.

He cried, "This is my beloved son!" and boomed out genial and genuine laughter, allowing them to comprehend that he both loved and owned, and finished the quotation in a burst of triumph, "Hear ye *Me!*"

And woke in a sweat of terror, with a sense of having trodden a precipice—and fallen.

The dream vanished in physical distress. Details faded. Something remained of vast sound and anger and an irrational conviction that a clamor in his deepest mind had been outrageous and wrong. He did not commonly remember dreams and was not given to nightmares; not since Fraser had there been phantoms to shake him into sweat.

But it was morning and the time to dwell on what the day might bring.

Bring something it would. Joe was an innocent but that young Peter, the expert with quick thoughts and rapid speech, had more than sociology on his mind. Raft would be disappointed with less than an attempted kidnapping. With the joke-like Lady in the limbo of the over-zealous and with John in charge, Gangoil needed him.

Just as he needed John . . . who would now be a very old man.

But there would still be room for the homing starman in that ancient tenderness.

—2—

Joe the Innocent believed with Poe that the obvious is the unnoticeable and, in 2052, he was possibly right. The note at Raft's breakfast setting read: "Gate. 0900. J." and nobody at the table queried what in a subversion-alert 2010 would have evoked at least an obliquely searching comment—his relationship with a civilian employee.

From the gate he watched heavy cloud scud in from the west, weighting the air, enclosing the heat, threatening half-darkness by day. *I had forgotten the smell and feel of rain.* A few bullet drops, ranging shots, did not deceive a man who knew his Melbourne weather; the downpour would hold back until humidity and tempers reached trigger-touch, then in moments swell the gutters to flash flood. Against the unholy competence of man a few traits of nature defied change.

Joe was waiting for him—and waiting, no doubt, like all his peers for his chance at running the world so eagerly prepared for him. Joe and peers would learn soon enough that what waited for them was involvement in nightmare. But the kids had always been used to fighting the wars; that was youth's place in history.

"You're the one," Joe was saying, "who can see this time from the outside, not caught up. That's why the kids look to you; they want to know what you see when you look at the world."

Did gadgeteer Peter want that? He thought not. He said, "I see a lot of indiscriminate violence."

Joe took time to realize what he meant. "That's a funny one. There's always brawling among the brat types, but you expect that."

. . . expect it . . .

How did they see it? Young blood, rising sap—those hardy excuses? Would they understand that dragooned, channeled intelligences sought outlets from repressions that had no easy psychiatric names? That revolt could be so disguised by the ethic of *laissez faire* that its very presence went undetected? Even the most primitive communities had not tolerated extreme outbreaks amongst their young, but neither had they suffered the modern pressures that caused them. Increasing sophistication and intellectualization grew ever more complex blinkers.

And this repressed but articulate, confident but emotional, educated but ignorant material was tailored for Campion's and Parker's visions. All the young Joes, openminded with the naïve hunger that gulps without question, would follow nose-to-tail like the marching caterpillars. *Roll up, suckers—but it's a shame to take your money.*

Guidance would be needed. Strong, unswerving, clearsighted guidance.

The bus arrived with Peter whistling and gesticulating from a window, very much the high-spirited youngster at play.

It was a regular public transport vehicle carrying passengers whose glances flickered over Raft, recognized the publicized features and flickered away in that agreement on privacy as discomforting as a frank stare. Their presence spoiled his intention of a barbed dialogue loosed on the boys, and the necessity for small talk irked his impatience to be doing.

The bus turned left into the old Princes Highway. That name still, with all royalty long perished . . . or had some Ombudsman cherished a dream of orb and scepter? No archetype was impossible where a huge democracy had collapsed into communism and the communist empire had withered away into a puritan theocracy.

He restrained a bursting surge, as if within him another cried for light and air; he focused his will to a stringent determination on absorbing and understanding.

The grass strips and trees flaunted the high green of summer; they had been preserved but the power lines had been torn down and the road's edges petered uncertainly at the footpaths where screens of trees concealed the decay beyond. In glimpses through gaps he decided that the destroyers had not rumbled their bulldozers and lasers and explosives through this area because it had been purely residential and not worth mass plundering. The houses had been screened off to rot. How much history, tradition and knowledge was crumbling because neither the time nor the manpower could be spared to save them?

The bus halted, he judged about three miles up the road. Peter said, "Out, fellers," and they were standing on a disintegrating, weed-penetrated footpath while the bus whipped silently on its way.

A few huge raindrops burst at their feet.

There was a sheet-iron fence, head-high, which once had been painted and now was a tatter of rust hanging from wooden posts and runners; behind it an enormous pittosporum hedge blocked the view, its mirror leaves clouded with summer dust. A gate had been knocked down or fallen down and been dragged aside; it opened on what had been a gravel path and was now a meander of small weeds and grasses through the tall desolation of a one-time garden.

To the right, beyond another ruined fence, rose a church, its grounds tended, itself plainly in use. Ahead of them was what once had been the church hall, its grounds overgrown, itself plainly out of use.

Peter said, "There are lots of these old halls. We use them. Nobody cares."

Like kids of yesterday playing secret societies in deserted houses. "And old churches, obviously furbished and attended?"

"Plenty. The Christ crowd look after them. They really mean this religion gimmick."

Some cared about Christ and some about tomorrow; the kids cared about their grievances and their elders cared about their ethical rectitude. But nobody cared about the totality of the world; that was Security's business.

Because nobody cared, you could plot empires to ruin in the middle of the street and probably at the top of your voice.

He knew what he would find in the mouldering hall— a floor for dancing and games, a tiny stage for concerts and the local amateur group, a store room for pews and seats and Ping-Pong tables and sporting gear, a pantry for tea-making and washing up, but mostly empty space waiting to be decorously filled—the parish hall the world over.

Lightning flashed, the air stilled expectantly for the thunder, and when it came the rain came with it, a dense, warm outpouring from the burst bag of sky.

They ran.

It was Joe, laughing and whooping in the rain, who threw open the door and stopped dead.

Raft, peering over his shoulder, saw Lindley's face and knew he had guessed dead center. He pushed Joe inside. "Get in, lad."

The boy hung back, gasping, "It's a trap!"

"And I'm the eager mouse." He turned to Peter, who had hung back. "You too, young Judas. Inside."

Peter muttered sulkily, "Nobody's going to harm you."

"You bet they aren't. They wouldn't dare now."

The appearance of the hall fulfilled Raft's dreary projection. The youngsters who used it for their intellectual spasms—bull sessions, he substituted unkindly—had made some attempt at tidiness but the windows were grime-dark and the rotting floor would not be danced over again.

The human furnishings were more exotic.

Behind a small table in front of the curtainless stage sat a dark, thin man whose receding chin suggested weakness and whose eyes suggested authority. On either side, two right, two left, stood impassively alert clone-brothers; identically dressed in khaki shirts and trousers, they resembled marvelously modeled dummies.

There were none of the promised youngsters, but they had been only the bait of Peter's rapid extemporizing.

Behind them all, Lindley sat on the stage apron, long legs swinging cheerfully, essential boniness exaggerated by his dress of singlet, shorts and sandals. He lifted his hand in casual salute.

"Hello, Albert."

Nobody else moved.

Then Raft dragged Peter forward by the scruff of the neck and asked Joe, "Did it not occur to you that someone amongst your acquaintance must almost surely be a Gangoil puppet? The sin of this age is innocence."

Joe lunged across him and connected once, cracklingly, before Raft pushed him back. "Not his fault, Joe; it was done to him. It could have been you." Peter dabbed his bleeding mouth silently. Raft stared at the silent man at the table. "And who can question anyone's loyalty with every one of you whittling at your own beliefs, night and day? Minds have to be made up."

The man at the table smiled briefly and some tension eased from his stillness. Raft let Peter go and walked down the hall. He nodded to Lindley. "Hello, Jim."

The clone-brothers exchanged their instantaneous glances and one spoke. "You are welcome, Albert."

"Shut up. You are of no importance. You never were."

"That is rancorous and untrue."

Raft ignored them but addressed Lindley while he indicated the man at the table. "Who's this rabbit?"

The dark head jerked and an extraordinary cinema film of emotions—shock, anger, mortification, self-restraint—merged in a revelatory tic. It was enough momentarily to distract attention, but in the background Lindley thought he recognized the role-playing Raft of *Columbus* and took the cue. "Commander Raft, meet Doctor David, head rabbit of the Gangoil biological warren."

David's mobile face contracted in instant agony of betrayal as he heard Lindley change sides before the game was properly opened.

Raft stared down at him. "What do you want?"

David did his best, as his planned approach collapsed around him, to answer coolly, "It is a question of balance of power, Commander," and got no further.

"Tell me in three sentences or I walk out of here and the police can have you. They'll get to you soon enough."

That was a more dire threat than he realized, enough to frighten David into snarling, "You won't walk out, Commander. The clone are as powerful and alert as yourself. As you know."

Raft smiled at him; in the arc at the apex of his vision Lindley was nodding encouragement, mouthing at him to stay on top. He said genially, "But not, I imagine, trained in what we called the martial arts. And the clone does not kill. I will kill. With my hands and quickly." He felt he could slaughter these dummies without qualm, in sheer disgust.

The dummy faces twitched slightly in controlled hints of angry contempt. A spokesman murmured, "We don't welcome death but we don't fear it." He spoke as if explaining to a child. "With the seeds of immortality available in John's laboratories, with even memory carrying on unbroken, why should we?" Raft's scalp crawled to an understanding of how far the Gangoil dreams had progressed, and Lindley's solemn nod assured him of epochal truths. "And while you kill one, others will restrain you. You must come to Gangoil, Albert." With sleight of hand a small syringe appeared between his fingers and disappeared again into his palm.

To the table Raft said, "Warn your golems not to irritate me. I intend to visit Gangoil, but on my terms. Be wise and treat me as a friend, whether I am or not—and you don't know that."

David's self-possession splintered; it had been held together only by will and stimulants. He beat his hands on the table and yelled, to himself as much as any, "What the devil does it matter who dominates? Let the ignorant idiot have his way if it will save Gangoil."

Raft looked to Lindley in silent enquiry.

"You'll be fascinated," the psychiatrist told him. "Fascinated and frightened. You were right—something will have to be done about biologists. But the thing that must not be done is that Gangoil be delivered over to any national government. *Any* government."

Raft ruminated. Outside, the rain had exhausted its first fit, but if it had been dropping in sheets his need would still have been to end this useless confrontation and be on the way to Gangoil. He said, "All that's understood, but it isn't enough. Jim, you'll have to stay behind." David's mouth opened and Raft told him flatly, "You need me and my price is high. Do as I say or try to negotiate with Campion and Parker yourself. Just try."

"Parker!"

"Surprise, surprise? He knows where you are, but for the moment he's following Campion's lead. And Campion will follow mine—and that's your hope of salvation. So this is what will happen: Jim will stay behind. Joe will take him to Ian Campion and he'll tell Ian everything he knows about Gangoil."

David was mumbling about his missing drivers and pilots.

"Then you can bet Parker has them."

"They don't know anything about the internal activities."

"Lucky you. If they did Parker would have it out of them and I'd be no use to you. Now, Joe, can you get transport?"

Joe, only half comprehending but exalted with a sense of being at the heart of great affairs, stuttered that there would be a bus along. "Or we can hitch a commercial."

Lindley objected, "This mightn't be the best idea. You aren't totally informed, Albert. There are facts you need to know before you get to the mountain."

"David can brief me. It'll pay him to brief me."

"Not as I can. Heathcote, for instance, is not the same."

"After forty-two years? Do you think I expect a bloody

youngster?'' He was tired of pressing his weight on them all; his temper slid off balance and he bellowed, ''For Christ's sake, Jim, do what I tell you and stop trying to push me.''

Then he was furious with himself for losing grip in front of a psychiatrist who knew him in and out, deep and shallow.

David said, ''Have your way, Commander. You intend to have it anyway. I will brief you en route. Now let us get away from here.''

''What about me?'' That was Peter.

Raft asked, ''Does Gangoil want him?''

David shook his head. ''I don't know him; I don't have contact with operatives. I'm a biologist trying to pick up the pieces, not the spider of the network.''

''Who is?''

''No one any longer.''

Raft grinned heartlessly at the boy. ''So do what you like, lad. Nobody needs you any more. You've been used up. Try the Security clinic and find out how much postcommand is crammed into your head.''

Lindley jumped to the floor and came to him and said, too quietly for the others to hear, ''I don't remember you as an unnecessarily cruel man.''

''Or as a sentimentally kind one. If he needs help he can get it, so let's not waste time on pity.''

He heard Joe, perhaps having second thoughts, say, ''Stick with me, Pete. It'll work out.''

Raft dismissed the youngsters from consideration. He was very satisfied that the unlooked-for presence of Lindley had solved a problem. With Jim at Campion's ear, plainly sent as adviser and deputy, there would be no fuss, no tension, if he vanished for a short time. He could not estimate how much time. Gangoil seemed a flailing, inchoate group; it could well take a day or two to establish firm control. Old John would be the key, easily turned by the fingers of affection.

He realized that Lindley thrust something at him, and recognized incredulously a monopole gun.

''Take it. You may need self-defense in that rubbish heap of unbalanced minds.''

The gun could have come from only one source in the world. For an instant he traveled in time, re-living the half-concerned, half-derisive moment when he had made the gift, hoping John could find the spirit to use it if the need arose.

Lindley's voice returned him to the present. "Don't be hasty with it. Gangoil needs understanding more than anger, but it can be dangerous. The magazine is loaded."

"I'd forgotten it existed."

Laughing, he thrust it into his belt.

David called out, his voice cracking, "What are you doing, Lindley? Is he to make peace with a gun?"

Raft answered him calmly, "I'm not that kind of a fool, neither am I refusing protection when it's offered."

The rain ceased briefly; by a miracle of contraction the clouds parted to admit the stroke of a blazing sun. Lindley and the boys emerged into bright and steaming air.

At the last moment Peter raced back to the hall door to shout, "His clothes are wired! Every word . . ." It penetrated at last that bugging and tracing and listening no longer mattered, that the fabulous Gangoil he had never seen was out of hiding.

Urging him away, Lindley surprised him wiping at tears and took him by the shoulders to shake without gentleness.

"I haven't time to purr and soothe. Just make up your mind that you've backed the wrong horse, that it wasn't your fault and that nobody's dwelling on making you pay for it. You brats have a world to build but not the one you think. The Gangoil caper's finished and if you knew what I do you'd be damned glad of it."

The boy sulked, which was as good a sign as any and better than having him afraid and unpredictable.

Almost Lindley turned back to give a message for Alice but thought of nothing that wasn't ridiculous or pointless. He had better accept that he had no future there.

He felt suddenly uneasy about Raft, sensing a hardness different in quality from the game-playing of a subtle commander. Something had happened to him, some internal shifting. Or, he thought, super-sensitivity was deceiving him, too finely honed by the rapid changing of his ideas as day by day the new world revealed new faces.

He had, he realized, been so occupied that he had not consciously thought of England in several days. Now he found the anger gone and only a grey sadness underlying his mind.

At the shattered gate thought fled as he was closed in on from both sides by grey uniforms. As if in sympathy the clouds began to draw together again; the light dulled.

"Doctor Lindley, I think."

"Yes." So soon the planning for Gangoil was ended.

"I suppose," Parker suggested with villainous brightness, "that Commander Raft and escort will vanish by rear exit to wherever their transport is waiting."

"I suppose so."

"Don't be downhearted, Doctor; I wouldn't arrest that gang for my hope of paradise. So let us exchange news until our instruments tell us in which direction our birdie flies. To Gangoil, I presume?"

Exchanging news should have meant a furious pumping by Parker, but first it was necessary to convince Lindley of his good intentions, which he thought he managed reasonably well. If Lindley received the impression that Parker and Raft were deeply involved co-conspirators with a common lofty aim, that was all to the good. It held some elements of truth.

His first direct question brought an answer that tumbled all deviousness out of his mind. The twenty minutes which elapsed before the double beep which represented Raft rose upward, airborne, raced by in agitated probing. He could wait no longer though he left a hundred questions unanswered; he must greet Raft on the High Plain and not leave him again.

Lindley he dispatched to Campion with a shower of instructions and a policeman in case the psychologist should have second thoughts and create difficulties.

Lindley, watching Parker's dragonfly rise from the middle of the road where it had arrogantly forced traffic to stop or crawl round it, recalled that he had not mentioned the monopole gun. Parker would be interested in that simple and foolproof weapon, not that there was any likely need for it unless the unpredictable clone-brothers turned mulish and dangerous.

—3—

The Gangoil party went by back gate and back lane, through overgrown streets of collapsing houses lurking behind shrubbery come back into its own.

David's dragonfly was hangared in a brokendown shed a mile from the hall, and turned out to be not a modern 'fly but an old helicopter-jet with a variable rotor design Raft recognized on sight. It had been the most ambitious design of 2003; this relic was in showpiece condition, beautifully maintained. It explained one puzzlement of Gangoil's transport facilities, for it was not possible that they mounted a hypno-hijack every time a vehicle was needed; this one had been with the complex from the beginning. Given an adequate fuel dump and operation by night on courses away from regular flight lanes, secrecy in a world with eyes inturned was relatively easy.

Carrying six, with a clone-brother piloting, it was roomy enough. In elbow-touching proximity, but with automatic reactions suppressed, Raft felt only a normal distaste for propinquity with persons he disliked. Now, studying their mask-similar expressions, he came on a fact that pleased him immensely—given line for line repetition, their faces still were not the face he saw in his mirror. In their midst he would be seen as the lone individual, alike but distinguishable, as the expert separates the original work from all copies. His internal self registered in his face, and his self was not theirs. He began to think of them as a tool he might impersonally use.

As the machine rose he looked over Melbourne Town, incredibly small and compact, bright-roofed and complacent. In the surrounding desolation a great city was skeletally present in the squares and curves of a dead planning, spectrally blurring where vegetation reclaimed the ruined land.

He checked the position of the sun; they were heading approximately north-east. "Where is Gangoil?"

David grumbled, "You said you knew."

"I said Parker knows. Where?"

"Beneath the Bogong High Plain."

He was jolted to childhood, to the yearly motoring holidays, those short happinesses when he sat alone in the back seat, unspeaking, watching the world without, happy because it changed and changed with the miles and required nothing of him save that he look, and because the two in front lived inside themselves and forgot him, allowing him to forget them.

The High Plain had been a favorite run, up from the valley, up thousands of winding feet where the monstrous conduits of the hydro-electric plant plunged to the valley floor; up to the High Plain, the plateau where the waters gathered, where the cattle fed in summer and whence they were driven down before the snow reclaimed it in winter . . . Once John had taken him there, the two of them only, in the one ecstatic summer when They had been too firmly occupied to consider the need of a lonely boy . . .

"It is the laboratory complex the last of the old governments built to hide Heathcote's work."

The name roused Raft from dreams. "What did Lindley mean about change in John?"

A few minutes of woollen greyness closed round them as the 'copter rose into the cloud layer; in near darkness David muttered that explanation was not simple, that Raft was not a biologist——

The word opened menace. "What have you done to him?"

He saw Raft as an overbearing thug, capable of any crudity, and retired into the face-saving of the non-violent man, a strained coolness proclaiming intelligence as a proper human weapon. "Not to him, but for him. You will be surprised at his youthfulness; he is probably younger-looking than you remember him."

That did not commit him to an uncomfortable exactness; he had to depend on Heathcote and sentiment to calm Raft when he faced the—"revenant" was the word he groped for but he had thought, "remnant."

"*What* did you do?"

David relaxed into lecture. "Studies of the ageing process were an offshoot of genetic manipulation, leading to experimental work in rejuvenation. Side issues of the cloning data opened new avenues, particularly with regard to the thymus and the immune system, which was really the key———"

"Agreed I'm not a biologist, but you weren't the first to see the immune system as basic to the study of senescence. So John permitted himself to be used for rejuvenation experiments?"

Sudden sunlight illuminated the cabin, revealing the clone-brothers intent on David's words. He was reminded of what Lindley had told him of Raft's loathing of the clone, of the cloning process and everything to do with it. His courage, a strictly intellectual trait, ebbed; he could not bear Raft's style of larrikin brow beating. And there was the gun, silently evil. He said, "Yes."

Something, not a movement but rather a sense of increased attention, passed over the clone-brothers. Raft's residual sensitivity perceived it and even made some interpretation.

"You're lying."

"Simplifying," David protested. "I can't sum up forty years of research in simple sentences."

The pilot spoke without turning his head. "John has the appearance of youth and the brain of age. But there are deficiencies."

They would not contradict him but he must not hide truth altogether; he improvised rapidly, smearing science fiction over science fact. "Doctor Heathcote was approaching senility when the treatments began. Some areas of memory were failing, and brain cells do not replace themselves." He found himself on the brink of another unnecessary lie, and said plainly, "His memory of life before rejuvenation is therefore imperfect."

"Does he remember me?"

"Yes, oh, yes."

"With love," said a clone-brother reproachfully. Raft behaved as if he had not heard.

David said eagerly, "He was greatly upset when he learned of The Lady's attempt to have you killed."

"Who is she?"

"A cult object. I don't know her name. Nobody knows." That was safe; for once the clone was not aware how much he knew. "John has forgotten. She was in Gangoil before I was born and she has always been The Lady. Even the clone don't know."

The pilot said over his shoulder, "She is a poor woman out of her wits. But she is the mother of the new world as John is its father."

Raft laughed, a short and ugly sound. "I am the father."

The immobile expressions surveyed him, betraying nothing, but David's revelatory tic ran its course from surprise to a scared wariness and lapsed into speculation.

It was not a long trip, perhaps a hundred miles in a blaze of sunlight on cloud, until the clouds also reached for the sky; at the last, Bogong was invisible and they moved blindly to the mountain. A point of light on the instrument panel told of a radio beacon hidden in the gloom and whispering in the pilot's ear, but it was the communicator grille in the ceiling that blared noisy panic.

"Davy! Davy! Doctor David! There is a strange 'fly on the High Plain! Answer me, Davy!"

The pilot said to the ground, "Do not shout, please. Be calm."

David spoke across him. "David. Report fully."

The voice, deprived of drama, complained, "It landed only two minutes ago, in zero visibility, on radar reflection. It's about a mile from the hangar lift. If you come in quickly you may get in undetected."

David turned to Raft. "Your friends?"

"Parker, I imagine. I arranged nothing, but how could he fail to take an interest?" He let David stew a little in the steam of the Controller's name; even navel-gazing Gangoil must know his reputation for dedicated ruthlessness.

The radio chattered, "He's lifted again. Moving towards you on a direct line."

Raft fingered his betraying shirt collar for David's sour understanding. "But he isn't after you, Doctor; he has you any time he closes his fist. He's keeping an eye on me. You might as well land; you've passed any possible usefulness of running."

David scowled. "Take us in." The 'copter began to lose height, groping slowly into the murk.

Raft slipped the monopole gun from his belt and, without looking at it, began with a soldier's familiar accuracy to take it to pieces. It came apart in a series of sliding motions, breaking the magnetic lines which were all that held it together. To David's eye the construction seemed impossible; the chamber pressures in firing should be sufficient to scatter it into its component fragments.

Even the barrel split in short segments like collars. The butt came off, dividing laterally into two flat pieces of casing and disgorging a flat plate which David recognized as a sophisticated power pack as well as a flat magazine holding what appeared less like bullets than small slugs without cartridge cases. The firing chamber also split apart. The pieces disappeared into Raft's pockets. Suddenly there was no gun.

David viewed the performance with an expression of affront at observing a known object constructed in impudent defiance of proper requirements.

Raft shook with quiet laughter. He moved his hands with conjurer's accuracy; in ten seconds the assembled gun was pointed at David's indignant head and as quickly was gone again into the Commander's pockets. Throughout the demonstration he had not once looked at the weapon.

The clone-brothers were not impressed, each of them being gifted with the same ambidextrous accuracy and speed. They averted their eyes, registering virtuous disapproval of the weapon's existence.

The 'copter landed in the grey gloom with little more than a cushioned bounce, the radio ejaculating useless reports until the pilot shut it off.

David asked him, "Are we on the lift?"

"Directly central."

"Then signal for entrance."

It was already too late. The cloud burst into diffused brilliance around them, the source racing in, separating into gauzy searchlight eyes as it came to rest only yards distant.

"Open up," Raft said. "We'd better be sure it's Parker."

David nodded moodily to the pilot and the door gaped.

Raft, stepping out on to the platform of the lift he could see only as smooth soil, felt he moved on a radiant seabed. Indistinct figures solidified at the limit of his vision, darkened and thickened as they approached, became clearly men.

"Parker?"

A dark column took a pace forward, became familiar in the haze. "Commander Raft?" Always punctilious.

"Come to see the sights?"

"As you say."

"And keep a restraining hand on Albert?"

"As you say."

"And do I see a bodyguard?"

"Call it that. Three men, adequately armed. Perhaps excessively, but we shall see."

"Wasted preparation, Controller. Gangoil wants only your good will. Shall we enter Aladdin's cave?"

"I came for that. Doctor Lindley made it sound most interesting. We, er, met—at the Parish hall gate."

"And?"

"I found your appreciation most estimable and sent him on to Campion as you suggested. And I kicked your barrack waiter's arse as punishment for the sin of naïvety."

David said peevishly, "It is wet and cold out here."

"Who's he?"

Raft made the introduction.

Parker stared into the flinching face. "As a biologist you are a global nuisance; as a chief administrator you shall offer us hospitality. How do we get in?"

A clone-brother spoke into a hand mike and the lift eased down into the mountain; it was as if a football ground sank out of the landscape with 'copter and men in a huddle in center field. It passed the ceiling of the sunken hangar and light flooded in as it dropped into a space to dwarf cathedrals and lit with the profligate brilliance of unlimited power.

Parker and his policemen took in the sight with grim unease, appreciating immense resources. The young men's impassivity failed momentarily; they made unconsciously reassuring motions at their concealed arms.

They saw—helicopter jets, including two immense transport vehicles, all of old-world design, all well-used and ready for further use

——commercial trucks and personnel transports, duplicates of official originals in use in the outside world, probably built on the spot

——a group of flying machines with folded wings, swathed in plastic whose ground-in discoloration said they had never been unsealed; beneath the covers they probably still carried their packing grease (Parker could not recognize the lines through the sheeting; Raft could—fighter planes, the most modern, of his day—Gangoil had fangs unused)

——solo transport of all kinds—bicycles, motor bikes, twentieth-century cars and trucks, even canoes, most seeming little used, probably prepared against anciently conceived eventualities which had vanished in the storms of disease, radio-active dusting and famine.

Gangoil had been designed not only to hide from the world but to make use of the world in its good time.

Parker wondered what had become of the young men assigned and trained to use this material. Dead? Grown old and efficiently disposed of as unproductive consumers?

He said contemptuously, "Tinware! Biology—life and murder hand in hand." He considered the lift platform and the huge hydraulics below it and the wastrel wattage of lighting and murmured to David, "A small nuclear plant? Power to burn?" David nodded, as much intimidated by the narrow-faced policeman as he had been discomforted by Raft. "We must not forget to see your very efficient heat disposal arrangements. I had a satellite take thermal readings and it couldn't pinpoint the area. You *are* efficient, in your fashion. I have a swag of your hypnoed people under question——" David winced "——oh, they know precious little; your field organization also is excellent."

"Not mine." Eagerly David found an involvement to disclaim. "The clone administrates outside operations."

Parker shifted his smile to Raft. "I should have known. The family touch, including the highly individual morality."

Raft's glance promised a reckoning, instantly veiled.

At the far end a door opened and a man came unhurriedly towards them; his green shirt and sandals, and shorts the color of sunflowers, were opulent in the stark hangar. Closer, he emerged as a big man, taller than Raft and slimmer, but plainly powerful. He advanced with the deliberate stride of one who is worth a second glance and intends to get it, but the effect was rendered bizarre by plucked eyebrows and bright green toenails. He favored the uniformed police with a skilled insolence: "Glory be, the cops! It's a raid!"

David squeaked, "Behave yourself, Arthur! Have you a message?"

"Not exactly, but John is practically pissing himself in anticipation of embracing his Albert and if we don't produce the boy soon he'll blow an artery. He really is being a bloody trial." His self-possessed gaze sorted them out and fixed on Raft. "What a relief that the original isn't another plaster cast. Nobody will ever mistake you for one of the simultaneous dancers."

The clone-brothers ignored him—really ignored him, did not admit his existence. Raft asked, "How so?"

"Your face is alive. There's a man behind it, not a conference."

"Thank you." He said to David, "Take me to John." David's expression said nothing remained in his hands; Raft would do as he damned pleased.

Parker came to life. "One moment. You! Arthur!"

Arthur smiled a slow and exquisite insult. "Wanting something, policeman?"

David shuddered. Parker grinned like a wolf. "What's your function here? Camp follower?"

"Please don't make tired *old* jokes. I am a member of an experimental clone." Even Parker's control slipped before that hint of demented possibilities and Raft gave a hyena laugh. "Shall we go now?"

"What's your name?"

"You know it. Arthur."

"Arthur who?"

"You mean for checking against the census computer in the Town? Now, that's difficult. You see, my mother was a humidicrib and my father was a set of genetic equations tagged to a flask of nutrient solution. Write me down as one who has had to learn sin instead of being born into it like the rest of you."

Parker's frown relaxed as though he actually appreciated this defiant comedy, but his mind had coolly separated from it the unlikely reference and he was not one to lose even a minor opportunity. "Are you a Christian?"

Arthur's insolence softened to a cautious puzzlement.

"I mean it. I want to know."

Raft paid unwilling tribute; in a few phrases Parker had projected peace terms and a sincerity which Arthur suppressed his sardonic contempt to recognize and accept.

"I don't really know. This isn't the environment for picking up cult affiliations, but I've read the New Testament and there are things in it I like. There's that—I can't remember which book, but there's that part on the mountain, a sort of long sermon. It makes good sense."

"The fifth chapter of Matthew makes very good sense. Remember it in the months to come." He turned to Raft. "I don't trust you an inch but I can take advice where I find it. God *is* a good gimmick. Now let's get on to Heathcote, the young-old man with the imperfect memory." (David started, and his gaze rested sourly on Raft's bugged collar.) "It is not given to all of us to goggle at the first exhibits of the imminent destruction of the human race."

In the startled silence Arthur clapped his hands, slowly, twice. "At last somebody has begun to use his brains."

The clone swung on him in stony anger; David's twitching glare could have killed him; the police watched them all with hands urging to unseen weapons.

Parker murmured, "Cast your bread upon the waters, Commander, and find it snapped up in the most unlikely places."

Raft urged Arthur away. "Let's get to old John, feller, before this lot declare open season."

—4—

A passenger lift fell with them through floor below floor; only governments could be so profligate. Only a government terrified or paranoid, Parker concluded, could have initiated the monstrous undertaking at all.

He caught passing sight of men and women, mostly of a single age group, the middle thirties, variously dressed, from laboratory smocks to mere decorative swatches. There were a few children, mostly under ten, but few signs of an in-between group. The pattern was plain—the children were the second generation bred in an artificial cultural fragment whose purpose had vanished in disaster and whose preoccupations had mutated in the eerily self-continent fashion of the isolated.

Eight floors down the lift stopped and the grille opened.

The clone-brothers marched—the only word for their concerted movement—straight down the long corridor ahead of them with David hurrying after. The five outsiders stepped out of the lift, saw what was before them and slowed for curious inspection. Arthur, last out, leaned against the wall, watching them with the patronage of an impresario approving a *coup de théâtre*.

This corridor was the first they had seen with a carpet, and the warm crimson spread wall to wall for three hundred feet ahead. The light here was not brilliant but diffuse and controlled, not the yellow of indoor lighting but approximating daylight. The light cylinders themselves were clamped to the upper edges of the frames of the paintings which stretched down the whole stunning vista of art.

Parker's reaction was first and perhaps predictable. "Luxury for the brass. Twentieth-century administrative morality."

His policemen stared without understanding. Twenty-first-century art was either functional or colorfully decorative; they had had no time to assess the aesthetic past or even to look seriously at it.

Some of the canvases were huge, but Raft stopped at one of the smaller ones, some twenty inches high by forty wide, a surge of gold cut by a double ribbon of green, rising into what might have been a sky of impossibly dark blue laid on in heavy impasto, both gold and blue bearing on their surfaces black flying things like stylized bats or a child's symbolic statement of birds.

Parker stared with him. "Some of that stuff—what did they call it? Surreal?"

"No." Gently Raft touched the thickly pigmented surface, muttering, "It has to be a copy."

"No copies here," Arthur told him. "Only old masters for the old mistress."

"The Lady? She used catastrophe to plunder the world?"

"You could say that. It was before my time; for me, the stuff's always been here. Can't say I care for it."

Parker looked more closely at the work which had caught Raft's attention. "What's it supposed to be?"

"I think it's called *Wheatfield With Crows*, and I think it belonged in a museum in Holland."

"Wheatfield! Even you didn't have wheat that color, or a navy-blue sky. The bloody man must have been mad."

"He was. His name was Van Gogh and the progress of his illness can be charted in the handling of the brush strokes. He was one of time's greatest artists."

"But your whole damned world was mad."

"Was it? If it helps your opinion. Van Gogh never sold a canvas in his life." He thrust his face into Parker's. "But your go-ahead, hell-for-leather, Johnny-come-lately, plaster-and-patch culture has a long leeway to make up in some directions."

Parker stepped back, refusing to quarrel. Arthur asked, "Is he the one who signed everything 'Vincent'? They're different; you can't help noticing, there are so many. The Lady is very rapt in them. But then she turned out a bit bats above, too, didn't she?"

Raft regarded him with what Parker saw as the look of yet one more madman. "A lot of Van Gogh?"

David, fifty yards ahead, wanted to know what held them up and Raft bawled at him that he wanted to see The Lady, now, this minute.

"But Professor Heathcote is waiting."

"After forty-two years an hour won't hurt him. I want to see this art-fancying priestess of the drug and clone scene."

He was too excited to notice David's kinetescope performance of surprise, doubt, calculation and decision that the meeting might serve as well now as later.

David turned a corner. "Down here."

Raft hurried, with Arthur after him scenting drama and determined not to miss a bar of it, and prodding, "There's one outside her door she always fancied a bit like her. Wrong coloring, but it is a bit like.''

Raft flung over his shoulder, ''Van Dyck's full length of the Countess of Southampton? All draperies and peachy fat flesh?''

''How did you guess?''

A hysterical edge sharpened the answering laugh. ''It was hung in the Melbourne Gallery. She'd stand in front of it, loving herself.'' The laughter stopped abruptly; he snapped, ''Which room?''

''There.''

Parker, running and shoving through a congestion of clone and police, bellowed, ''What are you doing?''

Raft ignored him and flung a snarl of contempt at the Countess of Southampton. He leaned an instant on the door, gathering anger to a head, then hammered on it with fists and feet. ''Open the door, you blazing bitch! Open the door for not so dead Albert!''

An arresting, unnatural sound of outburst matched his through the panel, the voice of a woman whose range could roar like a man's. ''Why can't you die? Must you live for ever?'' Her heavy panting was an animal's, hunted to a stand; her mouth must have been pressed against the door jamb. ''Go away! Away!''

The clone fell back in a common decision of neutrality; Parker pointed like a hound, scenting fresh truths; David watched with held breath as a plan exploded in his face.

Raft took a long breath and said with conversational menace, ''Just open it or I'll kick it in.''

A fascinated Arthur threw in the advice of the born meddler: ''It won't be locked.''

Nor was it. They faced each other with the naked venom of twisted lives.

''To the stars and back, and here's Mother waving her handkerchief on the wharf! You might at least have dressed for the occasion.''

Her reply whickered down the long walls—a prolonged reptilian hiss. Yet for once the vulnerable nature of nakedness reached to her, equating with the stripped mind able to hide nothing from the one man to whom her nudity meant nothing: reflexively she cupped her hands before her and took a short pace back.

Raft leaned against the door, ablaze with a spite as bare as her flesh, and sniggered at her.

Behind her, at the back of the scented and cluttered room—posed like escaped caryatids, one each side of the huge, luxurious Tiepolo—stood replicas of Arthur. There was nothing hesitant or unmasculine in their wholly dangerous watchfulness, but Raft's aggression centered in his mother.

He mocked her. "You look so well. Rejuvenation in this world beats resurrection in the next, eh? Think of centuries of bouncing the bedsprings—but not with Dad, I'll bet. What happened to Dad? New life for him, too? Not if Mama could help it!"

The jeering stiffened her. She unclasped her hands and clenched them at her sides, straining upright for a rigid majesty, head withdrawn to strike, a sculpted rage under a monstrously frizzed, brilliantly red coiffure. She tried to force words from a congested throat. "Your father——"

Her face darkened, convulsed. Unable to continue, she spat, and ineffective spittle dribbled on her chin. From the back of the room Francis came to her side, wiped her face, placed a hand on her arm, spoke quietly into her ear, trying to calm her. She swung a closed fist at him without turning her head. He slipped the blow with quick ease, still murmuring.

She calmed appreciably, even managed a wraith of smile and performed a feat of mental acrobatics between deep breaths. He was not deceived; she had always been capable of it.

"Your father and I separated after you left."

"After. It would have been bad publicity before—bad for your career as patron saint of the aborigine cause." He took a step into the room and Arthur warned quietly out of hard-earned knowledge, "Be careful."

Parker pushed forward to miss nothing; his impassive young men must have been bewildered by developments but for all they showed might have been another clone.

Raft was asking, "But why you? Why should John choose you for the gift of eternal—uh—middle age?"

The light of murder returned to her eyes and was as quickly replaced by a smiling, crafty triumph. For answer she drew her hands right and left across her full breasts and raised them above her head as if to challenge time. She could scarcely have chosen a less appealing, less erotic stance, fists flung up and legs stumpily apart, but she possessed sexual handsomeness, a touch of muted splendor that overrode flesh and muscle. Insane, evil or merely debased by indulgence, she breasted her world with a power of womanliness. If she was aware of watchers bewitched at the door she gave no sign; her victory smile was for Albert alone.

But he knew her; he could laugh. "You seduced old John? Really? Got him into bed and played strong-girl Delilah to little Samson? No wonder you wanted Dad out of the way." His chuckling turned ugly as he took another step towards her, his voice informed quickly with menace. "Did you do that to John? Pervert him and use him? Chisel him for a harlot's sucker?"

She answered with effervescent impudence. She clipped her feet together, turned a sudden swift and steady pirouette and made a half-curtsey, leering for his applause. His restraint broke and he stepped close, reaching for her arm.

She shrieked, but not with terror. Her clenched fists opened and fingernails filed to points raked across his face, right and left and back.

He leaned away, taken by surprise, and bleeding. Then it seemed that he would attack her, with death in his hands, while she opened a screaming mouth and advanced on him without fear. She was beyond consideration of hurt or ending.

Several things happened together. Francis and Eric came swiftly from the rear to restrain her; Parker started forward to grasp at Raft but Arthur was before him, taking the starman by wrist and elbow to swing him off balance. Raft's years of training operated reflexively, converting imbalance into a full turn and a fist lashing at the face so easily in reach. The face slipped the blow with amazing speed and instead he took a full-bodied punch, high on the cheekbone, that snapped his head aside and toppled him half across the room. Then Arthur and the policemen carried him down under them; his expertise heaved uselessly against weight and brute strength.

He lay still for perhaps half a minute, until he breathed normally, then said, "Get off me." Arthur rose, dusting his knees. The police hesitated until Parker said, "Let him up. Watch him."

He stood. He turned, stone-faced, to where his mother scowled and muttered, alternating between struggle and collapse in the grip of the red- and orange-clad figures who managed her with practiced gentleness. In the moments of struggle they needed all their strength not to hurt her, and the orange-clad one finally seized an opportunity to jab a needle into her upper arm. Her son watched, unmoved, as she relaxed and they guided her to the couch; then he turned his back on her and dismissed her from his universe.

He found Arthur at his side, surveyed him appraisingly and offered a compliment as condescending as an insult. "Surprise packet, aren't you? Quite the manly young feller, eh?" Getting no reaction, he said, "I need to clean up."

Arthur replied from depths of boredom, "That you do." He pointed. "There's a washroom across the passage."

"Thanks." Raft jerked a thumb over his shoulder to where his mother sank into sleep. "So you do have a job of sorts."

"Job? It is something we choose to do."

"To look after a maniac? Why?"

Arthur wasted no effort on hiding contempt. "We have pity. What did they have in your day?"

"Don't push your luck, Arthur-boy." Raft thrust by him and came face to face with Parker. Very softly he said, "I'm not forgetting you called me mad."

As if he had not heard, Parker spoke across him to Arthur. "Your lot would make useful policemen. Think about it."

It was a mistake; Arthur's acceptance of him stopped short of blarney. "That's sweet of you, but I'm going to grow up to be a criminal."

Parker acknowledged failure but Raft guffawed and pushed through them all until he came to David, in the corridor, apprehensive of bullying and now getting it.

"Why didn't you tell me? You knew who she is, didn't you? You knew damned well."

David nodded miserably and looked to the others for protection, but Raft only ripped at his incompetence. "You thought you could stage a mother and son reunion, all tears and slop—sentimental son forgives murderous bitch and scatters goodwill to all Gangoil. Either you didn't know the facts or you were out of your idiot mind. Well, you've earned me a faceful of fingernails and a smack that made my brains ring. If you've any more ideas, tell me first."

David was certain he would be knocked down and not a person present would move to help him. But he was not a prime target or even a subject for action; Raft pushed past him into the washroom and slammed the door.

Arthur looked round the group. "I've never seen so many stunned ducks in one pond. It all makes you wonder about that motherlove line the psychs hand out, doesn't it? Well, I suppose *somebody* had better see he doesn't rip the plumbing out."

He followed Raft.

—5—

A common distaste for what they had seen had edged the group into the corridor, where Parker might have restrained Arthur but thought better of it. "He's right and rather him than me. Is there another way out of there? No? That man's a case for total rehandle—limit question and remake."

David was apologetic. "How could I know? Lindley should have told me."

"He didn't know either. Raft has had question therapy; he's probably a trigger case."

"We don't use the question techniques here." He made it very superior and virtuous. "Is it a trauma affecting personality traits?"

"Basic traits, naked, nasty. We're seeing the real Raft, with the overlay wearing thinner every time he's jolted— the Raft who murdered Fraser." David's mouth opened and closed. "You didn't know? Didn't you think my office worth a snoop? Yet you must have known your confrontation would be a failure; Lindley says you have a recording of Raft's therapy session—the 'beloved son' dialogue and the wish fulfilment about killing mama."

David said unhappily, "Nothing of his mother. Only a maddening snippet neither Lindley nor I could understand. We did not know it belonged in a therapy session." There were no certainties left for him.

"Where did you get your snippet?"

"From the clone. They control the outside contacts."

"And they selected what they wanted you to know. I wonder why."

A spokesman said at once, "To prepare Doctor David's acceptance of the supreme importance of Albert and of Ian Campion. But he thinks the future will emerge from his glass wombs and incubators." The disinterested contempt would have withered grass.

"Why Campion?"

The clone-brother appraised him as if revising a judgement. "You who know him, you ask that?"

"He is thought to be the Commander's grandson."

"*Thought*?" The four glances flicked each to each, opened into smiles. "Some of us took wounds protecting him from the drugged children. It is our shame that he was hurt. Thought to be *grandson*?"

The smiles faded. He felt he had been grouped with David and all idiots. So—not a grandson. Then what? Did it matter except as a quiddity in the web of cross-purposes while there were nearer worries?

"Yet you left him by the roadside to die."

"To be found. Failing Albert's love——" the face convulsed momentarily "——he was best left in Melbourne Town."

Their loyalty was brick-hard with practicality, Parker decided, but in its abominable way it achieved results.

"Why did you conceal his child-wish to kill The Lady? You knew of it from the therapy recording."

"Conceal?" The word shrank Parker to smallness. "This was a clone matter, concerning no others."

"God give me strength!" He asked David, without

change of pace, "Is Raft carrying a weapon?"

Almost it worked, but he had half-turned his back to the clone and missed the instant blaze of threat and warning that cancelled David's desire to please. The biologist, sure that whatever he did could only intensify disaster, said unhappily, "I don't know."

"Nobody knows any damned thing that matters."

David wished he knew what mattered to the clonebrothers. Albert, as clone-father, must not be interfered with; so much would be axiomatic in their system of involuted loyalties . . . or perhaps only the clone might interfere. So if Albert carried a gun it must be allowed that he had reason. But if Parker said he was insane, that could not be allowed as reason because the clone-father was not subject to the conclusions of outsiders. The clone breathed an atmosphere of perfumed unity—togetherness at smothering point.

Parker asked their bland faces, "Is he armed?"

"He did not tell us." Another said, "We did not ask," and a third, "We do not question the clone-father." The fourth showed marginal life in the lift of an eyebrow and murmured, "Who can know what Albert does when Albert is solely Albert?"

Parker reddened; he could take Arthur's cheek better than the clone's contemptuous play. He would get nowhere with them, but had to try.

"You know his mind. You all know each other's minds."

"Not so." This was no flummery; a spokesman had been instantly elected.

"Yet one speaks for all of you, without conference."

"On matters of total agreement only."

"Telepathy." His tone said, "Deny it if you can."

"Not so!" Sharply emphatic. Parker believed him—believed, that is, that the clone did not recognize the talent as telepathy. "It is a stupidity which John once embraced because we think alike and in simple matters no speech is needed. One way of thought can have only one ending. Only scientists scratch for the intricate and difficult while simplicities escape them; truths are simple but their minds demand complication." He glared at David. "The clone could live with telepathy; you sniveling liars could not.''

Parker gave it up. Ask a silly question and get more answer than you bargained for, none of it useful. He closed his eyes to shut them all out while he considered Raft as the ''father of tomorrow.'' And then Campion as a further development . . . and Campion's children and children's children, all further developments . . . of what and towards what?

He opened his eyes to ask forcefully, ''Will you have the future of men grabbed by the descendants of a mad mother and a mad son?'' The clone faces did not change. ''He *is* mad—dangerously, fixatedly, paranoidally mad. In the manner of his screaming mother, blinded by the light of a supernal ego!'' The clone did not react; David made motions of distress like a harassed host with a rumbustious guest. Parker remembered the clone's pinnacle of moral purity and launched a torpedo at its base. ''Your Albert murdered his crewman. The clone does not kill—but Albert kills.''

The faces registered contemptuous unbelief. A spokesman said, ''As policeman you need a scapegoat. Albert is human. Humans do not kill.''

He conjectured dazedly that if humans—meaning the clone—do not kill, then they classify the rest of us as animals. In the midst of the dissolution of Gangoil the clone could speak of men as a species already supplanted.

The facts, then, were still to come, and they rested with a pack of philosophic amateurs who knew biology and who knew nothing, nothing, nothing else. He spoke on a note of hopelessness to David. ''I can only do what I must. Remember that I don't *want* to kill him.''

David merely looked outraged.

The scratches were long but superficial. Arthur produced something like a styptic pencil from a wall cupboard and applied it with finicky precision, talking all the time: ''——nobody believes she really wanted to rule the world. She just wanted to be top girl with no let or hindrance, and, with the clone to strongarm anyone who objected, she had the run of all the equipment in the place. Chin up!'' Raft lifted his head for an application where talons had caught in the angle of the jaw. "She really hated the clone, but mad and all she had her head screwed on straight and didn't let it show; she knew that without them she was nothing. They knew, of course—those bastards know everything—but power suits them. Would suit you too. Yes?" Raft's smile was any answer Arthur cared to make it. "And then, whether they liked it or not, they had this built in reverence thing, but *that* took a mighty tumble. No wonder she burst at the seams when they rated you above her! There; you'll do." He tossed the coagulant into the cupboard. "Not that you're my charismatic dream of the new Adam."

"You think that's what I am?"

"Scandal says."

"But you like your father figures more glamorous?"

"Let's say, more self-controlled."

"You've got a brass nerve; it's a pity about your bitching tongue."

Arthur followed him from the washroom, reflecting that like the rest of the simultaneous dancers Raft cared that people should fear him. He was more open about it; a sort of *primitive* simultaneous dancer, before civilization set in. Pity, really.

They found the corridor rippling with mixed uncertainties. Parker, domineering but not in control, faced David, sullenly cowed; round them the police and clone-brothers maneuvered fractionally, observing each other, unbelligerent but snapping small tactical advantages of position.

The strategic waltzing stilled as The Lady's door opened and into the tableau sailed the woman herself, unruffled as though she had never in her life screamed abuse or unsheathed a claw. Whatever tranquilizer had been given her had been no more than a suppressive of excess energies; she looked an ordinary, plumpish, not unattractive woman. Her hair had been rapidly arranged; she had lost the maenad appearance. She was clothed now, in high-heeled bedroom slippers and a white evening wrap trimmed with fur enough to winter a flock of ermine. But she had lost majesty; with eyes damped to dullness she was uncompromisingly vulgar. Behind her Eric and Francis attended in boredom.

At sight of Raft she slowed her progress, assumed an

expression of resigned suffering and spoke gently. "You have been a great disappointment to me, Albert; a great disappointment." The lip of the distressed mother trembled bravely. She was incredible.

Raft had recovered some equilibrium; he said cheerfully, "You stupid bitch, you hardly ever noticed me."

In fact she hardly noticed him now, but continued in character, "Your father never could control you, but he was a weak man who disapproved of corporal punishment. I feel it was a mistake."

"When you did notice me you belted me enough for both."

His statement did not exist. "And as a woman it was not my place to discipline a rebellious child."

"Rebellious, is it? I didn't dare open my damned mouth."

She completed her thought. "Only John could handle you. I must talk with John."

"Let's both talk with John." He extended his arm in mocking escort. She seemed then to see him clearly and started back with a revulsion which blazed an instant through the tranquilizer and went out.

She turned down a side corridor and all of them followed, like a retinue, with Parker grinning to himself at Raft's expression as his mother's moment of recoil ripped his self-possession like a switch-blade. Young conditioning dies hard.

It was a short progress. She came to a door and would have gone straight into Heathcote's apartment if Raft had not heaved close, between her escorts, and made to enter with her.

She cried out, "Am I never to be free of you?" and he answered like her mutinous child, "John has been more to me than he ever was to you."

"I suppose I cannot prevent you." She sighed with sublime self-pity. "I am too much a woman to use force on a man."

Parker cackled, and to Raft's glare remarked, "I'm coming in, too. My professional interest supersedes your jealousies."

Raft grunted, "You'll see John when I'm good and ready to let you."

Parker snapped his fingers and guns appeared in the hands of the police. The clone-brothers tensed and at once relaxed; their eyes turned to Raft for orders; one said, "Albert should decide. He has first right with John."

The Lady's glance should have swept them out of existence but Raft accepted primogeniture and chieftainship without comment; if his contempt could not alienate them, so be it. "I think we could take your boys, Controller, guns and all, but we aren't here for bloodshed and you have some right. But your men stay out here. And both clones."

David protested that he should be included. "All this is by my agreement and you need me. I should be fully informed on all developments."

Parker raised his eyebrows and Raft conceded, "Give an inch and you get a committee meeting. Let's go in— Mother."

She shrugged away from the word.

Arthur murmured in Parker's ear, "There's a back way out of John's suite," and to his suspicious glance explained, "I wouldn't trust that bull running loose any further than you would."

"Show two of my men the other entrance."

Two clone-brothers detached themselves without apparent discussion and followed Arthur and the policemen. No one contested the arrangement; Raft observed, understood and pointedly ignored it.

Francis temporarily took over Arthur's role of gadfly to remark on forty years of genetics achieving nothing better than a family brawl. One of the clone-brothers told him with uncharacteristic coarseness to keep his bloody mouth shut, surprising those who had not realized their individuals could occasionally speak for themselves.

Lindley had had neither the urge nor the time to lecture on Trollopian Victoriana, so Parker inventoried the huge room without understanding. Accustomed to light and color and usuform practicality, he saw only a clutter of somber and depressing furnishings; it was easy to ignore these oddities in favor of the apparition of Heathcote. He had gained from Lindley a sketchy idea of a gerontological miracle without evaluating the compressed and ambiguous facts; he was not prepared for fantasy.

The young man raging in the center of the ridiculously over-figured carpet could not, of course, be Heathcote; the aged and hysterical voice suggested that the youthful face was a mask.

"I'll not have it! Not have it! Entry without so much as token knocking! Doctor David, I'll not have that woman tramping through my quarters at will!" His ranting died in a reedy gasp as he realized that the clone face with The Lady was not one of her attendants.

"Albert!" His voice squeaked abominably. He ran down the room, arms outstretched, crying the name, almost weeping it, until he flung himself on the petrified Raft and to Parker's amusement kissed the Commander on the mouth, then stepped back to hold him at arm's length and slobber, "My boy, my boy!"

Raft seemed to doubt, like Parker, that this lunatic could be his ancient biologist. He faced David with ready accusation, then returned his eyes dumbly to Heathcote, recalling what he had been told and had passed over, absorbing now the impact of it. With a jerk of his body, a total reflex, he dislodged the grasping hands, rejected the ersatz creature; a burgeoning disgust invaded his face and vanished into an expressionless withdrawal.

"No!" he said, reclaiming a lifetime's affection, taking it back for ever.

Heathcote's pale fingers fluttered uselessly; his eyes took on an unutterable hurt; old age looked out of him.

Into the gap of silence The Lady, impervious to everything outside her intention, entered dignified complaint. "John, you must assert some authority over Albert. He has become unmanageable." In her self-absorption she was as fantastic as the changeling Heathcote. "He actually struck me," she announced, and probably believed it. She pouted and posed as a forlorn little girl, her tranquilized mind incapable of subtlety.

Heathcote buried his face in his hands. Raft stood over him without love, his judgement made. "I must be sure what you are. Are you a rejuvenated John?"

From between his hands Heathcote answered extraordinarily, "Not quite." He lifted his head and a young man looked out, as if a switch of bodies had been made under their noses. Old John had been retired to lick his wound in another place. "I am cloned from him and I have most of his memories. That is another process. Having memory, I sometimes think I am he." Something appeared of a bleak Victorian formality. "I regret having submitted you to indignity, Commander. Shock and emotion unbalance me. I confuse the living man with the dead."

"Old John is dead?"

"A body dies—so we say. John Heathcote's body died—as you might say. I have his mind. I have *all* his mind and most of his memories—not knowledge of him as another man, but memories. Tell me, Albert—Commander—who am I? Who is dead?"

Raft said coldly, "I couldn't care less, nor am I interested in ambivalent mockups." He turned restlessly, heel and toe, to scrutinize the room. "All this . . . The old man collected Victorian junk but he wasn't so far sunk in it as to retire physically into another age. Your clothes——" he searched for the word "——are Trollopian. He would not have done that."

"He did. The collapse of the world unbalanced him; his interests became obsessions. Sometimes I am aware of obsession; at others I am Old John and see nothing abnormal in these surroundings."

All of this might have passed unheard by The Lady, who said patiently, "John, I insist that you listen to me."

The young face surveyed her with a suppressed emotion Parker could not read.

"I remember you clearly now; Doctor Lindley supplied the triggering information. You are Mrs. Raft."

The unfamiliar address roused her. "I am The Lady!" She stretched her hands to him. "And you loved me, John."

Parker's mind gave a comprehending *oh-oh* as more jigsaw fell into place and Heathcote said, "I have remembered it."

"We can love again!" The actor's inflexion was mechanical; her dulled mind was dredging up weapons of habit, abridged and simplified to naïvety. "Remember, John!" She threw back the fur from her shoulders and lowered her hands to allow the wrap to slip down her body to the floor and stood naked before him, erect and in her manner appealing, an over-ripened Venus arising from a pool of trampled cloth.

To the spectacle of his mother as vaudevillian courtesan Raft gave only impatience, and Heathcote said with embarrassment, "It ended."

"To begin again!" Siddons, Bernhardt, Duse.

Heathcote, his own rejection still burning, answered with precision. "Love does not begin again, and our ages are no longer compatible with dalliance."

The cruelty, Parker saw, was meaningless. The Lady, wanting only a tool for the humiliation of Raft, was as unable to observe her own emptiness as to realize that Raft was out of her reach for all time. She would not suffer.

Only her stung vanity reached to turn the grotesque into comedy. She sat down roundly on her ample backside, squawking bitterness, and burst into rowdy tears.

Heathcote turned his back on her. "This is most distasteful. Cannot her catamites come for her?"

Raft said, "Let it wait. I have a question." His blandness promised no pleasure.

Heathcote made a plea curiously like a warning. "Remember, Commander—Albert—that to me, in any persona, you are the boy I raised and loved and sent away for his safety. And waited for."

Raft inclined his head curtly, recognizing the man's right and discarding it. "I am no longer the boy. I imagined I needed your affection. I don't."

Dimly Parker sensed the intolerable nature of the renewed blow, and gropingly sympathized. And there was more to the young Heathcote than a creature of confusions; he was able to admire the man who now shook off his reverse in a single display of pain and submerged it in dignity.

"Ask your question."

"Who is Ian Campion?"

Parker felt he had no right to surprise; he should have

guessed it. Yet the time elements were incompatible . . . He saw no surprise in Raft.

"Yes. Anything else was genetically impossible—mathematically improbable. So you kept faith. But how? Who was the mother?"

Heathcote had no chance to reply. The Lady shrieked from the floor, "Your daughter! He had your sperm in bank and bred her back to you like a stud animal!" Her mouth twisted in an attempt at virtuous horror. "Incest! Campion is your incestuous son!" Satisfied with her performance, she patted her hair and commented primly, "He'll go mad, of course. They always do."

Raft asked, "Where is she?" and behind him David answered, "Thirty years dead. It was a time when many were still dying."

"Even in Gangoil?"

"She stole the baby and left here. Escaped, if you like."

"With Ian? How did he come to—No matter; it will keep." He said to Heathcote, "I don't give a damn about the ethics of incest though I might have shrunk from it in the flesh. The point is that the union was genetically successful. Wasn't it?"

Everyone in Gangoil, Parker thought, was larger than life or displaced slightly to one side of it—or was he seeing reality from an unaccustomed angle? Perhaps his own attitudes, logical to himself, disturbed and repelled others . . . but surely not so profoundly as Heathcote's voice detailing cool matters of fact concluded before his young-man persona was born. If a cutting could be said to have been born.

". . . the reinforcement of useful recessives in your gene complex . . . valuable additions from the girl's mother . . . a multi-directional viability amenable to simple gene surgery . . ."

Campion, it seemed, was more than he could possibly guess—a gene bank for supermen—and the young-old monster was saying it plainly in his pedantic whine. "I promised you would be the father of the future and Ian was the first fruit of that promise."

I think, Parker mused, *that I also might be a little mad if someone had promised me that, and I believed him.*

Raft responded with suspicion. "I don't forget your

promises. But Ian was never brought back to Gangoil, was he? With him the matter ended.''

''I grew old.'' It was neither apology nor explanation, only an enormous and pathetic regret.

David intervened with an authority Parker had not heard from him, entering his own territory. ''The work continued.''

Heathcote snorted derision. Raft asked, ''Under your direction, Doctor?''

''Eventually. I was born in Gangoil; there were directors before me.''

''And?''

''Campion was an experimental line which could be duplicated if need be. There were others.''

''Tell me.''

''Those are what you came to see.''

Parker said, ''What I also came to see.'' The balance of forces should be kept before their minds.

An old Heathcote asked, ''Who is that man?'' and Raft told him sharply, ''He is a policeman. An ally of sorts, though I'd see him damned if I could. That will come. Doctor David, what have you to show me?''

''The future.''

''Large word. Where do we find it? In your laboratories? Then we're wasting time.''

David asked, ''Will you come with us, John?'' It was only the routine politeness of the usurper to the superannuated star.

''No.'' More than a refusal; the snapping shut of a mind.

''John is upset by our neglect of the lines of research he laid down.'' Perhaps fortunately for his peace of mind he could not see Raft's expression as he led the way to the door. ''I have never been able to convince him that his routine was too limited.''

They filed into the corridor, followed by The Lady's giggling farewell: ''Wait till you see what the doctor has for you!''

Parker directed Francis—or Eric—to get his men back from the rear exit. ''Then go in and collect your bag while she's quiet.''

There were too many tensions, he thought, pulling too

many ways, and grotesques like Heathcote and Mother Raft
only clouded issues. If one matter stood out as appallingly
touchy, it was Heathcote-God's promise to his clod of a
Jesus. Who could wear the magnificence of genetic messiah
from the stars? Lindley had been insistent about the harm-
lessness of the place with The Lady's authority broken, and
he hoped his men would not need their weapons, but their
presence comforted him.

— 6 —

The twelve of them not only fitted easily into the laboratory
lift, designed for portage of supplies, but maintained their
division into mutually watchful units, with David and Arthur as odd men out. Only Arthur appeared unconscious of
cross currents, but in Parker's view that sharp intelligence
missed nothing and might in its sheer lack of commitment
be of value.

The lift crawled downward. And who need hurry in Gangoil, built just outside the wall of its culture's time and
space? David remarked, like a tourist guide, on the half-
mile drop which would occupy six minutes. "That old Federal Government knew the value of what it hid."

No one offered congratulations.

Parker asked suddenly, "Who began the War of the Collapse? Who mutated the crops and diseases?"

"Who knows?" He sounded genuine. "And who wants
to know? I was not born; to me it's only an old horror
story. Do you want to blame Gangoil?"

"Gangoil might know. Such a long-term project must
have archives. And trained archivists."

"My department," Arthur said. "That information is not
in the archives, and I agree that it would be better suppressed if it were."

Parker suspected that he had been exquisitely evaded, but
by then Raft had taken center stage and history had to wait
on exhibitionism.

"Yesterday is over; forget it. Consider tomorrow." Having their attention, he told them amiably, "I am tomorrow."

The clone nodded in unison. The police remained stolid. Parker waited for revelation. David looked, for no obvious reason, uneasy. Arthur said, "Balls."

To Raft's insulted rigidity he extended ultimate impertinence. "If it were true it would have to be altered."

Parker tensed for intervention but Raft had captured a more urgent aspect of the speech. "If? *If*? What does he mean, David?"

David retreated into blustering panic. "Nothing! He means nothing! What in hell are you talking about, Arthur? You're ignorant of the program—ignorant!"

The unrepentant Arthur could not be stared down but Raft was after all concerned only with Raft. "Forty-two years ago John Heathcote named me father of the future, and it was no metaphor. I hold Gangoil to the promise. Am I understood?"

David made a gesture of cowed assent.

"I want more than that, Doctor. We are about to inspect the children of my body. Is that what in fact they are—the children of my genes?"

Definition of a madman, Parker thought, with his inner arm pressing on his shoulder holster: *a man stripped to the naked ego.*

"Let me hear you, Doctor David!"

David agreed desperately. "The children of your genes. Everything you will see—yours!"

The clone gave their unison nod and a paternal smile. Arthur said, "I bet you'll just love your pretties," and could not resist a swiping jeer: "Pack of bastards, I'd call them."

Clone breaths hissed inwards but Raft merely looked at David, who bleated with anger and fear. "He has seen some—some failures. His clone have acted as assistant in minor laboratories and he has seen—seen . . . in research there are always some failed results." He shook, convinced that he was being made answerable to a madman who could command the clone and that death could be dealt faster than Parker could prevent it. Arthur he himself could have killed, happily. "He knows nothing of the major laboratories. Nothing."

Raft flung over his shoulder, "Arthur, you make too much clatter with your cap and bells."

Parker speculated, in passing, what might be the reason for the existence of Arthur's clone. Experimental what, besides the obvious?

The lift halted gently and the doors opened.

The laboratory covered the same immense floorspace as the vehicle park far above, but its long reaches were deceptive; white walls faded into each other's planes and into the white ceiling, hallucinating depth. White smocks and shoes, white trousers and skirts moved against white tiles and cupboards and partitions. Splashes of flesh color were hands and faces; instruments were glints of copper and chrome; glassware gave glitter to the ubiquitous white.

Benches, tables, sinks, cupboards and aggregates of incomprehensible machines stretched in soldierly rows the entire length of the hall, with at their center a raised and glass-walled structure where white-clad figures fluttered white paper and spoke into white administrative telephones.

Only the grey-green filing cabinets were drab. From visits to Canberra archives Parker recognized them as relics of the old world public offices; no officer of his would put up with such arbitrary dullness in his work area.

"This is the primary laboratory." David was home, his voice asserting territorial right. Near-by heads swiveled in recognition but their eyes fastened on Raft. As Arthur had said, there was more than dress to distinguish him from the clone.

Raft said loudly, "They know who I am." He was pleased.

The faces turned away, detected in vulgar staring.

The unremitting egocentricity affected Parker like a filed glass. "Everybody on the damned planet knows."

"Who but not what, eh, Controller? Does it rankle, that your plans and Ian's must make room for the father of tomorrow?"

Parker cursed himself for making the opportunity, but Arthur stole the scene from both of them. "Really, Commander, what difference does it make who is Daddy? I get no special joy from being one of your fiddled-with off-shoots. I can tell you."

"You!" Raft began to absorb the implications of the relationships he himself had demanded.

David rushed his explanation. "Commander, I said every experiment has been designed to preserve and strengthen your line." He added, with menace for Arthur, "Not all were designed for permanence; ancillary attempts were required for testing of theories. Arthur's clone is six or seven stages of manipulation removed from the central line. It is a dead end, useful for service work in the complex."

The eagle let the rabbit go. "It isn't important."

Arthur bridled. "Oh, but it is. Look what can happen to you with the slip of a molecule!"

Parker stifled laughter, but assessed Arthur's consistent playing with fire; he would surely need protection later, if not from Raft then from the clone, who registered venomous recognition of sacrilege. But Arthur feared neither Raft nor clone.

With sharpened attention Parker measured Arthur's body against Raft's, point for point, and found the family resemblance inescapable there while it was lacking in the face. Arthur was perhaps not quite so big overall but where Raft's physique—and his clone's—was classically beautiful, Arthur's flatter and longer muscles and slightly different shaping of muscle groups gave a curious impression of . . . his subconscious supplied, a little to its own surprise, "engineering efficiency."

He filed the observation with his puzzlement; his capacity for multiple observation was becoming impossibly stretched.

Raft chose to behave now as if Arthur did not exist—possibly because the police guns were an unsolved problem—and asked David what was done in this hall.

"Non-specialist work. Cell cultivation and observation, radiological research on multi-specimen projects, common pathology routines. These operatives are the specialists' laborers, so to speak. There is little to see here."

He led them past the regimental benches towards the stairhead leading down.

From the corner of his eye Parker caught a movement of something white across the floor between benches and one of his policemen gave a hoarse, choked exclamation. He turned his head swiftly enough to catch a photographic glimpse and forgive the lapse of training.

It was about three feet high and mostly head, and it moved with the smooth flow of tiny footsteps on stumped legs under the floor-length gown. As it skittered between the benches it held aloft a kidney dish, like an offertory vessel borne from one research assistant to another.

Parker saw the huge lunar face clearly before it vanished behind the woman who held forceps over the dish to drop something into it. The tiny mouth and splayed nose were lost in the dish-shaped visage; the face was a disk of skin under sparse hair, for there were no eyes, none at all, nor depressions where they might have been, only a soft pudding-crust of featureless flesh.

He heard it mewling against the woman's smock. She listened intently, then put her hand on the thing's face, tapping and patting and soothing, and bent to whisper where the ears should be. The mewling stopped. It appeared, to race again to the opposite bench, kidney dish held high, to deliver the soggy scrap of contents to another woman who glanced indignantly at the intruders as she took the dish from its infantile hands.

"What in hell's that?" Whatever its understanding, the thing recognized harshness and hid afresh from Raft's voice; the second woman plainly wished them all to the devil as she repeated the patting and placating procedure.

David said coolly, "An error. As you see, it is not un-intelligent, and it likes to make itself useful within its limits. A sort of laboratory mascot, you might say."

Who might say it, Parker's thought ran, was a soulless golem, but it was a pleasure to hear Raft again disconcerted, asking. "Why don't you kill such things?"

A fine sighing of dismay came from the clone-brothers, and phrases: "The living flesh!" "All things part of us!" "Part of you, Albert, of you!" "Even the errors, sacred flesh!"

Raft turned on them with insult in his eyes and it seemed to Parker that there might be hope for the man if shock penetrated deeply enough. But the eyes hardened; he absorbed the brothers' attitude and accepted it. Parker's inward scowling deepened; the man would accept anything which could be twisted into an adulation, a hint of godhead.

David seized opportunity to marshal them onward. "Pollyanna enjoys her life, we believe. And it is 'she' by chromosomal definition. She's very nervous but laughs and sings a lot. We go down here."

On the stairs Parker dropped a pace back to mutter to Arthur, "What's your special talent?"

Arthur was bland. "Sleight of hand. Quickness deceives the eye."

That was all that was to be got from him—that and the recollection of the tiny flicker of the head which had slipped Raft's punch in The Lady's boudoir.

The second floor of the basement was more like the concrete galleries of the domicile floors, a similar gridiron of corridors and rooms, but more austere. Only functional items disturbed the walls—videophones, fuse-boxes, cupboards with contents incognitoed by symbols instead of words. Not a sound came from behind the closed doors and David's voice was an intrusion on the bleak air.

"The suites are soundproofed. We work here with live subjects in many cases and the sounds could often be disturbing."

Parker's young men were openly upset by the implications of this and David became defensive. "I don't know what chimerae you are conjuring, but this is an advanced biological laboratory—the most advanced in history—and the pursuit of knowledge is not like the peaceful construction of a work of art, though the end may be similar."

Parker glossed drily, "You mean that each perfected specimen is produced at the price of a few tormented monsters."

"That is a most biased recension of my words. We do not practice deliberate cruelties."

Raft said suddenly, "Doctor Moreau."

Only David took the reference. "Not so, Commander. I was given that romance during my indoctrinal training as a warning against falsified aims. Gangoil's business is to produce beings developed to their ultimate capacities, not meaningless sculptures in flesh."

They might have accepted his statement of dedication, however disapprovingly, if Arthur had not tossed in sweet poison. "Like Pollyanna—the ultimate brainless message runner. Just try to improve on that!"

David exploded. "Shut your poisonous mouth! Who attached you to this party? Get about your sycophant's business upstairs!"

Arthur smiled at Parker, openly inviting patronage. "I just thought I might come in handy."

It was an offer of some sort and Parker accepted it, on the principle of never refusing an ally. "Let him stay."

Raft watched the play impassively. The clone-brothers seemed perturbed as if they also wondered what Arthur offered. David calmed rapidly against an opposition he could not contest, conceding sulkily that he supposed he must do as he was told.

Raft intervened. "I don't think so, Doctor. A trouble-making failed experiment has no place here." He addressed Arthur, "You! Get back upstairs."

"You," suggested Arthur, "get stuffed."

Raft swept through the screen of clone-brothers.

Parker bellowed, "Be still!" and the guns appeared.

Raft halted with his fist rising.

Parker laid down the law. "No violence. And Arthur stays. Understand that I control this party."

David shrugged. Arthur nodded appreciatively. The clone-brothers looked mutinous but so far passive. Raft said very quietly, "Your guns persuade, but not for ever. What we have to do, you and I and Ian, needs more than a policeman's expertise." His voice strengthened. "You will realize yet that I *am* Gangoil." To Arthur he said, "You've chosen your master, bitch, but he won't save you. Let's get on, Doctor David."

Parker mulled over the fact that Arthur, with Raft in motion against him, had not observably tensed in his lounging against the wall.

David grumbled again that there was little he could actually show on this floor. "Unless you are prepared to undergo theater sterilization. The floor is divided into self-contained blocks, each entered through a sterilization chamber. The work is mainly ultra-microscopic probing, microsurgery by laser and pulse-radiation as well as chemical means, and experimental pathology. There is little to see in the demonstrative sense.'' Nobody spoke or moved; he felt the unspoken accusation of double-talk. "Unless you care to inspect the gestation sector. The incubators can be examined through glass without prior sterilization.''

Parker holstered his gun. "We'll see those. We want to observe results rather than methods.''

Arthur said, "So here comes one.''

From far down the corridor a woman approached. They assumed a woman because of the long brown hair and sarong-like garment, but became less certain. The bare torso did not carry the heavy breasts which would have matched the sturdy body and the outline appeared muscular rather than rounded.

From speaking distance the figure acknowledged Doctor David in a flat contralto, moved through the group without paying attention to them beyond a swift notice of Raft and disappeared into one of the experimental blocks.

David returned the greeting, calling her Mary, settling gender if not wholly the question of sex. She was a Raft, no doubt of it, a twin sister Raft carved from the family block but muddled in the differentiation. Her breasts were little more developed than a man's and her muscles far more so than a woman's; she carried the essential layers of fat tissue for her sex, but the distribution was erratic; her shoulders were too broad and her hips too stiffly articulated. That she wore make-up, and too much of it, was an aggressive error; the defiant need to be taken for a woman was a failed plea.

Parker asked harshly, "Another dead end?'' and David crackled in defense, "Can't you set aside emotional judgement? There's no result without trial and no trial without error.''

"I feel the world can do without the results I've seen. I begin to suspect that your work features a touch of art for art's sake.''

"That would make us sadists—animals.''

"You have a point. It would. And you have been secluded from humanity long enough to fall from the norm.''

Raft asked, ''Why don't you shut up, copper? You haven't much morality to cheer about.''

Parker prodded immediately. ''You quarrelled with Heathcote over the direction of his work. Now you see where the direction led, do you want to defend it?''

If he thought to put Raft in an impossible position, he failed. The starman said simply, ''I am Gangoil; I will decide finally what stays and what stops.''

The immense assumption frightened David into grey faced fear for his lifetime of dedication, but the clone brothers snapped little head-jerks of assent.

Arthur made conversation. ''However, there are compensations, and Daddy of All the Ages mightn't have to do too much deciding.''

The clone-brothers drew concerted breathy hisses and seemed about to close in on him, but Raft stopped them with a gesture. His authority seemed absolute. They halted with marionette precision.

''There's no need for anyone to die.'' Raft turned his head to Parker. ''Yet.''

Arthur had not moved. He said, ''The lady, forgive the word, who just passed, is genetically sterile. As am I and as are my brothers. And as are most of the pretties we are about to inspect. Be assured, Commander, that no little brood of Pollyannas or Marys will scuttle around the playgrounds of tomorrow.''

David would have interrupted if Raft had not cut him off. ''Go on, bitch. Your spite may show a dividend.''

Arthur inclined his head in gracious insult. ''Biology is not my dish of slops but you can't infest Gangoil without getting a splash here and there, and local scandal says it's all tied up with gene relationships. Traits aren't simple like one gene, one characteristic. It happens sometimes—I think eye color is determined by a single gene—but most are the result of interaction of groups of genes, which in turn have effect on the operations of other groups. Very complicated, you see; far too much for a simple soul like me. That's why the projects are worked out on computers, and even then the programer can't foresee all his long-range effects because he doesn't know what questions to ask until he sees the answers. So round and round it goes and most of what our tame zoo is demonstrating is what can't be done, while the commonest outcome of complex gene manipulation is an inability to reproduce. Not art for art's sake, Mister Parker, so much as manipulation for desperation's sake. They keep on mixing and hope something nice will float to the top.''

Raft looked at David. "Well?''

David, between fear and rage, ground out an answer. ''The biological information is over-simplified but basically correct. The commentary is a disgraceful attempt to create dissension.''

''Successful one, too,'' Parker said. ''Arthur, what is your dead-end trait?''

Surprisingly, Arthur turned sulky. ''Seven of us were cloned for isolation of homosexual influences. I suppose you could call that a success.''

David cut in waspishly, ''Each of them was also subjected to other forms of genetic engineering, without success. This one was an attempt to improve on Commander Raft's abnormally fast reflexes. A failed attempt. Arthur has never forgiven us for his not being a superman.''

Raft said speculatively. ''I think he's as fast as I am.''

Arthur's reaction was a tossed head and a snapped, ''Faster.''

Raft grinned. ''All right, dearie, have it your way.'' The grin was not fashioned for amusement.

Parker fancied a satisfied glint in Arthur's eye, but by now he was fancying innumerable peculiarities, including a feeling that the display of sulks had been a diversion permitting a less than total answer to his question.

They followed David to the gestation sector.

Parker expected a chamber of horrors; an anticipatory relish admitted the touch of the ghoul in all men. The reality was close to prosaic. What he saw was a bank of humidi-cribs behind plate glass, each crib holding a small form. Closer examination showed that not all were so small as would normally need the protection of the crib and in some the aged faces made it difficult to guess the relative state of development.

"What is the percentage of successful manipulation?"

David blinked. "I have never considered it in quantitative terms. Very small, of course. Thousands of pathological studies to determine a desired structure—perhaps hundreds of gestations to achieve it—and then no certainty of a viable structure. The number of satisfactory results is small. But the aim is only a single end product, is it not?"

"A final descendant?" David's face wrote largely that his thinking did not proceed along so narrow a line as Raft's question. "An ultimate child of my line?"

Parker intervened. "We take that for granted, Commander." Raft, after a second's thought, let it be so. Parker pursued, "There must be a great number of successful manipulations at large in Gangoil."

"Not so many. To most of them life would be a burden; even for science we cannot be totally inhumane."

Parker thought of Pollyanna and considered the meanings of "burden" and "inhumane." "And the—er—nonviable?"

"Euthanasia, naturally."

The idea was not controversial in Parker's world but he knew enough history to look for a reaction from Raft. There was none; Raft was interested only in himself as Progenitor Apparent. He suppressed a question about the nature of some part of Gangoil's protein supplies, not wishing to risk revolted stomachs in his policemen. Instead he asked, "What sort of improvements are you aiming at?"

"The usual dreams of men—longevity, an improved immunological system, control of reflexes, increased muscular efficiency, self-replacement in brain cells and others, regrowth of injured members and so on. The ultimate body should be virtually immortal, with total control of its autonomic system and even of cellular structures, but we are a long way from that. It will not be arrived at in my time."

"And all this is inherent in human genes?"

"We don't know. We think so. The combinations produced by the computers indicate extreme probability."

Parker found himself resenting Gangoil most powerfully. *A marvelous future seen from far away—but no room for us in it.* Change, even enormous change, he could face; that was what he and Campion conspired to bring about, but like any man he wanted miracles that would fit within his grasp, not outright destruction of his universe by an unimaginable other, however godlike.

Angrily he said, "We aren't interested in beginnings. Let's move on to the major work." Raft nodded. "Let us see the final product."

"Another floor down," David said stiffly, resenting the cheap-tour attitude to decades of achievement.

As they descended some old association cast up a phrase in Parker's mind—"nether hell."

—7—

"Results!" David tried a pallid jocularity over his cringing to Raft. "You might call this our warehouse display room."

Arthur chirruped, "Any buyers for tomorrow's pretties?" and for once caught no attention.

The area was smaller than the upper concrete caverns, with no more than a sixth of their floorspace. By the staircase a single white-clad figure sat at a console, a broad spread of dials and controls and miniature TV screens; he turned his head to see who entered and turned it away, satisfied.

New faces, Parker thought, should be an excitement in an ingrown community; but perhaps "ingrown" was a pivotal word, and with a psychic shiver he acknowledged the deadening outcome of an unrelenting conditioning in self-sufficiency.

The remainder of the space was taken up by another of Gangoil's constructions in utilitarian geometry. Three rows, each of nine waist-high, squat cabinets, stretched the length of the room, emphasizing the soulless perspective; each was about eight feet square, drearily white-enameled and surmounted by a flattened glass dome like a carapace.

"Slow met chambers!"

"Yes, yes!" David's voice pitched high in his effort to please. "You would recognize them, of course, Commander." He gabbled with awful brightness, "What better way to preserve an experimental model during periods of assessment and consideration?"

The man's terror was becoming excessive; something he had counted on to please, he was no longer sure of. And how right he might be, Parker thought, hugging the one piece of truly murderous information Lindley had given him.

Raft bent over the nearest chamber, examining the meters and button controls set flush in the casing. "Changes. Improvements?"

"Extensions of function," David chattered. "Control of growth rates, stimulation of specific factors, alteration of relationships between metabolic functions. The possibilities are endless. Some quite brilliant biologists and electronic engineers have collaborated on improvement over Doctor Heathcote's initial design."

"There was no Heathcote design."

"No, Commander?"

"There was a Heathcote conception and a Raft design." It could be true, Parker decided, but probably was not; Raft had moved into the foggy drifts of megalomania, prepared to assume any aggrandizing claim. "Heathcote was no genius. He was a headpiece, a pivot, competent and lucky in the men working with and under him. Without *me* there would have been no slow met, no star voyage and hence no Gangoil. Do you understand now how I *am* Gangoil?"

It was so smooth, so matter of fact, so much obvious truth; no wonder insanity could pass so many boundaries of fantasy before it was recognized.

"But Heathcote is dead and his effete replacement can be got rid of."

The clone-brothers spoke together, dissenting violently, subsiding at last into a single voice. "You are clone-father but John is the begetter. By clone he remains John, as we are you."

Raft answered them patiently. "You are mine—you are not me. The dummy John is not John. Get rid of fancies."

David pleaded across his fears, "But the work, the work! The memory transference!"

"That? A virtual immortality. The work can be transferred to the Raft strain." He bent over the chamber, dismissing a subject completed. "What's this?"

Parker did not much care what it was; his attention was on the patently unhappy clone-brothers. Raft was isolating himself from them satisfactorily and soon they might be leaderless. How to set about leading them? However, he crowded with the rest.

It was a male body, faintly clouded in the yellowish fluid, relaxed and blank, reminding of sleep and reminding of death while its condition was neither. The Raft resemblance was oblique; features seemed about to become Raft's or to have just failed to become. It was young, possibly in its early twenties and bigger boned than its many times removed clone-father; it was fleshless and tight-skinned to a skeletal degree yet without signs of malnutrition. Its peculiar musculature was large, anchored to every part of the over-massive bone structure available to it, but long and upraised and strangely angular in effect.

"So far a failure," David said, "but perhaps not eventually so. One of our computer patterning groups conceived the possibility of producing a more efficient muscle, a better heat engine, and this is the latest result. We have to be most careful with it; the thing is appalling strong. It has perhaps three times your strength, Commander."

Raft's eyes glazed and Parker's scalp prickled. Did the fool dream of memory-transfer, of his essential self grafted to this machine of flesh?

The fool was not utterly fallen between realities. "What's wrong with it?"

"The effects are ephemeral—titanic effort for a matter of seconds, then collapse. And the heart needs redesigning to absorb the strains. Work is proceeding on that. But the difficulties multiply; success brings new problems. This one has a convulsive symptom; it tends to break its own bones at peak effort."

"Continue that line, Doctor."

"It is dangerous because it is not very intelligent. Gene patterning is still more art than science, but we are learning the basic groupings and in natural phenomena there is always a key syndrome leading to a formula."

But Raft had given his order and moved on.

"This?"

They peered at an unremarkable child's body. "The hands. There was debate about the practical advantage of the little finger as an additional opposable thumb, but there

seems no value in it. The body is being preserved for pathological tests.''

Raft was away, uninterested, but stopped by the next chamber, arrested by an intense revulsion. ''Another Pollyanna!''

David hurried after. ''No, no; this is quite different, experimental work of an unusual kind. I don't encourage this
sort of thing—too much intuition allied to too little logic—
but the trio working on it are brilliant. It would have been
unreasonable to prevent them.''

''Stop yammering. What is it?''

''A search for embryonic senses. You may have heard
of people who can distinguish print or color through their
fingertips. Many can detect the near approach of an object
like a pencil which does not actually touch the skin. There
is the common awareness of being stared at. We can cite a
number of possibilities of receptor symptoms based on, for
example, fluctuations of potential in skin cells or detection
of airflow and air pressure variation. Experiment of course
involves suppression of the major nervous receptors in order to force use of the exotic——''

Parker ceased to listen and turned away from the thing,
the Pollyanna body with no face at all, not even the Pollyanna disk of flesh but a globular nub, a huge and shining
tumor, blue-veined under a circular crown of auburn hair.

Arthur's loud derision shocked his sickness into control.
''Nobody in his right mind wants to look at that subhuman
radar station. It doesn't work, anyway.''

Raft was sour. ''The bitch is right. Show me something
that works. A success.''

''Please! Science is not a simple puzzle game. Centuries
could pass . . .'' Only a frightened man would have lacked
the control to allow him to talk of centuries to Raft. He
said, despairingly, ''We have something that may be a blue-
print for tomorrow.'' He led them to the farthest slow
chamber in the farthest row. ''Here.'' He attempted pride
in his exhibit but was too dispirited to impress.

Arthur gave a high-pitched laugh, a mockery as deliberate as spittle in the face. He was close to Raft, who
flashed him a split-second glare of calculating rage, and that
perhaps inspired Arthur to crow directly into his ear, ''Look

what ingenuity and an absence of common sense can do to the beautiful Daddy body.''

It was scarcely possible that the lightning backhander could miss his out-thrust face, but it did miss. Parker was sure only that Arthur's head alone moved on his neck and that it moved no more than the fraction needed to swish Raft's knuckles in empty air.

Raft must have caught something of it from the corner of his eye, for he turned completely in a transcendent anger. His lips barely moved; Parker was close enough to apprehend rather than truly hear him say, ''Failure, eh? A failure to remember!''

David, with his mouth open for speech, froze in stupefaction, absorbed slowly what he had seen and blazed into stuttering fury at the only manner of betrayal which could touch his dedicated heart. ''Arthur! You withheld information—suppressed data . . .''

Raft snapped, ''Be quiet,'' and returned to calm with one of the intense nervous efforts of which he seemed endlessly capable. ''Later you can give him what attention seems necessary.''

But he was shaken, violently shaken at being outclassed on his own ground of flicker-fast reflex. And it would be better for Arthur that he should not fall into the hands of the stern-faced clone-brothers. Parker made sure two of his men were watching them before he looked at the exhibit.

It was hairless. Perhaps it was a man, perhaps a woman, for he could see no genitalia of any kind, but the hips were abnormally, most femininely wide and sloped sharply inwards at the knees. The vestigial breasts were ready to vanish from the genetic pattern but the apparent disposition of fatty tissue was female although the shoulders were masculinely broad and the muscles under the smooth layers of fat were large and powerful.

''This is the male specimen,'' David said. ''The female is practically identical, save that the hips are rather wider and the point of sexual ingress is readily apparent.'' He might have been discussing furniture but his nervous eyes never left Raft.

The head held their attention. The features belonged to Raft—a Raft glorified and transfigured, every flaw teased out into a handsomeness, a sweetness, a human splendor. It—he—bore the most beautiful face any of them had ever seen; even in the relaxation which drains faces to blankness it expressed a power they could perceive only in terms of wisdom and nobility. It looked up at them, sightlessly, from a perfect mask fitted to an ambiguous body—a mask because its forehead ended at the supraorbital ridge and the skull sloped back without a cranium. Its beautiful features were imposed on a brainless wedge of bone.

Raft asked, "Are you mad?"

Fright could not dim the sense of affront by ignorance. "Most certainly not! This is not beatified man to be judged by the standards of classic statuary; it is man as he can be! But man's standard of perfection is ridiculously based on himself." It was as close as he dared approach to a thrust at Raft, who merely held him wriggling on his glance and said, "No brain."

"Of course there is a brain, but not in the head, exposed and vulnerable. Between the thighs, in an armored pelvis, where the genitalia are also retracted until required. There is a small pseudo-brain in the head, little more than a relay station for the sense receptors, and even there the bone structure is reinforced. This model is to be largely self-sufficient; it should not require clothing save under extreme conditions because it can grow a fine pelt if necessary and also has conscious control over skin pigmentation."

"Shut up!"

David became rigid; through stiff jaws he enunciated a useless plea: "The specimen must be observed through the eyes of science. Today's man is not the evolutionary end."

Raft bellowed, "Will you be quiet!"

David was quiet.

Arthur came in like a gimlet. "This model really should be able to control things but in fact that strategically placed brain doesn't work too well." Raft remained still and silent. Arthur sighed great sorrow. "That's the trouble with your more spectacular descendants, Daddy—they're either sterile or stupid."

Raft uttered a sound Parker had heard once before, on the therapy tape—a scream blending rage and frustration, fear and desolation, torn out of him.

It seemed, astonishingly, to serve as an instant and complete release. He seemed to forget Arthur and said smoothly to David, "You must kill this thing."

David shook his head, unable to speak.

"It is to be killed."

David found a thread of voice to plead with a kind of hysterical determination, "Not destroy it; no."

Raft cocked his head as if listening to words behind the tone. "Dedication is not enough, little man; you must learn what may and may not be done. This line of manipulation is at an end."

David looked to Parker, but Parker's instinct was for once with Raft's; he did not fancy this vision of human glory.

Raft continued to lecture. "The quality of the work is undeniable but the direction unproductive. This——" he dismissed the thing with a flicking finger "——may serve in a million years or so; for today we must anticipate evolution rather than attempt total revolution. Old John was right and his memory-dummy may be of use after all; the direction lies through my son Ian."

The clone-brothers approved in their intense, soundless fashion. David's face cried out fears and frustrations. Arthur, for once, was quiet. Only Parker, excited by a meddling devil, threw out an irresistible bait: "Your beloved son, in whom you are well pleased."

No spark leapt; Raft was mildly surprised. "You quoted that before. Don't let religious ecstasy get the better of you." His mouth slackened and an inner sight invaded his eyes. "But he is beloved and I am well pleased. He is the key to tomorrow's humanity." His arm swept out as if to tip the contents of the slow chambers off the edge of the earth. "Well, Doctor David?"

"I have nothing more to show." He was sullen and uneasy and for Parker's money had every reason to be so.

"Nothing at all?" Parker asked, knowing his time had come. David held his eyes steadily while his face said he lied. "Nothing, Controller."

"Yet this hall is so small compared with the others. Where is the door to the rest of the floor?"

"There is no rest and no door. This was a small storage basement which we cleaned out to use as—as——"

"As a futurist zoo. But there is a door."

Raft asked, "What are you talking about, copper?" and David looked fearfully into the policeman's immense sureness.

"I talked to Lindley, Doctor."

David's fear burst out. "He had no right, no right! That was for Campion's ear. For Security only!"

"Why should he be loyal to your dreams? Lindley's loyalty is to men and women; he did what he thought best. Only the whole truth can prevent disaster, Doctor." He waited, but David was silent. "When everything is in sight, we can deal with it." The biologist registered only frightened misery. "Come, come, man—show us the telepaths."

His bomb did not explode, only fizzed a little.

Raft said contemptuously, "Telepathy's a fairy tale and one that I'm sick of. Old John used to rattle nonsense about it."

A clone spokesman said as from a vast height of superiority, "John was misled by our gift of communal empathy. There is no telepathic sense."

Parker did not doubt their honesty. Arthur was looking anticipatory as at a new and amusing gambit. Only the man at the console, forgotten at the other end of the hall, swung in his chair to listen.

David, with wary eyes on Raft, said, "Damn Lindley for ever," and gestured to the console operator, who stretched a finger and pressed.

Not ten feet from the group a shallow cupboard swung in from the wall on hinges; behind it a lead-sheathed door hissed softly as it slid aside.

The spidery nakedness that had crouched there, listening with its starved brain, shrieked at its vision of their minds and fled out of sight.

—8—

Raft asked, "What's that thing?" His charge of massive disbelief heartened them all; they did not want to believe; even Parker clung to a half-hearted hope that Lindley had been mistaken, that he had deliberately lied or that David had made some idiot error of enthusiasm.

It required Arthur's hard-headed frivolity to skip over fantasy to the problem. "My, my, but it takes real genius to keep a secret in Gangoil. Why, Doctor David?"

Yes, why? I'll have that one in the force if he has to be psychoed into it. Parker echoed, "Why?"

David seemed barely to hold back from stamping with rage. "You damned policeman with your terror of telepathy! You ask me that?"

"So not everybody in Gangoil approved and you were forced to hide the work?"

"Old Heathcote began it." Venom overcame fear for a fitful spite. "He had more intelligence than the raging ape whose accidental gene structure was the cause of it." Raft only listened with granite gravity while the brothers clicked disapproval. "He made the correct deduction from the Commander's reaction at the birth trauma but he wasn't geneticist to follow it up alone. His assistants argued against the research—like you they lived in terror of truth—and when mental decay set in it was easy to convince him he was wrong. But a few were impressed and there was a split in opinion. The favoring group, of whom the new Director was one, acquiesced with the majority but established their own complex down here in the supernumerary areas. I don't know just how the maneuver was managed, but it was a time of confusion, which probably helped. I was only a boy. I knew nothing of this until in my turn I became Director."

"And then went into it with a will."

"I had your doubts. But I am a scientist and know what every scientist knows—that what is discovered will be discovered again, that it is useless to hide a discovery."

"I think this particular discovery might well stay under cover for a few years."

David shrugged. "The time for anything is the time at which it happens. The lightning doesn't give warnings."

Raft spoke with a faint slur and the muscles of his hands quivered minutely. "You're a hick, Parker, a country boy who'll believe anything. This little man is all talk and no production, only a shambles of failures. Show us the quadraphonic think tanks, Doctor."

With nothing left to hide David had regained some composure; with faint derision he waved them through the door.

The clone-brothers pushed through in a body, for once less than co-ordinated in their angry interest; like their prototype they resented contradiction. Parker's trained young men followed them smoothly and disposed themselves tactically.

Raft stood aside with a movement of natural courtesy and Parker nearly fell for it. With his foot in motion he knew with certainty that with Raft behind him he was a dead man, with his police out of sight and the brothers waiting on opportunity. The brothers were not yet alienated to the point of not supporting Raft in a moment of decision.

He brought his foot down in a smart halt, half turning to catch the starman's grin that dared him to pass first through the door. He was slightly off balance and he thought Raft's big hands were at the instant of action when a polite cough reminded them that Arthur still remained behind.

Raft relaxed and Parker cheered silently at proof that the Commander did not trust his ability to deal with that particular failure.

Arthur dragged an affronted David between them. "Controller, Director, Commander, in that order. Arthur's new protocol. With himself trailing behind to see fair play."

Parker passed cheerfully through the door with David after him. "Fair play," Raft said thoughtfully and moved obliquely through without losing sight of Arthur, who giggled gently. "Cards on the table now, aren't they, Commander?"

They might have been again on the second of the basement floors, among rectangularly laid corridors and white experimental blocks, but these corridors were short and opened into a great partitionless space covering half the total floor area.

The greater part was empty but furnishings and equipment floated in it like jetsam; nothing, to Parker's eyes, seemed arranged in a specific order. There were chairs and tables, couches and island bookshelves, floor rugs and areas which seemed marked out for games, small cupboards and beds, television sets and a movie projector. Some small white-covered tables, banked with equipment, each with its set of folding screens, recalled both an operating theater and a deep-question laboratory. There were people he took to be nurses, all women, which might indicate that the patients—would that be the word?—were relatively harmless.

And the patients——

The spider-like one who had fled, a weakly slender structure of stick limbs and pigeoned rib cage, had taken refuge in a far corner of the hall, whimpering and pointing and trying to hide behind a harassed nurse. The girl cuddled and soothed and pitched her voice indignantly across some seventy yards. "Herbert says two of you tried to kill him."

David called, "No, Clara, no. He startled them and misunderstood." He dropped his voice. "He saw aggression in two minds and became hysterical. Yours for one, Commander, no doubt." Raft made no reply. "Which other? Not the clone—murder is conditioned out of them."

Parker shifted uncomfortably. "Me, I'm afraid. It was an immediate reflex, gone now. I could have killed it, like a snake—inbred reaction. It won't happen again; the shock is past."

Raft admitted surlily, "The same. A reflex, no more. It was upsetting."

"What was upsetting?"

Neither could answer; they had reacted, but to what? Raft had been shocked enough to attempt total denial.

Arthur spoke from the rear. "Funny, but I knew right away he had been there a while, listening to our minds. And when the door opened our thoughts hit him at full strength, as if the door had acted as a sort of insulator."

"It did. The area is lined with substances we have found to inhibit transmission. Can you be more definite?"

"I don't think so. I just knew that was it."

"Commander? Controller?"

Parker shook his head. "I didn't think to question; it seemed like my own thought."

Raft agreed tonelessly, "Just so."

"Proof of success, I think, in a small way. Herbert is very limited; he does little more than listen to emotions, but ninety per cent of people react to being listened to, which indicates some general sensitivity in the species."

Parker asked, snapping despite himself, "Effective radius?"

"Very small. About twenty feet. He can't hear you now."

Twenty inches is too far. (For a confusing second his mind darted aside to be astonished at possibilities in sexual encounter, to fall back before the probability that the talent would blight more unions than it blessed.)

He saw only two others besides Herbert. Each appeared to be male; they watched the invasion of their peculiar laboratory from opposite corners of the basement, only casually curious. A pattern in the furnishing emerged; each occupied a private island of single domesticity; the cupboards and laboratory tables fell into the spaces between. There was a fourth island.

"Where's the other one?"

"Robert? At the far end. Probably on the couch with its back to us. He doesn't like people near him."

"It looks as though none of them do."

"A matter of privacy, keeping out of each other's ranges. Insulating partitions are impracticable, and the insulations are not fully effective."

Parker barked at him, "Imagine a world of people fighting to keep away from each other. Worse, a world fighting to keep its distance from spies on whom it can't spy back."

Raft said negligently, "They'll kill them, of course. But you can continue that line, Doctor; now we know the thing is possible you must develop efficient shieldings and so on." Then he rounded on the clone-brothers, instantly raging. "Why were you made? If I'd had my way you'd never have come to term. See where your damnable sensivity has led!"

A spokesman was impassive. "Yours also, Albert."

Raft's face grew congested. "I disown you!" It was the voice of judgement dismissing the damned. "I am I. My name is not legion."

The spokesman did not reply, probably did not understand. There was altogether too much biblical reminiscence here, and of the wrong kind. Parker said to David, "Tell us about them."

"Joseph and Henry communicate in fragmentary fashion, the level of understanding not as high as low IQ vocal exchanges; they use speech to assist them. Their range is about forty feet."

"And they can't switch on and off?"

"How could they? The brain isn't an on-off switch-board. You only cease to think by dying."

"That makes an appalling prospect."

"So far. Of course we hope some form of control will appear." The implications really meant nothing to his insular intelligence.

"Do they try to find ways?"

"How? How do you think a quiet thought or a noisy thought or a thought in one direction only? Can you expect more of beginners, telepathic babies? The brain is an autonomic mechanism."

Parker jerked his head at Raft. "He has some control over his heart and glands, I believe. Those are autonomic."

"The Commander's control is limited and he cannot describe it in meaningful terms. Rather, the clone cannot. Can you, Commander?" Raft shook his head. "Nor can these novices describe what they do or how they do it."

An insinuating voice said, "I can control."

One of the telepaths had approached as they talked. He was about seventeen, vaguely a Raft in features but in body shapeless and flabby.

"You can't hear me yet because I'm not pushing. Now I'll push!" He clamped his lips, clasped his arms across his stomach and crouched; veins in his temples swelled. "Now you can hear me."

They "heard" nothing. A nurse appeared. "Joseph, come away."

"No. You can hear me, can't you?"

David said, "The others hear him faintly. Nobody else does."

Parker said, "An idiot. And the others?"

"All—disturbed."

Joseph burst into tears and stamped. "They're pretending! They won't admit——" He squealed and turned to Raft. "I heard you! The Doctor will have you killed for that!"

The nurse cooed in his ear, wheedling, "I'll play music for you." The effect was immediate; he left them precipitately, dragging the girl. When soft music started in his island he listened with his head thrown back and an expression of inspired stupidity.

David asked, "Commander, what was in your mind then?"

Raft spat but otherwise ignored him.

Parker said, "What about the fourth one?"

"Robert is best left alone. He—his nurse wears a shielded head-dress."

Parker had noticed her—and the girl was two hundred feet away—and the metallic something covering her hair, part helmet, part pudding-basin. "Is he dangerous?"

Raft's head swiveled intently to David.

"Discomforting. He broadcasts patterns."

"Geometrical patterns?"

"No, no. Patterns of abstract thought. At least, we think so; they come through as emotional effects and they can be very disturbing. Exciting at times, depressing at others, even frightening. I suppose that in unshielded company he could be psychologically dangerous. There's so much to be understood; it will be years before we achieve anything useful."

"Before," Raft said, "you produce anything but idiots in my name. In my name!"

At the far end of the hall Robert rose from his couch, disturbed by their voices and resentful. He was immense—immensely tall and broad and fat. He sagged with flesh.

His helmeted nurse ran to his side and he squeaked at her in a high counter-tenor whose words were indistinguishable. He pointed an elephantine arm and waved with imperial arrogance, apparently willing them to vanish. The nurse spoke inaudibly and he swung his ham fist at her, so slowly that she evaded it with ease. She spoke again and again he squawked, but lowered himself obediently from sight on the couch. She returned to her desk at the wall.

"Another of my sons? This abortion I must inspect." In mid-speech he was off down the hall, dodging through the pattern of areas. The police reached for their guns and Parker stopped them with a word. He saw a moment for testing his strength. He said to the clone-brothers, "You! After him. See he does no damage to it."

They hesitated for their voiceless conference, perhaps half a second, agreed with his decision and set off after Raft. Parker's opportunist soul hugged itself; he would have them yet as disillusionment with the clone-father grew. The elation faltered at a prick of doubt that he understood properly what took place in those outlandish minds. Swiftly as he had acted, so swiftly was he convinced that he had acted foolishly, but with all of them half-way down the hall fresh interference could only cause confusion. He patted the comforting gun in its holster.

Arthur came from the rear and silently placed himself at their head, knees a little bent as if he might leap after Raft.

"What is it, Arthur?" He was impelled to a paternal caution, "Don't do anything foolish."

Arthur sighed at him, "Shut up. Watch. Listen. And don't shoot."

Police eyes queried and Parker showed them empty hands; they accepted the order uneasily. Perhaps he had compounded error, but he was beginning to think that Arthur possessed the coolest mind of any of them.

Raft's footsteps were loud; his clone, plastic-soled, went unheard. Robert heard him and raised his great head over the back of the couch, resting his chin there, jowls spread like dewlaps. Perhaps because he saw five where he had heard only one he suspected some unholy intention and bleated out a baby's unreasoning terror, raising his blubber to its feet, shaking and shrill.

His nurse cried out to Raft, "Please go away. You're frightening him," and Raft proceeded as though she had not spoken. "You're upsetting him; you don't understand!"

It seemed that at once Raft did understand. Perhaps twenty feet from Robert he staggered and came abruptly to a halt, and lifted his hands to his eyes while Robert squealed and fluttered and the nurse at her desk made anxious signs to David. Raft retreated, a long pace at a time, until he found a bearable distance.

David shouted, "Stay where you are, Marion. Let his damned ignorance suffer."

Another mistake, however meant, for it focused Raft's attention on the girl. He moved sideways while the brothers halted, unable to approach Robert's radiant fear. She saw the intention and began to run and had the chance of a rabbit with a tiger. He went over the furniture in smooth, beautiful strides as she skirted round it, caught and swung her about, snatched the helmet from her head and placed it on his own.

He pushed her away and continued a curving course until he stood behind Robert, the squealing jelly rotating to face him, the huge flesh blocking him completely from their view. The entire maneuver had been carried out in seconds.

Robert's fear noises crescendoed to screams and the brothers retreated further; whatever the stripped-naked mind gave out was insupportable.

Parker mumbled shame and rage; with every advantage, he had let the man get out of his control. Arthur heard him and spoke without looking round: "Do nothing."

Raft was engaged in some complex action behind Robert's bulk; his elbows jerked in and out of sight in hidden manipulation. The nurse, who alone could see him from the side, shrieked unintelligibly to David, the words lost in hysteria. Simultaneously it seemed that Raft pushed Robert off his feet, toppling him on to the couch.

They saw him with bitter clarity now, the white metal in his hand unmistakably a gun even at that distance, its barrel trained on Parker.

Arthur cried in soft anguish, "Fool! And I let him do it!"

The voice of the Commander Raft of the parade grounds cracked down the hall.

"One of you moves and Parker dies. This is a monopole gun; once aimed, it cannot miss. *Cannot*. At two hundred feet or ten thousand. It is the ultimate gun."

Parker relaxed a trifle. He might have guessed—talk, talk, talk; that sort of man. But where had he obtained the disastrous thing?

"David, listen! You will transfer control of Gangoil to the dummy Heathcote at once. The dummy will work under my direction. The line of descent of the new men is from myself through Ian Campion, not through a farrago of freaks."

At least he knew what he wanted—a field officer giving an operation order. And Parker himself was not forgotten.

"You, Controller, will either make yourself useful or die here and now. The Prime Minister will be arrested, killed if necessary, and the State administration taken over by your police until Ian can assume control. Organization and coup should take no more than four hours." He paused. The nurse sobbed loudly and Robert's wails rose from his cover. "Well, Parker?"

"Campion to be front man, I take it, with you as the real power."

"Invent your own construction; Ian is my beloved son." They gained the impression that with the repetition he had surprised himself. He smiled, considering matters removed from them though he never ceased to watch, and Parker could have sworn that behind the flesh of his face began the ghost of a transcendental glow. For a moment body and personality reached for the superhuman; he said with the quietness of a final certitude, "You know who I must be. What I am."

Parker had no thought of dying. Best go along with the man and wait on opportunity, even if he required an occasional hymn to be sung. He had forgotten the brothers, and afterwards ruminated that in all the world only the clone, as crazy in their way as Raft in his, could have brushed aside the announcement of divinity to concentrate on private philosophies.

They protested with solemn sternness, "You must not order killing, or speak of killing. The clone does not kill."

The eyes of the god never left Parker but his face changed horribly. "I am no clone-doll to be stuffed with nonsense. Be quiet, because I kill."

The clone spokesman was clear, precise and unafraid. "You are Albert, the forefather. You live for ever if you wish, through us and through those taken from us. How should we fear to die? We regret death but need not fear it. But those with only single lives need them, having no other. If they kill, that is error and stupidity. If we should kill, it would be a cruelty. If you kill it will be a denial of the world yet to flow from you."

Raft's eyes left Parker at last and flickered to the spokesman. Parker thought that Arthur tensed. The monopole gun moved gently to cover the clone-brother. Raft said, "The good servant must understand his master."

He squeezed the trigger.

The superb, ultimate, infallible gun kicked wildly in his hand.

The round thudded loudly somewhere in concrete.

Raft, unbelieving, waited for the clone-brother to fall.

Finally his incredulous eyes dropped to the gun in stunned wonderment.

Arthur was off and running, and Parker had never seen anything like it in his life. Like Raft he went over the furniture, without breaking stride, at a speed that made Raft's a jog trot. Parker had scarcely grasped the fact of action when Arthur was half-way down the hall and Raft had not discovered that a man had moved.

As he flashed past the clone-brothers Parker thought the blurring stride broke, jerked, recovered. Perhaps it was there he entered Robert's radiating disturbance and took the shock of abomination. But his velocity then was unstoppable; at the last moment Raft became aware of him.

They calculated later that Arthur was moving at more than seventy miles an hour when he cleared the couch to strike Raft head on. Both of them died instantly in the shattering of their bones.

"David!" The biologist stared blankly at an urgent Parker who shook him until his brain rattled back to sense. "I want them alive, David! Both of them!"

"In the name of sanity, why?" Dispassionately Parker hit him, not too hard, hard enough. Professionalism asserted itself; he bellowed for the nurses, who came running. "Prepare two slow chambers. Instantly. You have ten minutes."

They ran.

Down the hall the brothers made futile dashes at the

couch and retired, stumbling; Robert was in hysterics.

David obtained helmets from a wall cupboard and gave one to Parker. They ran down the hall. "Put the helmet on, Controller."

Parker wanted to know for himself what manner of beastliness emanated from Robert. Swiftly he found out. His mind evolved fear when he was fifty feet from the couch, increasing with each step. It was an unfocused fear, without an object; he was simply afraid. He had no sense of being imposed on from without; it was he himself who feared with an intensity he had never encountered. Nor was it Robert's fear felt or reflected, but his own capacity for terror touched off and amplified. He retreated like a frightened animal until he recalled the helmet and placed it on his head.

Panic receded, fading to a generalized uneasiness. As he followed David the uneasiness increased, until he felt a tension like the familiar state of nerves before a possibly dangerous action. The insulation was barely good enough.

David swerved away to the nurse's desk and Parker rounded the end of the couch. He thought of knocking Robert out and doubted that he could succeed against such a sponge of flesh.

He bent over the bodies, sagged together in a crush of limbs. He had had no doubt of them as anything but dead. There was little blood; some trickled from Arthur's mouth, evidence of a burst of hemorrhage instantly stopped. Both necks were broken, and Raft's back.

He disengaged the aluminum gun from Raft's fingers.

David came running and Robert shrieked afresh at sight of the hypodermic. Parker had to hold him while he thrashed in slow motion, a physique barely able to support its own weight, until the needle went home. The shrieking ran down a lunatic scale and stopped; Robert pouted, slept and almost at once emitted a raucous, ponderous snore. They took off their helmets.

David signaled the clone-brothers and Parker wondered aloud how Robert's heart stood the strain.

"He has two excellent hearts."

Just dream up an unlikely answer and don't bother with the question.

The brothers carried the bodies into the slow-chamber hall. Their exaggeratedly reverent treatment of Raft was wasted; carelessness could do no significant harm to either of the wrecked carcasses.

Parker examined the gun. It looked and felt utterly useless; it was the slightest, most unbalanced weapon he had ever handled.

The perfect gun?

Well, it had failed.

Why?

Carrying it gingerly, his fingers well away from the unidentified buttons in the butt, he followed the carrying party.

The two slow chambers were ready. "Twelve minutes," a nurse said, expecting praise and getting it; it seemed that the preparation, including check of banks of instruments was a twenty-minute routine.

Installation of the bodies and cooling to preservative level occupied another half-hour. Too long for Parker. "There will be brain damage."

David, remote and a touch supercilious in his resumed role as Director, tut-tutted. "Cerebral tissue regrowth is a simple matter. There may be some trifling memory loss."

"Indeed!" *Not to worry; leave it to Ole Doc David.* He began to feel light-headed as problems resolved themselves.

Under the slow-chamber carapaces, square-nosed instruments were extruded from the walls and moved purposefully through the fluid on jointed arms, trailing thin cables and extending hair-fine sensors which felt the bodies and selected points for attention.

"X-ray cameras. There may have to be mechanical and electronic inserts before we can even begin to think of stimulation of the involuntary muscles—perhaps an external heart and lungs, temporarily, and some nervous system bypasses."

Parker had been about to ask whether specialist assistance from the Melbourne Town hospitals would be welcomed; he held his tongue.

"Then, perhaps, we will be able to induce slow metabolism and commence regrowth techniques. In ten or twelve days from now, perhaps. Once begun, we can apply speeded-metabolism methods to the injured areas and bring the whole organism to simultaneous recovery." Parker accepted the exhibitionism with grace; the man had humiliations enough needing compensation. "These chambers are, of course, a considerable improvement on the crude model used in *Columbus.*"

I shall enjoy repeating that to designer Raft some day. It was a pity to cut him short, but Campion and Lindley would be worrying. He held out the gun.

"Where did this come from?"

"Lindley gave it to him."

And hadn't mentioned it! But Lindley had imagined a Raft-Parker alliance, so why should he? There had been no time to explain the maddening subtleties of all the relationships involved. But David . . .

"You denied knowledge."

David indicated the brothers. "They threatened me."

Four heads nodded disinterested admission and Parker knew better now than to waste time disentangling their motives. "Where would Lindley get it?"

"I have wondered. He did not bring it to Gangoil with him, and the only persons he associated with here were Miss White and Heathcote."

Pawn-Alice he could ignore, but he would have to see Heathcote again.

David said with a new, gentlemanly distaste, "I am not familiar with guns, but that is surely a peculiar model."

"I know nothing like it."

"It comes apart into small pieces. That's how he carried it distributed in his pockets."

"So." Parker examined it closely and found plain seams everywhere; the whole ridiculous thing appeared to be held together by simple ball and spring tongues. Just twist and pull. As though it generated no firing pressures to shake it apart. Such a gun could not, absolutely could not, buck in the hand; it would have be recoilless to fire at all. He pointed it down, grasped the barrel, twisted and removed it from the butt, which he laid aside.

The barrel itself split further into four short cylinders. He held one to the light, curious as to the shape of its bore and lands. What he saw caused him to laugh immoderately.

"Didn't Raft examine this thing before he fired it?"

"I shouldn't think so. He disassembled and reassembled it in front of me as a threatening exercise, but never once looked at it. He held my eye, demonstrating his dexterity, showing superiority, trying to overawe."

Succeeding, too. "So he was familiar with it?"

"Most. He had it apart and together again in seconds."

"An artifact from the old world."

"I suppose so."

Parker tossed him a section of the barrel. "Look through it."

"It seems very dirty."

"Very dirty. Notice that he called it a monopole gun and that the only part of the weapon which is not aluminum is the barrel core itself, a sleeve of steel—monopoled steel I suppose—an annulus to channel the round. Assume that Lindley got it from Heathcote, your own artifact from the old world—peaceable Heathcote who would have had it lying around unused, possibly untouched, certainly uncleaned, for forty years. Think of that steel sleeve exposed to atmospheric humidity all that time! It wasn't merely rusted when he fired it, it was thick with rust. A bullet belted through it at high speed and had to push the grit out ahead of it. It's a wonder it didn't jerk clean out of his hand."

"So he died of vanity. Now I am puzzled as to why you want these unconscionable thugs reanimated."

"You could say that Arthur deserves some life, for services rendered."

David stiffened. "I shall have some unpleasant dealing for him. I very much want to know how he was able to develop beyond the point where his project had been discontinued as a failure, and why he chose to hide the fact."

"As to how, I don't know and will be as interested to learn as you. As to why—you shouldn't have treated very intelligent young men as menial scrap material. As to unpleasant dealings, remember that relationships have altered; it may be they who deal unpleasantly with you."

The clone brothers laughed in chorus. David colored and banged his hand on Raft's carapace. "And this one, mad and murderous?"

"You save his body; I'll attend to his mind."

"Save it for what?"

"There's work for him." He gathered the clone in a jerk of the head. "Perhaps for all of them. Now it's time we went; Campion will be chafing. Sleep tight, Doctor, in the knowledge that your telepaths have just ushered in the destruction of civilization for the second time in forty years, and that the murdering madman under your care has shown us how to begin to cope with it. You! Clone-brothers!" They attended, stony-eyed. "I leave you responsible for the welfare of Albert and Arthur. Are there enough of you in Gangoil to maintain control until Security takes over?"

"Enough. Gangoil is not hysterical Melbourne Town."

He had reached the lift door when David called out, "What will happen to Gangoil?"

"I'm damned if I know. As everyone keeps insisting, knowledge once discovered can't be destroyed, so I suppose we'll keep the place going for a while."

He saw with disgust that David blinked back a manly tear of relief; the idiot hadn't a single human clue to the meaning of his telepaths in the world outside. The clone-brothers also had little interest beyond themselves and Arthur; one asked him what work he had in mind for them.

"Who better to crew *Columbus* and more like her?"

A policeman had experimented with buttons until the lift doors opened; he kept them open while David protested, "You don't really mean you intend to reopen that wasteful business of stellar exploration! The world hasn't time for nonsense."

"This world, it transpires, hasn't found time for much else. As for stellar travel——" he glanced disapprovingly round the most advanced biological laboratory in all of terrestrial time "——your trouble is that you have a conventional mind."

The lift doors closed.

CHAPTER EIGHT

But Tomorrow Will Be Better . . .

We will now discuss in a little more detail the struggle for existence.

Charles Darwin:
The Origin of Species

—1—

The spires of St. Paul's Cathedral in Melbourne Town acknowledged God with a touch of brio when the demolition of their multi-storied neighbors allowed them to soar as the architect had intended. Not so high, as such ecstasies go, they reached high enough to hide from the viewer on the ground the existence of rampart balconies at those points where the square pediments gave way to the spires proper.

Soon after sunrise Lindley and Francis—or perhaps Eric or Donald, for the gay clone traded identities in the interest of personal convenience now that their color-coding had been discarded—ascended the narrow intramural stair to the south-west balcony. Francis—Lindley was prepared to believe "Francis" rather than risk a comedy-of-errors inquiry—carried the Allocation Board with its flags, buttons and name-wafers.

In a dawn whose clarity mocked his memory of louring cities Lindley surveyed the rally area. The city block facing the west porch had been cleared of debris, razed flat, as had the space diagonally to his left, once occupied by one of the world's busiest and ugliest railway stations.

Where the earthmoving machinery for this heroic task had come from he had not been told but he suspected Parker's unsubtle management. Parker, when he required action, had the morality of a mugger and the blunt charm of a successful blackmailer. As Controller of Police he was a breath of old-world corruption and a damned good policeman with it; as a noisily practicing Christian he was less believable in his ability to reconcile his ethics with his actions. But there was nothing new in that.

Francis opened the folded board and leaned it against the grey-yellow stonework. A couple of name-wafers sprang loose and fluttered down to the silent street. "It's the Sydney and Adelaide sections; I know where they belong." He made pencil marks in the appropriate areas.

"Small contingents," Lindley commented. "I'd hoped for better."

"But each person represents a group of dozens. And there's a surprise turn-up of New Zealanders; six of them flew in last night—as students, as if Security even pretends to believe that!"

"Put them with the interstaters. One of your clone can nursemaid them; they'll need someone to explain the banners."

Those banners—yellow on black for maximum readability—upset him more than was reasonable. Not for the messages they carried, because the messages were valid, but for the memories they revived. Thy hung from crosspieces on long poles that held them high overhead; they would face the rally like military standards. They recalled old photographs of Hitler's fabulous Nuremberg rally and made him unsure of the ultimate honesty of what he did. In the past months he had taught these political novices the alphabet of mass trickery, subversion and persuasion; he had become with natural ease the organizing arm of the Campion movement, while Campion and his advisers watched admiringly what a manipulative psychiatric coaxed from the forty-years-dormant techniques of rabble rousing and the lost expertise of Madison Avenue.

He was apprehensive of the power he had guided into the hands of a Campion who had unexpectedly displayed charismatic personality, bringing the youngsters to his feet while their elders looked on, appalled. He had said something of this to Parker, who had remarked without much interest that Campion could always be shot if he got out of hand. And that Campion knew it.

Lindley told Campion, who did know it—and laughed.

They could be terrifying men.

Mostly, however, Lindley had become emotionally removed from the operation. He moved the players, he mounted the speeches for emotional impact, he choreographed the confrontations and demonstrations—and always as a gamester playing on a board on which he could not be beaten. It was too easy. Each move succeeded because every simple propaganda *putsch* or dialectical gambit was new to people who had spent their lives following an undeviating line.

It couldn't last; in the end the whole foolish campaign must crumble and be laughed out of history. The position of Campion and Parker was finally as ridiculous as that of the dotty Lady (now being subjected to massive mental reclamation somewhere in the Town) who had set out to conquer the world with an idea and a troupe of simultaneous dancers. (That phrase had spread and stuck and the clone-brothers were unforgiving of their gay cell-cousins, who despised them cheerfully in return.)

And conquering the world would be a damned sight easier than teaching it to follow the most difficult psychological philosophy ever invented. Which was what Campion and Parker wished it to do.

The world had not heard the whole rigmarole yet, but the youngsters had fallen on the first hints and promises with starved eagerness; more, they had seemed to divine the magnitude of the task and to welcome it. It was only the clone-brothers' love-in-a-mist religion remodeled and updated and placed on a more secure emotional footing, but still . . . but still it couldn't work.

Yet the youngsters . . .

To hell with the youngsters and Campion and the clones! Best to concentrate on the job in hand and hope to avoid being swallowed alive at inevitable doomsday.

The sun rose with more splendor than men deserved. Dawns and sunsets were noticeable events; people actually watched them, perhaps because no monster city expunged horizons. The hot core of summer was past but there would be sweat enough to stain the air when the thousands gathered. There had been no time to plant lawns—no money for it either—and dust would stir to mix with the sweat and emotion, of which there would be plenty. This was the first major rally, the first emergence on to a world scene of cameras and recorders and correspondents. He must consolidate today or face a long and uphill grind.

"Oh, he'll win this one," Lindley said aloud.

Francis, as usual, picked the inconsequential reference out of the air. "But you don't really believe it, do you?" The gay clone missed little where human beings were concerned. "You scheme and make it work, but you don't believe in it. You don't really care. You look surprised when your foolproof arrangements pass off perfectly. As though continual success can't be real."

"Your world isn't real. It will blow down or fall down or melt. It shakes every time an old gimcrack con works on people who have forgotten how dangerous life is. I was born in a complex society; this toy-town stuff has no substance."

"We're trying to give it some, aren't we? And deciding how to handle a very substantial crowd is part of that. Which reminds me: Parker must get some of his horrible policemen out of uniform. Their presence is necessary but we don't want them rammed down everybody's throat. Nobody actually loves the bastards."

"I'll suggest it." He added distastefully, "And put an extra chair on the stage; he has decided to speak today."

Francis yawned. "Surprise, surprise! That'll send the temperatures up. And what will Hawkeye-never-sleeps talk about?"

Lindley did not know and was quietly furious at the decision made without consultation, passed to him at second hand as if he were servant rather than ringmaster. He improvised, "Perhaps he'll declare himself as a member of the movement."

It was, tactically, too early for that, but he could not imagine what else might be on the man's mind.

Francis was entranced. "Won't *that* upset the PM's Department! The poor dears will feel the state has been whipped from under them, all in the name of freedom of speech. And what will the hot gospeller do for an encore? The Sermon on the Mount?''

''Why that?''

''It's the only bit of his book of fairy tales that makes sense. We've all told him that and he just says that if we understand that much, then we've got the game by the balls. Marvelous expression! I wonder where he got it?''

Lindley had the grace to change the subject; Parker's enthusiasm for imported twentieth-century gutter idiom was as marked as Campion's austere refusal of it. ''There's word from Gangoil that Albert and Arthur are up and about.''

Francis said, ''Arthur's here; he came in last night.'' He did not mention Raft and Lindley detected a quickly glossed hesitation, but if the gay clone wished to withhold information their deviousness would baffle better men than he. Later he could ask Campion.

He asked, ''Is he——?'' A precise word did not present itself.

''Normal? Changed? Peculiar? Why do we feel death should do something strange to people? Arthur's all right except for some memory lapses, and he went right off the giggling deep end when they tried to treat him as a hero. It was all a bit of a mistake really.''

''Tell me.''

''He underestimated Robert. Anybody might have, first up. He reasoned that at full speed he'd go through the hysterics so fast that there wouldn't be much effect. He meant only to grab the gun and give Parker control of a wicked situation because he'd sized up our holy copper as a no-nonsense type with brains as well. But Robert's tantrum turned out to be a mental earthquake. Arthur says it was like running into the middle of a bomb blast. At that speed he couldn't stop, but he lost control of thought and action; he simply crashed into the Commander because the man was in front of him. He says there was a moment of most frightful pain.''

''We'd wondered. He's not the type to throw away his life.''

''No? Clone-group attitudes to death are not yours.''

''We'll talk about it some time, but I'd like to know what explanation he gave David, if any.''

"Why didn't you ask before? Any of us could have told you that. You see, Gangoil is very inefficient; there just aren't enough trained staff for all the work being done. Main lines only are followed; minor lines are discontinued unless some new application shows up, but how do you tell which is which before the answers are in? All six of us were gene-manipulated for various physical advantages. When the expected results didn't show up by age five or six, the work was dropped." He smiled with huge enjoyment. "They kept us as unskilled laborers. Mistake, wasn't it?"

"A boo-boo, a clanger, a bomb-out—I make you a present of those. The implanted characteristics showed up later?"

"It wasn't straightforward. You know how you may have a perfectly formed throat and mouth but won't sing properly unless you're taught; the latent possibility has to be developed. In adolescence we discovered that we did have the abilities we were programed for, in an embryonic way, but they had to be trained up. It took a lot of discovering how and why and what, but you can't live in that place without learning scientific method. And we aren't short of brains, you think?"

"I think. But why the secrecy?"

"Another thing you learn in Gangoil is what it means to be an experimental subject. Even looking after Great Bitch was preferable, and sooner or later there'd come a day when we could use our talents."

"Has it come?"

"Not yet."

"What are the other five talents?"

"Give us a new world we like and we may tell you. We don't want power and we don't want to live as freaks. So it's up to the revolution, isn't it?"

"The revolution may be a disaster. Historically they usually were, one way or another."

"Then we can dance on the ruins. It's a pity you don't believe in what you're doing. Why do it at all?"

"I suppose I want change. Any change. I detest what the world has become."

"Perhaps," Francis suggested, "you should see a psychiatrist."

—2—

Lindley knew, but refused to admit, that much of his unrest stemmed from basic lack of comprehension of the new world and from his resistance to believing that certain contradictory (to him) characteristics did in fact exist.

This rally, for instance.

He had wanted to hold it at night, to capture the drama of darkness and searchlights, the mild mysticism of figures appearing and disappearing from a stage lit as an amber pool in shadows; he had thought of a torchlight procession.

Parker had given immediate "No!" and Campion had backed him. Ideally, they pointed out, the meeting should be held in the late afternoon, when it would not interfere with working hours (extremes of politeness and considerations staggered Lindley at times) and would leave the night hours free for people to discuss and digest what they had heard.

Discuss and digest!

Campion assured him that would be the process, that it was the conventional, understood method of initiating change; a too radical departure might divert attention from the main theme.

Lindley began slowly to appreciate twenty-first-century education; it meant a thinking world. His conception of his usefulness changed—his business was to use special experience to expose and underline facts, not to hook suckers. (No? But who decided which were the facts?)

So be it. Psychiatrist Lindley knew people, but his two naïve revolutionaries knew *these* people.

They had not put a foot wrong since Campion, on the day of his return to full mobility, opened his campaign with the public announcement, through every available medium, of his resignation from Security—and followed it with the brief statement that Security was outmoded and should be disbanded. (Lindley's part in that had been the brevity of the statement; Campion had favored detailed explanation but had been persuaded to opt for impact, with explanation later. The impact of a statement tantamount to heresy had been explosive.) All else had followed in calculated series, with Lindley continually astonished by the reaction Raft had divined at first contact: the response of the youngsters. He had not expected their instant and furious understanding of Campion's depiction of their world as a monster of repression and dogmatism and convention, of unthinking acceptance masquerading as civilized restraint. (But, he reflected, you could always rouse the kids, in centuries AD or BC, by mocking the "done thing.")

Overnight Campion had become a godlet. With private satire for his man of straw Lindley had resurrected a forgotten word, "superstar," and seen it run wildfire across the country, irrespective of meaning. In a week it had leapt the ocean and was heard in the greater world.

Consideration of the greater world frightened him. It had been simple in Australia, protected by ocean and remoteness, but would it be so simple in the American Soviet or the ferocious Kremlin Hegemony or mysterious China? Might these not combine to excise a cancer in the south? Security was not likely to help or protect; present prognosis was that Security would, in such a case, abandon Australia, placing it under a trustful quarantine which any predator with transport and a gun could breach . . . unless Ian were proved right again and Security collapsed throughout the world once its dependence on co-operation was underlined. With the nations left to fend for themselves—and this was, after all, one major aim—there might be breathing space to be turned to advantage.

Faster and faster the tiny, tinny campaign moved towards a proliferation of "if" and "maybe."

The Prime Minister—who traditionally had little personal power and depended on the support of a now dumbstruck cabinet—had made his single attempt at control in the middle of Campion's second broadcast address—the reasoned explanation which bid fair to scramble the wits of his hearers. He had reached for his sole weapon of strength, the Police Force, to be told by a pokerfaced Parker that his men could not interfere with freedom of expression, any more than Security could interfere with the man who abused it in public. Campion was within the law. As Parker understood it and said, authority challenged must justify itself, not seek to apply a gag.

Reaction gave shocked tongue: Chaos is come again!

Not so, Parker assured; his police would prevent that. Which told them what Parker had refrained from spelling out: that the only remaining legal—and armed—authority in the country favored Campion.

Lindley wondered, with a lifetime of violent political memories crying out, whether Parker's grim young men would be able to adapt to new power and new style of law-keeping. Parker said "Yes," but Parker was a fanatic.

—3—

"HQ" was a group of tents by the artificial lake in what had once been "Albert Park," was now known as "Public Recreation Area 3" and usually referred to as "down at the lake."

As advantages, it was within walking distance of the town proper and it was a popular sporting and slap-and-tickle venue for the teenagers who were the main target of Campion's ideas. Also the lake, filled and cleaned by the Town Instrumentality, solved a water problem which would have been acute if he had moved into a disused dwelling with no public supply connections save the rusted dead ends of dead years.

Use of public demesne for private purposes was not illegal simply because no necessity for prohibition had arisen, but was frowned on as a breach of propriety; a public frown accompanied by modest social sanctions was enough to bring an offender to heel. Campion was not frowned on; he had counted, accurately as usual, on the goodwill of the youngsters to checkmate their elders, and now the elders also were observing from a distance and making tentative overtures.

Light and power could have been impossible luxuries had it not been for the overnight appearance of a dozen linked arrays of the tiny, longlife batteries which powered the public transport system. Lindley located one whose identification had been not too thoroughly removed, pointing to the Department of Civil Police as the donor; he knew better than to question Parker, but observed that failing cells were replaced by kindly fairies overnight. But there were always police around the place to keep a governmental eye on the strict legality of Campion's activities, to break up the frequent confrontations between the youngsters and their elders (incidents telling their own tale of societal misdirection), and to maintain unobtrusive communication between Campion's HQ and Controller Parker.

A final advantage was the open space permitting occasional use of an all-purpose vibrationary blind to block long-range bugging. The dampers were not illegal—for anyone who could afford the power load—but tended, in untrained hands, to overheat metal roofs and fittings, powder glass and loosen the bonding of cement. Tents were ideal.

Money had never been seriously lacking. By the time Campion's savings and severance pay had run out Lindley had become a major television attraction with personal reminiscences of the old world and tart commentary on the new; also, historical foundations across the planet inundated him with questionnaires whose general naïvety was mixed with queries which showed him how much he never had known about his own age. (The astronomers, he noted, were not interested in a psychiatrist's impression of another solar system and the psychiatrists were not interested in him at all.) But simple income was inadequate for the expense of Campion's television campaign appearances, until the contributions of the youngsters began to flow. The kids had little money, except for the supertalents who had moved into top jobs at impossible ages, but a few cents a day from each of several thousands became impressive in a culture where nothing cost more than it reasonably should.

Unexpected faces began to appear in HQ area and new tents were erected.

The defection of stolid, dedicated Senior Tech Colley

caused greater uproar in Australian Security than the resignation of Campion. Campion had resigned alone; Colley brought three other Techs with him.

Lindley and Francis returned to the camp for breakfast. Lindley went directly to Campion's administration tent, rankling with Parker's interference with his program.

A member of the gay clone came from one of the sleeping tents as he passed. Similar dress made them unidentifiable as individuals, but this one's skin was pale where the others had taken sunburn.

Lindley stopped. "Hello, Lazarus."

Arthur smirked lazy recognition. "I'm told I was much the best-looking exhibit in the slow chambers."

Death had altered little there. "Fully recovered?"

"Better than the original, actually. It appears I would have died even if I hadn't broken my silly neck against great-great-grand-uncle Albert's breastbone, because it was the biggest effort I'd ever made and it brought on a heart-seizure. So that unpleasantly attractive policeman of yours told David to do something about it, and so I've been provided with all sorts of ingenious muscular heartwall reinforcements and the poor thing can take any strain I'm likely to put on it."

"That was Parker's way of saying thank you."

An eyebrow twitched. "That one doesn't give even thank you for nothing; he'll find a way to get value out of me." Lindley had no doubt of that. Arthur added, "Albert's here too."

Lindley was struck with nostalgic affection for this last scrap of his world, changed though he might be. "Where?"

"Somewhere around, you'll run into him. You'll find him different."

"How?"

Arthur studied him a moment before he asked, "Were you close friends?"

Quite a question. Did Albert have close friends? "I suppose we were. In a way."

"Then he prepared to meet a stranger."

He shied from all but the most minor implication "Memory impaired?"

"No more than mine; they stopped degeneration pretty quickly. But Parker had him brought down here for a few days as soon as he could be moved. I don't suppose he told you."

"He didn't."

"Devious bastard, isn't he? I suppose you know about the Gangoil happenings—the god-delusions and what have you?"

"Yes."

"Parker had all that ripped out of him under deep therapy—memory channels repressed, emotional centers rebalanced, full scale rehandling to short-circuit the childhood traumas that drove him."

Lindley felt again the despairing anger that had taken him when they told him England was dead. "What's left? A vegetable?"

"Nothing like that. He's a charming and delightful man; you can't credit how different. Of course he no longer knows about the Gangoil débâcle."

"I see." No, he didn't see. He didn't see Parker's motive.

"I only thought I should warn you the mental scenery is changed."

"Thank you, Arthur."

With generalized anger degenerating into personalized hatred he went on to the admin tent. This thirty-foot marquee had been borrowed, stolen, smuggled from places unspecified. Most of the more expensive equipment testified to Parker's opportunist morality and Campion's ability to let his sleep. The attitude that good end justified arrogant means was the great link between all the revolutionary movements of history; it had much to do with Lindley's lost ability to identify with the work he had begun as an intellectual *jeu d'esprit*.

Campion was breakfasting as usual with casual company. Policeman, clone-brothers, assistants from the younger groups, news media people—he made himself approachable and hospitable at meal times.

This was to Lindley a new and unlikeably political Campion, though he knew that the character changes seemed great simply because he had not known the man well; they were not very apparent to those who had known better what to expect of him. Nonetheless his professionalism could not override the human sense of having been tricked, of having fallen into comradeship with a false face. The swift declension of the apostolic visionary into the planning, coldly seeing, often double-dealing administrator had impinged as creeping shock. He no longer liked Campion. He knew himself unreasonable, but a psychiatrist's emotional life is no more rational than the human norm and knowledge could not overcome his aversion for the revealed demagogue.

Possessed with his angers, he did not so much as look at the company as he strode from sunlight into comparative dimness. "What has Parker done to Albert? What have you bastards been at behind my back?"

Campion, thinner now and drawn with nerves but still unmistakably a red-headed Raft, rose to face him. "You have seen Albert?"

"No. I'm told you had him deep therapied."

"Not I; the Controller. It was necessary. Do you think I would have my father treated any way but well?"

Lindley rejected the emotional gambit; Campion had displayed much talent for that manner of persuasion. "I think you people—not only you but your whole nursery culture—would do anything to anybody where it served your purpose."

Campion refused the quarrel. "It seems like that, Jim, because your illusions are not ours. Wait until you have met Albert again. In the meantime we must not expose guests to our disagreements."

As his eyes adjusted Lindley saw that Campion did not entertain his usual company. Instead he played host to a group which in these years must be as rare as summer snow—three lined and ageing men, all probably septuagenarian. He was saying smoothly, "Our meeting has excited interest. Some major national groups have sent Ombudsmen to observe and report. It makes a great opportunity for us." He drew Lindley forward. "Gentlemen, this is Doctor Lindley, formerly a psychiatrist aboard *Columbus*, but who now calls himself my campaign manager. I hope the term is more familiar to you than it is to me.''

The short and fleshy one with mottled cheeks, wearing his age, as they all did, with the panache of gerontological buttressing, said without friendliness, ''A campaign manager was a paid liar who prepared the way for a confidence trickster.''

Lindley noted the tiny cross on the chain round the neck. ''As, for instance,'' he suggested, ''John the Baptist.''

Surprisingly the old devil laughed. ''You see that we had to be quick on the uptake in those days, Ian! Well, Doctor Lindley, I'm Bellamy, Ombudsman to the Prime Minister, and you are one of the current pains in my neck.''

''I recognize all of you, I think, from photographs. The gentleman on your left will be Mister Fomin of the Kremlin Hegemony. Or should I say *tovarich?*''

Fomin was bald and radiation-marred as Jackson had been. ''Not *tovarich*. In English the form is 'Brother in God.' '' He spoke plainly but haltingly, as in a language used long ago and laid by. ''My Brother in God, Piotr Kulayev, greets you through me.''

It might have been pity that flashed and faded in the reptilian eyes.

''Pete? Is he well?''

''I have not seen him. I am only a messenger.''

Stonewall. He turned to the third man, dressed with strange conventionality in an approximation of the business suit of the eighties. ''I know your face, sir, but not your name.''

The tall figure recalled portraits of Abraham Lincoln but the penetrating voice harked further back, to the Pilgrim Fathers and Salem. ''Datchborn. Of the People's Republic of New York in the Soviet of North America.''

Compulsively Lindley said the unforgivable: ''And have you a greeting from Tovarich Ewan Matthews?''

Datchborn's reply could not have been gentler. ''I am not a citizen of the Soviet, Doctor, but an Ombudsman, beyond and outside citizenship. On Doctor Matthews I was not consulted. Nobody was consulted. There was no time.''

''Do you believe that?''

''Does it matter what I believe? The thing is done and

men were punished for it. I believe the punishment served no purpose, but again does my belief matter? You, it seems, are taking strong action in an unfamiliar world. *That* matters. I hope *you* believe in what you are doing.''

He could not tell whether he had been intuitively detected or struck by a random shot. It hurt. He said dismissively. ''A man can only do what he believes in,'' which was not evasion enough and nonsense to boot.

Campion took over the conversation, leaving him to dissatisfaction and silence, but even his half-hearted listening perceived that the Ombudsmen's knowledge of the campaign was exhaustive. He had not thought about international espionage in this new springtime of history but saw that something of the sort must be well developed. Good luck to them, but there were shocks in store for spying eyes; Campion had not revealed his full batteries yet.

He was sickening of the whole affair. As soon as he decently could he pleaded pressure of work and escaped.

He had not thought that Campion would come after him, leaving his guests, but protocol was as yet undeveloped.

''Jim! You'll want to talk to Albert.''

''Yes.'' He needed the only remaining fraction of his world. The Ombudsmen, changelings who had renounced birthright, did not count. ''Where is he?''

''Having breakfast, I imagine. And, Jim!''

Lindley's suspicions came on guard. ''What?''

''Talk to him about *Columbus*. It's important.''

So that was it. The father-son relationship had stabilized on a level of common sense; Campion, raised without parents, knew precisely what his parent was worth to him and his crusade.

''You're in a hurry to get him out to the stars again. Doesn't a father mean a damned thing to you?''

''That's unfair, Jim.''

Yes, it was unfair. Campion had some affection for Raft, but his conception of the obligations of emotional attachment was the alien conception of another culture. Lindley had adjusted only to recognizably similar ideas in this time; its true basis was as hidden from him as the true faces of good and evil.

''I'm sorry. Perhaps I'm upset.''

"About anything in particular?"

"You and Parker are interfering, planning without me. I've worked out this rally in detail and now Parker seems about to set it arse over tip."

To his own ears it sounded petulant, and Campion soothed maddeningly. "Everything you planned will be done, but also some things you didn't plan."

"What things?"

"Leave the extras to us, Jim. You've three men's work on your shoulders."

"No more than I can handle."

Campion's patience wore thin. "We have to learn to run our own campaign sooner or later."

But nothing about Parker's intentions. He said, with prescience, "You're going to show them the telepaths!" He was right. Campion, averse to the outright lie, said nothing. "Ian, it's too soon. The kids aren't sufficiently prepared. You'll confuse them."

Pressured, Campion eyed him with dislike, became terse. "You know your repertoire of tricks but we know our people. Leave the kids to us."

It was one thing for him to recognize his limits, another to be told the recognizing had been done for him.

"You'll fail," he said as he moved away. "Story-book revolutionaries! I've always known the end must be failure."

He did not look back as Campion told him, "And we have known that you felt so."

He located a dozen clone-brothers at breakfast but could not see Albert. There was, however, a curiosity, a definite Raft but with sallow skin and straight black hair and brown eyes with the slight, tight slant of an epicanthal fold. He had heard of this small group whose racial traits had been remolded to allow them to live undetected in foreign regions when The Lady experimented vaguely with pointless and unintegrated planetary reconnaissance. They were being quietly brought home by a sulking Security which feared their discovery abroad might cause complications, possibly violent complications. Albert 43—they had never adopted names for themselves—had spent some years in

Korea, prodding uselessly at the closed frontier of China.

He was an exotic, a curiosity, but none of them had ever been true Albert duplicates. It was an utterly unlike spirit which informed their repeating faces.

They made a noisy group at table, almost human when behaving as individuals; if clone-consciousness had not reduced them to the status of animated dolls it would have been possible to think of them as people. They stood apart from their race where the gay clone, lacking the strong hiving instinct, were fully part of it.

He had to raise his voice to get attention. "Have any of you seen Albert? Where is he?"

They ceased instantly to be individuals; they . . . coalesced . . . and a spokesman was chosen. They rarely did this to him these days, accepting him as a friend. They started up a species of regimented laughter, a short bark of amusement that ran round the table to its beginning and stopped.

The spokesman said infuriatingly. "He's around somewhere; you can't mistake him."

"I know that, but where is he?"

"Around."

"Please, I'm not in joking mood. Where is he?"

The spokesman stood. "What's the trouble, Jim?"

But they always called him "Doctor."

"Jim? Don't you know me any more?"

The laugh ran back round the table. The small triumph of a successful deception severed the last link with the past.

He studied the—*simulacrum*, he thought—carefully. It was a perfect duplicate of—of itself. Anticipation dissolved; the meeting would never take place. He said, with measured meaning, "No, I don't know you any more."

The friendly doll gave superfluous explanation. "I've joined the family, Jim. It was the only rational answer, wasn't it?" He seemed momentarily doubtful, as if he remembered something, perhaps an old human attachment. Only momentarily. ".Wasn't it?"

Most logical. Parker had removed his trouble spot. Lindley's voice, separate from his weeping will, said cruelly, "If you never identify yourself to me again, there'll be no need for me ever to know who you once were."

He went quickly, hardening the recesses of his mind, not caring to witness the pain caused by his brutality . . . a pain which this submerged Albert might not in fact feel.

Almost he had forgiven them the tragedy of England, but now they had taken everything. He could have welcomed the fabulous Robert's ability to use his turmoils as weapons with which to beat and destroy.

—4—

Lindley did not set out to get drunk, for he was no drowner of sorrows, but he did not put normal restriction on his alcohol intake that day. By the time he was due to leave for the rally he was in that condition described in a forgotten legal code as "having drink taken," neither quite tipsy nor totally sober—and certainly in no mood for the company of the Ombudsmen for whom Campion had required him, simply because nobody else was available, to act as shepherd, glossary and guide.

He had accepted the briefing without grace, and without grace delivered his notice. "I'll see today out. In the morning I leave you."

The words came easily in an intention immediately irrevocable, though he had not consciously thought the move through.

Campion did not pretend surprise. "I know how you feel."

"You can't."

"No, Jim, I suppose I can't. What do you intend to do?"

As if he cared. No attempt to retain, no wasted gratitude. Practical people, these babies by survival out of future shock. "History Departments or Social Research organizations anywhere will take me."

"I suppose so." The farewell was over but Campion said, astonishingly, "I had thought you might be interested in going back to space."

"Returning every half-century or so to see what new cultural monstrosities love and logic can devise?"

"I think Albert is counting on you."

Apparently he had not been told of that meeting. Lindley answered with the venom of the betrayed, "Are you blind in your pumped-up charisma? Spend my life with zombies! I've seen what was done to Albert."

He spat. It made as good a breaking-off point as any.

—5—

Vehicles arrived, with food distribution insignia on their doors but driven by policemen in civilian clothes, obtained by only Parker knew what acts of ethical thuggery. One was for the Ombudsmen.

Climbing into the front seat, Lindley hissed at the driver, "You can't beat a moral crusade carried out by stealth, threat and misappropriation."

The youngster, about eighteen and scarcely out of recruitment, caught the smell of beer and pulled impassivity over his face.

It lacked two hours to sundown when they reached the rally area. Emerging from the tree-screened traffic lanes at the entrance to Princess Bridge, Lindley was able to survey the entire gathering on the far side. He had smiled at conservative cluckings over the, to him, modest numbers gathered for Campion speeches in the past, but today's attendance triggered tensions in his mind.

The mass of humanity beggared expectation. At this crucial point the movement had taken off.

Humanity flooded the cleared block in a ripple of color to the limits of the angles from which they could see the platform raised before the cathedral's west door; it flooded the broad old street to left and right and spread across the one-time station site to halt only at the green riverbank.

Twenty, thirty thousand, he guessed, multiplying his pre-estimate to a figure approaching half the population of Melbourne Town. They had been seeping in from the country areas for days, but there must be more than just excited youngsters here. Incredulity fell before the plain fact that the older generation also had begun the slide into Campion's hands.

The Ombudsmen were astounded.

Bellamy leaned over from the back seat, his voice a controlled storm. "What's this, Lindley? Conspiracy? Show of strength? What are you up to?" He studied Lindley's face and laughed as he fell back to his seat. "Bitten by his own dog, begod! He didn't expect this, doesn't know what to do with it." He tapped Lindley's shoulder with hard prodding fingers. "Don't imagine we didn't recognize twentieth-century techniques or that we didn't know who to thank for them. Now what?"

"I don't know." The flattening effect of the beer wore off under startlement; it would return, but now he was fully professional, worried but not confused. "I'd banked on eight or ten thousand—a monster rally in your terms, but this . . . I don't know. And now Parker——"

Bellamy exploded. "What about Parker? Is that sanctimonious bastard actively involved? Is he?"

The police driver was quietly furious, but there could be no harm in letting it out now. "He is."

"So it isn't simple persuaded change. It's revolution."

"Wrong word. More like tugging the mat from under you. I don't know what Parker is likely to do."

Datchborn said, with the ghost of a chuckle, "Sounds like back to square one, 1990 style. You've started something but you don't know what, and we've spent our lives trying to stop that sort of politics."

"And replace it with worse."

A confusion of old voices protested. The young policeman intervened, with small effort but tremendous vigor. "Shut up! You're here to see, not to argue. Argue after."

It was possible that no Ombudsman had ever been so addressed by a youngster. Lindley did not dare to look round at veneration savaged by time and change. Self-shocked, the policeman looked like a man who knew he should apologize and was determined not to. With the car nudging the rear of the crowd spilling on to the bridge, he said, "I can't go any further."

The Ombudsmen stepped down to the road in psychological disarray. They had known their day was dying but had not dreamed of having the omens spat in their faces. They peered at the crowd, old men uncertain of their standing, newly wary of the youth that as old men of the tribe they had taken too lightly.

Lindley said, "Parker is an unusual man who commands intense personal loyalty from his men. That young driver doesn't represent the crowd feeling."

It was probably untrue, but they had to penetrate the crowd physically because the stand arranged for them was eighty yards into the mob. *In 2010 such men would have had armed escort; now we rely on good manners. Hell!* He plunged into the mass, pushing, tapping shoulders, asking, "Would you mind letting us through?"

They knew him and greeted him. And saw who was with him.

Ancients could only be Ombudsmen, and Ombudsmen had in the past weeks become obscurely equated with Security as a repressive force, as "enemies of promise." (Lindley had dug the phrase out of his literary memory and turned it into a catchword.)

Habitual respect demanded politeness but newly taught dissatisfactions underlaid it with insulting reserve. The old men progressed through noise which died at their approach until they moved in oases of attention, not positively inimical but less than friendly. There was judgement in the air.

They mounted their platform and sat down; Lindley took position where he could see their faces as they assessed the scene.

The old stone of the cathedral glowed golden grey in the late sun, its solitude dramatic against blue sky. The crowd was noisy but orderly. The size of the gathering seemed itself an instrument of awe, restricting movement and gesture. Lindley, remembering soccer crowds in the English stadiums, found them unreal; that the Ombudsmen and Security had actually produced this generation of mild mannered, repressed hooligans was appalling testimony to their dedication and their ultimate folly.

The cynosure was the staging at the west door. It was not massive, just high enough to raise its occupants above the crowd level. It was empty yet the diaphanous sound screen—so fine-filamented that sunlight could not catch it as more than a lucent vapor—was the only moving thing there, swaying so gently behind the dais as to appear no more than a film of mist. In fact it was a very practical piece of electronic engineering whose presence ensured that every word spoken on the stage would be heard at the limits of the gathering without amplified distortion.

It would be the banners that shattered the old men. Burning yellow print on black velvet, they hung in insulting ranks.

They knew of them; news of them had girdled the shocked or intrigued or merely amused world. Now they saw them; the facts, uplifted, were more rawly real than newscasts. The twenty-foot falls stood four on either side of the stage. Directly behind it was another doubly huge scroll hung from the face of the building itself, new to Lindley, not of his designing. The wording of it frightened him, though not in the way intended.

Of those he had designed, on the right a statement was made and a topic discussed:

SECURITY	STATUS	NOBODY	IGNORE
IS THE	QUO IS	CAN	IT AND
ENEMY	A STATE	FIGHT	IT WILL
OF	OF	SECURITY	GO
PROMISE	RIGOR	BUT—	AWAY

On the left also a statement was made and discussed:

DATA	WHO	SECRET	CONTROLS
BANKS	GUARDS	FACTS	ARE GUNS
GUARD	THE	ARE	AT
US ALL	DATA	SECRET	OUR
BUT—	BANKS?	CONTROLS	HEADS

The wording of the new banner was less plain; the old men would take first shock from the blatant others. Lindley said, attempting lightness, ''Not pithy as slogans go, but your super-educated kids couldn't be hooked with bilge. I had to settle for talking points.''

Datchborn pulled at his Honest Abe sidewhiskers (in

early days he must have gained useful mythic power from the resemblance) and said, with the Pilgrim Fathers breathing down his nose, "You've done well according to your beliefs." The tone called his beliefs names beneath contempt. "Total destruction—then what?"

"First, no destruction!"

The voice came from the level of their feet, from a freckled girl who rested her elbows on the edge of the platform and gazed up at them with too much seriousness spoiling emerging good looks. Some of her peers, boys and girls, were gathered with her, considering the spectacle of so much age in one small space.

She said in no-nonsense tones, earnestly setting up a man to man basis, "I know you, Doctor Lindley——"

He cut in at once, recognizing the type, trying to head off a display of dogmatism. "Every kid in town knows me though I don't know you, but do you know who this is?"

"Of course I know who Mister Bellamy is." Her hand moved automatically to her heart and she caught herself in mid-gesture. And knew her peers had seen Lindley trap her so easily. She could not abort the salutation without open insult, and that was not permitted by her upbringing or by the new education Campion's area advisers dispensed. Blank-faced, she completed the movement.

"And these are the Ombudsmen of the governments of the Kremlin Hegemony and the American Soviet."

She bobbed her head angrily, owing them no more than politeness.

Datchborn had followed the play appreciatively and felt himself cued to continue it.

"Well, Miss——?"

"Waggoner," she said irritably. "Jenny Waggoner."

"No destruction you say, Miss Jenny. In the face of those!"

His waved fingers despised the banners and their messages. It was a mistake, giving her her chance.

"Nobody wants to destroy the data banks, only to limit the information preserved in them and to insure the removal of private, personal, unnecessary, destructive information."

Lindley recognized the wording—his own—and hoped she understood it; propaganda could be anaesthetic as well as informative. Datchborn did not know she parroted. He answered quietly, like a man in communication with himself. "My America will not fancy that. One people, one state, from crèche to crematorium . . . I don't think . . ." He lapsed into private thought.

Fomin spoke, with less antagonism than Lindley had expected: "You will make rules, eh? But who will keep your rules? Like the—the message—the placard thing there—who guards guardians, eh?"

The answer came pat, robot-taught; the girl had not yet begun to jab at dogma with intelligence. "All data in all data banks must be publicly available at all times. In this way retention infringements will be under constant random surveillance."

Some of her peer group seemed discomfited by the metallic quoting but no one tried to supersede her. Bellamy muttered, "Holy Jesus!" and fingered his cross as if he rubbed an amulet. The Russian was scandalized, the American amused.

Sympathizing a little with the naïve figure the girl cut, Lindley pushed the argument sharply under the aged noses. "In the old world, complex with energies at cross purposes, it couldn't have been done. In this one, still manageably small and relatively unsophisticated, it can." Bellamy nodded slightly and Fomin shuddered; Datchborn presented smiling contempt. He felt tired as latent alcohol continued its draining of will, and said dully, "At least, I hope it can." He should not be defending the campaign in which he had no faith, but his disgust with the Ombudsman system was as great as his other resentments.

The dialogue should have ended there, but Jenny was having her day, talking with Ombudsmen and a starman in heady importance. She said, probably more astringently than she intended, "You sound as though you hope it, Doctor, but don't believe it."

For a second, just long enough, the hectoring broke his restraint. His pent bitterness splashed her. "What would you know, you automated brat?"

His voice was low, pitched behind his teeth, but she heard and so did a handful near her. She stiffened to shame in an island of stillness. The youngsters exchanged glances

like—like the damned clone making a party decision—and
without a word turned their backs on the platform.

Datchborn shook his head with insulting sympathy, Bellamy looked distressed, Fomin impassively disapproving.
Nobody shamed a youngster save in necessity and love.

With a quite insane feeling of having struck a blow for
an obscure personal freedom Lindley said loudly enough to
be heard a dozen paces, "I behaved badly and should apologize. I'm not going to. I've had enough of this ethic-proud
culture that simpers morality while it murders minds. Let
it rot!"

He ran down, assailed by the conviction that nothing he
said or did could avert onrushing chaos. The youngsters
elaborately gave no sign of having heard.

Nobody, he thought as he clawed back to sense, had
queried the anti-Security posters. Perhaps they approved of
those; politics could come into its bedlam own with the
blinker-boys out of the way.

—6—

The cathedral venue had been Parker's suggestion. As the
doors of the west porch swung open on dimness Lindley
speculated angrily on mystery and symbol. Surely the man
did not mean to force his hardnosed Christianity on the
movement? He was capable of anything, but how would it
be relevant?

The door opening was stageplay. Lindley knew that
Campion already waited behind the drop of the central ban-
ner, whose lower edge was level with the back of the stage.
His first appearance would be on the stage itself. An advent.

A ripple of quiet rolled out to the limits of the crowd. A
huge, tensioned hush descended.

The youngsters, unaware of the sophistications of
twenty-five centuries of drama—the age had developed little theater yet, and that little was amateurish—were
involved by simple effects, the more easily on a day of
prepared, pre-ordained excitement.

Datchborn muttered appreciatively, approving technique. Bellamy was alert and not fooled. Fomin seemed unaffected; he leaned to whisper in Lindley's ear, "The very big placard thing—banner—what does it mean?"

Sooner or later it had had to be asked.

IS
THE THOUGHT
I THINK
MY OWN
THOUGHT?

OR

IS IT

ANOTHER'S?

WHOSE?

"I don't know." It meant what he could not explain until he discovered the extent of revelation intended. In any case it meant they had decided to lead enormous trumps and chance the game on a coup.

"Not know? Not your own words, Mister Entrepreneur?"

"Not mine. I am not fully briefed on today's—exhibition."

He caught the sidelooks of politicians recognizing another on his way down, probably deciding this as the strain behind his outburst of a minute before.

Their whispering brought turned heads and affronted glances.

At the stage something moved.

A rustle passed over the crowd as a ripple had passed before, an indrawing of breath, a powering for the hail of greeting.

It was not Campion. The rustle returned as a sigh.

A head, enormous, bloated, encased in a metal skullcap which covered the entire cranium, appeared above the edge of the stage, rising slowly.

Lindley breathed, "God forgive them; I never will."

The vast bulk of Robert, huger than life in the looseness of a silver-grey caftan, rose as though on a concealed lift—

which he probably was. As the size of him became apparent, six and a half feet of rounded blubber topping more weight than anyone was likely to guess, a sound of puzzlement rose in prickles over the staring heads.

At stage level Robert advanced with the tiny paces which were the best his muscles could achieve without leaving him blown red-faced and ridiculous, until he reached the group of three metal chairs placed for him. He paused a moment, gazing across the rally with amazed disgust, and sat—a single fluid collapse which spread him, amoeba-like, over the three chairs.

Lindley felt sick. So they had found a means of control . . . drugs . . . conditioning . . . In a world where such parodies did not survive to adulthood he was horrifying. Some might have doubted that he was human. Their voices rose, buzzed, roared, subsided.

Joseph and Henry, in white with heads also insulated, came quickly, not attempting to repeat Robert's stunning entry. They came on stage and sat, one right, and one left. To Lindley they seemed terrified; Robert, concerned with little but himself, would be unaffected by anything less than direct threat.

Datchborn asked, "Who are they?"

He said stolidly, "I don't know." Their very presence made rational explanation out of the question.

When silence had become absolute with expectation, Campion appeared. He also wore a type of caftan—cut with cunning to lend him height and power and to cling as he moved—in brilliant, electric blue.

They ripped the sky to welcome him.

Fomin frowned. Datchborn's condescension vanished. Bellamy hooded his eyes like a man measuring his enemy.

There were minutes of it. Campion waited, let it die away. To kill the last sounds he opened his lips as if to speak, and silence fell like sudden death.

Behind him the soundscreen glittered hazily, ready to throw his voice in the new ventriloquism.

He said nothing.

He half turned from them, looking to the back of the stage.

Another head appeared—a dark, narrow, angular face—

a figure slenderer than Campion's but erect as a spire—a caftan as craftily made in blazing scarlet to set beside the sparkling blue.

The rally did not at once recognize the man whose face was only occasionally publicized and whose name was so far only furtively muttered as sympathizer.

But some knew him, and the name swept back from the stage to the riverbank—and the meeting crashed into a sound of triumph that left Campion's welcome a rehearsal.

The messiah had produced a magician.

With the police—the only power which could oppose undeciding, wait-and-see Security—with the police to back them Melbourne Town was theirs and all the state for hundreds of miles around it. *Exultate, jubliate!*

Bellamy sighed, a bubbling sound of delivering his lifework up to the unknown.

Datchborn's gasp was a rattle in the throat, a premonition of wreckage, a foreseeing that it might engulf him.

Fomin's lips moved. Perhaps he prayed, not perceiving the miracle before his eyes nor conceiving yet that "miracle" does not mean "blessing."

Through pandemonium the newscasts sent out the scene to a world more puzzled than impressed by this incomprehensible Australian outburst. Suspicion lurked behind the puzzlement. Nobody really liked the Australians, who had emerged too healthily from planetary catastrophe. But the Ombudsmen were noticed, and if Soviet and Hegemony thought this uproar worth their attention . . .

Parker accepted his ovation in stillness, an absolute control of the flesh through unpredictably long minutes; he did not stir until the last whisper had faded. Then he moved his lips only, and the soundscreen flickered more brightly as the words activated it and were flung outward in a great fan, entering each ear as if the speaker stood at his elbow.

"Anger! A rage for peace in the heart!"

Of course they exploded all over again. The almost meaningless, gnomic phrase Campion had tossed at them one day had assumed semi-mystic significances which each clutched for himself. Cried out in Parker's unschooled, grinding voice it was as if a donkey had essayed a song. But the words were right and the gift of police support was right; it would not have mattered if he had assaulted them with a coloratura shriek.

With excitement roused to the pitch where they could be manipulated by any jackass, he sat down.

Campion waited because all through the crowd grey police uniforms had suddenly appeared, to become foci of welcome and demonstration.

On the outskirts black uniforms watched, having no power to do more.

When Campion was ready he spoke gently, not pushing it out for hysteria, like Parker.

"What is the first enemy of promise?"

An answer crashed from throats still amazingly capable of response—one word, incomprehensible in thirty thousand united bellowings.

Fomin asked, "What do they say?"

" 'Ignorance.' "

"Well, that is true."

Oh, but you'll learn, Brother in God, you'll learn.

Campion asked, "And where are the roots of ignorance?"

Lindley translated the howling. "In the hands of those who entrap knowledge."

Datchborn caught the point before the others and was not amused; the Soviet pivoted on centralized intelligence.

"How can the hands be forced open?"

"By refusal to co-operate."

"And then?"

"The state will wither."

"Unless?"

"Unless all knowledge is made free for all. Then we will co-operate."

Fomin muttered, "This sounds like worship perverted."

Doesn't it, Brother in God? Keep listening.

Campion asked, "Whose hands entrap knowledge?"

The confusion was impenetrable, a babel of answers.

Lindley transmitted drearily, having heard it all before. "Psychologists. Deep-question technicians. Political advisers. Statisticians. Security. Archivists. Data bank attendants."

Datchborn snorted, "Who the hell wants all that stuff in the public domain?"

"I do," Lindley said. "Who wants secrets wants power."

"You can't run a state——"

"You can!" Datchborn shut up, troubled.

The soundscreen made possible miracles of emphasis and inflection as Campion began again. "What is the second enemy of promise?"

"International Security."

"But are the Techs not men of good will?"

"Yes!"

"But?"

"We need freedom to make mistakes."

"Why?"

"To learn."

"Learn what?"

"To run our own lives for better or worse."

"And what of Security?"

Heads turned to the dark uniforms at the outer edges. "Security must abdicate."

"Or?"

"We will not co-operate."

"And?"

"Security will wither."

The black uniforms listened, motionless.

"And if Security abdicates?"

"There is a role for them, but servants must not be masters."

So much for Security—bend or vanish. The black uniforms held rock-steady, betraying nothing, but Lindley knew that Security was shocked to the core by the public eruption of the condition it had always known and ignored—that it was an expedience, and expendable.

Datchborn snorted, "Litany! The dead end of thought."

Bellamy knew better. "This is a receptiveness preparation. He'll snap them out of it when he's ready."

Campion was not yet ready. He asked, "What is the third enemy of promise?"

"Repression?"

"Of?"

"Of freedom of choice. Of the mind. Of the soul."

"Repression leads to?"

"Violence."

"Which is?"

"A madness."

On that Campion made a pause, turned heel and toe for his gaze to encompass the whole gathering, then folded his hands. He asked, "If violence is madness, what is the alternative?"

"Understanding."

He paused again, and said, "Consider it."

Silence covered them like private prayer.

Datchborn muttered disgust. "Love crusade!"

Lindley whispered harshly, "Like hell it is!"

On the stage Campion said at last, "Understanding. You who have been with me from the first have considered it often and deeply. We must desire understanding of each other because without it there is no future, only a progress of technology down the years, with no man knowing more than the first man knew. That killed the twentieth century and can kill this one."

He did not elaborate. It was preamble, and they knew it all. He moved instead towards new statement.

"We must consider what is involved in understanding each other. We must prepare to comprehend violence and cruelty and murder, deceit and treachery and hate, theft and fraud and extortion."

As if the catalogue of disgust had surprised himself he dropped back to an intimate note, with little hesitations, as if the ideas came extempore.

Bloody mountebank!

"It's easy to say, 'Love one another'—but it isn't enough . . . you can't actually love brutality and betrayal and double dealing. But you must—*we* must—understand them because they are part of the matrix of humanity. Perhaps saints exist, but I have never met one. Not being saints, we must accept ourselves as being privately stained with the same weaknesses that publicly we treat with contempt. That makes us hypocrites, doesn't it?"

He prodded at the question as if testing it. "Aren't we hypocrites? All of us, I mean? Little ways, big ways—

things we don't like to have known—habits, thoughts . . .
Even thoughts . . .''

A murmur spread, a groping at difficulty.

"Not one of us would like to have his private mind laid
open. Open at all times, I mean. I couldn't stand it. I'll
admit it. Could you?"

The murmur became articulate. They agreed with him
because what he said was true but they could not see where
he was leading: their answer held questions.

Campion let tension stretch, and broke it with a touch of
lightness. "Telepathy would be an unpopular talent, I
think."

It was a rueful geniality rather than a joke, and they
laughed gently with him.

*Oh, those poor, pre-damned animals seated behind him
in their helmets, half-stupefied, unaware how he readied
hate!*

An unexpected voice cut across the murmur—Datchborn's nasal tone, penetrating and loaded with histrionic
boredom.

"I didn't come from New York to watch a variety act,
Mister Campion. What have you got?"

*Excellent, excellent! Split his attention and his confi-
dence.*

The Ombudsmen's platform was not more than fifty feet
from Campion's stage; Datchborn's razor voice carried
strongly to faintly activate the soundscreen. Thousands of
heads turned like a single animal with a host of eyes; the
multiple mouth exclaimed against insult and danger rumbled below the protest.

Datchborn stood, a very tall old man, straight and dignified and most angry. "What have you got, Campion, that
needs ritual mummery to make it acceptable?"

Campion watched him, unmoving. Round the Ombudsmen's platform his followers surged menacingly; Jenny and
her circle closed in, staring enmity.

The girl called viciously, "We need to understand violence, mister, and not be ashamed of it. Do you understand
it? At first hand?"

Lindley rose and pitched his voice to carry over the angry applause. "Mister Datchborn is an Ombudsman of the American Soviet!"

The title still held magic to demand restraint. Voices—one was Jenny's—cried that the day of Ombudsmen was over, but they fell quiet again.

Lindley called out, risking the doubtful calm. "It was good question, Ian. Won't you answer it?" Campion's smile wavered. Parker's head pointed, hound-like, over his red robe. "After all, Ian, the Ombudsman wants only a plain statement." Excitement was seizing him, or perhaps the flat alcohol was stirring again. Resentments streamed to a node of anger—the quasi-humans in their helmets staked out for sacrifice—the so casual joke about telepathy—only Parker's role was still unclear—and Parker was ruthless when Campion might be termed merely practical.

He called recklessly to undercut Campion's parahypnotism, "Your litany and staging make it seem as though you're preparing a bluff."

Campion reacted at last. "*Your* litany and staging, Jim."

True, true. What now? He raised his voice to catch the soundscreen, to have his words carry, however faintly, to the limits of the rally. "I didn't design these meetings to have all you youngsters turned into chanting robots. Only months ago he saved you from the drugs of Gangoil, but now he's using you just as they used you——"

The rising growl cut him off in fear; excitement had carried him past sense. He saw Parker bend to speak to someone behind the stage. Campion remained still, letting him call down his own destruction.

The crowd rippled and rustled, as if the great animal twitched before the spring.

He could go on, without hope or effect, because there was no road back.

"Ombudsmen! Here's his simple statement!" A hand stretched over the edge and plucked at his ankle; he stepped quickly back from the line of furious faces. "He's been building up to this from the talk of all the secret information stored in data banks, the weapon that makes it possible to control the way you think and act." He was yelling because yelling was now necessary. "He's getting ready to bind you to him with fear!" Fresh action stirred in the crowd, a movement of big men from the stage towards his platform; Parker had set the clone in motion. "He's going to tell you there's telepathy loose in the world. It's a lie!"

Instantly Campion's voice, magnified with the full power of the screen, bore down in thunder. "STILL! ALL OF YOU! BE STILL!"

The crowd came to heel, assaulted by appalling noise.

Campion said coolly, quietly, "It is not a lie. Telepathy is loose in the world."

A section of the crowd swayed as clone-brothers pushed through them.

Lindley howled, knowing he had only moments, "He has three broken sticks of near-telepaths on the stage there. Three helpless mental cripples who he will tell you are the menace of the future. He'll tell you that the only way to hide your thoughts, to remain individuals, is to bond yourselves to a common belief. Not individuals at all is what he'll have you be, but a great sprawling hive of a single entity!"

Thunder struck. "ENOUGH! QUIET!"

At his feet a clone-brother said, "Come with us, Jim. You're making useless trouble."

"I mean to make more."

The edge of the platform was lined with clone faces. The one before him said, "You will gain nothing. Ian holds them in love. What better can you offer? Please come, Jim."

He was aware of the thousands poised in expectation of action. Spectators at the arena. *That* would not change quickly, for all litanies of love.

And the clone-brother had called him "Jim."

"Albert?"

"Yes, Jim. Come with me. There is no peace up there."

"There is no peace anywhere while your beloved bastard son betrays the tricks I taught him."

With triumphant accuracy he kicked Raft in the mouth.

He saw blood flow before his ankle was hooked and he was jerked from his feet. His head struck a chair arm as he fell; he was barely conscious of being dragged from the platform, of being carried head high by the clone-brothers while others of them fought off the youngsters who would have killed him with clawed hands. Perhaps someone came near enough to strike or perhaps he fainted, for there was an interval of darkness.

—7—

Cold stone under him—the mosaic tiling of the cathedral floor. The air cool and dim, none of the candelabra lit.

They had laid him at the base of one of the huge anchoring pillars which took the weight of the roof just inside the porch doors; his eye roved upward and along a curve of grace to the point of a gothic arch and upward again to the timbered vaulting of the ceiling. There the dark wood was palely luminous with the light of the setting sun beating through ranks of stained-glass saints in the high windows.

He ached. Crowd-murmur penetrated the closed doors washing round the edges of the soundscreen which flung the stage voices forward and blocked them behind.

He lifted his head and it throbbed abominably. On either side tall legs in khaki rose up to identical faces. Beyond them open floor stretched from wall to wall; there were no pews. Rotted and discarded? Stolen for firewood in the dogdays and never replaced? Did the new Christianity worship on tortured knees?

Facing him sat Parker—trust Parker to find one chair where no other existed—in his melodrama of scarlet robe and hawk face, chewing his lips. When he saw Lindley open eyes he rasped in a voice close to pain, "In God's name why couldn't you keep quiet?"

It would be interesting to know Parker's vision of God. A neat, businesslike type who didn't mind a little rule bending so long as you were honestly doing your best and who always listened to the prayers of the man who knew just what God wanted and didn't hold with sentimental claptrap? Better still: what did unbeliever Campion think about God? Campion was a demagogue who found a deity useful—good enough for the peasants, so to speak.

''I am oldfashioned. I love truth.'' *Is this Lindley talking such bull? But it's true, it's true.*

''Don't shit me, Doctor.''

''Tut, tut, Controller. In the cathedral!''

''What of it? God isn't petty.''

Nice to be certain. ''That's as well for an honest policeman who'll acquiesce in anything promising power and authority.''

Parker leaned forward. ''You think that of me?''

''Of both of you. Power-grabbers lining the kids up as blind babes!''

''You know better than that. We see the possibility but we won't let it happen. They're ours, yes, but they *think* when they're away from us. They don't follow blindly.''

Talking hurt but he could not contain the overflow of insight and betrayal. ''After today they'll have no chance to think. You mean to frighten their wide-open wits out of them. But if you think you can balance between fears and ecstasies for ever, forget it. You've loosed a beast you can't chain and the next step is what we called totalitarianism— revealed truth demonstrated by violence, and argument disallowed. May your morally obliging God preserve you from it.''

Parker had thought of all that and dismissed it. ''Today is exceptional. There's a long step to be taken.''

''Exceptional enough to justify the use of the methods you hope to outlaw?''

''Paradoxes have to be lived with.''

''There are no paradoxes, only false premises.''

''We're making history, not geometry.''

''Different rules?''

Parker said impatiently, ''Nobody knows the rules of history. Experience only tells you that you were wrong last time; it doesn't tell you where you went wrong or where to go right. To change history you choose the tools you need.''

''Hypocrisy's a rotten tool. You'll play up telepathy as the ultimate invasion of privacy, pretending it menaces the world. But it doesn't. There are no natural telepaths and there probably never will be. The Gangoil work shows it up as an anti-survival trait. It will not appear in a viable line.''

Parker stood, all scarlet impregnability, secure in his ethics and his God. ''For a twentieth-century expert with an ingrained flair for dirty tricks you're making a fine job of missing the point. I haven't time to argue; I've a part to play out there.''

Lindley struggled to sit up; with the pillar supporting him and a proper perspective, Parker was less impressive. ''What's going on out there? What are you doing?''

''Ian's running a demonstration of telepaths in action. Very neat, too.''

''Kept it bloody quiet, didn't you? Knowing I wouldn't play. But at least I might have designed something with less stink of trickery and time-serving.''

Parker was stung. ''The damnedest thing about self-righteousness with its back to the wall is its way of squawking, 'You're nastier than I am.' ''

He was gone in a swirl of red.

Lindley closed his eyes.

A Raft-voice said, ''We should explain.''

''Explain, dummy? Or excuse?''

''Explain, Jim.''

His eyes snapped open on the puffed and plastered face he had not seen at the shoulder-edge of vision. The voice, impeded by kicked lips, should have told him, ''Can't I be free of you?''

The face settled in the gentleness so at odds with its ill-matched lines. ''A sick soul can be healed. We were friends and will be again.''

From Raft remembered, this was intolerable, beyond reply.

A fresh voice approached from the door. ''Really, Albert, you should make the chorus line give up these love-and-sweetness gambits instead of falling for them yourself. You'd better all get out of here and help keep order before those poor bloody telepaths get torn up alive. Some demonstration! At any rate, get away from Jim while I patch him up.''

''Has Controller Parker asked for us?''

''That's what I'm saying, dearie. Now do piss off.''

Their footsteps receded.

"Francis?"

"No. Arthur. Where do you hurt?"

"Where don't I?"

"Tch! You did bring it on yourself, you know." He sorted bandages, tubes and phials from a first-aid kit. "But I agree that the whole thing is a bit sick-sick."

"You don't believe in Campion?"

"Come off it, dearie! Of course I do. I meant that you sometimes have to go an unpleasant way round to get a result."

"End justifying means again."

"A good end does. Doesn't it?"

"Never."

Arthur stopped sorting. "I don't follow. If you do the right things always, you'll always get slapped down by the types who don't. Stands to reason."

What stood to reason was that he would only waste time arguing ethics against practicality. Perhaps Parker's God was the logical moral authority for the time.

"Tell me about the telepaths."

"Up a bit while I ease your shirt off. What about them?"

"Ian can't use them as bogeymen. They'll never develop naturally."

Arthur swabbed his ribs with something cool. "So what, Jimmy boy? Now that Gangoil has learned how to make them, who cares about breeding? You make one good one and then clone like mad. And while nobody will like them everybody will use them. Talk about spy rings within spy rings! The globe will be crawling with them! And then there's the communications thing: once the range is increased and somebody comes up with an amplifier and tight-beam focus—and don't you fool yourself they won't—there'll be world linkage wanted. And it will lead to other things, bad as well as good—as you people used to say, spin-off. Now the game has started there's no end to it and no chance of stopping it."

"Then the preserved pryings of data banks will represent absolute privacy compared with the exposure of your mind to telepaths owned and operated by a paternalistic state."

"That's about it, bless us all. My, but you are a mess."

He unrolled a foot of bandage. "Hold the end—there."

Lindley held and asked, "Don't you care?"

"Dearie, I'm scared gutless! But dithering and complaining won't make it go away, will it? Ian and that bloody policeman—though he's quite nice when he isn't being dutiful—have an answer."

"To what?"

"How to live with your mind wide open. If we're to have a world without privacy, we'd better start practicing before it arrives, hadn't we?"

Answer? Some more bloody nonsense; and he didn't want to hear it. It was time he looked to his own future. The ache in his head had increased. Skull fracture? Fear and solitude spilled in a cry of weakness, "They don't care whether I run or stay."

"I think they do. But where would you run?"

Loneliness of world and time closed in. The crew climbing the light years had dreamed of change, even mutation, not of total alienation.

"Listen, Jimmy boy, you can make yourself a place in this world, but you'll have to face up to total loss. That's the trouble, isn't it?"

"Shut up."

Shadows darkened the door. A group of clone-brothers entered, half carrying, half dragging the bulk of a squealing, collapsing Robert. The helmet could not wholly suppress the uproar of his panic terror. They dropped him at Arthur's feet, letting him fall like masses of porridge congealed in a skin; they had no consideration for him as anything human.

Albert, thankfully, was not with them.

"Put him to sleep, orderly." The tone held an edge of contempt; Arthur also was non-human. Had he not killed the father and most unfairly shared resurrection? Only the Raft-clone was in the true line of descent.

Arthur used an ampoule. The bulk subsided in a spreading of flesh.

Lindley asked, as reasonably as his bursting head and animosity allowed, "What happened?"

The clone-brothers surveyed him somberly, letting him remember that he had attacked the clone-father. "Albert understands and forgives.'' First things first, apparently. As if he cared whether the zombie lived or died. ''As for the Robert-thing, son Ian arranged a demonstration by the telepaths,'' *which doesn't mean us, you understand, not us at all*, ''which was received by the faithful''—oh, dear Jesus, ''the faithful''!—''with anger and contempt. He was frightened by their enmity. He is quite useless for son Ian's purpose.''

''What purpose?''

''Demonstration of the mind as a weapon.''

There must be a limit to disgust and Campion might yet drag him to it. ''I didn't know of that. He said nothing to me.''

''Son Ian has realized your half-heartedness for many weeks.''

They went away.

Robert slept noisily.

''Even the dummies knew I was on my way out. Everybody knew but me.''

Arthur, working on his legs with a cream he claimed would reduce bruising, answered at length. ''I'm revising my ideas about your culture. You weren't so tough-minded; you only seemed so to yourselves. You were nasty and self-seeking and quite clever but you could only operate in your own psychological environment. No adaptability. You weren't a *practical* people. Ian must have seen your limitations right away, but he had to take what you offered before pushing you aside. And now the pushing aside hurts you like some sort of treachery after a promise, yet a clear mind would have seen that it was inevitable and made some sort of bargain. Did you get any kind of promise out of Ian?''

''I didn't try.''

''Tut! What did you bank on? Gratitude?''

''I suppose so.''

''Gratitude is only a prettied-up 'thank you' and your performance today has cancelled the debt. Ian should have foreseen that you would prance and carry on, but he really didn't understand your thinking any more than you do ours.''

Truth. No more to be said. So? "I'd like to see what's doing out there."

"I don't think you would, and anyway you shouldn't move."

"Give me a stimulant and something for my headache. I want to see what disgraceful mess I've stirred."

"Your skull——"

"That won't kill me."

"No; it's getting quite hard to die, isn't it? But the sensible thing——"

"Please!"

"Well, it isn't my business to force you for your own good. Besides, I'm curious too. I could give you a hyper shot. You'll regret it later of course."

In five minutes he felt well enough to walk to the door, Arthur at his side, leaving Robert alone and snoring. Nobody cared what happened to Robert. If he made a nuisance of himself he could always be shot.

—8—

The sun was low. Climax had come early and been sustained at hysteria pitch, technique triumphant.

From the back Lindley saw through the soundscreen—blue Campion and scarlet Parker gesticulating—but heard only a smothered burr of speech.

Arthur guided him where the edge of the audience made sharp demarcation between the zones of hearing and damped-down noise, and in the length of a pace sound became intimate at their ears—Campion in full cry.

Lindley was noticed and resented but way was made for him. He could be tolerated so long as he behaved himself.

Henry and Joseph were gone; he supposed the clone had removed them, but was prepared to believe that if the mob had torn them apart the messiah and his red eminence would simply have amended their approach to accommodate the incident.

Campion did not seem to have departed much from his original subject.

"We built a new world on principles we thought good and could not see that they were mistaken.

"We hoped to preserve the good of the past and yet escape the bad.

"We thought to keep the machines, the technology, the creature comforts, and not have our souls destroyed by them.

"Do not blame the Ombudsmen.

"Without them we might still be savages, killing for the right to eat and live."

It was not poetry but it had its rhythms; the short sentences built the mob's cumulative self-hypnotism more effectively than technical magicianry. *I taught him this, too.*

"We thought that if our hearts were dedicated, our minds would escape evil.

"We were too new in the world to perceive what evil is.

"We created Security—and saved ourselves the fatigue of honesty.

"We created freedom of allegiance—and did not realize we might give allegiance to stupidities.

"We refined the techniques of the past—but told ourselves our usages were beyond reproach.

"And we crammed the data banks—for the good of mankind!"

He delivered the last sentence like a jab in the face. The crowd responded with a harsh murmur of agreement—because he had willed it of them.

"My father came out of space and time to teach me truth.

"And it was my father who showed me what we had done with our legacy—that we had used it to bind ourselves to lies and cruelty as surely as our grandfathers did.

"They lived in a world where no man owned his soul.

"With good intentions we recreated their world—with a different face."

He made one of his long pauses, then gave them all the screen could deliver:

"WHO CAN LIVE WHERE HIS SOUL IS NOT HIS OWN?"

More quietly: "Where his very thought can be manufactured for him——

"Where what he has never thought can be inserted in his mind——

"Where one man with power can control the thought of a nation——

"With drugs——

"Psycho-surgery——

"Hypno-therapy——

"Data banks——

"And because we know that we are weak—that we are merely human—the end of these is coercion, blackmail, torture, fear!"

They screamed agreement.

He waited for mouse quiet.

"And the ultimate invasion—telepathy!

"What now must we do?

"How may we learn to live where the very thought may not be the thinker's own?"

The billion dollar question, Ian!

"What we cannot change we must accept."

Cliché of clichés! You'll have to do better than that, messiah.

The crowd waited for him to produce a miracle.

"How can we accept unless we understand? We know that lying and lust, treachery and fraud and the urge to murder and destroy are part of humanness. But the thought is not evil until it is acted upon. So we must accept the existence of these thoughts and admit that they are instinctive in all of us. We *will* accept them because with the psychological machines there is no denying them—and in the day of the telepaths there will be no hiding them. In that day a man will be judged by his actions—not by his revealed and helpless thinking but by his ability to control his actions despite the pressures of instinct and self-seeking."

Quiet. Most thoughtful quiet. Through it a voice called, "Do you mean that every private shame must be laid open for every man to see?"

(Cheap, crude, but effective. Campion had learned about planted questions.)

"No! Understanding must reach beyond shame! We must recognize *every* thought and impulse as part of the human psyche. We must stop hiding behind the face we turn to the world. We must turn from dissecting the universe to re-moulding ourselves."

The silence simmered with unease. No concealment? Shuddering, face-proud humanity exposing its coward guts in mental abasement? He demanded more than they had bargained for.

In the moment of hesitation, while the thousands tasted the impossible sourness of the proposition, Parker came from the rear of the stage, his scarlet deepened to blood color in the setting sun.

He faced them with arms upraised as if in invocation and cried out words which Lindley could hardly believe he heard:

" 'The light of the body is the eye: if therefore thine eye be single, thy whole body shall be full of light.' "

The sharp, ill-produced, crackling voice was not ludicrous. It reached them with an overtone of passionate belief, the touch of fanaticism Campion did not have in him though they had been readied for it.

So Parker's role was clear. But how many would recognize the provenance of the quotation, let alone perceive its meaning? The Sermon on the Mount was not altogether straightforward in the King James version. Near at hand Lindley heard muttered explanation ". . . means that where there's total illumination evil can't exist . . ."

His instinct was to protest the distortion. But Parker would have seeded the rally with the religious, ready with opportunist interpretation. The frustrating, unfightable circumstance was the man's maddening honesty in his deceptions and play-acting. *But history is scattered with the bones of well-meaning hypocrites.*

The explanatory spate died down. Parker dropped his arms. Campion took over with the warm and intimate smile he had practiced to produce with precise control.

"Do you think we're about to sell you a religion? Well"—quizzically—"we might do worse. But most of you don't know quite what a religion is, and what we need is really a philosophy. The one we offer is not new. It is two thousand years old in the words of a man named Yeshua, or Jesus, and it was not new when he propounded it. It is one of the oldest dreams of thinking man, and the time has come when we must attempt it or perish. Listen to what this man said of shame and self-righteousness.''

Parker's horrible voice crowed from the stage, amplified, flung out, sharpened—and redeemed by the depth of his passionate commitment.

'' 'Judge not, that ye be not judged!' ''

He had force and personality and hurled words like weapons. He caused listeners to stiffen and thrill.

'' 'For with what judgement ye judge, ye shall be judged: and with what measure ye mete, it shall be measured to you again.' ''

Wise, wise, Lindley granted, to use the old version with its immense majesty of words.

'' 'And why beholdest thou the mote that is in thy brother's eye, but considerest not the beam that is in thine own eye? Thou hypocrite, first cast out the beam out of thine own eye!''

To Arthur Lindley murmured, ''Some constructive editing there.''

''He discards what is not to the point.''

Arthur believed with a cool belief, which could be dangerous. Fanaticism could waver, be diverted and reversed because it swam with the emotions; cool belief would stand fast.

Whispering shreds of explanation rustled in the air.

Lindley's head ached again, but he ached more with anger at the talented misrepresentation which could seduce even Arthur's Gangoil-bred cynicism. They were close to the stage, so close that he had seen the tic of irritation with which Parker had noticed his returned presence. Knowing what he did, while he knew it to be reasonless and stupid, driven by miseries and lightheaded with fresh pain, he spoke to Arthur in a voice that carried clearly over the mutterings around them:

''This teaching has failed ever since it was first conceived and it will fail again.''

Eyes swung to him. *Yes, sheep, that man's back.* Arthur hissed something he did not hear because his senses were concentrated on the stage. Around him voices threatened and he did not care.

Instantly Campion bellowed, ''QUIET!''

They obeyed him. Campion was invincible. If he needed proof, that command gave it. He could do nothing here. He surrendered to his bursting head.

But Campion did not intend him to retire on a simple confession of enough. He called down from the stage, ''Why must it fail, Jim?''

Lindley gathered strength for hopeless dialogue. ''For the same reason it always did.''

''Tell us all the reason, Jim. Tell it loudly.'' The scorn was gentle. We'll hear what he has to say; we are nothing if not reasonable.

''It's a counsel of perfection, Ian. Beyond human capability.'' His head hammered in a fresh onslaught.

Campion was genial. ''Yeshua didn't think so.''

''He died for not thinking so.''

''Oh, no, Jim! He died because he started his revolution without first enlisting the law as his ally. There must be temporal as well as philosophic strength.''

Parker spread his arms and gave his crackling laugh and the crowd laughed with him, prompted to see Lindley as light relief.

''And even so, Jim, he had a victory in the end, didn't he? Even your materialist century admitted that.''

The crowd began to enjoy the exchange. A microphone appeared under Lindley's nose, giving him through it benefit of the soundscreen.

In pain and humiliation he howled, ''He gave the world the greatest single cause of venality and speciousness and hypocrisy and murder in all of history. And you'll do the same because you ask more than men can give. Utter honesty is a fanatical dream. The ability to lie is a survival trait.''

''Survival for liars, Jim! Men have imagined they could live without honesty, that hidden thought could be both shield and weapon. But now there are only two choices— honesty and understanding, or brutality and slavery to greed, machines and the rule of force. We must survive by honesty because there will be no survival without it.''

Parker seized the moment to throw them a slogan: ''No

man can serve two masters. Ye cannot serve Man and Mammon.''

The impudence of the substitution almost silenced Lindley. Then he shrieked and cawed again through his bitterness, ''You want to eliminate hypocrisy, yet every word you speak is distortion and double dealing! Try telling your crucified Jesus how the end sanctifies the strategy! From his cross he'd spit on you for turning him into a con man's trick on leaderless youngsters!''

The pain expanded and engulfed him; he was already unconscious when Arthur caught him. He did not hear Campion's explanation of how Yeshua himself had recognized that the road to heaven lay through hell, or Parker's inspired rehandling of the resurrection story.

—9—

He came to in the cathedral, in God's fastness of soaring stone forms and space for prayer to rise, but from which God most probably had withdrawn in favor of Parker's revised model.

This time they had found him something soft and warm to lie on. Arthur fussed round him, making the most of his position behind the scenes of excitement. His head was calmer, which probably meant a bloodstream awash with drugs.

Campion was with him, cross-legged on the floor, his favorite pose when talking with groups of youngsters. Light from the high brackets shed a mild patina on his red hair. His face was troubled with the first genuine feeling Lindley had seen in him that day.

''I may never see you again, Jim. After all, we have already parted in every significance. You'll go from here to hospital.'' The troubled look deepened to a determination on choice of words. ''When you recover there will be a job for you to do. Not with me, of course.''

''Thank you, no. I can support myself writing and teaching pre-Collapse history.''

Campion said—and he was ashamed—"We can't allow that."

Lindley struggled to sit up. Arthur tut-tutted but helped him. "I suppose you can't. Once you've started on the old game of rewriting history you can't afford a perfectionist at large. Is Parker still practicing New Testament exegesis out there?"

"Yes."

"When he begins to overtake you, will you have him crucified? If, that is, he doesn't wash his hands over your death first?"

Campion was unmoved. "Only losers destroy each other. We're starting with thirty thousand disciples and a country, not twelve simple men and a dream. You dislike our methods. In a way I see your reasons, but I don't follow your logic. So long as they learn tolerance and the love that eventually goes with it, what do the means matter?"

"You can't build truth on a lie, but you are far too committed to retreat. Forget the argument. What's your job for me? Where will you bury my inconvenient voice?"

"In the sky."

"The moon?"

"Aboard *Columbus*. Or one of the sister ships we will build."

Lindley exhaled on a rasping protest. "You can't be serious! Parker's project? Back into space? Not me. No. Not again."

Campion's unchanging face told him the matter was decided, and the bleakness of half a lifetime in black emptiness was insupportable.

"No, Jim!"

It was only a cry of despair, unrecognized, ignored. He had become an obstacle. Pity was precluded.

Campion explained, as if he had not spoken, "Computation tells us we will have, with our depleted resources, another impossible population problem in about two centuries. Resources we can mine to some extent from the planets, but living space . . . So the time to begin exploring for habitable systems is now. With the improvements already proposed for the ramjet there should be thirty or forty within reasonable reach. Earth-like planets."

Lindley conjured a poor laugh, a chatter of revengeful contempt. "Who's been fooling you? The astronomers? Bouncy amateurs like young Peter? Do you know what an astronomer means by an Earth-like planet? He means a planet roughly the same size—plus or minus a factor of two with all the gravity differences implied—with a suitable inclination to the ecliptic to provide seasons for an Earth-like ecology—with suitable concentrations of the essential elements in accessible strata—at the right distance from the solar body and in an elliptical orbit not too narrow, not too deep—and with an atmosphere that will sustain life.''

"We know the mathematical limits to the possibilities.''

"But there's a joker in the pack. It's called 'atmosphere that will sustain life.' What sort of atmosphere, my hypocrite Brother in God? You don't find primitive planets with free oxygen in their atmospheres. And the few that have them may be pretty thoroughly occupied.'' Campion's emotionless attention was deflating but he ploughed on. "Life comes *before* oxygen. Oxygen is strong poison to primitive proteins; they have to evolve to deal with it, a little at a time. They are born in methane and ammonia in conditions of constant ionization; after millions of years they mutate into forms which break down oxygen-bearing rock into just the quantities which will support them without poisoning and eroding the planet. It is life which *creates* the liveable atmosphere—and it takes about three thousand million years from the birth of the planet. What are your chances of finding one that fills the requirements, including being the right age? The universe is full of Earth-like planets, but you can't live on them. You can scour the sky with ten thousand copies of *Columbus* and Earth will choke to death before you locate the new paradise.''

Campion said, "Gangoil.'' As he expounded, Lindley realized how little he had ever been trusted, that he had known nothing of the extent of the dream. "Doctor David has already a group preparing bacterial and algal forms which will separate oxygen from suitable compounds at accelerated rates. We aim to terraform—I think that's the word—suitably positioned planets in a few decades instead of millions of years. Then, of course, we will be able to produce colonizing types to exist under abnormal conditions and make intelligently directed adjustments to hasten adaptation to the requirements of normal men. Genetic manipulation will coexist with and support evolution. If even one or two worlds are marginally ready by 2200 we will have won the gamble. The prize is worth the trial."

Lindley was aware of tears—of weakness, disappointment, vulnerability, loneliness. He mumbled, "Parker will crew the ships with Raft-clone, won't he? I can't live with them. It isn't possible."

Campion rose straight up to his feet, with the muscular grace of his father. "Of course it is. We'll attend to that."

"Life imprisonment with zombies!" Irrelevant complaint faded as the meaning of the words penetrated. "No, Ian! No!"

"It's for the best, Jim. You'll see that when you think it over. You'll never be happy in this world, and to adjust you to it would create a vegetable nonentity. But we can fit you to be contented within a small group, like a space crew, no matter who they are. It's the best I can do for you and I doubt if anyone could do more."

"Best!" He struggled to his knees, pleading, abject, divested of pride. "No, Ian! Kill me, please kill me. Don't take my identity, my mind! I'd rather be dead!"

"You wouldn't rather anything of the sort. I didn't expect to hear such rubbish from a psychiatrist. Oh, for Yeshua's sake!"

He turned in disgust from the abandoned animal that wept at his feet.

He was on a stretcher, arms and feet constricted by straps. Clone-brothers carried at his head and heels and Arthur moved ahead, apologizing a way through the crowd.

He was at peace, purged by the climax of spiritual cowardice.

Nobody paid attention to him. He was past, completed, historical, and they were enmeshed in Parker's crackling declamation. The man seemed to be hammering the idea of all-embracing tolerance still.

" 'For if ye like them which love you, what reward have ye? Do not even the publicans the same?

" 'And if ye salute your brethren only, what do ye more than others? Do not even the publicans so?' "

Poor bastards. Perhaps some of them dream of the perfect communication—the feast of love. Wait till the telepaths—the monsters they manufacture for their convenience—show them what humanity is like!

Lindley recited quietly, " 'Therefore all things whatsoever ye would that men should do to you, do even so to them.' That's in the Sermon on the Mount, too. And it's two-edged. You'll find out, kids."

Arthur bent over him. "What did you say?"

They came out through the fringe of the crowd and he saw the brazen upper rim of the sun barely above the horizon in a red sky.

"I pronounced a curse on your generation."

The last arc of sun drowned in a welter of blood.

"Well, I must say! We're only doing our best for you. Some people are never satisfied!"

AVONOVA PRESENTS
AWARD-WINNING NOVELS
FROM MASTERS OF SCIENCE FICTION

MIRROR TO THE SKY
by Mark S. Geston   71703-4/ $4.99 US/ $5.99 Can

THE DESTINY MAKERS
by George Turner   71887-1/ $4.99 US/ $5.99 Can

A DEEPER SEA
by Alexander Jablokov   71709-3/ $4.99 US/ $5.99 Can

BEGGARS IN SPAIN
by Nancy Kress   71877-4/ $5.99 US/ $7.99 Can

FLYING TO VALHALLA
by Charles Pellegrino   71881-2/ $4.99 US/ $5.99 Can

ETERNAL LIGHT
by Paul J. McAuley   76623-X/ $4.99 US/ $5.99 Can

DAUGHTER OF ELYSIUM
by Joan Slonczewski   77027-X/ $5.99 US/ $6.99 Can

NIMBUS
by Alexander Jablokov   71710-7/ $4.99 US/ $5.99 Can

THE CONTINUATION
OF THE FABULOUS
INCARNATIONS OF IMMORTALITY
SERIES

PIERS ANTHONY

FOR LOVE OF EVIL
75285-9/ $4.95 US/ $5.95 Can

AND ETERNITY
75286-7/ $5.50 US/ $7.50 Can

THE FANTASTIC ROBOT SERIES

ISAAC ASIMOV'S

by Hugo and Nebula Award Nominee
William F. Wu

EMPEROR
76515-1/ $4.99 US/ $5.99 Can

PREDATOR
76510-1/ $4.99 US/ $5.99 Can

MARAUDER
76511-X/ $4.99 US/ $5.99 Can

WARRIOR
76512-8/ $4.99 US/ $5.99 Can

DICTATOR
76514-4/ $4.99 US/ $5.99 Can